20 YEARS LATER

E.J. NEWMAN

E.J. Newman was born in a tiny coastal village in Cornwall, south west England, during one of the hottest summers on record. Four years later she started to write stories and never stopped until she penned a short story that secured her a place at Oxford University to read Experimental Psychology. She now lives in Somerset with her husband, her son, and her books, where all are loved dearly. She runs her own copywriting business and a free short story club at her blog Post-Apocalyptic Publishing at www.enewman.co.uk.

*"For my grandparents, both here
and on the other side,
        but especially for my Nana,
who always believed in me."*

ISBN 978-0-9844981-2-3 (hardback)
ISBN 978-0-9844981-1-6 (ebook)

Dystopia Press
3615 Franklin Ave., No. 237
Waco, Texas 76710

www.dystopiapress.com
dystopiapress@gmail.com

Publisher: Mark Roy Long
Editor: Kayla Allen (kayla_allen@baylor.edu)
Cover design: SoroDesign (http://sorodesign.com/)
Interior design: Stacie Buterbaugh (smbuterbaugh8@yahoo.com)
Author photo: Harry Duns (www.harryduns.com)

Special thanks: Scout Flowers, Annabeth Parrish, Joy Cozby, and Steve Tiano

First edition, first printing

Printed in China by Asia Pacific Offset

**Publisher's Cataloging-in-Publication
(Provided by Quality Books, Inc.)**

Newman, Emma, 1976-
    20 years later / Emma Newman. -- 1st ed.
    p. cm.
    SUMMARY: Twenty years after a plague has wiped out most of humanity, four friends in London seek to discover the secret behind this catastrophe.
    Audience: Ages 12-18.
    ISBN-13: 978-0-9844981-2-3 (hardback)
    ISBN-10: 0-9844981-2-5 (hardback)
    ISBN-13: 978-0-9844981-1-6 (ebook)
    ISBN-10: 0-9844981-1-7 (ebook)

    1. Teenagers--England--London--Juvenile fiction.
2. Plague--Juvenile fiction. 3. London (England)--Juvenile fiction. [1. Teenagers--Fiction. 2. Plague--Fiction.
3. London (England)--Fiction.]   I. Title. II. Title: Twenty years later.

PZ7.N47976Twe 2011   [Fic]
                    QBI10-600137

20 YEARS LATER

E.J. NEWMAN

DISTOPIA
PRESS

PROLOGUE

London wasn't always a dusty, ghost-filled monument to the dead. It was once an intense city with toxic air and the constant din of millions of people talking, consuming, shoving past each other. Perhaps it's impossible for you to imagine so many people alive in this place but, I assure you, it's true. After all, where do you think all the bones littering the streets came from? Each one of the skulls you step over every day was once a person, alive as you are now, and that skull was filled with dreams and fears just like yours. Terror was probably the last thing all those poor souls felt. God knows it was for me.

I can only guess that you're in London, unless this book has had its own adventure too. For a moment more, indulge me, I like to try to imagine who you are. Of course, I can only make some educated guesses. It's likely that you're older rather than younger, as so few children read now. But perhaps you are young, and if so, you must have one of the survivors caring for you, someone kind enough to teach you how to read now that there are no schools. I hope so, it makes you one to treasure.

Perhaps you're trying to decide whether to burn this book now or read it first. Are you weighing up which is more important to you: a few more minutes of heat or the hours of another person's voice reaching up to you from these pages?

Wait! Let me speak to you, let me tell you this tale! Don't you want to know about the Red Lady's rise to power, or perhaps how she fell? Have you heard the name "Joshua" whispered in dark places and wondered what exactly he did? Or is it David the King who fascinates you? No, what am I thinking? It must be the Four you want to know about, the four who changed the world. Well, I was there, watching as it all happened, so if you burn this now, you'll never know.

I shall start after It happened, some twenty years later, when London was divided between the gangs: the Gardners, the Bloomsbury Boys, the Red Lady's Hunters, to name but a few. Yes, I shall start in the place where it all began: Miri's garden.

You may not have heard of her, but one of the most important people you need to know about is Miri. In the year I begin this account, she was in her forties. I'd like you to try to picture her, hair long and dark with some silvered strands. Some of the lines around the edges of her large brown eyes were no doubt left by the horrors she experienced when It happened, but most of them were carved by smiles.

Miri's garden, at the centre of Queen Square, Bloomsbury, was one of the most beautiful places in London. Not dangerous and wild like the big public parks with their beasts and thorns, and not overgrown like the small house gardens are now. Well kept and orderly, Miri's garden kept her and many others alive.

Her home was part of an old school with arched windows where the housemaster once resided. The other choices were old offices (too impersonal) or one of the hospitals that surrounded the square, but nothing on this earth would make Miri step into a hospital for a second time since It happened, let alone live in one.

The old schoolmaster's house was where her son, Zane, was born and raised. Ah! I can imagine your eyes widen and hear you say: "Yes, I've heard of him!" Well, yes, of course, everyone alive has but, at this point, very few knew of Zane. He learnt about the healing arts at her side, which is why I start with her. Without Miri, there would have been no Zane as you know of him.

Zane was always a sensitive child, with his mother's dark, soulful eyes and the thick brown hair of her youth, uncut since the day he was born. At the time I have in mind, he was almost fifteen and his hair reached his lower back. He was becoming a handsome young man, so yes, everything you might have heard about him in that regard is certainly true.

At that age he knew very little of life outside the garden, but despite everything his mother did to protect Zane, his innocence was still taken from him. Not by one dramatic event, but gently, like each day steals one's youth. The first little piece was stolen the night the Giant came.

Chapter 1
THE GIANT

On the night Zane first saw the giant, the summer moon was almost full. A figure approached Miri's house slowly and fearfully, keeping well within the shadows and ducking behind anything nearby whenever the clouds parted. The visitor crept up to the house and paused, looking carefully at both ground floor windows several times before finally making a choice. Standing on tiptoe, he cast one more fearful look around the shadowed square before tapping insistently on the glass.

After a few moments, Zane opened the window as quietly as he could, held up a lit candle and peered down with sleepy eyes.

The trespasser bounced on his tiptoes. "Hullo!" he whispered.

Zane smiled at the Bloomsbury Boy standing in front of him. "Hi Dev, what's wrong? It must be the middle of the night." The candlelight shone off Dev's teeth revealing the large gap between the front two. Even though it was only illuminated by one candle, Dev's shock of unruly hair was clearly bright ginger.

"Come with me," he whispered. Dev was shaking, as if scared as well as excited. The Bloomsbury Boys' territory was only five minutes to the west from Miri's garden, in Russell Square, but Dev rarely came over at night.

"But it's dark!" Zane said, looking past Dev. The garden in the square, so familiar in the daylight, looked forbidding. His mother never let him go out alone once the sun had set, and that had never bothered him at all. The routine was always the same; packing up tools half an hour before sunset, then filling three buckets of water from the pump in the garden.

1

Once everything was safely inside, she had taught Zane to go to every door and window in the house, locking and checking each one, before lighting candles in the kitchen and living room. It was then Zane's responsibility to ensure that all of the curtains were closed perfectly, lest the candlelight shone out of a gap into the darkness. He had never asked why, it was just the way things were. Unlocking the window to talk to Dev had been bad enough, the thought of climbing out and into the moonlit garden was just ... absurd.

"But you got to come with me! I seen sommat ... sommat weird ..."

Dev's apparent agitation stopped Zane from sending him away. "What do you mean by 'weird'?"

"A light ... in one of the windows, high up. I saw it. Was like it was movin' too."

Zane was fully awake in an instant. "A fire!"

"No, not fire. I know what that looks like, an' it weren't that. It weren't like nothin' I ever seen before. Weird light ... we got to check it out, might be sommat important, we got to keep you and Miri safe. An' I don't wanna wake Jay up, in case it's sommat ... stupid." Dev hung his head, recalling the last time that had happened. "You're clever. I thought you should come look-see too. Jay'd be dead chuffed if you did."

Zane considered this carefully. Within the Bloomsbury Boys, a strict hierarchy was in place. Jay, at the top, was the biggest, the one who had lived the longest and the one who had survived most fights with the Gardners. He could also be charming when he needed to be. Miri had once said he had Irish blood in him but Zane looked carefully the next time Jay was cut and his blood looked just like everyone else's.

The only ways that a boy could impress Jay were to either fight a Gardner up close and win, or get a Token, a physical trophy to prove a Boy's ability to steal from the enemy in their own territory and get away afterwards. Tokens earned a Boy status within the gang: the more Tokens, the more re-spect and the better claim to food, the ultimate Token being the black tie of a dead Gardner.

Dev, approaching fourteen (a guess, as none of the Boys knew when they were born and didn't mark birthdays), didn't have the dexterity or coordination to survive close combat with a Gardner and mercifully knew that fact. Unfortunately, he also didn't have the luck or the wits to be able to obtain any other Token, and every day had to watch Boys much younger and smaller rise higher in Jay's estimations. Jay was the axis upon which Dev's world turned and Miri had patched Dev up several times after varied attempts to win his favour.

Zane frowned. "If there is something weird there, it might be dangerous." He took a deep breath. "I suppose it's up to us to make sure this isn't a threat, right?"

Dev beamed at him. "Too right!"

Zane and Dev stood outside of the hospital at the far corner of the square. His house couldn't be seen from here, the line of sight intersected by the dark garden.

Zane shook his head. "I'm not going in there."

Dev, a good six inches shorter, looked up at him with large hazel eyes. "Go on, honest-like it'll be worth it, you ain't seen nothin' like what I saw, you wanna see it too. Your Mum won't know; she's asleep."

Zane tensed as pride tugged at a string in his stomach. "It isn't my Mum I'm worried about," he lied.

In Zane's life, the rule to *Never Go Into Hospitals* was as fundamental as *Don't Touch The Fire* and *Wash Your Hands Before You Clean The Wound*. Miri had instilled him with not only a respect for nature, but also a pathological fear of the dark concrete buildings that lined the square. It hadn't taken much; only a few cautionary warnings, a tearful reprimand when she had found him entering the lobby to look for fuel on

3

a bitterly cold day, but the *Never Go Into Hospitals* rule was proving hard to break.

"Then you must be scared," Dev stuck out his chin as a clear challenge.

Zane thrust his shaking hands into his pockets and stood straighter as Dev pulled his favourite woolly hat out of his pocket and jabbed his hair under it. The ginger fuzz defiantly poked out of several holes across the crown as Dev meticulously tucked in wayward strands away from his forehead and ears. Everything that Dev wore had holes, like all of the other Bloomsbury Boys. The skill of the well-dressed Boy was to make sure that each thin layer had its holes in different places. Lots of layers not only kept out the cold, but also made them look stouter than they were. It no longer worked on Zane as he and Miri had dressed too many wounds on their scrawny arms and legs to be fooled by such a simple trick.

Dev took a deep breath, drew himself up to his full height as he faced the double doors and strode towards them.

Zane's clammy hands clenched deep in his pockets. The old glass of the doors was filthy and cracked, beyond them the hospital was as black as the inside of a poppy. He read the words on the faded blue sign hanging lopsidedly over the door. "National Hospital for Nee-ur-ology and Nee-ur-osurgery," he sounded out softly as Miri had taught him.

Dev, trying to seem braver than his clever and more handsome friend, reached out with shaking hands and pushed the doors open. He and Zane wrinkled their noses at the stale air that wafted out, carrying a fine dust on it that made Dev cough slightly.

Inside the lobby fingers of moonlight began to tentatively pick their way across the floor. A thick layer of dust covered everything in sight with gentle undulations immediately recognisable from some of the alleyways between the garden and the Boys' square. Bones.

Zane swallowed hard, not noticing that both he and Dev were holding their breath. Their eyes darted around the space, taking in the strange looking doors, how so many things were broken. Internal windows and doors had been smashed and many were hanging off their hinges. Strange wheeled beds were further in, some blocking a corridor in their haphazard arrangement. There were many things neither of them had seen before: signs, symbols on the walls, fire extinguishers, faded and grubby posters from the time before It happened.

A large, rotting staircase was at the farthest point ahead of them, but it was blocked by several pieces of furniture that had been used as some kind of makeshift barricade. Two pillars that were once white stretched up to the ceiling, now grey and streaked with dirt. To the right was a large reception desk, the wood intact, thanks to Miri keeping the Boys out of the hospitals too. Any other building and it would have been scavenged and burnt a long time ago. To the far right, Zane caught a glimpse of an attractive woman with short blonde hair looking out from a painting. He stared at her for a long moment, until Dev finally moved forward, taking a step inside.

Zane followed close behind him, both still enraptured by the alien space but also the sheer sense of adventure. He jumped as the door began to swing closed behind them, and paused to brace it open with an old clipboard he found on the floor near his feet.

"We need the light," Zane whispered.

Dev frowned. "We need to find another way up," he whispered back, with a slight tremor in his voice. "Them stairs are no good."

Zane looked around for another way out of the lobby and saw a sign reading "Stairs to upper floors" with an arrow pointing to the right.

"This way."

"How'd you know?"

Zane pointed at the sign and began to move forward. His illiterate friend shrugged and fell in behind him, stepping where Zane stepped as Jay had taught him to do when exploring new places.

They clambered over the bones and wreckage, taking care not to touch anything unless they absolutely needed to do so. The corridor to the right was extremely dark; the moonlight could only penetrate so far in, and at several points they could only progress by touch alone. It was only by chance that Zane leant against a door out of the corridor that swung open to reveal a stairwell, lit by moonlight streaming weakly through a skylight high above them. It was sufficient to sketch out the shape of the stairs stretching up above them and the door to the first floor.

"It were four windows up, where I saw it, and on the other side," Dev whispered. Zane nodded in response, gritting his teeth to stop them chattering. It meant that the light would be impossible to see from the garden or their house.

As carefully and as quietly as possible, they both began to climb the steps. It was slow work, as the steps were also blanketed by the awful grey dust and many of them were littered with bones and skulls. They were careful not to send any crashing down the stairwell. Both boys were used to seeing remains bleached by the sun on the roads that hadn't been cleared by Miri or the Bloomsbury Boys, but somehow the darkness and the knowledge that they really shouldn't be inside this place conspired to make it scary to step over them here.

Zane counted the doors as they went up and thankfully the dim blue-grey light got slightly stronger the further up they went. Finally, he stopped outside the door to the third floor. A small round window was set into it and he stood on his tiptoes to peer through. A long corridor with many doors leading off it on both sides could just be made out through the filthy glass. It was also very dark.

He turned back to Dev. "Can't see anything."

"It'll be further along, the window was in the middle."

There was an awkward pause. "Shall we go and have a look?"

Dev nodded. "Come this far ..."

He stepped in front of Zane and slowly pushed the door open. It creaked as if it hadn't been opened for years and they both froze.

Nothing happened.

Dev let out the breath he hadn't realised he was holding and stepped through. A large murky window at the far end of the corridor let in enough moonlight for them to progress. Their shoulders hunched with tension, they both began to creep down the silent corridor, their footsteps muffled by the thick carpet of dust. Thankfully, there seemed to be fewer bones up here.

The clouds outside cleared and the grey-blue light strengthened into silver, describing the streaks of dirt on the window as it reached through. In that moment, Zane saw something that made him grab Dev's shoulder, half to stop him but half out of fear. With a shaking hand, he pointed out the large footprints in the dust that lay from a door at the other end of the corridor and led up to one of the doors just to their left. Only one set. Whoever had made them was still in that room.

In that moment, they both heard a strange rasping sound, like someone struggling to breathe in the winter after running in the cold. Only it wasn't entirely like that; it was slow and it had an edge to it. There was something odd about the exact regularity of the breaths and a slight click that sounded as it changed from intake to out breath. It came from the same room that the footprints led up to.

As they both turned to the door, the crack beneath it was suddenly illuminated by a bright yellow light that spilled out from underneath and into the corridor to fall over their shoes. Zane and Dev clutched at each other wildly, but the light faded just as quickly as it had appeared. They finally began to relax but froze again when the the light returned and the door handle started to turn.

A footfall with a heavy metallic clang made them both jump, the shock spurring both of them to back away from the door as it swung open. Both boys gasped at the figure emerging from the room. He was huge, at least seven feet tall, but what drained the colour from their faces was the shape of the Giant's head. It was as wide as his shoulders, like a huge square sat on top of his frame. The Giant lurched out of the room as if his feet were made of iron and turned to face the boys. Before they could make out any features on his huge face the bright yellow light swung around to shine on them. Dazzled, they both shrieked in terror and sprinted down the corridor back to the stairwell.

They hurtled through the door and raced down the first flight of steps as the heavy footfalls approached and the yellow light burst through the round window above their heads. They listened to the bizarre breathing as the Giant approached. He stopped on the other side of the door and both boys held their breath, hoping desperately that he wouldn't come into the stairwell after them. After agonised seconds of tense listening to the regular, horrible wheeze, they both sagged as they heard him walk away in the opposite direction. The steady, slow, clanking footsteps grew quieter as the light swept away from their door.

Chapter 2
THE NEW BOY

A long time ago, Russell Square, the heart of the Bloomsbury Boys' territory, had a garden in the middle of it just like
Miri's square. But since the Boys had claimed it, the garden
had gradually died, unable to withstand the constant assault
of small, destructive children. When his predecessor had died,
Jay ordered it cleared of the last big shrubs to give a clear view
across at all times. Now all that was left was a few stubborn
trees, tattooed with the markings of every Boy who had lived
there.

The concrete area in the centre, where a fountain once
entertained small children before It happened, was where the
Boys tended to gather. News was exchanged there and the
spoils of scavenging were pooled and inspected and fought
over. On the mud around the concrete area they kept bits of
metal, piles of junk too big to put easily anywhere else after
having been cleared out of the rest of the square.

There was also a small fleet of rusting shopping trolleys
that provided hours of amusement. None of the Boys had any
concept of what they'd originally been designed for, so for every
Boy they had only one purpose: racing, with one Boy inside and
two to push. The shopping trolleys, or "Wheelies" as the Boys
called them, had been responsible for three broken arms, two
sprained wrists and countless scrapes and cuts. All of these
injuries had been carefully cleaned, set, and bandaged by Miri
as she listened to a detailed account of who had smashed into
whom and who had won. Not even a broken arm would stop
a race.

Almost the entire gang had gathered to hear what Dev
had to say after he'd come running into the square yelling for

9

Jay. Zane had waited at the edge to be invited into the territory, and Grame waved him in, also eager to see what the commotion was about. Zane hung back, giving Dev the spotlight as the Boys drifted in to surround him. Dev's eagerness to impress them and raise his profile was palpable.

"He was twice as tall as you Jay, and at least three times wider ... and he couldn't breathe proper-like, he sounded like Tim after he runs lots –"

"Hey!" Tim protested, admittedly one of the shortest and weakest of the Boys. The rest of them sniggered.

Jay had been rubbing the sleep from his eyes when Dev and Zane reached him. Zane had persuaded his friend to wait until dawn before going back to report to Jay, knowing of his bad temper when woken too early. Dev tried to catch his breath and calm down before starting, giving the others a chance to collect around him. The only ones not there were those on watch, but they would soon be filled in.

Jay stood a head taller than the rest of the Boys, even Grame and Mark. It was this, and his thick black hair that he liked to shape into short messy spikes, that made him so easy to spot when the Boys were all together. When the Boys looked up at Jay, they stood straighter, and he only needed to shout "Oy!" once to make any of them stop whatever they were doing and come running if he wanted it. The gang leader walked with the swagger of a young man who knew he was on top. Never afraid to make and hold eye contact, he had the cockiness of one who could fight well and knew it.

A vast array of items adorned the young leader's wiry body. First was his belt, made of several thin black ties plaited together. Then his jacket, made of faded and scuffed black leather, with a variety of patches, some fabric, some metal, sewn over various holes left by different knife fights. Zane's mother had stitched on several of them, usually after sewing up the wound acquired at the same time. On the inside of that jacket was a collection of small metal badges coveted by all of the other Boys. Jay gave them out as a special reward whenever he felt a Boy should be publicly lauded. Almost all of the Boys had at least one; Grame and Mark both had ten each. Dev had none.

Two knives hung off Jay's hips. They had worn handles and battered sheaths but Zane knew that the blades were sharpened every day. Jay had a spot in the square where he liked to do that, opposite the main barricade at the top of Montague Street, the place where the Gardners attacked the most. His pale blue eyes, framed by long black lashes, stared at that point where he had personally killed several Gardners with the very knives he was sharpening. All the Boys knew never to disturb Jay when he scraped the metal with his special stone, for when he was doing that, all Jay saw was Gardners and blood. When they were sharp enough, Jay would trace a finger lightly over the flat of the blades, still staring at that point, his lips curving into a smile that made anyone who saw it shiver and hurry away.

Jay concentrated on Dev's tale, but when he finished his eyes flicked to Zane.

"This all true?"

Zane hesitated before replying. "He was really big." He wanted to be truthful but not to discredit his friend who had exaggerated slightly.

"Bigger than Luthor?" Jay was frowning. Luthor, the largest Hunter of the Red Lady's gang and the one she called her Champion, was very tall and very strong, setting Jay's standard for "people to be concerned about."

"Oh, much, much bigger than Luthor," Zane replied with certainty and a ripple of wonder spread through the circle of Boys.

Dev sighed in frustration. "I told you he was, Jay, honest-like!"

Jay frowned. "But he didn't follow you?" Both boys shook their heads. "And you didn't see him in Miri's square afterwards?"

"Nothin'!" Dev confirmed. "Was like he disappeared. Outside the hospital we couldn't see anythin' of him or them weird feet of his."

"We could see footprints in the hospital," Zane explained, "but all the dust blows about outside, so we don't know which way he went."

Jay looked down at one of the smallest Boys who tugged at his jacket hem. He leant down and the sandy-haired Boy whispered into his ear. Jay nodded and straightened up. "Seb here's got a good question. How did the Giant have a light that wasn't fire?"

The gang murmured as Seb looked proud. Zane and Dev shrugged in unison.

"Maybe he put some fire in a jar like we do when it's windy," Mark proposed, scratching his lank brown hair.

Zane shook his head. "It didn't look like that. It was too bright, and not shaped like a jar either. It was a perfect circle."

The murmuring increased. "Maybe the Giant caught the sun in a bottle," one of the younger ones called out from the back.

"Nah," Dev said, "would've been hot, and it weren't."

No more theories were forthcoming. Jay kept frowning and that made the Boys nervous. "Grame, Mark, we need double shifts tonight, and everyone needs to stay sharp, ya hear?" All assembled nodded, even Zane, who then blushed. "Anyone hears anything weird, or sees anything weird, come to me right away."

"Even if it's Dev?" one of the Boys quipped. They all sniggered again, apart from Dev and Jay.

"Shut it," Jay said and silence fell. "No messin'. This is serious. Maybe them Gardners have got sommat goin' on with the Giant, so we need to stay smart-sharp. Got it?"

There were few things that Jay took more seriously than the threat from the Gardners. Named after their matriarch's surname and that of her three sons, the Gardners attacked his Boys at any opportunity. Brutal, ruthless and cruel, with a territory boundary that expanded and contracted according to Ma Gardner's daily whims, they were always on Jay's mind.

Dev watched Jay closely, like a hungry puppy hoping for scraps from a table.

"Now scarper you lot. Check the square and the edges of the territory. No wheelie racin' or fightin' 'til I got the all-clear. Go on then!" The Boys scattered to all of the places they knew to check, but Jay grabbed Dev's collar and held him back. "Nice one, Dev."

Dev grinned as he saw Jay reach into his jacket and pull out a badge. "Ta Jay!" He scampered off after beaming a gap-toothed smile at Zane.

Jay turned to Zane. "Your mum know about this?"

Zane looked down at his scuffed shoes, his dark hair falling to hide his guilty face. "You know how she is about hospitals."

Jay nodded, remembering the last time some of his Boys had been caught trying to pilfer old mattresses from the hospital on the corner of Miri's square. He wouldn't have believed their story if she hadn't marched them over herself to hold him to account. "She should know though. If I were in her shoes, I'd wanna know."

Zane sighed. "I know, I –"

He was cut off by three sharp whistles from the northeast corner of the square. Jay took off at a sprint with Zane following close behind. It was some kind of alert, but not a full-blown Gardner alarm.

"Jay! Jay!" A Boy called Smudge (because of a small birthmark on his forehead) was waving frantically for his attention. He was pointing at a low wall in front of one of the abandoned houses. "Another boy, a new one! Behind that wall!"

Jay ran and peered over, then vaulted it effortlessly. Zane hurried over, eager to help, tying his long hair back out of the way in case he was needed.

Huddled against the wall, shivering and deathly pale was a scrawny boy with very short mousy brown hair. He was dressed in the strangest clothes: thin pale blue cotton pyjamas, almost pristine in condition, no patches or holes and hardly any dirt. Zane shuddered when he saw him, not knowing why.

"Hey there," Jay said. His voice was soft and calming and the little boy lifted his head. "I'm Jay, this here's my patch, but boys are allowed to stay so you're alright." As he spoke, the boy visibly relaxed, and Jay slipped off his leather jacket to place it gently around his shoulders. He seemed to notice something as he did so, and beckoned Zane over. "Come look-see, Zane. I reckon he's hurt."

Zane clambered over the wall and went to Jay's side. The little boy's eyes widened when he saw him, and the trembling started again.

Zane knelt down to his level and, just like his mother would, he smiled warmly at the boy, even though a chill spread through him that made him shiver.

At that moment, the boy's face crumpled into an expression of utter terror. He shook violently and his breath became ragged. Stunned, Zane drew back as Jay threw him a confused look.

"I only smiled at him," Zane said apologetically, just as confused, as Jay gathered the boy up in his arms.

"I'll take him to ya mum," Jay said, as the petrified boy buried his face into his chest and clung to him desperately.

Zane sagged, watching them go. Smudge peered up at him. "Whatcha do to him?"

"Nothing! I've never even seen him before!"

Smudge raised an eyebrow. "Looked like he'd seen you before."

Chapter 3
DEV'S TOKEN

Zane kept busy in the garden for the rest of that day, steering clear of the house whilst his mother tended to the new boy under Jay's protective supervision. At supper that evening he was quiet, not wanting to talk too much about anything, in case it led to the tale of the Giant in the hospital. Zane wasn't ready to face her anger about that yet.

For her part, Miri assumed he was brooding about the new boy's reaction that Jay had mentioned, and left him to it. The boy had clearly been distressed and disoriented, and she couldn't understand why Zane was so shaken up by his behaviour.

The next morning she was relieved to see that he was back to his old self. Not only was he cheery and pleased to see her, but he had risen early and stoked up the fire to boil the day's drinking water. He kissed her on the cheek, just like every morning, and she hugged him tightly.

"Everything alright?"

Zane rested his chin on her shoulder, it still being a novelty to be able to do so and thought for a moment. Somehow it still wasn't the right time to tell her about the Giant, but there was something else to talk about. "I had a weird dream last night."

"Tell me about it whilst I make breakfast."

Zane leant against the door frame, his back to the living room, as his mother began to chop the fruit he had picked the day before. The kitchen, like the whole downstairs of the house, was tidy and clean, worn and patched. Small, meticulously labelled pots and jars containing ointments, seeds, preserves, and dried fruit lined every work surface. The dark-red tiled floor, swept daily, was marked with scrapes from the wooden stools tucked under the table in the corner. The wooden cupboards, full of mismatched crockery, also showed signs of age, but it was all well cared for. The oven was treated as the best mouse-proof cupboard, as all of the cooking was done on a trivet over the fire in the living room. The back door into the small court-yard at the rear was open to let in the pleasant morning breeze, a thin muslin curtain pinned over it to keep out the summer insects.

"I dreamt I was in a house, not this one," Zane began. "I was living there but it wasn't my home. Everything was very dusty, and all the picture frames I could see were turned face-down, so I couldn't see the people in them." Zane glanced back into the living room at the framed pictures on the mantel piece over the fire. All were old photos of his mother with her parents when she was younger. All Zane had heard about them was that they died when It happened; Miri didn't like to talk too much about the past.

Miri looked up at the pause and he continued. "I could see a rug that had been rolled back, and there was a weird sort of door in the floor and steps that went down."

"A cellar," Miri said, her knife halfway through an apple as she frowned a little. "You've never seen one before ..."

"Oh. Well, there was one of those there," Zane continued, unconcerned, "but I didn't go down it, I knew some-one was down there, but not a bad person. Anyway, the really weird thing was that I looked in a mirror in the dream, and I had strange purple eyes."

"Purple eyes?! Like you'd get from a fight?"

"No no, the um ... the bit that's brown –"

"The iris."

"Yeah, that bit, they were like a pale purple, the same colour as those flowers that grow on the right-hand side on the way to Jay's square."

"Violet," Miri's hand was still poised on the knife halfway through the apple. "Like Elizabeth Taylor's eyes."

"Who?"

Miri shook her head, starting to chop quickly again and Zane knew she had thought about before It happened.

"Isn't that a weird thing to dream about?"

Miri nodded. "Do you remember if your face was the same?"

Zane shook his head. "I can only remember the eyes ... and that was all that happened, but it was so clear, it felt like I was really there."

He watched her chop the rest of the fruit and then mix it all together, remaining silent. Miri glanced over at him expectantly a few times but didn't press him to talk about the day before.

"The little boy was alright in the end," she commented as she served the fruit into Zane's favourite bowl.

"Oh, right ... that's good."

Miri frowned at him and sighed. "Are you sure you're alright?"

He nodded hurriedly and took the bowl she offered. "What do we need to do today?" Miri didn't press further.

As the days went by, Miri noted that Zane wasn't visiting the Boys, but she didn't worry too much about it–the same had happened in the past. Sometimes Zane would want to be close to others his age, sometimes he preferred her company; either way she was sure he would drift back there soon. Besides, summer was always very busy, and she was glad he wasn't being distracted from all that had to be done. And the less time she spent worrying about what he might be getting dragged into with the Bloomsbury Boys, the better.

The night of the next full moon brought Dev to the square again. Zane was much more alert this time when he opened the window. "Is it the Giant again?"

Dev shook his head and Zane smiled with relief.

"Ain't seen you for ages, don't you wanna be friends with us no more?"

Zane looked away, feeling guilty for avoiding them, but then fired back, "You didn't come over here either."

"Couldn't. Jay's got us busy at the moment. We heard noises on the other side of the barricade few days back, and what with the Giant an' all ..."

"So why couldn't you wait until morning to visit?" Zane yawned.

"Because it needs to be dark to do what I'm gonna do, not too dark mind you. But tonight's perfect, and I need your help." Zane listened with apprehension. "I'm gonna get me a Token, best one ever. Ever." Dev puffed up his chest, the moon-light glinting off his highly polished metal badge.

Zane was far from keen. "It sounds dangerous."

"Course it is!"

"It's not something from the ..." Zane swallowed hard. "The Gardners is it?"

Dev shook his head. "Nah, too hard – anyway, loads of the others have got stuff from them. I wanna do something better, something *different*." At Zane's raised eyebrow, he continued. "I'm gonna get sommat from the Red Lady's place."

"What?!"

"I'm gonna get one of her banners. I went and had a look-see at 'er patch last night, and I reckon if someone kept watch for the guards, I could grab one and run with it."

"You're mad."

"No, really, it'd work, Zane, honest-like! I just need you to keep watch, not go close or anything."

Zane knew that the Red Lady's territory, with Gray's Inn at its heart, was only ten minutes from the garden to the south-east if one were stupid enough to attempt to walk there out in the open. He'd never been there himself, but he'd heard from the Bloomsbury Boys that the territory was marked by daubs of red paint on the buildings around the perimeter. Some said it was blood, but he wasn't sure he believed them.

"They kill people who go near, Jay told me, and Mum too. They both said to stay away."

"Aw, c'mon. Don't be like that. They only kill people they catch."

"That doesn't make me feel any better."

Dev sighed with frustration. "I thought it all through and it'll be fine. They don't expect anyone to do this, that's why it'll work. C'mon, help me out. I gotta get another Token. Len got one the other day from the Gardners, and he's half the size of me. Everyone laughs at me all the time; I gotta show them that I'm worth sommat."

Zane listened to Dev's pleading and his face softened. "It doesn't matter what people say about you, Dev."

"It's alright for you, you ain't one of us. You got Miri and the garden. It's different 'ere." Dev hung his head. "If I don't show 'em I'm worth sommat, they'll kick me out. So I'm gonna do this. Tonight. And if you 'ent gonna help me, then I'll go on my own."

Dev turned and began to march off purposefully. Zane watched him, worried, and then called him back with a loud whisper. "I'll ... I'll watch for you. But I'm not going close."

It was the nearest that Zane had ever been to the Red Lady's territory, and he was shivering despite the warmth of the summer night. Dev had posted him on the corner of Northington Street where it met Gray's Inn Road, the best place to watch for the patrol that guarded her and the inner territory. From his position, he could see the large gates, shut fast, and the white-washed walls that shone silver blue in the moonlight. Interspersed at regular intervals were long banners of silk that billowed gently in the summer breeze, stretching from the top of the wall down to the ground, some forty feet or so in length and about ten feet wide. Dev had described them to him on the way, in the moonlight they looked black, but he knew that they were blood-red.

The street that ran along her walls was completely clear of debris and wreckage, just like the areas around his own home and the Boys' territory too. But the street seemed even cleaner here, like it was swept regularly, and the walls were immaculate.

He held a piece of string that he fed through his hands from a ball that he cradled to his chest. Dev had tied the end around his wrist, and given Zane instructions on what to do. One sharp tug if Zane caught sight of a guard on top of the wall, two if the guard was looking in Dev's direction. Three sharp tugs for a guard at street level and that would bring Dev back and abort the mission. One slow pull on the string was agreed as an all-clear.

He watched Dev inch along the wall, crouched, staying in its shadow. His attention flicked between his friend creeping towards the closest banner and the top of the wall. When Dev was about halfway, Zane caught sight of one of the Red Lady's men appearing at the edge of it and gave one urgent tug on the string. Dev froze and crouched even lower as Zane watched the man's silhouette carefully. He could make out the drawn bow and the notched arrow, and the size of the man's muscles even in the dim light. However, the guard didn't look down at Dev's position and simply walked slowly along the wall, occasionally glancing into the street below, but nothing more. Finally, when he turned away at the end of the wall to patrol another edge of the perimeter, Zane finally let out his breath and gave a slow pull on the string to indicate the all clear. Dev began to creep along again.

Dev reached the first banner and turned to give Zane an eager grin and thumbs up. Dev seemed to detach the bottom of the fabric from something obscured by the darkness, then stood and gripped the dark material tightly. The silk rippled and creased as his fists grasped it, then after a brief nod back to Zane, he pulled down with all his strength in an effort to detach it swiftly and cleanly.

The sound of several tinkling bells rang out into the night and both Zane and Dev gasped in shock. The banner didn't detach, despite Dev's desperate attempts. Even hanging all his body weight off it, the jangling only got louder with each wrench.

Zane gave two sharp tugs on the string as he watched three heads appear above the banner that Dev grappled with. In an instant, arrows were trained on him and Zane tugged urgently on the string, the code forgotten in his blind panic. He heard the heavy bolt of the gate slide slowly open and saw more guards spill out onto the street only metres away from where Dev was standing.

Dev, panicking, began to sprint back to Zane's position as arrows rained down, hitting the ground where his ankles were but moments before. The string went slack, and Zane dropped the ball as he began to back away, not being able to tear his eyes away from the disaster befalling his friend. He could see the Hunters on the ground gaining on him easily, and then in one horrible moment, he heard an agonised cry erupt from Dev as one of the arrows fired from above hit its target and the Boy tumbled to the ground. One of the Hunters jumped on Dev, his drawn sword gleaming in the moonlight, and Zane froze as the man noticed the string trailing from Dev's arm. The Hunter's keen eyes followed it in moments, all the way back to where Zane stood, mouth agape, his face the colour of the moon.

Then he was running, not daring to look behind him as arrows began to hit the corner of the building he darted behind. He pounded down Northington Street, his heartbeat booming in his ears. The footsteps of his pursuers echoed off the walls of the street, this one filled with rusting car wrecks, drifts of dust and debris. Cold sweat beaded on his forehead as the arrows whipped past him. He threw himself around the corner at the end of the road into John Street, chest heaving.

He knew the Hunters were gaining on him, and that knowledge pushed him to run headlong down the street not thinking about where he was going, only about getting away. He was so fixed on the end of the road that he didn't notice that the door of one of the dark buildings was slightly ajar. Nor did he see the arm reach out from it as he shot past to grab him firmly by the wrist and pull him into the black entranceway.

It happened so fast that he fell as the door behind him was shut silently. A sour smell assaulted his senses; it seemed the person who had grabbed him didn't wash often. A malodorous hand clamped over Zane's mouth before he could yell out and a voice breathed into his ear with a scent of something sweet on it.

"Don't speak, don't move."

There was a lilt in the male voice, sounding like no-one that Zane had ever met before. Shaking violently from fear and exertion, he did as he was told as the Hunters ran past the doorway.

"My name's Callum," the voice whispered. "Do as I say and you'll live to see your mother again. You've upset some strong people there, my lad. Now we stay hidden and silent, until the storm has passed. Understand?"

Zane nodded, blinking into the inky darkness around him. The building was cold, the floor felt dirty and littered with rubbish, and its windows were too filthy for any moonlight to penetrate. He couldn't see what his rescuer looked like, but his deep voice sounded kind.

"Can't do anything for your friend now. Let's get somewhere more safe, then you can sleep."

The smelly hand left Zane's mouth and moved to his shoulder, then patted down his arm to catch hold of his left hand. He was pulled to his feet and then guided slowly across the room, blind as a newborn mouse, deeper into the abandoned building.

Chapter 4
FAILURE

It was late in the evening of the next day by the time that Zane was returned to his mother. The sun had coloured the sky a deep red that reflected off the taller buildings of the square, the same colour as Miri's puffy, bloodshot eyes.

She was waiting outside the house, twisting a handkerchief in her hands. After the initial panicked search of the house and garden that morning, she had gone to Jay's square, only to find him searching for Dev. They both suspected the worst. Jay had sent Boys out searching the edges of the territory, even in the hospitals, despite Miri's insistence that they couldn't be there. In the end Jay had told her to wait, that they would come back, as it was too risky to push out into no man's land or the enemy territories.

The waiting was the worst. She had tried to keep busy, tried to focus on the garden, but found herself grinding to a halt, seized by terrible thoughts and imagined scenarios where his body had been found. All afternoon, the slightest sound had brought her running to the edge of the garden, until she had given up altogether and just stood there, waiting, simply incapable of doing anything else. She had spent fifteen years worrying about Zane's safety, but this was the first time she'd thought he could be dead.

When she saw him emerge from the far side of the square she ran to him and crushed him to her, as if trying to absorb him back into her own body. She didn't even see Callum who stood back respectfully, and neither did Zane notice Jay and Grame lurking near his house. For a good minute or so Miri clutched him tightly, and then held him at arm's length, tears streaming down her cheeks as she checked him for injury.

"I'm not hurt, Mum," he mumbled, trying hard not to cry. Zane had also wept that day, both for his dead friend and for his mother, who he knew would be distraught.

"Where were you what were you doing why did you go without telling me?" The questions gushed out of Miri's mouth as fast as the tears sprang from her eyes. Zane just stood there, unsure of what to say. A tiny gasp escaped from his mother as she saw his new friend.

"Mum, this is Callum. He looked after me."

Miri looked uncertainly at the man who stood a few metres back. Callum was fairly tall, but it was hard to tell the size of his frame as he wore so many layers of filthy clothing that all stank of sweat and dirt. His face was mostly obscured by a huge, matted beard that reached down to the middle of his chest. At the edges it tangled with his long, wild hair that had clumped together into long knots, in places looking less like hair than dirty grey rope. His kind eyes, sparkling like wet polished slate, were incongruous with the sheer mess of him. The beard twitched slightly, and from the crinkling around his eyes Miri deduced that he was smiling at her.

Pale and shaken, she simply nodded at him and said "Thank you" in a wavering voice, pulling Zane towards the house where she could lock the door and keep her son close.

Callum gave a brief nod back, acknowledged Jay with a quick raise of his bushy eyebrows, and then shuffled out of the square. Jay touched his own forehead briefly with his right hand in a curt salute to the old man and then focused on Zane as he was steered towards the house.

"Was Dev with you?" he asked, and frowned as he saw the tears well in Zane's eyes. "He coming back?"

Zane simply shook his head, allowing Miri to guide him into the house. Jay's right fist clenched into a tight ball and he began to follow them in, but Miri stopped him. "Tomorrow, Jay, we'll talk tomorrow."

Jay's jaw tightened as he fought back the urge to just push past Miri. But he respected territory and after a moment nodded in capitulation.

"Zane, I want answers first thing tomorrow," he said and turned on his heels, beckoning Grame to follow.

Miri shut and locked the door, steered Zane to the sofa, and went into the kitchen wordlessly. In moments she returned with a bowl and served some of the soup from the pot hanging over the fire into it. As Zane began to eat, she went into her room and re-emerged with a blanket from her own bed to wrap around him.

She sat in the armchair opposite and watched him devour the soup, not saying anything as she filled it again for him and watched him eat that too. He scraped the spoon around the bowl, scooping every last chunk of carrot and potato into his mouth. Only when he was finished did Miri say, "Tell me what happened."

And Zane did, his voice croaking and faltering as he related what happened to Dev. He could barely bring himself to look at his mother's face, her lips and cheeks whiter than he had ever seen them. He broke down as he told her how he had abandoned Dev's body and ran, thinking only of himself and his own survival.

Miri went to his side and wrapped her arms around him, rocking him gently as if he were a small child again, and let him sob into her hair. As his distress subsided, she moved away from him to look into his eyes.

"Zane, there was nothing you could have done. You were right to run. Dev made his choice and knew the risk–there was no point losing you too." He wiped his eyes and nodded weakly. "Where does this Callum come into it?"

"He pulled me off the street when the Hunters were chasing me. He knew the building really well, actually quite a few buildings. He knew how they were laid out by heart and could move around them in the dark and everything. And he knew how to move between buildings in a clever way, through really narrow places, like it was between gaps in the walls. It meant that we could hide off the street until they stopped looking. He smells terrible but he's actually really nice. He just doesn't have you to look after him."

Miri seemed distant for a moment and then asked urgently, "They don't know it was you, do they, Zane?"

Zane shrugged nervously. "I don't know ... it was dark."

Miri chewed her lip, frowning down at the rug in the centre of the room. "No ... if they suspected you they would have come here today. They must just assume that you were one of the Bloomsbury Boys. I need to go and speak to Jay about this right now as there may be retaliation." She stood and grabbed her shawl from the armchair. "Light the candles. It'll be dark by the time I come back. Lock the door after me, and do not leave the house, do you hear?"

Zane nodded, not used to such a stern tone of voice from his mother. Just as she was about to turn the handle of the front door he called to her. "Mum?"

She turned to look at him, her mind clearly focused on her task, "Yes?"

"Are you angry with me?"

She sighed. "I was, but now I'm just glad that you're home and safe. Promise me you won't do anything that stupid ever again."

"I promise."

Zane didn't leave the house for a couple of days and either Grame or Mark was always present at the edge of the garden square, watching over Miri, as all feared some kind of retribution. But no Hunters from the Red Lady were sighted, and so the tension gradually subsided into a quiet grief. Jay checked on Miri personally at the end of each day, only

27

stopping by for a quick conversation as he was reluctant to leave the Boys for too long on their own. They'd only end up fighting, mucking about or trashing something, and he needed to make sure their energy was focused on survival, not seeing who could pee the highest up a wall.

On the third day Zane finally went outside and helped his mother in the garden. He was still withdrawn, but Miri was relieved that he was at least starting to get on with things again. They worked close to each other, comfortable with the silence between them filled by the birdsong, the sound of digging, and the pulling up of weeds as they harvested the latest crops and herbs.

When the sun hit the corner of the garden, they paused for mid-morning tea as usual, made from a blend of herbs created by Miri that was both refreshing and restorative. Later that day, as they were about to lay down tools, they heard a sound that froze Zane and spurred Miri into action. It was the alarm from the Boys' square that was only sounded in the worst kind of emergency: a Gardner attack.

Miri scooped up her tools into her skirt and grabbed Zane's hand to pull him into the house. She then bolted the door and instructed Zane to check that all of the windows and the back door were also locked as she drew the curtains of the living room.

It had happened many times before, but this time Miri was more on edge. The loud clanging of the metal bar on the rusting car roof in the Boys' square was muffled indoors but still audible, carried easily across an almost silent London. Then it stopped, and both Miri and Zane knew that now, as they hid, the Boys would be engaged in a brutal fight for survival.

After a few moments, Miri went to pack her satchel with fresh bandages, needle and thread and then gathered her pestle and mortar with a selection of fresh herbs to make the poultice that would inevitably be used on some kind of wound. Whilst she did this, Zane tied his hair back and washed his hands in the bucket of water drawn from the pump that morning.

Then there was nothing to do except wait, poised, listening intently for the sound of the all clear. Some minutes later it was sounded, and Miri cautiously peeped out from behind the curtains.

They both knew not to leave the house until one of the Boys called round, just in case a rogue Gardner strayed into their square. It had happened only once since Zane had been alive, but that one time was enough to establish the rule firmly.

Sure enough, a short time after the all clear, a knock of three rapid raps, then three slower ones hit the front door and Miri rushed to open it, recognising Jay's code.

But it was Grame who stood panting at the doorway, a gash above his left eye sending a steady flow of blood down his white face.

"Quick, come to our patch," he gasped and turned and ran. Miri and Zane hastily followed.

Both Miri and Zane expected to see wounded Boys, both had even steeled themselves for the sight of ones that had died, but neither of them had prepared for what met them on arrival in Russell Square.

Most of the gang was clustered tightly around the corner nearest to the barricade. As they both ran over, they heard the sound of sniffling and whimpering of injured Boys, some calling Jay's name, some of the older ones calling for Miri. She went straight to the nearest, Smudge, on the edge of the crowd, who was clutching his arm, blood seeping out between his fingers that were clasped over the wound.

Zane instead pushed through the crowd, intent on seeing what was drawing all of the attention. The Boys parted when they saw it was him, and then he saw Jay up ahead, still tense with both knives drawn, looking down at a body on the ground in front of him.

Zane paused mid-step as he approached and blinked in surprise; his eyes were drawn down to the body on the ground, and he pushed past a couple of the bigger Boys to get a better look.

The Gardner's face was an awful ashen grey, and his breath was rapid and shallow. He wore the familiar black suit and black tie, but the crisp whiteness of his shirt was spoilt by a deep red bloom spreading out from a point high on the right side of his chest.

Zane gawped at the sight of him, then dropped onto his knees to swiftly loosen the man's tie and unbutton his shirt.

"What are you doing?" Jay demanded in a low growl, but Zane ignored him.

"Finish him off, Jay!" shouted one of the Boys and then others agreed with eager shouts: "Kill him! Get him Jay!" The many voices began to settle into a chilling chant as Zane trembled on his knees, his hands poised above the Gardner's chest. "Kill! Kill! Kill! Kill!"

Zane, not knowing why–only that he should–placed both of his hands on the Gardner's skin. The moment he made contact he drew in a sharp breath and what little colour was left in his cheeks drained away rapidly. His eyes darted all over the man's chest, sometimes focusing on the large stab wound, but mostly lingering in the region of his heart.

"Zane!" Jay yelled above the bloodlust chanting. "What the hell are you doing?"

"I can see it!" Zane said back, barely audible above the yells of the crowd around him.

The man's eyes fluttered open, rolling around briefly before settling on Zane. "Help me," he croaked, the breath gurgling and rattling in his failing lungs.

Zane gritted his teeth and took a deep breath, letting his eyes fall upon the wound. Many of the Boys watched as the blood seeping out of it started to slow.

"He's going!" one of them yelled joyfully, thinking that the failing heart was no longer forcing the blood from the wound.

"It's not enough!" Zane muttered, unheard above the jeering.

None of the Boys noticed the sweat break out onto Zane's forehead; they only saw the Gardner's dying breaths. With delight, they rejoiced in the moment when the tension in his agonised body drained away to leave him lying there, staring up at Zane with glassy eyes. Zane cried out in despair and pulled back, as if the body had suddenly become very cold and was freezing him.

An ecstatic roar leapt up from the Boys and Jay held the knives, still coated with his opponent's blood, high above his head for all to see. Several of the Boys nearest to the body began to kick it, and Zane crawled away to let them close in around it, desperate for air. He managed to emerge from the crowd and stagger to his feet only to double over and vomit into one of the drains nearby.

Chapter 5
JAY'S CHALLENGE

Once again Zane found himself on the sofa, a blanket wrapped around him, and a mug of his mother's tea in his hand. Miri watched him stare into space, her forehead furrowed with deep lines of concern.

"Drink the tea, Zane, you've had a shock."

He sipped at it obediently and looked up at her. "Mum, I think something weird is happening to me."

"It's just shock, it'll pass."

"No, I don't mean that, I mean ... the Gardner earlier today, something weird happened and I don't know what to make of it."

Miri perched on the sofa next to him and rubbed his back slowly, reassuringly. "Why don't you describe how it felt to me and we'll see if we can work it out together," she said gently.

Zane searched for the right place to start. Miri watched his hands shaking the mug, threatening to send the hot liquid spilling over the edge. She wrapped the blanket tighter around him as the shivering started again. "Sip the tea," she whispered and he did so.

"Today, the Gardner ... I know they're horrible. I know they hurt and kill the Boys, but I couldn't stop myself from trying to help him. Even before I saw him, I sort of knew he was down on the ground and in pain." Miri listened intently, stroking his hair like she did when he was small and had woken from a night terror. "I ... could *really* see him, like normal but clearer, but then I had the urge to touch his skin, so I did and then it was like I could really see him. It was like he had a kind of blue glow around him that was fading, and I could see the blood rushing

32

out of that stab wound, and how his lungs were filling with blood and how his heart was starting to give up." The words rushed out of him in a torrent, his eyes fixed on the floor in front of him as if he were seeing it all happen in front of him again. "Even though I knew he was a bad person, I couldn't stand that he was in pain, and I wanted the wound to close and ... and ... it started to. In front of my eyes, and I knew I was doing it. I knew it. But it was too late, and he died, and when he did, it was like putting my hands in snow, and I felt cold. It was just horrible."

Miri was silent for a few moments. She cleared her throat quietly and then said "It's hard to see a person die for the first time. It's natural for you to feel odd at the moment."

"No, Mum, I feel normal now, just a bit wobbly. What I'm saying is that I felt odd *then*." He sipped more tea. "Do you see inside the Boys when you bandage up their cuts?"

Stunned by such an odd question, at first Miri simply shook her head. "No ... never," she eventually said. Zane was disappointed, lost, and in the moments of silence that followed, she composed herself. "Zane, you're a bright, imaginative boy. I think that you're really talented at helping and healing people, and when you're there with someone that is hurt, you really feel what they do. You empathise with them."

"What does empathise mean?"

"It means that you put yourself in their place and know how they feel so much that you begin to feel it a little bit yourself too. I think that you're so good at that, that you begin to think you're seeing into them. You know enough about the human body to be able to imagine these things very clearly. I don't think you're odd." Miri paused as she thought about this and then said more firmly, "No, you're not odd at all, just very involved. That's all."

Zane let the confidence in his mother's voice

soothe him.

"Finish your tea," she said, "and I'll make us some lunch."

And with that, Miri went into the kitchen. As she peeled vegetables, the deepest part of her mind took what Zane had confided in her, threw a dark cloak over it, and like a magician worked to change it into something safer, more normal, and less frightening. By the time soup was ready his story had already begun to fit much more comfortably into the slot reserved for products of her son's overactive imagination. With its newly acquired shape, she found it easier to ignore; after all, she was constantly working on the hard business of survival. They needed to eat, plants needed to be picked and pruned, and just as she had through all of the trials life had brought, she clung to that distraction like heather clings to an Atlantic cliff.

By the next day, things were almost back to normal. Zane tried hard to convince himself that the extraordinary moments with the Gardner had been nothing more than being "very involved" by busying himself in the garden and changing the dressings on the injuries sustained by some of the Boys. One by one they drifted to Miri's door, sent by Jay to be cared for, relating the tale of how they got the cut or gash and what Jay had said about it. Mercifully it had been a small attack of three Gardners and only two of them lived to return home. Zane shuddered when each Boy gleefully described how Jay had stripped the dead Gardner down to his underwear and dragged his body to the top of the barricade single-handedly to throw it over to the other side.

After the Boys had left, Zane sat alone in his room, gripped by the nausea caused by their delight in the violence of the day before. Not even the familiar comfort of being in his small room filled with books, conkers, and dried curiosities found in the garden was enough to comfort him.

Not for the first time, he wondered if there was something wrong with him. He was a boy, like those in Jay's gang, so why didn't he enjoy the fighting like them? As hard as he tried, he just couldn't understand how they could hate being hurt themselves, yet delight in another person's pain. Perhaps he was too much like his mother. When that occurred to him, he realised he didn't think that was a bad thing. Perhaps it was the other way round; perhaps the Bloomsbury Boys were strange because they didn't have a Mum to make them kind. That helped him to pull himself back together, and he went into the garden to find Miri. He hugged her fiercely whilst her hands were still deep in the soil, saying, "I'm so glad I have you, Mum."

That evening, as Zane was tidying away the day's work whilst Miri made dinner, he noticed a familiar figure at the corner of the square. He dropped the tools and ran over, excitedly calling, "Callum!"

The beard twitched and a dirty hand emerged from the bundle of clothing to shake Zane's warmly.

"How are you, my lad?"

"Ok. You?"

"As fine as can be. I was wondering how your mother is now. All calmed down again?"

Zane nodded and smiled. "Why don't you come and say hello? There might be soup too."

Callum's bright eyes looked down at the ground shyly. "That's kind of you, lad, but I'm no company for a lady."

"Oh. Alright."

Callum cleared his throat and said, "I found this. I thought she might like it." A small bundle of fabric was produced from amongst the mass of layers and Zane took it from him gently. "Only a tiny thing, but, well, I thought …" Callum shrugged and shuffled a little.

Zane smiled. "I'll pass it on to her."

"And I hope you've not been wandering off again?"

Zane shook his head solemnly. "I know not to do that."

"Well, at least one lesson learned is some good to come out of it. Something's brewing over in the Bloomsbury patch, so you tread carefully there. Jay's worked up about something."

"Do you know Jay and the Boys?"

The beard and matted hair moved up and down. "Ay, I know them. You be careful around them, Zane. Ask yourself why there are no grown-up Bloomsbury Boys."

And with that, the old man shuffled off, this time heading east towards the area where he had saved Zane from the Hunters. Zane watched him go and then ran into the house.

"Mum! You've got a present! From Callum!"

Miri emerged from the kitchen. "The man who looked after you?"

She took the package from Zane as he nodded and watched eagerly. She carefully unravelled the scrap of material to reveal a dainty shawl pin in perfect condition. It was made of bright silver that had clearly been polished carefully. A delicate Scottish thistle decorated the top of it, and Miri smiled broadly when she saw it. "How lovely!" she exclaimed. "Is he Scottish?"

"Huh?" Zane asked, bemused.

"Never mind," she said and pinned it to her favourite shawl that lay on the armchair.

"I'm going over to Jay's for a little while, ok?"

Still smiling at the gift, Miri nodded, saying, "Be back before dark" as Zane slipped out of the door.

Callum had been right. When Zane arrived, most of the Bloomsbury Boys were clustered tightly around Jay in the middle of the square. Grame was posted on the edge of the territory, and even though Zane smiled warmly at him, Grame's greeting was colder than usual.

"I reckon Jay wants to see ya," he said, hands deep in his pockets, shoulders hunched.

"Okay," Zane replied, remaining sunny despite the reception. Perhaps he could help fix whatever was making him so bad tempered.

The murmur of the gathered Boys dissipated as he approached, and the ones nearest to him moved apart to open a way to Jay in the middle. Zane noticed the absence of nods and smiles and regretted coming to visit.

"Hello," he said, smiling despite his nervousness.

"Zane," Jay said, straightening to his full height. "Funny you should come over now. We were just talkin' 'bout you."

The Boys closed in behind Zane, forming a tight circle around him and the young gang leader. Zane's mouth went dry. "Me?" he replied, trying his best to stop his voice cracking under the tension. He failed.

"Yup. See, we was wonderin' sommat, and now you're 'ere, maybe you could give us some answers."

"Um, okay."

"Yesterday, you did sommat weird. That Gardner, when he was dyin', you touched him. On the chest."

Zane nodded hesitantly. "Yes, I did." There was no point denying it; they had all seen it happen.

"The thing with Gardners," Jay said louder, with more showmanship, "is that the only way to touch them is with the sharp end of yer knife, right, Boys?"

"Right!" several of them cheered.

"And, the thing about that," Jay continued, "is it ain't to do nothin' but kill 'em. We don't stick 'em with our knives to be nice, do we, Boys?"

"No!" more joined in, some snickering.

"You ain't got a knife, Zane," Jay rounded on him. "And you didn't look like you were tryin' to kill 'im." He let the statement hang in the air. "So what I wanna know is, if ya didn't wanna kill 'im, what the hell were you doin'?"

Zane's stomach cramped with tension. He curled his hands into fists and thrust them into his pockets so Jay wouldn't see them shaking. "I … I don't know. He was hurt –"

"I know!" Jay interrupted. "I was the one that done it!"

There was a mixture of cheers and laughter from the assembled, but Jay didn't look amused. Zane swallowed, peeling his tongue from the roof of his mouth.

"Mark 'ere," Jay jerked a thumb at one of the tallest Boys, "says you threw up when the Gardner died."

Zane nodded slowly. "Y-yes … I was sick."

Jay scowled. "Why?"

"Um … because of the … the blood," Zane replied, unable to think of anything else to say that wasn't the truth, and he didn't feel that here, right now, was the time to tell them about his strange experience.

"Bollocks!" Jay exclaimed. "You an' Miri stitch us up all the time–you see blood nearly every day!" He took a step closer. "I'd 'ate to think you were lyin' to me, Zane. I can't stand a liar."

Zane struggled to draw a breath; it felt like his chest had seized up. Jay stared at him and the circle of Boys closed in a step. Zane could feel a tremor in his knees.

"See, Zane, I got a problem 'ere," Jay continued when the boy said nothing. "Cos I like ya, and I think ya mum's ace. And that's good for you, cos if that weren't true, you'd be pasted on the side of that buildin' over there." Mark picked that moment to crack his knuckles. "But the thing is, you looked like you were goin' soft on that Gardner. And that worries me, Zane, it worries me."

"I … I don't want you to worry, Jay," Zane replied, his voice wavering.

"That's good, Zane, that's good," Jay said, planting a hand on his shoulder and gripping it firmly. "None of us want that.

But I know what I saw, and so I want proof you're not gonna start goin' soft on them Gardners when they start on us again."

Zane's throat felt like it was closing. "Proof?"

"Go get one of their ties for Jay!" said Grame, sparking a round of jeering agreement from the circle.

"Don't be daft," Jay dismissed. "He's too soft to stab a live one." As the Boys laughed, Jay pointed at the barricade. "But he could practise on the one they left behind."

Zane's throat burned as bile rose up from his twisting stomach. He'd never been near a dead body before; his mother had made sure of that. But he had read about it in the medical books at home. He thought of the Gardner Jay had tossed over the other side the day before, how the body would be cold and stiff by now.

Zane swallowed hard as Jay continued, a chilling smile spreading across his face like a dark cloud on a spring day. "I'll letchya borra me knife, can't say fairer than that." Jay drew one of the pair, tilted the blade to capture the last of the evening sunlight. "Go over and stab the body, Zane."

"Yeah! Stab it!" Boys yelled around him, building themselves up into a chant. "Stab it! Stab it!"

Jay leaned in close to him, holding up a hand to quiet the gang. "You bring the blade back clean, I'll know you're soft on 'em. We'll all know."

The Boys looked from Jay to Zane again, the tension twisting its thick strands tightly between them all. Zane looked at Jay's belt, thinking of all the men who must have been hurt or killed for Jay to have that many ties. He thought of his mother and what he'd promised her. He saw her face when Callum brought him back, how worried she'd been. What if there were Gardners on the other side of the barrier, hiding, waiting for a Boy to climb down and get rid of the body?

"He can't hurt ya!" Mark yelled, frustrated by Zane's hesitation. "He's dead already!"

The Boys laughed and the shoving resumed. Jay turned the knife to present the handle to Zane.

"Do it, Zane!" Grame yelled and the Boys echoed him. "Do it! Do it!"

Jay's face twisted into a cruel sneer. "Why don't you just say that you're too scared?"

Zane took a deep breath, mindful of the Boys closing in around him. Jay needed his mum too much to hurt him, but he also knew that if he didn't do this, they would make his life miserable. Swallowing down another surge of nausea, he reached for the blade.

"JAY!" The bellow came from the north end of the square. Jay's head snapped around to see Callum cradling a limp body in his arms with a familiar shock of ginger hair. "Jay! Come here! I've found Dev and he's alive!"

In moments the knife was sheathed and the challenge forgotten as all raced over to Callum. Jay snatched Dev from his offering arms and shook him gently.

"Dev? Dev!" he called but Dev didn't stir.

"Cor, what's that on his face?" one of the Boys exclaimed as Zane struggled to push his way past them all to see how his friend was.

The Boys made it hard for him; elbows jabbed into his sides, and they were slow to move aside as he pushed at them. He finally broke through to see two gashes, one on each of Dev's cheeks, describing a line from near the corners of his mouth to the outer edges of his cheekbones. The cuts didn't seem too deep, but what was alarming was their intense red colour, too garish to be just blood. It not only sat within the line of the cuts but had also seeped out into the skin of his cheeks, tiny cracks of dark red like fractures on the porcelain glaze of his pale face.

"She marked him!" Jay snarled with such rage that many of the Boys closest to him backed away without even realising what they were doing.

"Let's take him to Mum," Zane suggested and Jay nodded, immediately breaking into a run.

"You lot stay 'ere," he called back to the gang. "And keep watch for that bitch's Hunters."

Callum drifted after Zane and Jay as they hurried over to Miri's square, keeping his distance but eager to see what was happening.

Zane wasn't surprised to see his mother opening the door as they arrived; the sound of their footsteps had reverberated off the surrounding buildings like heralds' trumpets.

"He won't wake up, Miri!" Jay exclaimed, and she beckoned them into the house.

They gently laid Dev down on the sofa, the front door left open in their haste. Callum stood just outside of the door frame, looking in but also trying hard not to be noticed.

Miri carefully checked Dev's airways and breathing, monitored his pulse, and loosened the layers of clothing as best she could.

"He's dead pale," Jay said, hovering nearby like a nervous father.

Miri simply nodded, glancing at Zane and noting how intensely he was staring at Dev. "Check his leg, Mum, it's hurt," he muttered whilst pointing to his left calf.

She pulled up the trouser leg and revealed a clean, tightly wrapped bandage. "Perhaps this is where that arrow hit," she said. "They've bandaged it well."

Zane nodded, staring at it intently. "The wound's clean," he said quietly as Miri shuddered at his odd behaviour.

Jay looked at Zane, confused. "How'd you know? You can't even see it."

Dev moaned quietly, and Miri caught hold of his hand gently, distracting Jay. She stroked the back of it, very softly calling Dev's name.

Dev's eyelids struggled open and he looked up at the trio with bloodshot eyes. "Watchya," he murmured in a shaky voice.

"Thought you were dead, Dev," Jay said affectionately.

"Nah," Dev croaked back, "but I think I might've been for a bit." He began to reach up to his face but Miri caught hold of his hand and gently pushed it down again.

"Your cheeks are cut. Don't touch them or they'll get infected."

"That why they're itching?"

She nodded, smoothing back hair from his forehead tenderly. "They'll get better soon."

"Whaddya remember?" Jay asked, kneeling down next to Miri.

"I nearly got it Jay, honest-like!" he murmured sleepily.

"Never mind that now," Jay replied, fighting a smile that tugged at the corner of his mouth. "You've been gone a few days – what happened?"

Dev seemed genuinely surprised. "I have? Only remember the banner ... and me leg killing me."

"Nothing about the Red Lady?"

Dev jolted like a tiny bolt of lightning had hit him, and his eyes opened wide. He began to speak, but his voice was devoid of any of its normal inflection. "If one of the Bloomsbury Boys enters my territory again, they will be killed on sight. Let the marks on this one remind you of that every day."

All three of them drew back, staring at Dev warily. But then he relaxed and looked around at them after blinking a couple of times. "What?" he asked confused, with his normal voice.

Jay and Miri exchanged a look. Callum tugged at the bottom of his beard and shuffled a little. Zane mustered a smile and said "Nothing, Dev. It's alright. We're just so glad to see you again."

Chapter 6

AN UNWANTED INVITATION

After she had fed him and fussed over him for a while, Miri insisted that Dev spend the night at her house in front of the fire. Jay agreed reluctantly, promising to return to collect him the next day. Callum slipped away before anyone had the chance to thank him, much to Zane's disappointment. As Dev slept on the sofa, he brooded over Jay's challenge but didn't tell his mother. He didn't want to see her worried face again.

The next day dawned bright and clear, the weather holding fine and promising a good harvest. Jay kept to his word and collected a groggy and still mostly bewildered Dev from Miri's care. Zane hung back, nervous that Jay would hint at the day before, but he said nothing. But just as he was leaving, he said, "Zane, give us a hand with Dev 'ere, will ya?"

He obeyed, wanting his mother to think everything was fine. He said nothing as he steered Dev out of the house and along the garden.

"I spoke to the Runners," Jay said quietly as they reached the edge of Miri's square. Zane nodded. The Runners were a good choice, being the only people who could move between gang territories. They took messages between the gangs in return for clothes, food, and sometimes shelter in the winter. He was glad it wasn't the life he led. "I got them keeping an eye out for your Giant. I wanna know if he's been in any other places." Zane breathed out in relief, thankful that the challenge wasn't revived. "My Boys are watchin' for him too," Jay added, then lowered his voice even further. "They'll be watchin' you too.

I ain't forgotten." He tugged at Dev's collar. "C'mon you, keep up."

Shaken, Zane returned to his mother, relieved that away from the Bloomsbury Boys the morning was taking on the feel of any normal day. He knew that he would have to face Jay and the rest of them again at some point, but right now, all he wanted to think about was the soil and the plants and his mother's instructions. Everything else just felt confusing and difficult.

Together they worked in the garden, focused on the business of survival. Only a shadow falling over them stopped their industry. Miri plunged the trowel in the soil and left it there when she saw who it was.

The man nodded to her and she stood, wiping her hands on her long skirt and glancing over at Zane nervously. It was one of the Hunters from the Red Lady's gang, none other than the Red Lady's Champion, Luthor. He stood over six and half feet tall with calf muscles wider than Zane's whole thigh and biceps as big as Zane's head. Like all of her Hunters, he wore leather trousers that were deep red, rumoured to have been dyed by the blood of slaughtered enemies. His stout boots were made of the same red leather and he wore a plain hand-woven linen shirt underneath the red leather bracers on his arms. He was clean shaven and his dark blonde hair was scraped back tightly and plaited into a thick braid that reached the top of his thighs.

Luthor turned up like this once every two months without fail, coming to the garden with a small wooden box tucked under his arm. Usually, he would ignore Zane, but go with his mother into the house, and she would put something in the box. Then he'd leave, often without saying one word to Zane. He had given up asking what was put in the box; his mother always said that it was a "private arrangement" between her and the Red Lady. His favourite theories were that it was tea or herbs to treat some terrible disease; though what that could be, he had no idea. He had never seen anyone be ill, not like in the medical books he read anyway.

Zane never ceased to be fascinated by the weaponry Luthor carried at all times. A bow on his back next to the quiver always full of thick arrows fletched with red feathers. At his left hip hung a huge sword in a scabbard, and strapped to his left thigh was a long dagger. Another smaller one, for skinning, hung from his belt.

This morning, the box was tucked under Luthor's arm, as usual, but something was very different. Luthor was looking at Zane in such a way that pinned the boy to the spot as if the Hunter had thrown a spear through him.

Miri's sharp eyes rarely missed anything aimed at her son. "You're early," she said. "I wasn't expecting you for a while yet."

Luthor made a dismissive grunt at the back of his throat and held out the box to her. She took it and, voice quivering, said, "It may take a little while. I haven't prepared everything."

He nodded curtly, still staring at Zane, who began to squirm under the pressure of his gaze. Miri lingered, uncomfortable with Luthor's focus on her son.

"Is there something else?" she asked in a quiet voice.

Luthor pursed his lips as if he had tasted something sour, not taking his eyes off Zane for a moment, and said, "The Red Lady wants to see your son. Now." It was the first time Zane had ever heard his voice. It was even deeper than Callum's but didn't have any kindness to smooth away its harsh edges.

Miri wanted to speak, but the words died on her lips before they could be heard.

Zane stood, very slowly, watching his mother's panic. "Why does she want to see me?" he asked as confidently as he could manage.

Luthor's brow formed into a deep frown, casting an even darker shadow over his deep-set eyes as if they were overhung by a treacherous cliff. "That is for the Red Lady to speak to you about," he said gruffly, as if personally offended by the question.

Miri regained control over her tongue once more and said, "If you wait here, Zane can help me get things ready more quickly."

Luthor raised a suspicious eyebrow at her, but then shrugged, ultimately disinterested. "I leave in five minutes, with Zane and the box." He looked at it held in her shaking hands and added, "He will be returned to you by nightfall. I will escort him there and back. He will be safe."

His words did nothing to reassure her, but under the pressure of his gaze she caught hold of Zane's hand and pulled him into the house. She shut the door behind them and locked it. After carefully placing the box on the sofa, she caught hold of Zane's shoulders, turning him to face her and hold him in place.

"Zane, if she asks about Dev and the other night, deny any knowledge of it. Do you understand?"

"But you said lying to people is bad."

"This isn't people, Zane. This is the Red Lady, and this could save your life." She gripped him tightly with shaking hands. "Make an exception in this case. When you're there, be respectful, polite, and tell her as little as you can without being rude."

"As little as I can about what?"

"Anything. Everything."

Her fear began to leech into him. "Mum, why would she want to see me? Is she going to mark me like she did with Dev?"

Miri swallowed hard and tried her best to look brave. "I'm sure she won't do that ... why would she?"

Zane shrugged uneasily.

Miri glanced at the box and then said more confidently, "She won't mark you, Zane, I'm sure of it."

He nodded with relief.

"And whilst you're there," Miri continued, "don't eat or drink anything. Not a thing."

"But it's nearly lunchtime!"

"Not a thing, Zane. Promise me."

Zane searched her fearful eyes and nodded slowly. "I promise."

"I'll make you your favourite mash to have when you get home, alright?" Miri drew him into a tight embrace. "Now wait here whilst I get the box ready."

She kissed his cheek and then scooped up the box and rushed into her bedroom. Zane listened to the sounds of drawers in her apothecary chest being hurriedly opened and closed.

He shifted from one foot to the other until she called out, "Put on some clean clothes and wash your hands! And comb your hair too!"

He obeyed, and by the time he re-emerged from his room, she was waiting by the door, the box tucked under her arm.

"Mum, what if I don't want to go?"

Miri sighed. "I don't think that's an option, Zane. The Red Lady is very powerful. Try not to annoy or upset her ... just be lovely like you always are .... but less ... chatty ..." Miri frowned at herself and then leant forward to kiss his forehead tenderly. "I'll be here waiting for you."

She unlocked the door to find Luthor waiting nearby. She gave him the box and he gave her his usual brisk nod in return. Then his attention shifted to Zane. He squeezed his mother's hand briefly, stood as tall and straight as he could, and went to the Hunter's side to walk with him out of the square.

"Um … is it true that you're the Red Lady's Champion?" Zane took the first minutes of the journey to muster the courage to ask the question.

Luthor glanced down at the youth and nodded.

"What does that mean exactly?"

Luthor's face distorted into an unfamiliar smile. "It means I am the fastest, the strongest, the best Hunter, the one the Red Lady turns to first," he announced proudly. Zane had the feeling that he was about to say more, but nothing followed.

"Oh. That must be … nice."

"Nice?" Luthor scoffed. "Nice is how a woman would describe a dress. What I speak of is the highest honour." He drew in a deep breath, expanding his chest so much that it blocked the sunlight falling onto Zane's face. "No other man will ever take my place."

Zane remained silent, now too unsure of his choice of words to say anything more. He had to hurry to keep up with Luthor's huge strides.

It was the first time Zane had travelled so far from home in the daytime. Even though it was really only a short walk, this was a route that he had only dared once, that night with Dev. He had been taught from a very early age that anywhere except the garden and the Boys' square was unsafe, and so walking between two territories in broad daylight was a very odd experience.

The buildings lining the streets they walked through were similar to those in Miri's square; built several storeys high with dark bricks and large sash windows. His mother said the houses used to be some of the smartest in London, but now they were grey and dilapidated, nature having found every crack and crevice through which it could reassert itself. London's buildings were losing the quiet war with plants and he wondered if one day there would be any buildings left at all. As they walked past,

Zane was particularly fascinated by the curious shapes of the rusting ventilation system that lay behind the hospital in which he and Dev had seen the Giant. What could that have been for? How did people make metal into those shapes when it was so hard? How did it all get here in the first place?

Luthor walked with the confidence of a man who knew that no sane individual would dare attack him. As for any lunatic that might try, it was clear that he could slaughter them as easily as Miri would wrench a weed from the ground. His eyes scanned their surroundings constantly and he attended to any change in noise or distant sounds as they walked, but without any nervousness.

Before long they reached the edge of the Red Lady's territory, marked by huge daubs of red that looked like dried blood on the corners of the buildings at the end of Gray's Inn Road. Zane looked at them and his paced slowed; they hadn't been visible that night he had ventured into the territory with Dev. Luthor must have detected his fear and said to him, "I grant you entry into the Red Lady's territory by her command, so you have nothing to fear."

Zane looked down the road, the whitewashed walls coming into view, resplendent in the summer sunshine. The impressive red silk banners, stretched taut against the walls, were spotless, the same red as the fletching of Luthor's arrows. Knowing that he was permitted to be here did nothing to allay his fears.

Luthor escorted him to gates made of stout wood set into the wall. They were over twice the height of the Hunter, with no visible spy hole or any discernible point of weakness. Luthor signalled to a Hunter watching their approach from on top of the wall, who in turn signalled to someone below him, out of sight. In moments there was a loud thunk and scraping sound as the bolts that held the gates shut were drawn back.

Zane's legs were becoming uncooperative and he was

half escorted, half pushed past two guards on either side of the gates, both with arrows notched. They were dressed in the same linen and leather clothing as Luthor and were clearly also strong, but without his bulk. The guards watched Zane enter, and then one with dark brown hair drawn back into a long braid like Luthor's withdrew the arrow, slung the bow over his shoulder, and approached purposefully.

The Hunter reached out with both hands towards Zane. Startled by the intrusion of his personal space, Zane said, "Hey!" and backed away, only to feel Luthor's hand catch the back of his neck and hold him in place with a firm grip.

"Stand still. He is going to check you for weapons," Luthor instructed, not removing his hand.

Zane tensed as the other Hunter ran his hands over his shirt and patted his legs. Zane didn't ever carry a knife and he was appalled that the Hunter thought he would. Only the Bloomsbury Boys did that, and only the ones who knew how to use them. Jay was very strict about that.

"Strange prey that you bring today." The guard's dismissive voice rumbled over Zane's head, aimed at Luthor.

"Just check him, David," he replied curtly, making no attempt to hide his dislike of the Hunter.

The man finally gave Luthor a nod and Zane was released. He tugged his shirt down, annoyed by the mocking looks that the guards had given him. He straightened himself up as best he could, but they simply looked back at him steadily until he lowered his eyes. They laughed at him.

Embarrassed, he let Luthor push him farther in as the heavy wooden doors were slammed shut behind them.

Chapter 7

THE RED LADY

Few people had seen the interior of this place, and Zane was acutely aware of this. None of the Bloomsbury Boys save Dev, who couldn't remember anyway, had stepped foot into the inner part of the Red Lady's territory. He recalled being told that the Red Lady was the last person that a trespasser would ever see, as soon after being condemned by her they would be blinded or killed. Zane had always thought that these were simply scary stories that the Boys loved to frighten each other with at night, but now that he was actually here, they came back to him with a visceral quality. Images of the way the Hunters pounced upon Dev and the new scars on his face flashed in his mind.

The courtyard through which Luthor steered him was surrounded on three sides by tall, four storey high brick buildings, not unlike those in his mother's square, but these were all well cared for and clearly still in use, as several of the windows were open on the upper storeys.

The smell of food wafted from one of the open windows of the large building along with the gentle clamour of many people eating within. Zane's own stomach growled and he longed for a taste of whatever it was that smelt so good.

Luthor directed him to a large set of double doors with a steady pressure applied to the small of his back. Zane felt that Luthor didn't want him to have time to take in all of the details of the place.

A small set of steps led up to two grand wooden doors that looked heavy and thick, proportioned as if for men twenty feet tall, with two huge polished brass handles too big for any mere mortal to grasp in one hand. Again, they were flanked by two guards, both just as strong as those on the gate and with their hands on the hilt of the large swords hanging from their belts. Luthor nodded to both briskly, and they opened the doors for them to go through.

The interior was cool and shadowy after the glare of the noon sun. The floor alone arrested Zane's attention, as the pale marble shone unlike any surface he had ever seen; it was a world away from the wooden floorboards and faded rugs of his own home. A pair of large doors stood to his left, a grand staircase swept up in front of him, and a corridor stretched away to his right. The air smelt sweet as Zane recognised lavender, but it was laced with something else, something musky, unlike anything he had ever smelt before.

Luthor propelled him towards the doors to his left. A single guard, the biggest yet, but still not as impressive as Luthor, looked Zane up and down with barely disguised surprise and then opened the door at Luthor's nod. As the heavy wooden door was swung open, Luthor's hand went to the back of his head, pushing it down so that he faced the floor as if in deference. Zane wanted to shove him away, but was mindful of how much stronger Luthor was.

A beautiful polished floor, the colour of dark honey, stretched ahead of him. He was aware of the size of the room and how light it was. One large window was to his left in his peripheral vision; it was open and thin gauze curtains were teased by the gentle breeze.

That heady, unfamiliar scent was stronger here, and Zane felt the presence of someone at the far end of the room, but with Luthor's hand still firm on the back of his head, he couldn't look up to see who it was. He was manoeuvred further in and heard the doors shut behind them with a loud, deep thud that briefly drowned out his thrumming heart.

"Bring him closer, Luthor," a voice said. It was soft yet commanding and floated from a place beyond where he could see. His heart splashed against his chest. It was the first feminine voice he had ever heard that wasn't his mother's, and something rich in its tone made him desperate to look up and see what its creator looked like.

Luthor did her bidding, and a shallow step in the same gleaming wood as the floor came into Zane's field of vision.

"Mmmm ..." The silken voice murmured a hint of approval and Zane felt immensely self-conscious all of a sudden. It was a novel sensation. He wanted to know what she was thinking, wanted her approval somehow, before he had even seen her. "Hello, Zane," she said quietly, lingering over his name in the same way as he would savour the last bite of his favourite meal. "I've heard a lot about you."

Strangely, he was thrilled to hear this. "You have?" he replied, immediately annoyed at his voice not sounding as deep as he wanted.

"Mmmm, yes. Let him go, Luthor. I want to see his face."

The pressure lifted from the back of his head and Zane finally did as he craved, but slowly, now fearful that the sight of her wouldn't match the promise of her voice.

Three more polished wooden steps came into view, then a slender foot, wrapped in a sandal of thin strands of leather that crisscrossed their way up the smooth, shapely leg above it. Then red silk, draping its way across to cut off the upward track of his eyes. Unable to stop, he drank in the rest of her like a thirsty man would sweet wine.

The Red Lady sat at the top of the dais in a throne-like chair so wide that she half lay across it, accentuating the curve of her hips and her slim waist. Her long, straight hair framed her face like rich satin, a deep blonde with occasional auburn streaks. Her eyes looked back at him, hinting at something playful yet dangerous. Their colour reminded him of spring leaves with sunlight filtered through them. Her skin was flawless, creamy, and smooth, as if made to be touched. He wanted to rush forward and run his hands over her arms, left bare by the silken red dress that alternately draped and clung to her in all the right places. It was held up by two thin straps that looked as if they may slip off her shoulders at any moment, and without even realising it, he wished that they would. When he saw the deep cleft between her breasts, his mouth went dry, and in that moment he decided that if he ever saw another woman again, she couldn't possibly be as beautiful as the Red Lady.

She watched him, amused, as he blinked and his mouth hung open. Her full, red lips curved into a slow smile and she allowed him a few moments more before saying, "You act as if you've never seen a woman before."

"I haven't," Zane replied stupidly, and then hastily added, "I mean, not one that wasn't Mum. Miri, I mean ... she's my mum."

Her smile melted into a brief laugh that in his stupor reminded Zane of melodious birdsong. "I know."

He remained silent, watching her eyes slowly move up and down him as she seemed to study him, appraising him as one might a fruit tree that needed to be pruned. He became painfully aware of how small he seemed in comparison to Luthor.

"Zane's a strange name. Were you named after some-one?"

He wished he could tell her he was named after some kind of great hero, but all he could truthfully reply was, "I don't know."

"No matter." She caught a wisp of hair in her fingers and twisted it. "Luthor, you never told me how handsome Miri's son has become."

Zane heard the leather of Luthor's armour creak as he tensed at the comment. Zane smiled to himself. Handsome! She said he was handsome!

"Leave us now." She waved a hand dismissively at the huge man as she would a stray dog. He paused, as if needing a moment to understand the unexpected command. When he didn't immediately obey, the Red Lady's eyes flicked to him and it only took a moment of her glare to make him bow deeply and reluctantly withdraw.

She watched him leave and then her attention fell back on Zane.

"So what do you think of my Hunters?"

Zane fumbled for words, most of them having been pushed out of his mind by the vision of her. "Um … they're very strong."

She smiled. "I like my men to be strong. And big."

Zane thought of his skinny arms and legs and sighed to himself.

"I would think," she began slowly, continuing to torment the strands of hair caught on her finger, "that you would like to be big and strong one day too."

He nodded rapidly, completely unaware of how transparent he was.

"Perhaps you could be big and strong enough to be one of my Hunters."

Zane nodded again. "Yes, I'd like that," he replied without thinking.

She sighed. "But I don't see how you will be."

His stomach tightened at the prospect of such a personal tragedy. "I'll try really hard," he retorted, making silent oaths to get up at dawn and run and lift heavy things until his arms were as big as Luthor's.

"It's not that," she smiled, "I'm sure you'd be very motivated. It's just that the reason why my men are like that is because they hunt and eat the meat they catch."

Zane was crestfallen. "I don't know how to hunt," he said sadly.

"Oh dear." She let him wallow in his misery for several heartbeats and then leant forward, as if something had enthused her all of a sudden. "I have an idea!" Zane almost took a step towards her, she was so magnetic. But then her face lost its excited joy and she shook her head sadly. "I'm not sure your mother would like it though."

"Oh! How about you tell me anyway? I know her better than anyone – it might be alright."

"Well, perhaps we could strike a deal," she replied. "Let's see … I could send one of my Hunters to train you every day so you could learn how to catch meat and get stronger."

Zane gasped in delight at the possible end to his inadequacy. "That would be wonderful!" he gushed.

"But Zane …" She released her hair and held up a hand. "This is something I've never offered to anyone outside of my gang before. I'm not sure I should …"

Zane was about to say that he would join it, then and there, on his knees in front of her, unaware of how effortlessly he was being manipulated. Mercifully the memory of his mother telling him again and again to never join a gang chose this time to surface. Crushed by guilt at having forgotten her until now, he lowered his large brown eyes and said, "Mum would never let me join a gang … not without talking to her first."

The Red Lady leant back in her chair. "Well … I could make an exception in your case." She smiled at the way his head snapped up and his eager eyes searched her face for salvation. "Seeing as you show such … promise, I will offer you this. I'll send a Hunter to train you, and in return you'll give me a quarter of the meat from every kill you make. I'll offer this to you only once, Zane, so think carefully."

He didn't.

"Yes!" he said immediately. "It's a deal! That would be great. I'd happily do that – no problem. Thank you!" She laughed again, delighting in his open captivation.

Zane took a deep breath and said, "When the Blooms-bury Boys make a deal, they spit on their palms and then shake each other's hands. Do you do that here?"

She looked down at his hopeful face. "Goodness, no!" She stood, smirking at his disappointment and then held out her right hand down to him. "But I'll shake your hand *without* the spitting to seal the deal. And as you're an outsider, I'll release you from a blood obligation."

With trembling legs, Zane climbed the steps and reached out to clasp her hand. It was cool and so soft, so different to his mother's calloused hands. He held it a little too long before shaking it as firmly as he could, just like Jay had taught him when he was much younger.

"Well, your handshake is strong enough," she commented, and his chest swelled with pride. She smiled and said quietly, "You can let go now, Zane. The deal is made."

Blushing, he let go of her hand and she returned to the chair. When she turned her back to him to do so, he couldn't help but admire her skin and the curve of her back, the deep cut of the dress drawing his eyes to the lowest part of it just above her hips.

"I look forward to hearing of your progress," she said, draping herself across the chair, the silk of the dress falling from the slit cut at the side of it, revealing a little more of her thigh.

All Zane could do was nod, dumbstruck.

The Red Lady's smile played across her lips, but Zane failed to notice that it didn't reach her eyes. She clicked her fingers and the doors at the end of the room opened. It surprised Zane; surely that was too quiet to be heard through such a thick door.

Luthor and the other guard appeared at the doorway. "Escort my guest home, Luthor," she commanded. As he was entering, she turned back to Zane. "Unless you'd like something to eat before you go?"

At that moment, another Hunter carried in a large bronze platter, two crystal glasses at its centre, surrounded by a selection of cut meat and salad. He climbed the steps and knelt at her feet, presenting it to her with a bowed head.

Zane's stomach growled so loudly that Luthor raised an eyebrow at him. Zane swallowed and through gritted teeth said, "No thank you," whilst staring with longing at the platter. He and his mother so rarely ate meat.

"Ah well," she sighed and shrugged at him. "I suppose you should get back home to your mother. Goodbye, Zane."

Zane sighed wistfully, not wanting to leave at all but realising that it wasn't up to him. He was about to move when he felt Luthor's hand grip the back of his head again, this time more roughly than before, and push him down into a bow before Zane could resist.

"Be more respectful," Luthor growled in his ear and Zane conceded to the bow.

Luthor let him go and then bowed deeply himself. The Red Lady barely seemed to notice as she cast her eyes over the offerings in front of her. Zane was half pulled away by his escort before finally tearing his eyes from her and allowing himself to be led to the door.

Just before stepping through, he broke away from Luthor. It was so unexpected that Zane slipped from the Hunter before he had time to grab him; evidently no-one had ever dared return to her once dismissed.

Zane raced back to the dais as the other man hastily laid the platter on the floor to partially draw his sword. The Red Lady was also surprised, but maintained her composure, waiting to see what the boy wanted.

"I just remembered," he blurted and she raised an eyebrow in curiosity. "I didn't kiss you goodbye!"

"What!" Luthor roared in fury at his impertinence and began to storm his way across the room to drag Zane out by his hair.

But the Red Lady stayed him with her hand, still looking at Zane, fascinated. "I never said you could or invited you to do so," she said, amused.

"But … but I always kiss my mum goodbye, so I thought …"

A spontaneous ripple of laughter tilted her head back, exposing her milky throat. He ached to touch it. "I have never heard …" Her words unravelled back into her delighted laugh.

Luthor hung back, uncertain at what to do when he saw her amusement at Zane's effrontery, but ready to leap on him at a flick of her finger.

Zane also stood poised, not knowing what she wanted. He eyed the Hunter crouched between the two of them, who stared back at him balefully. The Red Lady put a hand on his shoulder, still chuckling. "Put it away, Leo. He isn't a threat." The Hunter dropped the sword back into its sheath and backed away.

Zane looked up at her hopefully, his muscles straining to be close to her once again. She looked at him with renewed interest.

"What a charming young man you are, Zane. Yes, I'll let you kiss me goodbye if you wish." A spluttering cough burst out from Luthor behind him, which she ignored. She turned her face slightly and tapped her left cheek.

Zane bounded up the last three steps like an eager puppy and then, holding his breath, leant forward to plant a tender kiss on her slightly flushed cheek. It felt like the petal of a newly opened rose beneath his lips, and he lingered there for a heartbeat longer than when he kissed his mother.

She pulled back and smiled almost mischievously at him. Grinning like a Bloomsbury Boy with his first Token, he practically floated back down the steps, walking backwards to the door so that he might steal every last moment of the encounter. He waved at her as he withdrew, a glowering Luthor ensuring that this time he really did leave.

Chapter 8
THE FRAGILE BALANCE

All the way back to Miri's square, whilst skirting around car wrecks and stepping over gentle mounds of dust collected by the clusters of bones, Luthor seethed. Zane was in a glorious world of his own, head crammed full of images of the Red Lady. He rolled each one around his mind like a sweet berry in his mouth.

A silly smile danced across Zane's face as he ruminated on what she had said to him. He fantasised about being a great Hunter and returning to her, bloody from a kill, to have her clap her hands in delight and then kiss him in gratitude, his young heart providing a loud percussive background all the while.

Luthor's face was twisted into a grim scowl, his eyes occasionally taking in the expressions on his charge's face; the happier they were, the more angry he became. He stopped at the farthest edge of Queen Square, eager to discharge his duty as soon as possible. Zane didn't notice for a few steps, but when he did he smiled at the massive man happily, making Luthor's teeth grind.

"Thanks, Luthor!" Zane chirruped and then dawdled on to his home, not feeling the keen Hunter's eyes fixed on the back of his head like sword points.

Zane drifted into the square, eyes drawn to the garden of one of the abandoned houses, in which an intensely red wild rose grew. He was surprised that he hadn't really noticed it before. Dreamily, he took a circuitous route through the central garden and finally emerged opposite his house.

"Hello?" he called as he opened the front door, and his mother hurriedly emerged from her bedroom, a small muslin bag of dried herbs in her hand. Her relief at seeing him was palpable, and she flew over to wrap him in her arms, smiling.

"I'm so glad you're back! She didn't keep you long–what did she want?"

"Mum, am I named after someone?"

She pulled away. "Why do you want to know about that?"

Zane frowned at her, sensing that there was something in this. "The Red Lady wanted to know."

Miri looked surprised and confused all at once. "That's why she wanted to see you?"

"Oh, no ... she just wondered, that's all. She said I had a strange name." The thought of that made him fretful. "Is it strange?"

Miri didn't want to be sidetracked in this way and answered in a frustrated voice. "It's rare, I suppose. That's not important though!"

"It's my name!" Zane retorted. "It's important to me!"

Miri sighed heavily and ran a hand through her hair, this conversation not going the way she wanted. "I didn't mean that. What did she want?"

Zane was about to answer and then frowned. "I don't think she wanted anything in particular ... just to meet me. For a chat I think."

Miri's eyes narrowed suspiciously. "The Red Lady doesn't invite people around for chats, Zane."

"Well, she didn't say what she wanted," he replied peevishly, the rosy glow of his visit being threatened by this interrogation.

Miri drew back, calming herself down in an effort to manage her son's emotions. She looked at him with a mother's critical eye and frowned. He didn't quite seem himself.

"So what did you chat about?" She lightened her tone to one of casual interest and the tactic worked, as Zane's face brightened immediately.

"Oh Mum, it's brilliant! She's going to send a Hunter to train me so I can catch meat and get big and strong!"

Miri blinked rapidly, struggling to take it in. "What!"

In his excitement, he misinterpreted it for amazement at how lucky he was. "Yeah, isn't it great!"

"No!" Miri cried, bursting the bubble around her son. "This is terrible! She's sending a Hunter *here*? Here, to my square!"

Zane's face rapidly lost its radiance. "Yes," he said hesitantly, watching his mother's hands cover her mouth, eyes wide in panic. "But that's good, right? I mean, then I can catch meat for us here. That's a good thing!"

Miri shook her head in disbelief. "Oh Zane, what have you done!"

He floundered. "What? I ... I thought it was a good idea!"

Miri dropped into the armchair and held her head in her hands. Zane hovered, utterly confused, watching his mother trying to calm down, her hands shaking. After a few moments she spoke, not lifting her head. "Who is it going to be? How long will they be here?"

"Um ... she didn't say ..." Zane replied quietly.

Miri tried to collect herself. "Tell me *exactly* what happened. Was this a suggestion? An offer?"

Zane fidgeted. "It started as an offer ... then it was a deal." His mother looked up at him, as white as the gauze at the windows in the Red Lady's room, and his voice became quieter.

"One of her Hunters will train me, and I'll give her a quarter of anything I kill." By this point, his voice was little more than a mumble. "We shook hands on it."

Something inside Miri snapped and she leapt to her feet. "You didn't think to ask me first?" she yelled.

Zane stumbled back a couple of steps. "I ... I thought –"

"No, Zane!" his mother interjected, her voice loud and harsh with anger. "You didn't think at all! Don't you know how fragile what we have is? Don't you see what you've done!"

An uncomfortable lump rose in Zane's throat and his eyes stung with tears, but then anger rose to squash it down as he struggled to preserve his dignity. "No!" he shouted back. "I did what you said! I didn't tell her anything! And I was polite! Why are you so angry with me?"

His voice began to crack and he fled out of the house as his vision misted with the tears he was determined not to shed. He ran to the garden of the abandoned house to hide in the long grasses behind its rose bush, trying to push away his distress with ragged breaths.

Zane brooded there for hours, his appetite destroyed, alternately thinking of the meeting with the Red Lady as he toyed with one of the roses, or wrestling with the first real argument with his mother, playing both again and again in the theatre of his memory. He was so absorbed in his private distress that he didn't notice the sun beginning to set, nor did he hear Callum shuffle onto the overgrown path. It wasn't until he sat, crumpling the grasses a couple of metres away that Zane noticed him.

Callum's beard twitched and the slant of his eyebrows indicated his sympathy. "Perhaps ears as old as mine have heard similar troubles before," he said in that deep, lilting voice. "Why don't you try telling them, and I'll see if I can remember."

At first, Zane couldn't speak. It was as if all of the words and emotions were crammed behind a small door and trying to get out all at once.

"I don't understand!" he finally exclaimed and then related the argument with his mother to the old man. Callum nodded slowly when Zane searched for an indication that he was listening, as he sat so still. Then Zane told him what had happened with the Red Lady and the deal, and somehow that turned into an exposition on her beauty and generosity.

Callum waited patiently for the natural end to Zane's account. For a minute that seemed like an hour to Zane, he tugged at the bottom of his beard, in deep thought.

"Zane," he finally said. "You're of an age where you need to understand what women can do, and that's nigh on impossible when you've only met two in your whole life, especially when one's your mother."

Zane nodded sadly. "I don't understand my mum right now, and I usually do."

"I mean the Red Lady too," Callum added gently.

"But she didn't confuse me at all!" Zane replied hastily and Callum sighed, shaking his head.

"But she clouded your thoughts. If I told you this morning that you would visit her and make this deal straight away, without talking to your mother, would you have believed me? Think carefully now."

Zane looked up at the twilight sky, considering the question. He shrugged and then reluctantly confessed, "No, I don't think I would."

"So what happened between this morning and when you made that deal?"

"I met her."

"And?"

"And she was so beautiful." A slow realisation spread across his young face. "Oh."

Callum let it sink in. "And did you really think about anything else when you saw her?"

Zane hung his head in shame. "No, I don't even remember what I thought about really."

Callum nodded and watched Zane frown to himself. "Don't be too hard on yourself, young Zane. To meet the Red Lady is an event that could make even the most experienced man into a fool. I've heard tell of what she does to men and how beautiful she is. Never seen her myself, but I can believe it. You know why?"

"Because people said it?"

Callum's beard twitched and the skin at the outer corners of his dark grey eyes crinkled with his amusement. "That's something that never makes me believe anything. No, I believe that she's as beautiful as they say because I've seen her Hunters." At Zane's confused look he continued. "Men as strong and powerful as them could easily take over, so there has to be something that keeps them loyal, keeps them in check. A beautiful woman can do that with only a smile. Just a look in her eye can make even the toughest man forget everything save pleasing her."

Zane mulled this over as Callum waited. Eventually he nodded and then pounded the grass with his fist. "I should've been more clever!" he exclaimed. Then just as quickly he looked confused. "But I still don't see why Mum is so upset. I mean, she must be angry because I didn't talk to her first, but I think it's more than that."

Callum nodded. "You're a bright lad, but you don't know all that your mother does. She's tried so hard to keep it all from you, to keep you happy and safe, but things are changing,

Zane. When someone like the Red Lady takes an interest in you, blissful ignorance has to end."

"What does blissful ignorance mean?"

"Not knowing what's going on and being happy because of it."

"But I like being happy."

Callum sighed. "Your mother likes you to be happy too, but you've already been drawn into this, and it's a dangerous game. The Red Lady is a clever woman. She used your ignorance to seal a deal with you that you couldn't possibly have understood the consequences of."

Zane looked down at the ground, crumpled.

Callum tilted his head in pity for the boy. "How old are you, Zane?"

"Mum thinks I'm nearly fifteen."

"Before It happened, boys your age were much older in their minds. They lived in a world where people grew up quickly. The Boys have a harsh life that hardens their hearts, and I imagine your mother didn't want that to happen to you too. But I think it's time you understood what you've done. Do you agree?"

Zane nodded and looked at Callum apprehensively.

"Away from this place, the rest of London is very dangerous. And one of the main reasons is because of the gangs. You only know of three, but there are more, and your mother knows this too. So she's made friends with the two gangs that live closest to here to make sure that no-one can come along and spoil everything for you both. Being useful to both gangs means that they have an interest in keeping her, you, and this garden safe. But she had to make friends with both the Bloomsbury Boys and the Red Lady. Do you see why?"

Zane thought hard, not ever having considered anything like this before. "I suppose if she only helped the Boys, the Red Lady wouldn't like it. And the same if it were the other way round too."

Callum nodded. "And more than that ... if one day the Boys decided that they didn't like Miri anymore, the Red Lady would help and protect her. And the other way round too. Do you see?"

Zane gasped. "Oh no! That's why it's so bad!" he exclaimed. "If one of the Red Lady's Hunters comes here to train me, Jay will think that we like her more than him, and he'll be upset when one of them comes so close to his patch."

"And that Hunter will tell her all about what you do here and how close you are to the Boys," Callum added.

Zane slapped his palm against his forehead, groaning at his stupidity. "Oh, why did I make that deal!" he moaned.

His and Callum's eyes met and they said in synchrony, "Because she was so beautiful."

Zane bit his lower lip. "I need to say sorry to Mum. And I need to find a way to break this deal."

"No!" Callum held up a hand blackened with dirt. "You can't ever back out of a deal made with a gang leader. It could make life very difficult for you. But I do think that an apology to your mother would go a long way, and I should think she's probably feeling very bad about shouting at you too."

"Alright then." Zane stood, charged with the desire to act on his new knowledge. "I'll say sorry to Mum, then I'll work out what to do about Jay finding out about the Hunter, and then I'll find a way to make sure I think properly when I next see the Red Lady. I should go home anyway. It's almost dark and Mum'll be worried."

Callum slowly rose to his feet. "She knows where you are," he said, and was about to add something when a loud clanging of metal against metal sounded out from the west. Callum listened to the rhythm of it and his brow furrowed. "Trespassers in the Boys' territory," he interpreted and began to hurry off towards Russell Square, Zane close behind him.

Chapter 9
TRESPASSERS

As they arrived at the end of Guildford Street, it was apparent that something extraordinary was happening. For one thing, there was no-one posted at the edge of the square, a huge oversight on Jay's part. For another, there were shrill whoops and yells coming from one of the roads off the square to the north, sounding like all of the Boys had congregated there. It seemed they weren't scared of the trespasser.

Zane ran into the square, aiming to go up Bedford Way to see if they were there, but Callum stopped him with a gentle hand.

"No, Zane, best they don't see us. We don't know what's happening yet."

The old man steered him towards an alleyway next to what Zane called the "Husbuc" building. It was an old HSBC bank that stood on the corner, long since stripped of anything flammable or useful by the Boys, with only the facia left intact. Callum took hold of Zane's hand and steered him through drifts of rubbish and foul-smelling places up to a fire escape at the far end.

He lifted Zane up to the lowest rung, the bottom ones having been lost through a combination of rust and vandalism on the part of the Boys, and then hauled himself up. Zane watched him, amazed. Even though he could only make out his outline in the last of the rapidly fading light, it was clear that underneath all the smelly layers Callum was really quite agile.

They both climbed, Zane shaking as much as the ladder that rattled in its rusty fixings against the wall. But soon they were at the top, outside a door into the highest storey of the building which Callum opened and stepped through cautiously.

After a few moments, he pulled Zane in too and shut the door behind them, plunging them into total darkness with only Callum's surefootedness to lead him through.

After picking their way round various obstacles and passing through several doorways, they reached a room on the other side of the building. The clamour of the Boys got louder as they reached the window. By the time they got there, night had fallen, yet the room was illuminated by flickering amber light. Zane realised that the Boys had lit torches. Jay only let them do that on rare occasions, so he knew there must be something interesting to see.

Callum deftly unhooked the window latch and opened it enough to be able to peep down into the street below. Zane was desperate to look too, but Callum's mass obscured the view.

The din grew louder as the window opened and Zane heard Grame yell out, "Is it really a girl, Jay?"

Callum finally opened the window more, now certain that they wouldn't be seen, and let Zane come forward and kneel at the windowsill so that both of them could look out.

Zane looked down and to the right. The Boys were clustered in a tight group around an open doorway of one of the buildings opposite the one in which he and Callum were hidden. They were all jostling, trying to shove each other out of the way to be able to see whatever it was.

Zane caught sight of Grame easily enough, as he held one of the torches. The other was held by Mark, a little farther back. Jay soon came into view, pulling someone out of the building. Grame pushed the Boys back to let their leader out, and Zane saw that Jay was actually holding on to a person with each hand, both struggling desperately to free themselves. One was much taller than the other, and in the guttering light it was clear that they were both thin and not openly part of any gang he knew of. Their clothes were mismatched but well cared for.

"Let us go!" the taller one cried out, sounding furious rather than scared. All of the Boys, and Zane included, gasped – the voice was high and most definitely female. The ones closest to her stood back a little, forming an untidy circle around Jay and his prisoners.

"It *is* a girl!" Dev said, in a voice somewhere between reverential and scared.

She was almost the same height as Jay and just as slender. Her shoulder-length hair was messy from her struggling. It was hard to make out the colour of it in the torchlight, but it was dark, probably brown. He couldn't see much of her face as she was twisting and clawing at Jay's hand, but Zane could see that she wasn't as shapely as the Red Lady and probably not even nearly as pretty.

In his fixation on the girl, Zane almost overlooked the other captive. The boy also struggled, shorter than the girl by about a foot or so, with very short dark hair. But he was much less interesting than the girl. Jay seemed to think so too.

He laughed at her, which seemed to only incense her more. "Whoa, whoa!" he chuckled. "I'm stronger than you, but if you want to keep doing that, I don't mind." She gradually stopped, realising its futility. "That's better," he said, his voice lowering in the way that always made Zane nervous. "Now, you two are trespassing on my patch."

"I didn't know it was your 'patch,'" she spat back at him and Jay's mouth formed into a theatrical "O" for the benefit of the crowd who began to jeer.

"You stupid or sommat?" one of them yelled.

"Everyone knows this is our patch!" another cried, and other Boys shouted "Yeah!" in agreement.

"Just let us go and we'll leave right away," she yelled above the mob and Jay whooped with enjoyment.

"Let you go?" he said, the mass of Boys quietening to hear his response. "You think it's that easy? Don't you know what we do with people who come into our territory?"

For the first time Zane saw her face. She was fairly plain, her features betraying only a little of her fear at his words. Zane admired her as she was certainly being braver than he thought he would be in her place.

"But this is a special occasion!" Jay announced loudly. "Don't remember the last time I saw a girl, let alone in my patch. So perhaps we'll find a way to have some fun first. Get to know each other a bit, whaddya say?"

Before she had the chance to answer, he pushed the captive boy away from him into the crowd. The girl yelled "Titus!" in desperation as she watched him being dragged away, the Boys swarming around him like bees.

Zane looked behind him up at Callum, standing still as stone. "Callum!" he whispered urgently, horrified at the events unravelling below them.

Callum looked down at him and shook his head grimly. "Stay silent, Zane."

"But ...!" he started as Callum put a hand on his shoulder. He wasn't sure if it was to quiet him or comfort him.

Back down into the street, Jay wasn't in the same place. Zane frantically scanned the road until he caught sight of him on the edge of the lit area. His right arm was around the neck of the girl, dragging her away from the mob. He couldn't see where his left hand was, but was thankful to see that both of his knives were still sheathed.

"Callum!" he said again in a panic. "What's Jay going to do?"

Callum didn't respond.

"He's not going to kill her is he?" Zane demanded. "We can't let that happen! And the boy, they'll –"

"Zane," Callum said, a little louder, cutting him off. "This is their territory. If you want you and your mother to be safe, best not interfere."

"But!"

Callum squeezed his shoulder gently and said in a sad voice, "Only way to stay alive, Zane. I know it's hard, but think about what would happen if you called out or went down there. Everything has consequences. Everything."

Zane turned back to the violence unfolding below, the Boys shoving their victim between them like a stuffed toy, the terrified child trying to protect his head. Jay was out of sight now, and a wave of nausea hit Zane, not knowing what was happening but fearing that it was very, very wrong.

He gripped the windowsill, burning to stop what was happening but paralysed by Callum's words. He was right; to challenge the actions of a gang leader in his territory was tantamount to suicide. But it didn't make it easier, and it twisted Zane's guts into tight cramps as he struggled to remain still and quiet. He wondered if his mother would stay silent if she were in his place now.

Down below the boy cried out as he was hit. "Lyssa!" he called out weakly, but then a knee in his stomach doubled him over and he collapsed, gasping for breath.

At the same moment, Zane gasped, blinking rapidly as his vision shifted. All he could see was crisper; the torchlight's glow was more vibrant, the windowsill's cracks and dirt were suddenly visible in far more detail than before. But it wasn't those that arrested his attention.

The boy at the centre of the violent pack had a soft blue aura all around him. In places it was dim, one place his stomach where he had just been hit. As Zane focused more closely, bruises began to bloom on his arms, face and legs, even where clothing obscured his normal sight.

Visible to everyone, a sudden flash of intense blue light far up the street in the direction that Jay had taken the girl illuminated the buildings, casting shadows as strong as if it were noon, and then disappeared just as quickly. A high-pitched scream sliced through the darkness. Another scream followed soon after, but this one was cut off suddenly and an eerie silence fell.

The distraction pulled Zane's focus away from the boy and his vision returned to normal. Callum crouched down quickly at the sight of the flash, keeping his hand on Zane's shoulder protectively.

Another burst of the same light, a huge arc of bright blue lightning leapt from somewhere up the street, far too low and disturbingly horizontal for it to be anything natural. The end of the arc struck Grame in the chest like a whip. He flew into the air, thrown several feet backwards to slam into an old lamp post. The torch was knocked out of his hand and snuffed out when it landed, casting most of the street into darkness. Grame's body thudded to the ground.

There was absolute silence for a moment, as all the Boys stared in horror down the street. Then in the next, there was pandemonium, the Boys scattering, yelling, and screaming as they ran back to their square. Mark waited until they had all left the street, not caring about the unconscious child left where he had fallen. When he was sure all the Boys were away, he took a deep breath and shouted "Jay!" as loud as he could. When no response came, he began to run towards where he had last seen him, taking his own torch with him.

"Stupid boy!" Callum hissed to himself.

They both watched helplessly as another crackling finger of lightning flicked out to him. It pitched him into the air with a cry, flinging him into one of the buildings. They heard the loud crack as his head hit the stone, and the last of the torch-light revealed a smear of blood as he and the torch fell to the ground.

Zane shivered violently, staring out into the blackness fearfully, so very grateful for the protection of the building. Nothing happened for a few moments, and Callum kept him still. All he could hear was the sound of his own rapid breathing and distant noises of the Bloomsbury Boys scrabbling into their hiding places.

"Keep still. We're safe here," Callum whispered in his ear. "We'll wait a little longer, then they'll be gone."

"What *was* that?" Zane whispered back, his throat tight and mouth dry with fear.

"Nothing good," Callum muttered back grimly.

No more lightning came. Callum kept them there for what seemed to Zane to be an almost unbearable length of time. He wanted nothing more than to get home to his mother.

Finally, the old man stood slowly, drew him away from the window, and began to steer him back through the building, down the fire escape and to the end of the alleyway. The waning moon was low in the sky and Zane was thankful for the pale light it gave. Callum stopped him from going on into the square.

"Wait here," he whispered, and then slipped out into the shadow of the old bank. Zane waited, twitching and jumping at the slightest noise.

Callum soon reappeared, this time cradling to him the beaten boy, who was moaning quietly with every movement. Zane stared at him and then looked at Callum.

"Two of his ribs are broken," he told the old man, whose surprised expression didn't quite move his beard, only one of his eyebrows.

Callum hurried to Miri's house, Zane beside him, to find her in the doorway waiting for them.

"I heard the alarm," she said, the argument earlier that day forgotten as she saw how ashen their faces were and the state of the boy in Callum's arms.

Just like any Bloomsbury Boy would be, he was laid on the sofa. Miri had prepared bandages and ointments already, and water was boiling over the fire.

Zane directed her attention to the various injuries faster than she could diagnose them. Callum lurked in the doorway for a few moments before saying very quietly, "I'll see if I can find the others," and slipping away.

The boy seemed older than Zane had first thought him to be, maybe the same age as he was, now that he could be seen by the light of several candles. He helped Miri tend to him as he murmured and frowned, barely conscious. His face was scraped and his lip cut, but aside from the broken ribs he was only bruised elsewhere. When Miri had done all she could, she told Zane to stay close to him as she made some tea to treat the shock.

Zane knelt next to the boy, watching him closely with concern. He was struggling to raise his head and trying to get up, but was too dazed and hurt to do so.

"Stay still," Zane said quietly. "It'll hurt less."

The boy tipped his head towards Zane, and through his bloody lips croaked, "Lyssa."

"Callum is getting her," Zane said but the boy frowned, still very disoriented.

"Lyssa," he mumbled again and his eyes fluttered open to look at Zane. Zane's back straightened when he saw them and he shuddered. He'd seen them before in a dream, looking back at him from a mirror. The boy had violet eyes.

Chapter 10
TITUS

The next morning Zane wandered out of his bedroom to find Jay lying on the floor on a blanket and his mother having a hushed conversation with Callum at the doorway.

Zane looked down at Jay, lying on his back. His jacket was missing and the t-shirt he wore was blackened from the chest downwards. A large hole gaped over the right-hand side of his torso, the edges crisped as if it had been burnt. One of his mother's poultices was smeared onto a large burn that spread from the top of his right hip to his ribs. Jay's mouth was slack and eyes shut, his long eyelashes especially black against the pallor of his face. He didn't look so scary now, and Zane found it hard to remember how he could have seemed so threatening the night before.

The boy had gone from the sofa, but Zane peeped into Miri's bedroom to see that he had been placed on the top of her bed and was sleeping too.

Miri and Callum were so involved in their conference that they hadn't noticed him.

"They'll have her now," Callum was saying as Miri leant against the doorframe wearily.

"I can't believe it was so close to here," she replied. "Poor girl."

Callum sighed. "Not sure what the boy had to do with her, but they were close."

Miri nodded. "He kept asking for her. I have no idea how to tell him."

"Tell him what?" Zane made his mother jump.

Both she and Callum looked at him with the guilty faces of interrupted conspirators.

"Nothing," she lied.

"Who has her now?" Zane focused the question at Callum, making him shuffle awkwardly.

At a pointed look from Miri, he coughed and mumbled, "I'd better get over to the Boys. They don't have anyone watching them at the moment."

Zane watched him withdraw from the doorstep and slip out of sight. Miri shut the door and turned to Zane.

"Are you hungry?" she asked, using an old distraction tactic.

Zane shook his head. "What's going on?" he asked, frustrated.

Miri's eyes flicked around the room, searching for something to concentrate on other than her son's suspicious look. They settled on Jay. "Jay's badly hurt and he may be here a while." She came over to Zane, moved his long hair off his cheek and smoothed it affectionately, sadly. "Zane ... Mark and Grame died."

Zane looked past her, through the window and into the garden, the day taking on the quality of a strange and rather unpleasant dream. "Oh ..." was all he managed to say. His mind ran over the events of the night before, how Mark had slid down the wall, how Grame had slammed into the post. He wasn't surprised, but it still made him feel odd. He hadn't been particularly close to them, but they'd always been around. Boys died in fights with the Gardners with depressing regularity, but none had ever been killed like this. He wondered how Jay had survived.

Miri kissed his forehead and went into the bedroom to check on her first patient. Zane stood there for some moments, looking down at Jay's injury, feeling numb.

"Good morning," he heard his mother say, and he surmised that the boy had woken. "I'm Miri, and you're in my house. Don't worry, I'm looking after you. No, stay still. You've got a couple broken ribs and that's why you're hurting."

A pause.

"What's your name?"

Silence.

"I have a son–I think he's about your age–called Zane. Do you know how old you are?"

Nothing.

Zane went to the entrance to her bedroom. She was sitting on the edge of the bed. The boy lay still, staring up at the ceiling. "I think he's called Titus," he said. "The girl said it last night." Miri grimaced at his insensitivity and he mouthed "Sorry" to her silently.

The boy looked across at Miri. "Where's Lyssa?" he whispered plaintively.

Miri sighed heavily. "I'm afraid Callum couldn't find her … she's gone."

Zane watched the flash of panic in his eyes, and then all of a sudden it was gone. He simply stared back up at the ceiling, his blank expression forming a mask.

Zane and Miri exchanged a worried look. She drew a thin blanket over Titus and stood slowly. "I'll make you some food," she told him quietly. Zane followed her to the kitchen.

She began to chop fruit earnestly, the pregnant silence hanging between them. Zane sulkily picked at a rogue splinter of wood in the door frame, resentful of being kept in the dark. Miri focused on her task with the fervour of one avoiding an unpleasant conversation.

"Did Callum tell you about last night?" he finally ventured.

She nodded and then stilled the knife for a moment to look at him. "Zane, I'm sorry I shouted at you yesterday."

Zane gave a lopsided smile. "I'm sorry I made the deal. Callum explained to me why you were upset. I know how bad it is."

"Well … it's done now," she said as lightly as possible. "We'll just make the best of it."

Zane watched her struggling to keep her brave face on. Several times he almost spoke but the resolve left him. Then he decided to jump in. "Mum … that wouldn't have happened if you told me more about what's going on."

"It's best for you not to know these things, Zane, else you'll only worry, and I can do that enough for both of us."

Zane puffed out a frustrated breath. "Mum, that girl, Lyssa, what happened to her?"

Miri chopped rapidly.

"Mum!"

She stopped, hanging her head over the chunks of fruit. "I don't want you to know. I want everything to stay as it is!"

He stepped towards her. "But it can't … Callum said it can't be like that anymore. I want to know."

She looked at him as if seeing him for the first time. "You're so tall now, Zane," she murmured. "You look so much like …" Her voice trailed off and she laid the knife down. She wiped her hands on a cloth, looking tired and worn. "We think that the Unders have Lyssa," she whispered.

"Unders?"

"Shhh." She pointed at the way to her bedroom and the open doors in between. "Someone else, a friend of Callum's, called them that, but I don't know why. I've never seen them, but I've heard of them. I thought they'd gone away, but it seems not."

"Are they a gang?"

"Maybe. I'm not sure."

Dissatisfied, Zane pressed further. "What do you know about them?"

"Only that they take women," she continued reluctantly. "And they're never seen again. No-one knows what happens to them, where they're taken, nothing."

Zane was horrified. "And no-one does anything about it?"

"You saw what they can do, Zane."

"They won't take you, will they?" he said, suddenly frightened.

She smiled as she shook her head. "I have two gangs who like me being here. They look after me, both of us."

"Is this why there are only Bloomsbury Boys and not Bloomsbury Girls?"

Miri considered this. "Maybe. Probably. I'm not sure where most of the Boys come from anyway. They don't know themselves."

Zane perched on one of the wooden stools lined against the wall. "So there's only you and the Red Lady left?" he said incredulously.

She shook her head, smiling. "There are women in the Red Lady's gang too."

"There are?" he exclaimed. "They were all indoors when I went."

"Hmm, I wondered why she picked a mealtime to invite you over," Miri murmured to herself.

She went back to her task as Zane pondered. Only weeks ago, everything was so normal, but now he was finding out just how much had been happening without his ever knowing. He watched his mother, thinking over what she'd said, about her niche in the world, about how people depended on her and so kept her safe. Not for the first time, he wondered what was in the box that Luthor brought to her regularly. Herbs of some kind probably ... but for what?

Jay was barely conscious for several days, waking only to eat and drink small amounts and moan in pain when the dressing on the wound was changed. Despite many attempts by both Miri and Zane, the other new patient, Titus, didn't say a word to them. He ate, slept, and lay as still as possible in the bed, any movement causing him a lot of pain. Miri slept on the sofa, wanting to be close to Jay if his condition changed and mindful of giving Titus some space.

On the third day Titus tried to leave by climbing out of the bedroom window, but they found him passed out on the floor beneath it. Miri put him back to bed without any fuss. She was concerned that the trauma of the beating and the loss of this Lyssa girl had just been too much for him and that nothing was going to reach him in his silent world.

On the fifth day, however, something changed. Zane had been talking to Miri as she prepared breakfast and trailed after her into her bedroom to watch her give a bowl of food to Titus.

Just as he had since he'd arrived, Titus took the offered meal after a few moments of staring at it and sniffing it a little, still distrustful of his caregiver. He winced as he moved, and Miri fetched some willow bark for him to chew on afterwards for the pain. As she did so, she noticed how Zane was holding his right arm as if it were hurt.

"What's wrong with your arm?" Miri asked Zane, watching him rub it.

"Huh? Oh," he shrugged, "Just a bruise." He lifted up his right sleeve and looked at it, a large red welt that curved across his bicep. He frowned. "That's weird ..." he mumbled. At his mother's curious look, he said "I had a dream last night, where Luthor was fighting with me. We both had big sticks and he hit me on the arm, just here ... he said I needed to be quicker."

Miri looked at it. "Maybe you hit your arm in the night, and it made the dream happen. Sometimes –" She was interrupted by Titus coughing on a chunk of fruit. He was staring at Zane in surprise.

"Is this Luthor someone real? A big man, very tall?" he coughed.

After the initial shock at hearing him finally string some words together, both Zane and Miri nodded. Titus lifted the sleeve of his shirt to show an angry red swelling curved across his bicep in exactly the same place. "I had that dream too," he said in his quiet voice, amazed.

Zane gawped at it. "You did?"

Titus nodded, looking at Zane with those violet eyes. "But I've never met him before ... I thought it was just a dream, 'til you described it."

Miri swallowed hard. "Perhaps ... it was just a coincidence."

Titus looked unimpressed. "There's a very low probability of that."

Miri didn't know what to say, surprised by his academic tone, as Zane tried to remember whether his mother had ever told him about probability.

"The dream was very vivid," Titus continued. "It felt as if I were being trained, but I was a bit scared too."

No-one said anything for a few moments until Titus finished his breakfast and laid the bowl on the bed. "Thank you," he said quietly. "That was very nice. Tasted strange, but nice."

Miri smiled at him, relieved that he was talking at last. "Where do you come from?"

He considered the question for the best part of a minute, as if weighing up whether to reply or not. Eventually he began. "We ..." His voice faltered briefly. "From northeast London, quite a long way away. It took us a while to get this close to the river."

"What river?" Zane asked and Titus looked at him disbelievingly.

"The Thames," Titus said, as if it were the most obvious thing in the world.

Zane shrugged good-naturedly. "I've never been very far from here."

Titus accepted that and scrutinised Zane as he chewed on the willow bark. "Did that horrible man die, the one who found us?"

"I think he means Jay," Zane said quietly to Miri. "He's not normally that bad, but you were in his territory ... he doesn't like that."

Titus scowled darkly. "Did he die?"

Zane shook his head and the scowl deepened. He then looked at Miri. "Why are you looking after me?"

Miri blinked. "Because you're hurt, and ... well, it seems to be the right thing to do."

"Mum always looks after people that are hurt," Zane added.

Titus frowned, not taking his eyes off Miri. "What will you want in return?"

She shrugged. "Nothing."

The frown didn't leave Titus' face and he didn't seem very reassured, but he didn't pursue the issue. "Lyssa will be back soon and then we'll go far away," he muttered.

Neither Miri nor Zane felt it was the time to correct him. "Is she your friend?" Miri asked.

"My sister," Titus replied. "She's brilliant. She'll come back for me when she knows it's safe. It might be a few days ..." He looked at Miri shyly. "Will you let me stay here until then? It seems safe here."

She was about to reply when a loud groan erupted from the other room. "Ah ... oh shit that 'urts! Oh ... oh ... Miri? Miri! You 'ere? Oh ..."

She grabbed more willow bark and hurried off as Titus' eyes narrowed. He struggled to climb off the bed, clutching at his side where the broken bones complained. Zane tried to tell him to stay still, but he was ignored. Titus made his way to the living room with grim determination and Zane followed, anticipating something dreadful.

Titus stopped in the doorway, watching Miri tend to Jay, who was now chewing willow bark frantically and grimacing as she cleaned away the poultice and began to treat the wound with fresh aloe. Titus' shoulders were high and tight with tension, and Zane was confused when he didn't say anything. Titus didn't rush in and start to batter Jay; he simply watched.

Zane edged past him and into the living room. He studied Jay's wound, frowning. "I've never seen a burn like that before," he commented quietly. He glanced at Titus. "It must really hurt."

"Course it bloody hurts!" Jay exclaimed testily, and at a glare from Miri went back to chewing the bark. "This twig 'ent workin', Miri. It still 'urts."

"Good," Titus muttered bitterly.

Jay noticed him and struggled to recall his face. "Oh, it's you," he finally said and squeezed his eyes shut in pain.

Titus stared at him, as if willing Jay to spontaneously combust before him. Zane was amazed that he wasn't shouting at Jay, screaming accusations at him. But the thin boy simply maintained a steady, hateful gaze.

"What happened?" Jay croaked, and Zane filled him in on the lightning, and then at a nod from his mother, what had happened to Mark and Grame. Jay gripped the edge of the blankets, lips pressed tight together. "Someone should be at the square!" he said suddenly but Miri pressed him back down.

"Callum is there."

Jay relented, tucking his hands into his armpits. Zane had the urge to try to heal Jay, like he had with the Gardner, but with Titus' baleful glare focused on the patient he felt it was the wrong time.

A loud rap on the front door made them all jump, so

intensely were they watching Miri's ministrations. It opened before Miri had a chance to reply and Zane span around when Titus gasped at the sight of the visitor.

Luthor filled the doorway, peering in to look with cold interest at Jay lying prone on the floor. He stepped inside a pace before Miri invited him, irritating Zane and Jay immensely. Zane caught a glimpse of someone else behind him, but it was impossible to see whom.

"Luthor ... what a ... surprise," Miri said cautiously, getting up and standing protectively between him and Jay.

Luthor did not look like he was in the best of moods. His attention switched from Jay to Miri, then fell on Zane, the muscle in his jaw clenching.

"I'm here to train you," he said, clearly not happy about the fact.

As Zane's eyes widened in disbelief, Jay spluttered out the bark while struggling to get up and yelled, "What!"

Miri shut her eyes and paused a moment before kneeling to push Jay back down again. "Luthor, please go outside," she said calmly, authoritatively. "Zane, go and talk to him. Jay, stay still!"

Zane didn't move straight away until she said his name again firmly, then he and Luthor stepped outside. Titus followed, still staring dumbstruck at the figure from his dream.

The person who was standing behind him at the doorway was a girl in her early teens who moved forward to stand next to Luthor. Zane saw an immediate resemblance between the two. She had Luthor's scowl, certainly, and the same steely eyes. Yet her features were softer, her lips a little fuller, and her hair, scraped back into a ponytail, was mousey brown rather than Luthor's dark blonde. Without any conscious intention, Zane compared her to the Red Lady and the girl seemed very plain as a result. She was as tall as Zane, slightly taller than Titus, dressed in an ill-fitting white sleeveless top, brown linen trousers that were too long, and the same type of boots as Luthor wore.

She reached across to brush a stray strand of hair from her cheek, the movement revealing more of her arm. Both Titus and Zane shot a look at each other. The same red welt that they shared also marked her arm.

Chapter 11
AN UNEXPECTED DAUGHTER

"This is Erin," Luthor said, without warmth.

"His daughter," she added proudly, seeming unconcerned by Luthor's flat tone.

Zane's eyebrows shot up. He couldn't imagine Luthor having a child, as he seemed too hardened for that. After recently meeting the Red Lady as the only woman other than his mother, Erin was the second girl Zane had ever seen in as many days.

He remembered his manners. "I'm Zane. This is Titus."

Erin wrinkled her nose. "Those are weird names."

Both boys frowned at her, mildly offended, and Zane didn't know what to say. She wasn't endearing herself to him at all.

Luthor's scowl was set in like a long day of persistent rain. "Why is the leader of the Bloomsbury Boys in your living room?"

"Because he's hurt, and Mum is looking after him," Zane replied matter-of-factly.

"I could see that," Luthor rumbled. "I need to speak with her."

Zane sighed. "I'll see if she's free now, shall I?"

At Luthor's nod, he went into the house to find her speaking to Jay in a hushed voice. Jay threw him an angry look. Zane tried his best to ignore it and said to Miri, "Luthor wants to speak to you. Really a lot, I think."

Miri squeezed Jay's shoulder. "Try to relax. I'll be back soon."

Jay seethed as she left with Zane. She invited Luthor to speak with her in the garden, leaving the two boys with the new girl.

Titus pointed at the bruise on her arm. "Did you get that after you had a dream?" he asked.

She looked at him as if he were an idiot. "I got it from my dad," she replied, unimpressed by the question. "We were training yesterday ... I didn't move fast enough."

"Did he tell you to be faster?" both Titus and Zane asked in unison, and then looked at each other in mild surprise.

She stared at them. "You two are weird."

"Did he though?" Zane pressed.

Erin shrugged. "Yeah, I think so. Why?"

Zane rolled up his sleeve to show her his bruised arm and Titus did the same. Erin raised her eyebrows. "You both been training too?"

"The bruises are exactly the same!" Titus exclaimed impatiently. "Exactly the same place, and both Zane and I had a dream about your father training us and hitting us here, and saying we need to be faster."

Erin briefly looked shocked but then her eyes narrowed. "Are you two winding me up?"

"No!" Zane replied, appalled at the idea. "Why would we do that?"

Erin shrugged again. She thought a moment and then said, "That's weird, if it's true."

"It *is* true," Titus said as he and Zane rolled their sleeves down. "And you're right, it is weird."

They all looked at each other for a few moments.

"How old are you?" Zane asked her.

"Nearly fifteen, I think," she replied, and Titus and Zane both exclaimed, "Me too!" at the same time.

This time they smiled at each other, amused at their synchrony whilst Erin looked at them uncertainly.

"Do you know my father, then?" she asked hopefully.

Titus shook his head as Zane replied, "I've seen him lots of times, but only spoken to him a tiny bit."

Erin looked disappointed. "Oh."

"Why?"

"Just wondered what you thought of him ... what he's like."

Zane's brow furrowed with confusion. "Don't you know? He's your dad after all."

Erin looked down at her boots. "I've only known him a few days. He didn't even know about me until a couple of weeks ago."

This piqued Zane's curiosity. "So you didn't grow up at the Red Lady's place?" Zane asked.

She shook her head, eyes distant and shaded by a pained expression. "No, I grew up with –"

"Erin!" Luthor shouted from behind her at the entrance to the garden, and all three of them jumped. "We are here to train, not chatter."

She hung her head and Zane suddenly felt sorry for her. "Sorry, Father," she said quietly.

"Don't mumble like that!" he said sternly, marching over. "A warrior never mumbles. Eyes straight and chin high if you have something worth saying, or say nothing at all."

She lifted her chin and looked at him, yet said nothing. Zane began to chew his lip, brooding. Of all the people she could have sent, why did the Red Lady have to send Luthor?

Miri emerged from the garden, deep in thought. She passed a brief, worried glance over the three children and then slipped back into the house, drawing as little attention to herself as possible.

"That's my mum. She's called Miri," Zane whispered to Erin.

Luthor was looking at Titus. "The Red Lady didn't mention you as part of the deal."

"This is Titus," Erin said helpfully.

"I don't care what he's called. She said I was to train Zane."

Titus patted the air with his hands. "That's fine. I'm not fit to train anyway."

"Good," Luthor said tactlessly and then turned to Zane. He looked him up and down critically. "Practically no muscle … no stamina either, I should think. No power there at all."

Zane fidgeted, somewhat humiliated in front of the others.

Luthor nodded to himself. "I'll need to build you up before I can do any useful training with you, otherwise you'll drop a spear from the fatigue of aiming before you can throw it."

Erin snickered and Luthor's gaze fell on her. "I don't know why you're laughing, because you need it just as much." She fell silent.

"Do ten circuits of the square to warm up," Luthor said and Erin sprinted off happily. Zane, slower to respond, finally set off at a similar speed, trying to catch her up.

Whilst they ran, Luthor watched, shaking his head in disappointment at the way that Zane began to slow down after a couple of laps. Titus leant against the wall. He looked on as Luthor went to run behind Zane, quickening the boy's pace with his menacing presence. Titus rubbed his eyes and, pale-faced, went back into the house to lie down, leaving his fitter companions to their exercise.

Over the next few days, everything settled into a routine. Titus became marginally more comfortable around Miri and let her have her bed back. He elected to sleep in Zane's bed, with

Zane on the floor, as Titus refused to sleep or eat in the same room as Jay. Soon after the two boys breakfasted together, Luthor and Erin would arrive and then all morning Zane would be drilled through various exercises with her. Erin took to it all very well, revelling in the exertion, whilst Zane struggled to keep up. It was only the promise of a kiss from the Red Lady for his fantasy delivery of meat that sustained him. Sometimes Titus watched, sometimes he read any book that Miri could lay her hands on for him, but occasionally, throughout the day, he would pause at whatever he was doing to turn and stare at Jay, hate-filled, just for a few moments, and then return his attention to his previous task.

The afternoons were filled with frantic work in the garden, Zane tired out and slow, Miri desperate to extract all she could to feed the extra people in her care. The Bloomsbury Boys intermittently brought canned offerings to her door, but she was adamant that the healing process would be improved by lots of fresh fruit and vegetables.

All the while, Jay swore and moaned with pain and frustration but kissed Miri on the cheek every morning and every night, thanking her quietly for her kindness when no-one else was looking.

A couple of times Zane approached Jay to try to help, only to be knocked back by his bad-tempered refusal to have anyone except Miri near him. In the end Zane gave up, letting the healing take place in its own time.

On the fourth day after Luthor's arrival, halfway through one of the training sessions, Luthor called a halt to announce that he was going to pick up some equipment from back in his territory. He gave Zane and Erin a set of exercises to complete before his return and then left at a jog. As soon as he was out of sight, Zane flopped onto the ground and groaned. Erin laughed at him.

"You're so soft!" she said.

93

Zane pouted. "You don't have to dig for the rest of the day when we finish here."

"I have lunch and then I practise with knives and swords," she replied, coming over to sit next to him on the old pavement. "After dinner I practise fletching."

"What's that?"

"Making arrows," Titus answered for her as he came over to sit with them.

"You do all that every day?" Zane asked incredulously.

Erin nodded. "I want to be strong." Her jaw was set in a way that reminded him of Luthor.

"I just want to be able to hunt," Zane sighed. "That's all. I didn't realise it would be so hard."

"My father's being thorough. Besides, you should feel proud to be trained by him. He's the Red Lady's Champion, so you're really lucky."

"Yeah," Zane sighed, unconvinced.

"Are you in the Red Lady's gang?" Titus asked after a few moments.

Erin shook her head. "No. I think my father wants me to be one day, though. I think he's hoping that if I train hard, I'll be good enough to join." She looked at Zane. "Are you training so you can join?"

He shook his head and explained the deal to both of them. Erin looked surprised. "I heard she doesn't make deals with other gangs."

"I'm not in a gang," Zane retorted. "And anyway, she said it was a special thing." He puffed his chest out proudly. "Just for me." He noticed that Titus' attention had drifted. "You ok?" he asked.

Titus blinked himself out of his deep thought. "I was wondering when Lyssa will be back."

"Who's Lyssa?" Erin asked and for the first time in days Titus' face became animated.

"She's my sister. She's clever and ..." His voice trailed off and he became distant again. His fingers dug into his palms. "Jay stole her ... I haven't seen her since."

"It wasn't Jay that took her away," Zane said hastily and Titus' glare fell on him.

"It was! I remember, he dragged her off and she didn't want to go with him."

"But it wasn't Jay who took her away afterwards. It couldn't have been–none of the Bloomsbury Boys can make lightning like that."

"Huh?" Erin's eyes were wide. "Someone made lightning? Did they make a storm come?"

Zane described the events of the evening that he and Callum witnessed, and it became clear to him that Titus hadn't fully realised what had happened. "So it wasn't Jay. He's alright really," he concluded, although he felt uncomfortable. He wasn't certain what Jay had been planning for Lyssa, but he didn't think that was helpful to mention.

Titus' eyes were shadowed by the depth of his frown. "They wouldn't have had a chance to take her if he'd left us alone," he muttered. Then he looked up. "So if he isn't hiding her, and it was these others, who are they? Why'd they take her? And where is she?"

Zane looked down, uncertain about what to say. His mum hadn't wanted to talk about the Unders, and what if she and Callum were wrong anyway? Before he could decide how to respond, he was distracted by Erin, who reached out unexpectedly and squeezed Titus' hand. "I know how you feel, worrying about someone ... it's hard."

"Do you have a sister missing too?" Zane asked nervously, fearing that such a degree of coincidence would just be too freakish.

She shook her head. "No ... not missing, and not a sister." She looked at them both watching her and seemed surprised, then defensive. "It doesn't matter, and anyway it's none of your business and I don't want to talk about it," she gabbled, jumping to her feet. "We'd better do something useful," she announced and began to sprint around the square, focusing completely on the exercise and doggedly avoiding their gaze.

Titus watched her thoughtfully. He glanced back to the house and then leant closer to Zane, lowering his voice.

"Do you think the Red Lady would make a deal with me?" he asked hesitantly.

Zane shrugged. "We could ask her. What do you want to make a deal for?"

Titus' eyes looked into that faraway place once again. "I need to get strong too. I need to learn how to fight."

"Oh. Ok." Zane also watched Erin changing her activity to go through strengthening exercises. His mind began to fill with the thought of speaking to the Red Lady again, leaving no room to consider what Titus could be planning.

Titus prodded Zane's arm. "Can you do it, Zane? Can you ask her to include me on your deal?"

Zane thought for a moment and then beamed. "I think we should go and ask anyway." Titus looked satisfied as Zane grew excited, already drifting off to his favourite memory of the Red Lady. He resolved to see her, as soon as possible, forgetting his conversation with Callum. All he could think of now was seeing her again, hearing her voice again and kissing her rose-petal skin.

Chapter 12

THE FIRST HUNT OF THE SEASON

Three days later, Zane and Titus were escorted to the Red Lady's territory by special invitation. Zane's steps were quick and eager, but he was slowed down by Titus, who was still sore from his injuries. Erin accompanied them, it being the end of the morning's training, and she also was excited.

"Do you know what happens today?" she whispered when Luthor had gone up ahead to investigate a noise. Both Zane and Titus shook their heads. "It's the first hunt of the season," she said excitedly. "It's a big deal there. Dad's been training really hard."

"First hunt for what?" Titus asked. "I thought they hunt all year round."

"They do, but today is the first day of the season for red deer. I think the Red Lady must want you to see it, and that's why she said you could come over today."

Zane's grin broadened. "That must mean she likes us, if she wants us there for something so special."

"She hasn't even met me," Titus reminded him.

"Then that means she really wants to see me!" Zane exclaimed, not noticing Erin roll her eyes.

The rest of the journey was in silence once Luthor returned to them, and Erin was all too aware of his foul mood. Luthor was never the cheeriest teacher, but today they had all noticed how quick to anger he had been.

The buzz of an excited crowd was audible before they even got to the Red Lady's inner territory. Zane's anticipation peaked as the wooden gates were unlocked and they were waved through. This time when he and Titus were checked for weapons, he was distracted by too many things to be bothered.

Close to thirty people were thronged in the courtyard, all in the same red leather armour that Luthor wore, all armed with bows, knives, and swords. Many of them were checking the straightness of their arrows, the alignment of the flights, and the tension of the bows. An excited chatter filled the air, creating an infectious atmosphere of keen anticipation.

Zane had never seen so many adults in one place at a time and, judging by Titus' large eyes and tightly pressed lips, his friend hadn't either. Zane's attention jumped from one to the other, admiring how strong they all looked. Everyone there had their hair plaited into a single long braid, just like Luthor's. There were several women, all of whom were dressed exactly the same way as the men. None of them were striking enough to hold his attention, his mind full of the Red Lady.

His eyes fell across the dark-haired Hunter who had checked him for weapons the first time he had come here. The Hunter stared at Luthor, as if he were willing the Champion to look over at him. Luthor glanced across the crowd and the intensity of David's stare also caught his eye. The leather of Luthor's armour creaked as he flexed his shoulder muscles in an effort to make himself look even broader as the other Hunter approached with a wide grin playing across his features.

"Feeling fit?" David asked cheerily. Luthor said nothing. "Don't get your hopes up too high," David continued. "I'm stronger than ever ... you know it too. This year, it'll be me."

Luthor guffawed loudly, making several people near them look over. He stepped towards his challenger, making a point of looking down into David's eyes. Even though Luthor remained silent, Zane found himself growing nervous as the Red Lady's Champion stared his opponent down. Unwilling to back off immediately in front of the crowd, David stood his ground, the baby finger on his left hand twitching. When Luthor leant forward a fraction of an inch, David eventually looked away and stepped aside, the muscles in his jaw working as he kept any insults locked in his mouth.

"Don't go anywhere." Luthor jabbed a finger at the children, not taking his eyes off David, and then marched away, leaving them on the edge of the crowd. David muttered something under his breath and moved off towards the main building that Zane had been in before.

Zane pictured the Red Lady and revelled in there being only one wall between them. That and many Hunters, but he didn't really care about them. He was too swept up in the mood of the crowd, his eyes fixed on that huge door made for the gods, waiting for his goddess to walk through them.

Luthor soon returned, fully armed, and the crowd parted to let him walk through to the front of it. Many envious eyes were upon the Champion, but Zane, too young and naive to notice, remained oblivious. Luthor stood like a mountain, eyes also on the same doorway as a hush descended over the crowd.

The last sliver of the shadow cast by the building disappeared, and in the next moment, the doors were pushed open by two male Hunters, slightly older than those assembled in the courtyard.

Silence reigned as the Red Lady stepped out into the noonday sun, red silk clinging to her, describing her curves with its luxurious drapes. The sun sparkled from a blood-red stone at her throat; her hair was swept back and tied, revealing more of her neck. As she walked a few paces out towards the crowd, the slit in her dress that ran from the floor to her thigh parted just enough for Zane to see most of her legs, smooth and long amongst the dark red silk.

For a moment, Zane ceased to see or hear anyone else. His eyes feasted on her, glorying in how she looked even better than he remembered. He watched her scan the crowd, feeling a twist in his stomach when her eyes lingered on Luthor. But then it was like the sun shone only for Zane when her gaze moved away from Luthor onto him, and she smiled. Smiled! He was almost lifted into the air with ecstasy. He was too busy smiling back at her like a fool to notice Luthor turn and see the target of her attention. Neither did he see how Luthor gripped the hilt of his sword hard enough to make the leather of his bracers creak under the strain.

Then she looked elsewhere, and Zane's heart slowly floated back to his body to hammer inside him.

"Hunters." Her voice filled the courtyard, loud but not harsh. "It is a year and a day since I last laid down this challenge." Luthor turned away from Zane to look back at her. "Today the hunting season for the red deer begins. Whilst no shadow is cast, I loose you like arrows upon this city." She reached back and pulled the strip of red silk which had tied her hair, freeing it to fall around her face like spun gold. She held the silk high in the air. "The one who brings the first hide to my door will be the one permitted to step through it." And with that, she let the fabric fall to the ground as gently as a sigh.

When it folded at her feet, the gates were unlocked and the Hunters poured out like water breaking a dam. Zane began to run with them but then remembered himself and stopped, watching them leave, crushed.

"I wish I was a Hunter!" he exclaimed and Erin rolled her eyes again.

The Red Lady turned and went back into her building, but the doors remained open. "Zane," she called with the same tone that a person that hides might tease the seeker. "Bring your new friend. I want to meet him."

Titus looked at Erin and she shrugged. "I have chores anyway," she said indifferently.

Zane began to pull Titus with him, hurrying towards the steps as Titus nodded to Erin and said, "See you soon."

When they reached the lobby, Zane told Titus to bow his head as he entered. Titus looked unimpressed. "But then I won't be able to see everything."

"It's just what they do here," Zane replied impatiently and began to walk through the inner doors that were being held open for them, head bowed respectfully.

Zane walked to the place where he had been brought when she had asked for him to come closer. He hoped desperately that Titus was doing what he told him to and that he wouldn't embarrass him in front of her.

"So, you must be Titus," she said, her voice honey-sweet. "Do look up, both of you."

She was on her throne again, smiling. Zane swallowed hard, his mouth dry.

"I am," Titus replied with a steady voice. "You must be the Red Lady."

Her smile broadened. "I'm told that you're living in the same square as Zane and Miri."

Titus nodded, seeming very calm. Zane marvelled at how serene he appeared to be, as he looked no different than when he talked to Miri. How was that possible?

"And I understand that you have no allegiance to any other groups."

"That's right," Titus paused. "Only one person. But that isn't a group."

"Who would that be?"

"My sister."

"And where is she?"

Titus paused for a moment and then said, "I don't know. But she'll be back soon."

The Red Lady's gaze fixed on Titus for a few moments. Her eyes then flicked to Zane, who brightened at this. Titus watched his reaction closely.

"How delightful it is to see you again so soon, Zane."

Her eyes sparkled like peridot. "I see that the training is going well."

"You do?" he asked hopefully.

"Oh yes," she breathed, her gaze playing across his unchanged shoulders. "I can see the benefits already."

Zane flushed with pleasure. "I'm trying really hard."

She nodded a little. "You wanted to discuss the deal with me?"

He nodded, glancing at Titus. "Titus would like to train with us when his ribs are better."

The Red Lady looked intrigued. "Is that so?" At his nod she turned her attention back to Titus.

"He can give you a cut of the meat he catches too," Zane added hopefully.

"Well … I think I'll have all the meat I need once you start hunting, Zane," she replied, not taking her eyes from Titus. He looked back at her with a steady gaze, face impassive. "And I can't let just *anyone* be trained by my Champion."

"But Titus isn't just anyone!" Zane blurted. "He's really clever, and he had the same dream as me, and I dreamt of him before I met him too!"

The Red Lady leaned forward slightly. "Really? Well, that is interesting."

Zane glowed with pleasure.

"Do you have lots of dreams, Titus?"

"I don't remember all of them," Titus replied warily.

"I see. Do you remember any from last night?"

Titus tensed slightly and he hesitated before saying "Yes … I do. But it was a strange one."

"Those dreams are always the most interesting."

Titus remained silent.

The Red Lady smiled to herself and then said, "I like to hear people's dreams as much as I like to hear stories. How about this: I will allow you to be trained by my best Hunter, if you agree to tell me all of the dreams that you recall the most vividly."

Titus considered this. "On the day I remember them?"

She nodded. "Luthor can escort you so you'll be kept safe."

The boy thought hard, much to Zane's disbelief. He wished he had the same deal; then it would be much easier to come and see her.

"Alright," he finally said.

"Starting with the one you had last night," she said, sliding from the chair to glide down the steps towards them.

Titus nodded. She held out her hand to him.

"Zane asked to shake on the deal we made," she said, and Titus shook her hand. Zane wondered if his grip was better. The Red Lady sighed. "If only everyone outside of my gang were such a pleasure to deal with."

She returned to her chair, much to Zane's disappointment, and looked at Titus expectantly.

"It was in Miri's garden," he began. "Close to one of the gates. There's a stone birdbath there, next to the water tap. It has a bowl shape on the top of it that collects the water, but in the dream it was dry."

Zane watched how attentive the Red Lady was and tried desperately to remember a more interesting dream than having violet eyes.

"There were strange balls in the bowl instead, going round and round it in a line, like they were strung on an invisible thread and being pulled by someone. They were only as big as my fist, and they looked like they were made from glass, but the sound they made on the stone was like a sound that a very heavy rock would make." He blinked and then paused, watching the Red Lady intently. She waved a hand for him to continue. "There were three of them. One red, one green, and one purple. It looked like there could have been one more in the line from the way they were moving and how they were spaced out, but I couldn't see it. They were strange because they moved by themselves, but also because they glowed a little bit."

He frowned slightly at the Red Lady. "Carry on," she said.

"I reached in and took the three I could see, but the sound carried on, like there was another in the bowl that was invisible. When I thought about that, it felt like I was covered by a kind of heavy black cloth, and it was hard to breathe and I woke up."

The Red Lady was studying his face. "What do you think it means?" she asked.

"I don't know. But it might be symbolic."

She looked impressed and – Zane's heart sank – excited?

"But I don't know what they could symbolise. Do you have any ideas?"

She smiled and shrugged in an exaggerated, playful way. "Who knows what dreams mean?" she said lightly, but Titus' frown deepened.

"Um ... I have a question," Zane piped up at the pause, eager to take her attention away from Titus. "You said outside that the first to bring a hide to your door would be allowed through it." She nodded. "Well, we didn't have hides, but you let us through."

She threw back her head and laughed melodiously. "Oh Zane," she sighed as the laughter ebbed. She pointed to the entrance behind him. "I didn't mean *that* door." Zane was confused but she didn't explain. "Time for you to leave me now," she said. "I look forward to hearing your next dream, Titus."

Titus nodded, somewhat distant, and then turned to leave. Zane took a deep breath and said "Goodbye then," and took a hesitant step towards the Red Lady. She laughed, remembering, and moved so that her left cheek was facing him. He bounded up the steps and carefully planted a firm, tender kiss on her warm skin, eyes shut, savouring every single moment of it.

He withdrew, lingering slightly to breathe in the scent of her as long as possible. When he reached the bottom of the steps she clicked her fingers. The doors opened and one of the Hunters stepped in. "Arthur, escort my guests home."

Zane, walking backwards as before, followed Titus out of the room and didn't turn until the doors were shut in his face.

Not a word was spoken as they returned home. Arthur, an older man with hair greying at the temples, didn't make conversation. Zane was lost in memories of silk and skin, and Titus remained silent, deep in thought. Only when they were left at the square, the Hunter gone, did Zane notice how quiet Titus was.

"She's amazing, isn't she?" he sighed.

Titus frowned. "You think too much about the way she looks."

Zane smiled. "I don't."

Titus sighed with frustration. "When we next go there, you need to think before you speak. You shouldn't have told her about the dream stuff."

"Why?"

Titus tried to respond but couldn't seem to find the right words.

Zane scratched his head. "Don't you like her?" he asked in disbelief.

Titus didn't reply immediately. "I ... I just had the feeling that she was much more in control than she let on. And I think she knew about my dream already. When I was telling her, it was like she had already heard it."

"Maybe other people have had the same dream. Like we both had the one about Luthor."

Titus shook his head. "No, it was different ... not like she'd heard it before ... it was ..." He frowned. "It was like she was checking if I told all of it, like it was a test."

"How do you know that? She looked interested to me, like she'd never heard it before."

Titus looked away. "I just know," he mumbled and went into the house.

Chapter 13

PICTURES FROM THE PAST

Zane woke with a start, confused and disoriented in the darkness of his room. It took him a moment to remember that he was sleeping on the floor. Then he realised that there was a hand on his shoulder, shaking him gently.

"What?"

"Shhhh," Titus whispered in his ear. "Keep quiet."

Zane did as he was asked for a moment before whispering, "What's wrong?"

"Shhhh."

The room was utterly silent, as were the square and garden outside. That was normal since the boys had grown up in a London that was quiet, save the sounds of wildlife. They knew nothing different.

Then a noise rang out through the darkness, tensing all of Zane's muscles in an instant. He recognised that metallic clang.

"The Giant!" he gasped and sat bolt upright, fumbling desperately for the matches and candle that were always at his bedside.

"Giant?" Titus hissed under his breath. "What are you talking about?"

Zane struck a match, lighting a candle that revealed the fear on his face and Titus sitting on the edge of the bed. Zane checked that his curtains were completely shut, afraid that the candlelight might escape and attract the Giant to his house.

"Yes ..." He paused, both of them listening hard to the sound of the footsteps moving away from the far side of the square into the distance. "Me and Dev saw him at the hospital." He related the events to Titus in a low whisper as the last of the footsteps faded. "I haven't thought about it for a while," he said finally.

Titus pondered. "It sounds like he came back. What did Miri say about it?"

"I haven't told her."

"Are you going to?"

Zane squirmed a little. "Don't know. I don't want her to worry. She doesn't like hospitals and I'm not supposed to go into them."

Titus lay back down carefully, mindful of his healing ribs. "It doesn't sound like the Giant is coming here. We should sleep and do something about this tomorrow."

With that, he drew the covers over himself and Zane listened to his breathing slow and become steady, marvelling at how easily his friend had returned to sleep. After pinching out the candle flame, he lay there for a long while, fretting about the Giant, wondering about the hunt and who would bring back the hide. He assumed it would be Luthor and that made him more restless, having realised by now which door she had meant. It was some time before sleep smothered the noise of his mind.

Erin arrived early the next morning whilst they were still having breakfast. She tapped on Zane's window and he opened it to find her panting as if she had been running. She looked tense and kept checking behind her.

"Can I come in?" she asked urgently. At Zane's nod she scrabbled over the windowsill, dropping lightly into his room. Both boys noticed the knife in her hand.

She shut and locked the window behind her. Seeing their eyes on her knife, she slipped it back into the sheath at her belt.

"I borrowed it from a friend," she said, her posture betraying her tension.

"Is everything alright?" Titus asked.

She nodded a little too quickly, glancing back into the square. Zane and Titus exchanged a worried look.

"Is there someone out there?" Zane asked, fearful that the Giant had returned.

"No-one's in the square," she replied, in a tone that suggested that she didn't want to speak further on the topic.

"Who won the hunt?" Zane enquired as nonchalantly as he could manage.

"No-one yet," she replied, sitting on the edge of the bed.

She looked around his room. It was neat and clean, like all of the other rooms in his mother's house, containing simply a bed, a chair, and a chest of drawers covered over the top with a collection of nature's curios acquired over the years from the garden. There was also a wall full of books ranging from those that he'd had as a child with which Miri had taught him to read to encyclopaedias of herbs and medicinal remedies. He realised it was the first time a girl had been in it, and that made him feel strangely awkward.

"The deer aren't so far east yet, so the Hunters have had to travel further west from what I've heard. But it'll be my dad that wins," she stated confidently.

Zane picked at a thread hanging from his trouser hem. Titus stood purposefully. "Well, seeing as Luthor is still away, this is the perfect time. Zane, tell Miri we're going over to the Red Lady's and then meet us at the far corner of the square."

"Did you have a dream?" Zane asked, getting up eagerly.

"No," Titus whispered, beckoning them both towards him conspiratorially. "We're not going to her place at all. Erin, I'll explain whilst we wait for him. We're going to the hospital to find what this Giant is so interested in."

"I'm really not sure about this," Zane whispered as the three of them crouched next to the round windowed door on the third floor of the stairwell. It was still fairly dark even though it was bright outside and he was convinced that it would be darker still in the corridor.

Erin sighed. "Stop saying that."

"But I really do think this is a bad idea," Zane persisted. "What if the Giant is in there?"

"No-one is here," Titus said with absolute confidence. When Zane didn't relax, he added, "If he breathes as loud as you say, we'll hear him before we get to the door."

Zane chewed his lip. "Mum says it's a bad idea to go into hospitals. Maybe we should go."

"Shut up, Zane!" Erin whispered. "Look, I'll scout ahead, ok?"

Before they had the chance to respond, she drew her knife, opened the door a crack, and peeped through. She opened it more then slipped through, knife in front of her, keeping her centre of gravity low and moving carefully as her father had taught her. She followed the footsteps to the room that the Giant had entered, the tracks clearly visible in the dust. Pressing her ear to the door, she listened for a few moments and then crept back.

Zane jumped as she came back into the stairwell.

"Clear," she whispered.

Titus stood and went into the corridor as Erin waved Zane through, bringing up the rear.

They went towards the door. Titus examined the prints in the dust. "Strange shoes," he commented, and then looked at the door. He pulled a sleeve down over his hand and wiped at a piece of metal positioned high up at eye level. He squinted to make out the letters in the gloom, found it impossible, and so struck a match from a box in his pocket. "Doctor Z. Al Siddique,

Doctor J. Shannon," he read out loud. "I suppose this room belonged to them."

"What's a doctor?" Erin asked.

"Someone that makes people better," Titus replied. "Like Miri and Zane."

"Doctor Zane," Zane whispered to himself, trying it out. "Sounds weird."

Titus turned the handle and slowly opened the door, Erin poised behind him with her knife. He looked first and then stepped inside, beckoning to his companions to follow.

Once inside, Erin put away her weapon as Zane shut the door behind him and looked around the room.

It contained two large wooden desks, two leather swivel chairs, one of which was on its side, and two walls full of files and books. A grey metal filing cabinet stood in the far corner, one of the drawers open, and all around it pieces of paper were strewn, left where they had fallen. Blinds at the window that practically filled the wall opposite the doorway were drawn, but Titus opened them and daylight filtered through the streaks of dirt into the dusty room. Both of the desks were positioned under the window, so that whoever sat at them could enjoy the view. Computer monitors, grimy and dark-screened, sat atop them, their keyboards covered with dust. None of the children had the faintest idea what they were.

Titus pointed at the Giant's footprints. By the look of it he had been to the filing cabinet a couple of times and also along the book shelves. There were several gaps where books seemed to be missing. Titus picked up a sheaf of papers from the floor and Erin went to the window to look outside whilst Zane hovered near the exit, ready to run.

"You can see loads of stuff from here," Erin commented, peering through one of the clearer patches. "Zane, come and see."

111

He shook his head. She shrugged and carried on admiring the view. Titus flipped through the pages in his hand, frowning.

"There are lots of words I don't understand," he said quietly. "I think it might be something to do with someone being ill. It talks about a patient a lot."

Zane fidgeted, eager to go home. Erin turned around to see the rest of the room. When she faced the wall opposite, her eyes widened.

"Look at all that!"

The wall was completely covered in pieces of shiny paper of various sizes. The one at the centre was a large rectangular grid of tiny squares marking out the days of the year with faded writing on most of them. Next to it was a poster of the brain of a yellow cartoon man that looked very odd to the children. All over the rest of the wall were photos, several hundred of them, pinned so close to each other that they often overlapped. It was these that drew Erin's attention. She was first over to the wall, carefully wiping the dust from them with her sleeve.

They peered at them, seeing another world of clean smart clothes, fresh, healthy faces, lots of smiles, and glasses held in hands with all manner of different coloured liquids in them. Everyone in the photos looked happy, all of them older than the children but much younger than Miri. Most of the locations were indoors, in places strangely lit with crowds of people in the background. There were many women, dressed in a kaleidoscopic array of dresses and outfits, some of which seemed to sparkle in the light.

Erin gasped. "Look, Zane! He looks just like you!"

The two boys hurried over to see the one she pointed at. Two men, dressed in crisp suits reminiscent of the Gardners, but without the long black ties, were seated at a table with the whitest cloth they had ever seen covering it. They were both smiling broadly and holding up a glass each. Both had neatly cropped black hair, but one had skin that was much darker than the other. The white man had a neat goatee beard and brilliant blue eyes that sparkled out at them. Zane couldn't take his eyes off him.

"He does look like me!" he whispered.

"Even more when you tie your hair back," Erin said. "If you had blue eyes and a hairy face like him, you could be brothers. I wonder why the other one has such dark skin. He must have spent a lot of time outdoors." Even as she said it, she didn't believe it, but having never seen anyone with skin like his, she couldn't think of another explanation.

Titus scanned the other photos. "They're both in lots of these pictures," he said, pointing some out. The children moved from one to the other, examining them closely. "I think they were good friends," he commented. "And there are lots of girls with them." He pointed out three photographs taken at different times. In each one, a different woman had her arms around the men's arms or necks, in some they were even kissing.

Erin shuddered and looked behind her, shrugged, and then went back to the pictures.

After a few moments, Titus unpinned one from the wall to take it over to the window. "Look!" he said. "This one was taken here in the hospital. I recognise the painting of the lady from downstairs."

The others came over to look at the photo of the same two men, this time dressed in long white jackets with more sensible smiles on their faces. They looked proud, and the dark-skinned man was holding up a piece of metal in front of them.

"It's the thing from the door!" Zane cried. "They must be the doctors whose room this is, I mean was."

Titus nodded at him, clearly having reached that conclusion some time ago.

"They look like nice people," Erin said quietly, almost wistfully.

Both Titus and Zane agreed. "Happy too," Titus added.

"Do you think he could be my dad?" Zane asked hesitantly and his friends nodded. Zane stared at the picture. "I wish I'd known him," he sighed, and swallowed down the lump rising in his throat. "Mum said he died when It happened."

"Lots of people died," Titus said.

Erin started and looked behind her, hand flying to her knife. Zane jumped and Titus looked alert. "Did you hear that?" she demanded nervously.

They both shook their heads. Erin shuddered violently and looked to her right sharply, as if seeing something from the corner of her eye.

"There's no-one here," Titus said, trying to calm her. He assumed Zane's nerves were getting to her.

"How do you know?" Zane said, voice cracking.

"I just know," Titus replied confidently.

Erin swallowed hard, slowing regaining her composure. "Have we finished here?"

Zane wanted to leave too, Erin's tension leeching into him, but Titus was beginning to pick his way through the papers on the floor and showed no signs of being finished yet. He tried his best to be patient while Erin returned to the window and looked down at the road below. She seemed to spot something and rubbed a patch of dust away from the glass to get a better view.

"Hey look, isn't that one of the Bloomsbury Boys?" she said, pointing down.

Both Titus and Zane followed her gaze to the shock of ginger hair bright against the grey dust of the surrounding street. "It's Dev," Zane replied. "I wonder where he's been— that's nowhere near Jay's patch." He watched him run. "It looks like he's heading to the garden. Let's go see what he's excited about."

Erin needed no persuasion and when Titus realised he'd soon be left alone, he decided to abandon his search and follow them down. They managed to intercept Dev on the corner of the square before entering the garden, and when Dev caught sight of his friend he flapped a piece of yellowed newspaper in his face, barely able to get the words out.

"I found this, you gotta look-see!" he gabbled and Zane took it from him to peer down at columns of text in faded newsprint. "No, the other side!" Zane turned the scrap over and his jaw dropped. "See!" Dev exclaimed. "Told ya! It is, isn't it?"

Zane simply nodded dumbly, staring at the torn image. Titus and Erin peered over his shoulder in curiosity as Dev whooped with excitement. "I done it!" he yelled, punching the air wildly, the flush of his cheeks deepening the red scars further. "I found a picture of the Giant!"

Chapter 14
AN UGLY THREAT

"That's the Giant that was in the hospital?" Titus asked, and both Zane and Dev nodded. Titus gently took the scrap from Zane and scrutinised it. Only the top half of the person could be seen, but the large square head and featureless face were easily recognisable. "Did you tear this from a newspaper?" he asked Dev, who watched his handling of the picture very closely.

"Nah, was like that when I found it. I was just looking for stuff to burn and I saw it and then I come here. Now I gotta show Jay."

Titus ignored Dev's urgency and peered at the corner above the top of the picture. "Some of the date is still on it," he mumbled. "I think it's from 2012."

The other three simply looked back at him, clearly not registering the significance of the year. Titus sighed. "That was the year that It happened." He was about to continue when Dev whipped the scrap from his hand and began to run off towards the garden. "Come on," he yelled, "Jay'll wanna look-see too."

"Wait!" Zane grabbed his collar. "Mum's around, and she doesn't know about all this ... let me make sure she's not in the house. Wait here."

It took only moments for him to establish that Miri was in the garden and to let her know that they were back and that Dev had come to visit Jay. Engrossed in her work, she smiled and nodded, pausing briefly to wave at Dev as he was ushered past and straight into the house. When they were all inside Zane shut the front door as Dev rushed over to the sofa where Jay was sleeping, yelling "Jay! Jay! I got a picture of the Giant!" It didn't take long for the patient to become fully alert and inspect the find.

"He looks like this?" he asked in disbelief and watched both Zane and Dev nod earnestly. "What happened to his face – why's it all smooth like that?"

"I think it might be something over his face," Titus replied. "But it's hard to tell from that picture."

Jay frowned. "Don't seem that clever if it is. How could he see properly?" He looked at Zane. "And he was very tall?" Zane nodded. "And he must be old for him to be on this paper," Jay muttered. "It 'ent right that someone like this is nosing round Miri's patch." He grabbed Dev's jacket and pulled him down so he could speak to him quietly. "Go back to our patch and show this to 'em all. Tell 'em that I want all eyes out for this Giant, and put up a strip to call a Runner. Meet them when they come tomorrow, show 'em this picture and tell 'em I want them to keep lookin'. This might help."

Dev listened to the instructions carefully and nodded frequently, eager to demonstrate his attentiveness. He went to move when Jay finished, but his gang leader didn't let go.

"Dev," he said in a slightly lower voice, "Don't mess this up. If any of the lads give you any jip, send 'em to me."

With that he let the Boy go, who quickly dashed out of the house, clutching the picture tight in his fist. Jay lay back on the sofa, shutting his eyes. "Don't like this one bit, Zane. That Giant don't look right to me. You told Miri yet?"

Zane shook his head reluctantly. "Not yet, but I ... I will."

The front door opened again and Miri breezed in. "Everything alright? Dev looked excited about something."

"Yeah, it's fine," Jay said coolly after glancing at Zane and seeing the tiny shake of his head.

Miri smiled at the three children and continued through to the kitchen with a basket full of herbs.

"Tell 'er soon Zane," Jay whispered, "She should know."

Titus remained silent and then looked down at his hand, realising he still had the photograph of the two doctors. "Here, I held on to it," he whispered to Zane as he handed it to him. Zane looked at it and sighed heavily. "I need to talk to Mum."

"Mum," Zane said, shutting the kitchen door behind him. "Why didn't you tell me that my dad was a doctor?"

The empty dish in Miri's hands slipped from her fingers and smashed on the tiled floor.

"Miri?" Jay called from the living room. "You alright?"

Miri stared at Zane, the curved fragments of earthenware rocking slowly at her feet. "How did you find out about that?"

"So he *was* a doctor?"

"Zane, how did you know?" She sounded panicky.

He stepped towards her, holding out the photograph. She took it gingerly, as it if were about to explode, and looked at the smiling men. Her eyes filled with tears and her hand flew to her mouth. Zane immediately regretted raising the subject, her reaction was so immediate and intense. She sat on one of the stools, staring at the picture, tears beginning to roll down her cheeks.

"Miri?" Jay called again with more urgency.

"It's alright, just a dish," Zane called back, seeing that his mother was unable to answer.

"Where did you get this?" she finally said, breathless with tears.

Zane fidgeted. "From his room in the hospital." He waited for the shouting, but none came. She just looked at him, speechless. "I didn't go by myself," he added. When the silence continued he added, "There's a whole wall of pictures there." She looked back down at the photo, her breath ragged as she tried hard not to break down completely. "I look like him, don't I?"

She nodded and then was on her feet, pulling him into a tight embrace, fierce and strong. He felt his shoulder grow damp as she sobbed into it. He just held her a while, not knowing what else to do. Slowly she let him go to fish a handkerchief from her pocket and blow her nose.

She sat back on the stool and handed the photo back to him. "He was called Doctor James Shannon. The man he's with was his best friend, Doctor Al Siddique. *Zane* Al Siddique."

Zane's eyes lit up. "So I *am* named after someone!"

Miri nodded, becoming tearful again. "One of the last conversations I had with your father was when he asked me to name you after him, he missed him so terribly."

"He died too then?" Miri nodded. "When It happened?" She nodded again. "And then Dad died after that?" Her eyes flicked away briefly and then she nodded.

Zane looked down at the doctors, smiling at him as if he were standing there in front of them.

"Why is his skin so dark?"

"Because his parents were born a long way away, where most people's skin looks like that."

Zane puzzled over this briefly but let it go. "What was Dad like?"

"He was very charming," Miri said quietly, with a pained expression. "Very clever too. I didn't ... I find it hard to think about him, Zane, so I haven't told you anything about him. I'm sorry, that was wrong of me ... it just hurts, that's all."

Zane nodded at her sympathetically. "It's ok. I'm just glad we're doctors like he was."

She smiled weakly. "We're not doctors, Zane, we just help to heal people."

"But Titus said ..."

"Doctors knew lots more about bodies and diseases than we do. And they took a special oath too."

Zane was thoughtful, his mind full of questions about this echo from the past. But he didn't want to dredge things up for her as she so rarely talked about before It happened. "I'm sorry I upset you," he finally said. He briefly considered telling her what else had happened at the hospital but decided that this wasn't the most sensitive time. Besides, he'd had an idea about something else that was pulling his attention elsewhere.

Erin returned to the square at the normal time the next day, but alone once again. "The hunt is over," she told the boys, who had been waiting for her in the garden.

Zane couldn't bear to ask the question, so Titus spoke. "Did Luthor win?"

She nodded and Zane bit his lip. "Did he go through the door?"

"Oh yes. He didn't even notice me when he turned up at the gates with this huge stag over his back. There was blood all over his shoulders and he just marched right up to her rooms." She paused. "David's really upset. He says that Luthor deliberately hit his ankle to make him lose when he should've won because he caught the first stag. He was yelling and shouting, but Father just ignored him."

"Do you think he did it?" Zane asked, intrigued by the possibility that Luthor would cheat.

Erin looked appalled. "Of course not! Why would he? He's the best. David's just jealous. He wants to be with the Red Lady." There was an awkward silence, but then Titus straightened suddenly as if he had heard something.

"There's a Gardner in the square," he whispered to them both and Erin was on her feet in moments, knife drawn.

Zane shook his head. "They wouldn't dare come here—they never do." He looked at Titus then and was frightened by the conviction in his friend's eyes.

Erin's hand shook. "They're not here for you," she whispered, alert and tense.

There was a noise from the southeast corner of the square, a very soft footfall. Zane grabbed Titus' arm, saying, "We've got to tell my mum!" He began to pull up Titus, who was staring in the direction of the noise as if trying to see through the plants and trees that obscured his view.

Something flew through the air from that same direction and hit the ground barely feet away from them. Zane cried out from surprise, then horror, as he saw what it was.

A skull, bleached white by the sun with shadowed eye sockets, had landed in a clump of plants. The children stared at it as Titus allowed himself to be pulled to his feet.

Then it moved.

All three of them cried out in fright and backed away as it scraped sideways before tipping off the leaves to roll upside down onto the dark soil. It rocked back and forth a couple of times, then a snout and whiskers appeared from the internal cavity, and a rat poked its head out.

All three breathed again, Zane immediately embarrassed that he'd thought the skull had moved itself. As the creature scrabbled out, Erin took aim and threw the knife, impaling it through the spine.

"Yuck!" Zane exclaimed as the rodent twitched a couple of times and then went limp.

A man's laughter, devoid of any warmth, echoed around the square. Erin drew in a sharp breath, trembling.

"Not long now, Erin," a deep voice taunted, drawing the words out like a cat prolongs the death of a captured mouse. "We know where you are ..."

"HEY!" It was Jay, from the direction of Zane's house. "Get gone, or get dead, Gardner filth. You got the time it takes for me to draw my knives to decide."

"I'm gone, whelp," the Gardner called back. "I did what I came for."

They could hear Jay moving now, round the perimeter of the garden, sharpening his knives on each other with a menacing scraping of metal. "You even cough in this direction again, you piece of crap, and I'll send your guts back to your old Ma tied in nice bows that she could wear in her hair, if the old bitch had any."

Zane tensed, expecting that to kick off a fight, but they heard nothing more from the Gardner. Jay shuffled into the garden through the south gate moments later, sweating with effort, knives glinting in the sunshine. "He ran off, worthless sack of ... You ok?" he asked them and the boys nodded. Erin stared at the dead rat, shaking.

"Bastards," she muttered, and then rushed forward, scooping the skull into her hand and throwing it as far as she could out of the garden. It smashed into the wall of the Royal Homeopathic hospital and then clattered to the ground. She knelt down to pull the knife out of the rat's corpse, wiped its blood on a leaf plucked from the nearest tree, and then picked it up by the tail as Zane's nose wrinkled in disgust. "I'll get rid of this before your mum sees it," she said and walked out of the garden.

Jay nodded to himself, impressed. "You know, she's alright, for a girl."

Titus was silent as he watched her go. Jay sheathed the knives and sagged. "Gotta lie down, feel like shite." With that he shuffled off, the adrenaline of the encounter fading and the pain of his injury returning fast.

When he was gone, Titus turned to Zane. "That answers one question," he said quietly. At Zane's blank expression he said, "Where Erin comes from. She was one of the Gardners."

Chapter 15
ERIN'S SECRET

After Miri had been reassured, the rat disposed of, and Jay returned to the sofa, the three children gathered once again in the garden, unspoken questions lingering between them. They sat on the only patch of grass in the centre of the garden, next to the small bronze bust of a mother cradling her child. Zane believed it was of Miri and him as a baby, as only someone without the knowledge of where things come from could believe.

Erin picked at the grass, Titus watched her, and Zane worried the thread on his trouser hem. It was Erin who spoke first.

"I suppose you're wondering what all that was about ..."

Zane nodded. "They've never done anything like that before. Mum's really freaked out."

She nodded sadly. "I'm sorry."

"It's not your fault," Zane replied, but Titus didn't show any support for his statement.

"I thought people never left gangs," Titus said, scrutinising her face.

"I was never in their gang!" Erin fired back hotly. That threw Titus off track. Zane looked confused and she sighed. "If I tell you stuff, I might get into trouble."

"We won't tell anyone," Zane assured her. "Really, I'll spit and promise on it, just like the Bloomsbury Boys do, if you like."

"I'll just promise," Titus offered.

"Promises are rubbish," she muttered bitterly. "Everyone who makes promises breaks them."

"We're not everyone," Titus and Zane replied in tandem which made Zane smile to himself.

Erin looked at them uncertainly and said shyly, "I think you are two of the nicest people I've ever met." Zane beamed at that. She thought for a few moments and then took a deep breath. "Ok then, swear an oath that you won't tell anyone. Not even your mum, Zane. And definitely not my father."

He nodded earnestly. "I swear I won't tell anyone about what you tell us."

Titus did the same and they both waited expectantly while Erin fidgeted.

"My mum is with the Gardners, but she isn't one of them, she's just … there." She shrugged. "I don't know why. She's a bit …"

"Weird?" Titus suggested her favourite word.

"Yeah." Erin stared down at the grass she plucked fiercely. "She hardly speaks … she's all broken because of them I think. There are a few other women there too. Once one of them tried to run away but they caught her." She shuddered. "I never saw her again, but I think I heard her crying once, a long while after."

Titus and Zane glanced at each other, Zane in particular disturbed by what she said. After a few more blades of grass were added to the small pile by her foot, Erin continued.

"Mum made a deal with the brothers. I think that's what kept them away from me whilst I was growing up."

"Brothers?" Titus asked.

"The Gardners are men, quite a few of them, but the ones in charge of them are three brothers: Jonathan, Harry, and Doug. It was Harry who threw the skull into the garden just now." Her face took on a grim stare as she recalled him. "Harry's really nasty. He's the worst one because he can seem really nice, and then the next second you've got a knife in your belly. Jonathan's the eldest of them. He and Harry are more in control. Doug is really big and really stupid. He does whatever they tell him to. But they all listen to their mum, old Ma Gardner.

She's *really* horrible." Erin glanced up and saw them gripped by her account, encouraging her. "She's big and fat." She curved her arms out away from her body and blew her cheeks out for a second to illustrate. "She has this big stick to help her walk, but she hits hard with it too. And she's only got a tiny bit of hair on her head. And she is so old. Her skin is all wrinkly and baggy." She shivered in disgust.

"I've never seen anyone like that," Zane murmured. "She sounds like a monster from a story."

"She is a monster. She has a really croaky voice, but you can still hear it from a whole street away."

Zane tried hard to picture the hideous woman in his head. Titus remained silent, a small furrow between his eyebrows being the only clue to his deep thought.

"How can Luthor be your father if your mother is with the Gardners? And how did you end up with him now?" he questioned.

"He came and got me one night," she replied. "Mum always wrote in this book. She hid it from them, especially from Harry … he would sometimes throw me out of the house and tell me to go away for a few hours." She paused and frowned to herself. "She'd always be worse when I was allowed back. One day he found it and went crazy." She trailed off as her bottom lip started to quiver. Zane reached out for her hand, but sensing her tension as he did so, he pulled back again. She set her jaw and looked up to the sky, eyes watery. "He said the deal was over, and he …" Her voice cracked.

Titus' frown deepened as he looked at her, and then a brief flash of grim understanding flickered over his face. "You don't have to say any more," he said softly.

She swallowed hard. "Mum wrote a note that night and sneaked out. I followed her. She left it on the edge of the Red Lady's territory and then went home. The next day, when the Gardners went on a run to the Boys' square, Luthor turned up, killed a couple of the ones that were outside our house, and broke in. Just like that, like it was easy. Mum said he was my dad and that I had to go with him. It was the most she'd said in months." She bit her lip, trying so hard not to cry that Zane's eyes began to mist with tears for her. "And then I was with Luthor. I mean ... Father ... he prefers me to call him Father. He took me to where he lives ... it was only a few days before we starting coming here." She sighed. "So now you know."

Nothing was spoken, only birdsong filled the garden. She looked at Zane and his tears threatening to fall. She rolled her eyes. "You're so soft, Zane," she chided, but not harshly.

"I think it's sad," Zane said, defensively, blinking rapidly. "Don't you cry when you're sad?" Both of his friends shook their heads.

"You shouldn't cry. It shows you're weak," Erin stated firmly.

"Boys don't cry," Titus said, "At least, not grown up ones. And girls who are tough, like Lyssa and Erin, don't either."

Zane looked down at his trouser hem and tried to swallow away the lump in his throat. Titus also looked down at the grass, watching a ladybird struggle up one of the blades.

"She's not coming back, is she?" he asked as he watched the beetle open its hard outer wings and fly off. "Lyssa, I mean."

Zane shook his head slowly, filled with sorrow for his friend. "Callum thinks bad people took her away. No-one said anything because they didn't want to upset you more when you were so badly hurt." He couldn't bring himself to say, "The Unders." Somehow he felt it would make it worse.

Titus pressed his lips together and nodded to himself slowly. "I'm going to go and lie down, I'm aching." He stood carefully. "Thank you for telling us, Erin. And you don't need to worry–I won't tell anybody."

Zane watched him walk away, wishing fervently that he could bring Lyssa back for him. But he knew he was just a boy, and boys can't do anything to people who make lightning. He looked at Erin. She was also watching Titus leave.

"He's tough," she commented. "Wonder what he's all about."

"What do you mean?"

She looked back at Zane. "You haven't noticed how he knows stuff when he really shouldn't be able to?"

"Huh?"

She rolled her eyes again. "Just now, when we were here, he knew there was a Gardner in the square, even though we couldn't see out of the garden at all."

Zane thought about this and his eyes widened. "Yeah! And after we saw the Red Lady, he said some stuff that was like he knew her really well. He's really clever. And he reads, too. I wonder how he knows how to."

"Maybe Lyssa taught him," Erin suggested.

Zane agreed. "Can you read?"

Erin shook her head. "No-one ever showed me. Don't see the point really."

"Reading's great, and it's really useful!" he smiled at her. "You'd be able to read street signs and place names, and books and all kinds of stuff. I'll teach you if you like."

She narrowed her eyes at him. "What do you want in return?"

Zane's face was open and honest. "Nothing. I thought it might be nice for you."

"You're so weird," she replied, but then smiled. "Ok then."

The following day Luthor returned to the square with a confident swagger and training resumed. Zane was convinced he was silently gloating but tried his best to ignore it. Titus and

Miri had a long talk, and that evening Titus announced that he was going to move into the house next door once he was better and could clean it out. Zane was thrilled at the prospect and Erin seemed pleased too. It felt good somehow when the three of them were together.

The days quickly settled back into their old routine of training in the morning and work in the afternoon. In snatched moments Zane taught Erin a new letter and sometimes when Luthor wasn't looking she would trace them out on the ground to demonstrate her progress.

Zane told them both about the Gardner he'd tried to save and what he saw when Titus was attacked, which fascinated Titus to the extent that he hardly said anything for the rest of the day he was so lost in thought.

Every night before blowing out the candle, Zane looked at the picture of his father and his namesake and thought over the idea he'd had after speaking to Miri about his father. He never asked his mother another question about him, even though at times he burnt to do so. He just couldn't find it in himself to make her feel so sad again.

Jay slowly recovered, Miri insisting he stayed so that he would rest and the wound would stay clean. Callum dropped by every couple of days to report on the Boys, often accompanied by a couple of them bearing some kind of offering for Jay or Miri. A few times Jay tried to speak to Titus, but got nothing but a baleful look in response.

Callum also brought a gift for Miri one evening: a new earthenware dish to replace the one that Jay had mentioned as being broken. Zane grinned when he saw him present it to his mother and loitered nearby as they spoke quietly to each other. When he left, Zane sidled up to her.

"Mum, do you like Callum?"

She nodded. "He's a nice man."

"I think he is too," he lingered. "I think he likes you too, Mum."

She chuckled dismissively. "That's nice."

"I think he'd like to spend more time with you."

Miri put the dish away and turned to face him with a quizzical look. "What are you heading towards, Zane?"

He put his hands up, feigning innocence. "Nothing. I just think he's nice, that's all. And that he's kind to you. And I like that."

Miri kissed him on the forehead and began to sort the day's harvest. "He is nice, like I said. I just wish he'd wash more often."

Zane frowned and wondered off, another idea beginning to blossom.

One morning when Zane woke, Titus wasn't there and the window was unlocked. As he dressed hurriedly, he feared that Titus had gone for good until he returned with Luthor and Erin. Luthor looked particularly bad-tempered.

Zane pulled Titus to one side as Luthor went over to Miri, who was pruning a tree at the edge of the garden. "Did you have a dream?" he asked. Titus nodded and Zane's brown eyes broadcasted his disappointment.

"How was she?"

"Fine. She asked how you were."

Zane's disappointment was usurped by joy. "She did?"

Titus nodded patiently.

"Why didn't you say you were going? I would've come with you!"

Titus shook his head. "Sorry, Zane … I can't say why I didn't take you." He paused and then added, "But I might be able to tonight."

Before Zane could respond, he was interrupted by his mother. "What!" she exclaimed, staring open-mouthed at

Luthor. "She can't! You can't!"

"It's for your protection," Luthor said, louder than her. "I'll choose one of the houses at the southeast corner. Besides, Erin will like it, I'm sure."

"Jay won't," she said, shaking her head.

"The Red Lady cares little for what he thinks," Luthor growled. He glanced at Zane and then back at Miri, leaning towards her slightly. "She would be very offended if you rejected this generous offer of help." He looked more pointedly at Zane and back to her again. "And if she couldn't ensure Titus and Zane's safety here, she'd have no choice but to invite them to live in our territory and leave more of us in the square to look after you and the garden."

Zane tensed, appalled at how he bullied her, and went to storm towards him in a burst of reckless courage, but Titus held him back, shaking his head quickly. "No," he whispered. "Not this fight, Zane. There's too much behind this–you'd make it worse."

Zane watched his mother look at him, torn.

Luthor savoured her struggle. "I'm sure you'd agree that it's better that Erin and I stay and keep the Gardners out."

She lowered her head and nodded, defeated. Luthor straightened, a triumphant sneer twisting his mouth as he turned away from her. Titus held on to Zane's shoulder tightly until he was out of sight and then let him rush to his mother.

"I'm sorry, Zane," he whispered guiltily under his breath, knowing that the Red Lady was far too interested in them to leave their survival to chance.

Chapter 16

A REMARKABLE DREAM

Zane woke standing up, which confused him thoroughly. When he saw he was no longer in his bedroom, he rubbed his eyes fiercely, struggling to wake fully.

"It worked!" Titus cried and Zane opened his eyes again. He was in a room, not much bigger than his own bedroom but very different.

"What's going on?" he asked Titus in a bewildered voice.

"I brought you here!" Titus dashed over to him and shook his hand energetically. It was the most animated Zane had ever seen him. "You're really here! This is fantastic!" He even laughed out loud with delight as Zane watched him, bemused.

"Where is 'here'?"

"It's a dream. I *knew* it! I knew it was a special place."

"A dream? But ... this doesn't feel like a dream. It feels too real."

"It's a special dream, a clever one," Titus replied, calming down. "I didn't tell you about it today because I wanted to test my theory. And it worked. I just had this feeling that I could bring you here. I have no idea why I felt that, but I did and here we are."

"So we're still asleep?"

"Yes!"

"Is this the dream you told the Red Lady about?"

"Yes," Titus replied regretfully.

Zane scratched his head and examined the room more closely. Beneath his feet were polished wooden floorboards, swept clean and devoid of imperfections. A desk and chair sat in front of him, not dissimilar to those in a ship captain's cabin from one of his favourite childhood books. The desk was large, with green leather inlaid into the top and four drawers with large brass handles down each side of the gap where the chair was pushed in. The chair looked comfortable, made of wood with arms and a leather cushion set into the seat. Above the desk were two long shelves running the width of the wall with a diverse collection of objects placed upon them.

To his right was a window, and outside was a night sky empty of stars. To his left was a plain plastered wall, clean and pale in colour, with a curious design painted on it. At its centre was a white circle, and radiating out from it were four evenly spaced spokes, each one ending in another circle, each a different colour. One was red, one green, one purple, and the fourth yellow.

Zane pointed at it. "This is a strange picture."

Titus agreed. "It reminds me of the first dream I told the Red Lady about. The balls in the birdbath were the same colour as three of those ones on the wall."

They both stared at it for a few moments, then Zane turned to see a door set into the wall behind him, a large wooden door that looked sturdy, with a bolt and chain and a brass door knob. Just like the other, the rest of the wall was plain plaster. Above him, hanging from the middle of the ceiling, was a light bulb, but what shocked Zane was how it shone so brightly that he couldn't look at it for long. He had seen so many of them, several in his own house, but had had no idea that they could glow like that.

Aside from the desk, chair, and shelves with their objects, nothing else was in the room apart from Titus, who was still very excited.

"Is this a real room?" Zane asked.

"As real as it needs to be I suppose."

Zane didn't feel satisfied with that answer and drifted to the window. His stomach lurched when he saw that it wasn't a night sky, but instead a big Nothing: no sense of ground or sky, just void. To the right was a large oak tree, floating in the inky blackness, as if in the height of summer with lots of deep green leaves and a thick, healthy trunk. He could see it as easily as if it were illuminated by sunshine, even though there was no light from any external source. But what disturbed Zane most of all was how all of the roots were also visible, simply hanging in the air with the rest of the tree as if it had remained after all of the soil and sky had been blown away. Frightened, he turned his back on it all and focused instead on the room, which was much less disturbing.

The objects on the shelves drew his attention, his eyes skipping from one to the next, some that he recognised, others that meant nothing to him.

Amongst the objects that he could understand was a crystal bowl, cut to catch the light and large enough to hold several pieces of fruit, though it was empty on the shelf. There was also a gold ring with a fine gold chain tangled around it and looped through a pendant of a glittering red stone shaped like a drop of blood. A small book bound in worn leather sat underneath a length of dark brown beads. There was a knife with an ornate handle and some kind of coat of arms set into the hilt. A large iron key with an elaborately decorated grip lay near to a small, white porcelain figurine of a dancing woman.

It took him a few moments to recognise a tube-shaped object as a telescope, but the purpose of several other objects eluded him. He pointed at one.

"What's this?"

Titus came and stood next to him. "It's a sextant," he replied, and continued when he saw that Zane didn't seem any the wiser. "It's a measuring device, used to calculate the angle of elevation of a celestial body, such as the sun, above the horizon. From that reading and a note of the time it was taken, a sailor could calculate their position on a sea chart."

Zane blinked at him. "You sound like a book."

"That's because it was from a book," Titus replied matter-of-factly.

"You remember what it said exactly?" Zane asked, amazed.

Titus merely shrugged. "I find it easy to remember things I read."

Zane wished he did too. He went on to ask Titus to identify a square and drawing compasses and a standard navigational compass that was a rather fine specimen made of brass resting in a smart wooden box.

"Why are all of these things here?" Zane asked.

"I don't know, but they're interesting, aren't they?"

Zane nodded in response, feeling very much out of his depth. "They were all here last night," Titus continued, "the first time I dreamt about this room, in exactly the same places as they are now."

Zane looked at the door. "Does that go anywhere?"

Titus shrugged again. "I haven't tried to open it ... things look very odd out of the window, so I haven't dared to yet."

Zane agreed with his caution. "This doesn't feel like a dream because we're talking like we do when we're awake," he commented, fathoming out why it all felt so strange.

Titus nodded. "I think it's called a lucid dream. They're supposed to be rare. I'm going to find a book about them and learn some more."

Zane was about to respond when a sound interrupted his train of thought. It was distant and somehow familiar. "Is that you, Mum?" was all he had time to say before the room disappeared around him as he woke up to the sound of his mother calling him for breakfast.

He looked up and across to Titus, who sat up quickly and then groaned at the twinge from his ribs. He looked down at Zane and grinned. "Do you remember?" he asked.

Zane nodded eagerly and Titus looked pleased. "Good. Tomorrow night, I'm bringing Erin in too."

Miri and Jay were both bad-tempered that day, and for the same reason. After training, Luthor explored the houses just off the square to the southeast to find one suitable for him and Erin.

The children made sure that they discussed the situation out of adult earshot. Erin was pleased to be close to her new friends, but told them that Luthor was very unhappy about it as he liked to be near the Red Lady. Zane explained how carefully Miri had broken the news to Jay, and how much strain it was putting on the delicate balance between the gangs. Titus stayed very quiet when they speculated about the reason why the order had been given, concluding that it was Erin's description of the Gardner event to her father that must have brought it to the Red Lady's attention.

That night Zane was pulled into the dream room again. All was as it had been the night before, but this time Erin was there too. She was just as disoriented as Zane had been, but she had two guides to show her the different objects and discuss the curious nature of the room.

She also was interested in the strange picture on the wall and Titus told her about his other dream. She nodded when he said that he thought the spheres represented something else. "Well, that's obvious isn't it?" she said. "They're us."

Titus blinked at her and then urged, "Go on."

"Well, that birdbath dream was in the garden, where we all spend time together. And there were three balls, and there are three of us. And they were moving together, like we do."

She said it as if it were the most obvious thing in the world, but it was clear that the insight hadn't occurred to Titus.

"Of course," he murmured. "Why didn't I think of that?"

Zane smiled. "You think too hard."

Erin agreed. "I think you thought it was more difficult than it was."

Titus pondered over this as Erin went to the window and said "Wow!" as she looked out at the tree suspended in the void. "Weird ..."

"But what about the sound of the other ball that I couldn't see?" he wondered out loud. "Does that mean that there are other people that are with us that we can't see?"

Zane shrugged and Erin remained quiet, staring out at the tree. After a few moments she moved to the shelves.

Zane watched her inspect the objects, picking several of them up, clearly not feeling as he had that it was wrong to do so. When Erin examined the necklace he said, "That reminds me of the Red Lady," and she nodded in agreement.

She picked up the dagger next and looked at the coat of arms. She frowned slightly as she tested its grip but put it down again quickly.

"I like this room," she announced once its features were fully taken in. "It feels safe and private."

Titus nodded. "It means we can talk together without anyone listening in. I think there's quite a lot that we need to talk about."

His companions agreed. He was about to elaborate when once again a distraction from the waking world tore them from the dream.

"Damn!" Zane exclaimed as he opened his eyes. "I hate it when that happens!"

"Shhh," Titus urged and Zane listened carefully.

The light at the curtains suggested it was barely dawn, but they could hear the sound of someone banging on their front door. It was a familiar rhythm, one of the Bloomsbury Boys' codes. Zane began to put on his dressing gown as he heard Jay groan and answer the door.

"Watchya, Tim," he said sleepily. "Better be good ... it's too early for any ... stop hopping up and down like that and tell me what's up."

"Jay!" the Boy said as Zane emerged, leaving the bedroom door open so that Titus could listen in. "Someone's signed in our patch! 'Ent never seen it before, don't recognise the gang that done it. Whadda we do?"

"What the hell?" Jay exclaimed, the news being tantamount to a rival gang claiming part of his territory from under his nose. "Where? Show me."

Gangs marked their territory in many different ways, but the most common was to draw some kind of symbol, commonly called a "sign," onto a building at the edge of the territory to indicate to anyone approaching that they were about to enter a held area. Jay's sign, two crossed knives, marked the Bloomsbury Boys' territory, whilst the Red Lady favoured her chosen colour more than an actual shape. Her signs resembled daubs of blood more than anything else, something that Jay suspected was deliberate. The Gardners never bothered with signs. He knew that they liked keeping their borders as vague as possible. He'd heard of several witless idiots that had just kept walking south, thinking they were safe, when they were already deep in the area the Gardners patrolled.

Zane helped Jay put on a shirt and trousers, slung low on the hip to avoid the dressing over his wound. "Can I come and see too?" he asked and Jay nodded.

He hurriedly dressed and ran to catch them up after Titus had urged him to tell him everything upon his return.

Tim took them up into Guildford Street and west, towards Jay's square, crossing to the other side of the road. Barely metres away from where they had entered the road, Tim stopped and pointed up to a spot on the edge of the huge red-stoned building that was the impressively run-down Russell Hotel, a place of luxury before It happened.

At a level about twice the height of Jay was a softly coloured pattern. It wasn't clear what it had been painted on with. The colours were fresh and there was no dripping; in fact, it was pristine and appeared almost mathematical in its precision.

Jay swore when he saw it, personally offended and furious at the unknown perpetrator, whilst Zane gawked in disbelief. His large eyes traced it out several times, but sure enough it really was there: a perfect replica of the four coloured spheres in their familiar design, exactly the same as the one from the dream.

Chapter 17
REPARATIONS

By the end of the day, all of the Bloomsbury Boys and also Titus and Erin (closely escorted by Jay) had been to look at the strange marking. No-one really knew what to make of it. Jay posted extra Boys on the territory perimeter and tried to return to his square, but Miri stopped him, having been tipped off by Titus. All evening he lay on the sofa, grumbling that his patch was going to be taken away from him whilst he lay around doing nothing. He didn't notice all the times that Titus smiled to himself smugly.

That night, Titus drew them into the dream room once more.

"This is so great!" Erin exclaimed when she realised where she was. "How do you do this, Titus?"

He shrugged. "I just stand still and think of you both very hard and then wish that you were here with me. And then you appear."

Zane scratched his head. "It would be good if I could do that for your ribs, just wish that they were better and then have it happen. All the other times it just happened by itself. I don't have any control over it."

"Why don't you try?" Titus suggested.

Erin snorted. "Wishes don't come true in the really real world!"

"Are you sure?" Titus asked so seriously that she actually paused to think about it. She threw her hands in the air. "Whatever, try it–nothing will happen. This is a dream, so weird stuff is bound to happen here."

"But people don't normally share dreams," Zane said quietly. "At least, I never have and no-one I know has ever said

139

anything about it."

Titus nodded. "I think this is very rare. In fact, I know it is." He leant against the windowsill as Erin drifted back to the shelves to fiddle with the objects. Zane pulled the chair out and sat in it before Titus continued. "I think we're different from everyone else."

Erin glanced back at him. "Everyone is different from everyone else."

"Yes, I didn't mean that … I mean that I think we're special in some way. Don't you feel it?"

Both Zane and Erin shrugged. "Mum says I'm special all the time," Zane commented.

Titus frowned and let it go.

"I wonder who made this room," Erin said, twisting the figurine on the shelf to make the dancing woman twirl.

"I don't know," Titus answered. "I just woke up here the other night."

Zane looked at the drawing on the wall. "Maybe the same people that drew that on Jay's building."

"But why do that?" Titus said, puzzled. "And why paint it so high?"

Zane gasped. "Perhaps the Giant did it!"

Titus shook his head. "The Boys would've heard him if he were that close."

The three of them pondered a while until Zane said, "I've had an idea about something, but I'm not sure if I should make it happen. Can I talk about it with you two?"

The next morning, as soon as they woke, Zane sat up quickly. "I wish I could make Titus better!" he said in a loud, eager tone. Titus watched him carefully, remaining silent, waiting for something dramatic to happen. After a few moments Zane sighed. "Nothing."

Titus shrugged. "Never mind."

Titus sat up, twisting too much, and winced in pain. At that moment Zane's expression transmuted into surprise.

"It's happening!" he whispered urgently, eyes darting around the room.

"Just go with it," Titus whispered back as Zane stood slowly and then went over to his friend. "Don't be scared, do what you feel is right."

Zane looked down at Titus, concentrating on the area of his broken ribs. Gingerly he reached down and touched the bandages. Titus drew in a breath as Zane's face strained with increasing effort.

"I can see it healing!" Zane gasped as his forehead began to glisten with sweat. Awestruck, he saw the blue haze around Titus, but not only that, into him, past the bandages, through his skin and muscle, to his very bones! Entranced, he watched the tiny fractures in three of the ribs very slowly begin to close, the bone knitting itself back together again. It was like watching the natural healing process, only sped up. In less than a minute, the bones were fused back to their rightful state, and as Zane's mind withdrew, he noticed the inflammation around the area and willed it to subside. Before his eyes, the tissue swelling began to reduce, and then all of a sudden his vision was outside Titus' body. Zane staggered back and sat down heavily, shaking as if he had run a marathon.

He rested his head between his knees as Titus sprang up out of bed and hurriedly began to unwrap the bandages. "I think it worked!" he said excitedly as Zane pulled himself up to flop on top of the bed with an exhausted sigh.

The bruising on Titus' chest was only a pale yellow and less swollen that it should have been. He bent from side to side experimentally and stretched up towards the ceiling, then down to touch his toes.

"Brilliant!" he cried and rushed back to Zane. "Oh." He deflated slightly, seeing that his healer was fast asleep.

It took a day for Zane to recover. Titus got to work clearing out the house next door, on the other side of the arched alleyway that ran down the side of Miri's house. When she commented on the speed of his recovery, he assigned it to her excellent care.

Luthor and Erin began to move into a Georgian townhouse on Boswell Street, just off the southeast corner of Miri's square. It made Jay even harder to live with. He seethed as he heard them clearing out rubbish that clattered into the street. He snapped at anyone who tried to talk to him, even Miri, whose previously bountiful patience was starting to wear thin.

In the afternoons and evenings Luthor would patrol the nearby streets to the south and then go hunting. He brought meat to Miri every day, which she genuinely appreciated. In an effort to improve the situation with Jay, Miri cured any leftover meat and sent a portion of it to the Boys. Jay was young and proud, but not stupid, and he could see that there was more to lose if he alienated the woman who cared for his gang so well. He was satisfied when Miri secured a promise from Luthor that the Red Lady still respected the boundary of the Bloomsbury Boys' territory and would make no move to encroach any closer to it. Jay evidently hated Luthor, but it was clear that the Hunter was a man of his word and that it would be a serious matter for the Red Lady to retract such a promise. Miri reminded him pointedly that they hadn't taken over her garden, only posted one person in it, but it was obvious that she feared the same as Jay.

It didn't help Jay's mood that, despite many creative attempts, the Boys couldn't scrub the sign from his building. However, over the next couple of weeks, no more of them appeared, and Callum reassured him daily that no trespassers had been seen.

Titus began to train, much to his relief, and the daily routine, if occasionally strained, settled back down again.

The day finally came when Jay was given the all clear to return to his own territory. He hugged Miri tightly and told her that she was the best, waved to Zane, and hurried off. Both Titus and Luthor cheered up when they were told of his departure. Zane, however, was despondent; the house felt too quiet now that both Jay and Titus were gone.

Later that day, Jay reappeared, to Miri's surprise. She was even more taken aback when he asked where Titus was. She directed him to the other side of the square where he and Zane were sitting on a wall talking in hushed voices.

"Alright," he said, striding over confidently. Zane smiled and Titus fell silent, watching the gang leader with suspicious eyes. "Wanted to ... er ... I'd like you to come over to my patch, Titus," he said and both Zane and Titus blinked in surprise.

"What for?" Titus replied warily.

"You'll see. Nothin' bad, honest-like."

Titus looked to Zane who shrugged and nodded. He looked back up at Jay. "Only if Zane can come with me," he replied.

Jay nodded. "No problem."

When they entered the square, it was strangely quiet, with most of the Boys gathered in the central area. Zane picked up on Titus' tension, even though his face betrayed nothing. He understood why; the last time Titus had been here they had beaten him and his sister had been stolen away.

Jay led them to the motley collection of Boys, several of whom were lined up in a row looking bad-tempered. Jay nodded over to Callum, who had been standing so still that at the far side of the square he'd escaped Zane's notice. The old man gave a brief salute and shuffled off.

Jay turned to Titus. "Sommat 'appened that I wouldn't normally be that bothered about, but I've been thinkin' that I 'ent happy with it, so I'm gonna put it right." One of the Boys in the row sighed loudly and Jay shot him a threatening look that soon quietened him.

"A while ago Titus 'ere and his sister came onto our patch and so we gave him a bit of a shooin'. You all know what else 'appened that night." His eyes flicked over to two long mounds of earth in the far corner of the central square. "Since that night, Titus has been taken in by Miri, so I reckon Titus must be alright."

Zane was astonished and smiled reassuringly at Titus, but his lips remained pressed tightly together.

"Now I 'ent sayin' that he should be one of us," Jay continued. "But what I am sayin' is that we should try to make up for what happened when we didn't know he was alright."

He picked up on a movement near the back of the group. "What is it, Tim?"

"But Jay!" the Boy cried out. "He came into our patch! We didn't do nothin' wrong!"

Jay put his hands up. "I 'ent saying we did. What I'm saying is that he's alright, and that I'm gonna give him a second chance. You know I don't normally do that with those that 'ent one of us, but in his case I am, so shut it!"

The Boys fidgeted, clearly not happy with the turn of events, but still respectful enough of Jay to go along with his wishes.

"Go on, Smudge." Jay poked the first Boy in the line and he sulkily approached Titus. He produced a small rucksack from behind his back that Titus clearly recognised.

"Sorry we nicked your stuff and walloped ya," Smudge muttered, holding the bag out to him.

Titus took it and looked inside.

"Everything there?" Jay asked, keeping a close eye on the row of Boys, all of whom were staring at the bag resentfully.

Titus shook his head.

"Smudge!" Jay yelled and clipped him around the ear. "I told you to get everyone to put it all back in the bag."

"I did!" the Boy yelled back, rubbing his ear furiously. "It 'ent my fault!"

Jay's pale blue eyes scanned the gang, most of whom stared at their shoes. "What's missing?" he asked, not taking his eyes from them.

"A jumper," Titus replied. "A good one. It's blue."

One of the shortest Boys at the end of the line began to raise his hand in the air reluctantly.

"I gave that to Squeak, the new Boy," he said tremulously.

"Squeak, come 'ere." Jay beckoned to the far back of the group.

Zane tensed as he caught sight of the child peeping from behind one of the other Boys. He was dressed differently now, most notably in a blue jumper that came down to his knees. He was slightly less pale, but still watched Zane fearfully.

"Come 'ere!" Jay raised his voice slightly as the child shook his head. "Bring him over, Dev," Jay said, and the ginger-haired Boy pulled the reluctant child with him despite his dragging his feet.

The Boy shook and Jay softened slightly. "You're new, so I'll let you off this one time," he said and then frowned. "Nothin' to be scared of." He followed the Boy's frightened gaze and then chuckled. "No need to be scared of Zane! He's the last person that'd hurt ya! This your jumper?" he asked Titus, who nodded.

Jay pulled it off the Boy to reveal a tatty t-shirt and handed it over. "Dev, give 'im one of yours."

"Aw, Jay! That's not fair!" Dev complained.

"Shut it!" Jay growled and Dev withdrew, the little Boy scurrying away to hide behind the crowd again. Satisfied, Jay turned to Titus expectantly.

There was an awkward silence as all of the Boys looked at Titus too. *Thank him!* Zane thought, desperately wishing he could prompt him out loud.

"Thank you," Titus finally said through gritted teeth.

Jay nodded in satisfaction. "Good. If you wanna come over with Zane, any time, you're welcome. Hear that, Boys?"

The assembled muttered back their assent and Jay strode off, several of the Boys breaking away to trail after him with disputes that they wanted to bring to his attention.

Titus and Zane left the square in silence, Titus holding the bag to his stomach tightly. When they re-entered Miri's garden square, Titus asked, "Why was that Boy scared of you?"

Zane told him about what had happened the day the Boy was found and how terrified he had been. Titus stopped in his tracks.

"You're sure you've never seen him before?" Zane nodded. "And when did your mum say that your dad died?"

Irritated by how insensitively Titus asked the question, Zane reluctantly answered, "When It happened."

Titus' eyebrows shot up. "That's a lie," he said, matter-of-factly.

Zane immediately took offence. "Don't call my mum a liar!" he cried.

"But she must be," Titus interjected calmly. "If you're the same age as me, either he isn't your Dad or she lied about when he died."

Zane looked thoroughly confused.

"*It* happened twenty years ago," Titus explained. "You were probably born about five years later. And seeing as how you look so much like him, I think she must have lied."

Zane blinked, taken aback.

"In fact," Titus continued, "judging by how frightened that Boy was, I'm starting to suspect that your dad isn't dead at all. I think that he's met him, and that somewhere, your dad is still alive."

Chapter 18
CALLUM'S TRANSFORMATION

"No!" Zane replied forcefully. "I can't do that!"

Erin sighed, flipping the ornate iron key over and over in her hand in frustration. Titus leaned against the captain's desk and frowned at Zane, who was sitting in the corner of the dream room, knees under his chin.

"But don't you want to know why she lied?" he pressed.

Zane bit his lip. "Of course I do, but you didn't see how upset she was. She cried when I showed her that picture."

"What about how upset you are!" Erin retorted.

Titus held up a hand in an effort to calm her and she put the key back on the shelf. Titus tried a different approach. "We could show the photo to Squeak–I think that was his name–and see what he can tell us."

"We can't do that!" Zane gasped and Erin looked up at the ceiling, trying to control her irritation. "He was scared of me and I only look like my dad. Imagine how he'd be if he saw a picture of him!"

Erin spun around. "Zane, this is your *dad* we're talking about! What about how you feel? Don't you want to know where he is, or what he's doing? Stop worrying about everyone else and think about what you should know!"

Zane shook his head. "It's not right to upset people. I've been fine without knowing up until now, and I'll carry on being fine. And maybe Mum'll tell me one day … it's up to her." He couldn't bring himself to tell them that he was more frightened of what he might find out than curious to know it.

147

"Are you for real?" Erin exclaimed and Zane looked back at her, puzzled.

Titus put a hand on her shoulder. "I think if everyone were as concerned for other people as Zane is, London would be a much friendlier place." She rolled her eyes.

"You're too soft," she muttered.

Zane looked down at the floor and a heavy blanket of silence descended over them. "I want to wake up now," he said softly, and the room faded from around him. He turned over in his bed, lit the candle, and looked at the photo. It was crumpled around the edges from being carried in his pocket and stuffed under his pillow each night. He stared at the image of his father for a few minutes before pinching out the flame and sinking back into a restless sleep.

The next day, the children trained quietly, grateful to have Luthor's lessons on setting snares to concentrate on rather than the uncomfortable conversation in the dream the night before. When the morning was over, Zane went over to Jay's square and sought him out.

Jay made time for him, sending some of the Boys away so that Zane could speak freely to him. He listened patiently to Zane's idea and when he was finished, scratched the edge of the bandage still left around his torso.

"You sure he'd like that?" he asked doubtfully. "Don't see why anyone would meself."

Zane nodded. "I know people used to really enjoy them before It happened. Can you help me, Jay? Please?"

Jay paused, thinking it all through. "I haven't got all that stuff ... I'll have to trade with the Weavers for it," he mumbled aloud. The Weavers were more a group of business associates than a gang, residing in Berwick Street, Soho, once renowned for its fabric trade. After any disaster, there's always someone who finds a way to turn a profit from it, and the

Weavers were expert at this, widely known as the first people to approach when searching for any rare goods. Rumour had it that the Weavers had filled every order ever placed with them, enjoying relative freedom from the more violent gangs due to their usefulness. Jimmy the Weaver, the nominal leader, may have seemed friendly enough but he was a shrewd fellow and one to take care around if you ever strayed that way. Jay knew never to go there at night as it was close to Gardner territory, and it was better to make first contact through a Runner for your own safety.

"You sure that's okay?"

Jay nodded. "Callum did right by us when I was laid up. I'll send one of the lads over when it's all set up ... might take a while, though."

Zane nodded, smiled, and then ran home, not noticing Dev wave at him hopefully as he raced by with his mind on the Weavers. He had never met any of them, of course, and Jay never sent any of his Boys there as it was so close to Gardner territory. If it wasn't for the Runners, and the risks they were prepared to take to survive, the Weavers would probably have gone out of business. Zane had the feeling that so much happened in London beyond his mother's garden.

Jay was true to his word, and three days later Tim was sent round to let Zane know that everything was ready.

He and Titus hurried to the square, leaving a message with Miri to let Erin know where they'd gone as she had been summoned by the Red Lady. Luthor was out hunting, so they didn't have to worry about him seeing anything.

A huge bonfire was lit in the east of the inner square, and a tightly controlled operation stretched from its edge right into the Russell Hotel. Jay had a constantly moving stream of Boys carrying buckets of water from the rainwater butts nearby which were then poured into metal saucepans, heated over the

149

bonfire, and carried finally into the hotel. He waved Titus and Zane over.

"Almost done, and Callum's on his way. Go and check it's all ok if you want."

Zane and Titus went into the hotel to find the lobby lit with candles in jars, the filthy windows alone not letting in enough of the daylight. Very little remained of the reception desk; its wood had been taken and burnt a long time before. The former splendour of the walls and ceilings was now eradicated by years of neglect, the coffee tables smashed and the sofas stripped of their cushions and fabric. Now only a collection of springs and metal frames was left scattered around the edges of the area. The marble of the floor was revealed in the path where Boys had walked back and forth, brushing away the thick dust. More jars of candlelight spread up the large spiral staircase to their right, made hazy by the grime that clung to the glass wall that curved around it. Zane and Titus followed the light up the stairs, dodging small Boys either staggering under heavy pans of steaming water or scurrying back down the stairs with empty ones. It was easy to see where the small army was heading to and from, and Titus and Zane made their way to the same room.

The bedroom had been stripped of fabric, wood, and paper a long time before, leaving only a large plastic box with a smashed glass screen that no-one knew the reason for and an old mattress that had been too heavy for the Boys to get out of the room. They had opened the windows to let in as much light as possible, but more candles were in the suite's bathroom, which had no window of its own. Trying their best to keep out of the way, first Titus, then Zane peeped in as one of the Boys tipped his pan of water into the newly cleaned bath. The air was full of steam and fragrant with herbs that Zane had picked from the garden. The list of items that he'd asked for were laid neatly in a row, along with some that Jay had added, and sure enough it was all there, the Weavers living up to their reputation.

Titus looked at Zane doubtfully. "I hope he likes this."

"If he doesn't, Mum will," Zane replied. "Let's go and wait for him outside."

By the time they had re-emerged from the hotel, Callum was entering the square, marvelling at the frenzy of activity.

Jay beckoned him over, telling the Boys to stop and rest, which they did gratefully. "Callum! Glad you were nearby. Zane here has set sommat up for you, and I let him do it on my patch to say thanks for lookin' out for my lads whilst I was laid up."

Callum's eyebrows were high as he heard this, and he shuffled over to Zane and Titus, who were waiting for him at the steps of the hotel. "Is this all your doing, young Zane?" he asked uncertainly.

Zane nodded eagerly. "I was talking to Mum ages ago, and she said that one of the things she really missed from before It happened was having a hot bath, especially after a long hard day. And you've had lots of long hard days looking after the Boys, so I thought you might like one too."

Callum blinked at him from under the eyebrows. "You did, hmmm?"

Zane nodded. "I picked lots of herbs for the water to make it smell nice ... I think Mum might like you more if you smelt better."

Callum took it well, seeing that the boy didn't mean any offence.

"A bath, eh?" he scratched under his long beard. "A hot one, you say?" Zane nodded enthusiastically. "Well, I better get moving, else it'll get cold."

He ruffled the top of Zane's head as he went past him into the hotel and up the stairs. The remainder of the Boys spilled outside, chattering and pushing each other, to gather under the window of the room Callum had gone to.

A few moments went past. The Boys fell silent, all craning their necks to see if Callum was going to come out running in disgust as many of them expected him to.

"Will he really get in the water?" Dev asked quietly.

"Course he will. We didn't take it all up there for him just to look at!" Jay replied.

"Won't that kill 'im?"

"Nah." Jay sounded less certain.

"Will he take all of them clothes off?" another Boy asked in a nervous voice.

"I bet some of 'em are stuck on," another quipped and got a clip round the ear from Jay.

"Less lip!" he growled. "Callum's alright."

A noise from above hushed them all. It was deep and resonant, like nothing any of them had heard before.

"Is it hurting him, Jay?" Paulie, one of the smallest, asked nervously.

Jay shook his head. "Nah ... don't sound like it."

The sound began to stretch over words, floating down to them all melodiously. "He's singing!" Zane cried out in delight. "It means he really likes it!"

Some time later, a different man emerged from the hotel. Jay jumped to his feet when he saw him, reacting as if someone had strayed onto his patch and Callum was still upstairs.

The man smiled shyly and Zane ran up to him. "Callum!"

Several of the Boys gasped. One cried out, "It made his hair fall off!"

Zane hugged him as everyone marvelled at how different he looked. His beard was gone, as was his long knotted hair. He had cut both away, leaving only an inch or so on his head, and had even shaved with the new razor and mixture secured from the Weavers. He was dressed in the new clothes that Zane had asked for and, much to Zane's relief, smelt fresh and clean.

"You look so much younger!" Titus remarked and Callum laughed, the skin around his mouth so much paler than his cheeks.

"You have to come and show Mum!" Zane urged, pulling him down the steps.

Callum stopped him at the bottom to go over and shake Jay's hand. "Thank you, Jay. It was high time I stopped hiding." He smiled at the Boys, a couple of whom were still gawping at him open-mouthed. "And thank you too, Boys, very kind of you to carry all those pots. I'll collect my things later. "

He then let Zane usher him to his own square. As he left, one of the Boys shook his head. "I 'ent never having one of them bath things," he mumbled. "Not if that's what it does."

Titus hurried after them, curious to see how Miri would react. Callum walked differently, with a body less encumbered by many layers. He was still broad in the shoulder, but with a sturdy body and strong-looking arms which had been impossible to see properly before.

Zane burst into the house, calling for his mother. She came to the doorway still holding her pestle and a handful of herbs and looked at the man in the doorway as if he were a stranger.

"It's Callum, Mum," Zane cried and her jaw dropped. "We gave him a bath!"

Callum smiled back somewhat awkwardly as Miri struggled to find words. "Would you like a cup of tea?" she finally managed, and Callum nodded with a shy smile, stepping into her house for the first time.

Chapter 19
ONE DEAL LEADS TO ANOTHER

The next morning Zane was surprised to find that Titus wasn't waiting for him in the garden as usual first thing. His friend soon emerged from his house, but he looked distant and tense.

Zane wondered over to him, noting the dark circles around Titus' eyes and the pallor of his cheeks. "What's wrong?"

Titus was scanning the garden for Luthor and Erin. "I need to go to the Red Lady. Right away."

Zane brightened at the thought of seeing her again. Before he had a chance to say anything, Luthor and Erin came into view and Titus hurried over to the Hunter. "Wait!" Zane called, "I'm coming too!"

Zane tried hard not to look too excited to see her when the Red Lady bade them look up. The breeze teased the voile drapes to his left, carrying her scent to him, and he breathed it deeply. Zane felt a huge sense of relief when Titus had asked that he and Erin be allowed to stay and it was granted. He heard the doors shut as Luthor left and watched her eyes take her visitors in. He was sure they lingered a little longer on him.

"Always a pleasure to have you visit." She smiled warmly. Zane was certain that she was directing that specifically at him, but then she shifted her attention to Titus. "I take it you have a dream to tell me about?"

The boy nodded. "I saw Lyssa."

Both Erin and Zane looked at him in surprise. The Red Lady leant forward slightly in her chair. "Your sister? Go on."

Titus was frowning at the floor, his hands clenching as he struggled to find the best place to start. "I know it was important ... I was planning to go to the room I told you about, but I didn't wake up there. I mean ... I didn't start the dream there–I was somewhere different, and I could hear Lyssa ..."

His voice faltered and he swallowed hard. The Red Lady stared at him intently before saying in a gentle voice, "Tell me about where the dream started ... was it another room?"

The tactic worked and Titus focused on the question. "No, it was a corridor, a strange one. The ceiling and walls were grey and smooth. The light was bright, like sunlight, but it came from thick lines on the ceiling that made a humming noise."

Zane glanced at the Red Lady to gauge her interest and was surprised by its intensity. She had paled slightly, and her hands, usually loosely draped over the ends of the chair arms, were instead gripping them tightly.

"Go on," she prompted, voice hushed.

"There were lots of doors ... sort of set into the walls in an odd way. There was no gap anywhere around them like normal doors and they were all shut. There were covered panels in them, but it looked like the cover could be slid back so you could see into the room. The floor was shiny."

There was a pause and the Red Lady adjusted her posture, sitting more straight in her chair. "What could you hear?"

Titus seemed reluctant to answer. "Crying ... but muffled, coming from the rooms, I think, but the doors were thick. Then I heard Lyssa calling for me and I was moving down the corridor ... like I was being pulled almost. I came to one of the doors and I could hear her ... hear her crying and calling for me. Then I sort of just moved through the door and ..."

His description broke off. Zane couldn't help but reach over and put a hand on his shoulder. Titus looked at him, his eyes blinking rapidly as he took a deep breath. Zane had never seen him so unsettled before. He looked back at the Red Lady.

"Lyssa was lying on a bed and she was held down by some straps and ... and her hair was all cut off and she looked sick. I tried to speak to her but I couldn't ... it wasn't like the clever dreams we have in that room. She was ... really upset and scared."

Zane squeezed Titus' shoulder gently as his friend shook, trying to convey his presence and support, but was uncertain whether Titus even felt it. After a few moments he regained his composure and continued in as strong a voice as he could muster.

"The door opened behind me and ... and the Giant came in."

Zane gasped. "The Giant comes from the Unders?!" he exclaimed.

"Giant?" The Red Lady rose and came down the steps to their level. She then looked at Zane with surprise. "You know about the Unders?"

Zane felt the pressure of the three of them staring at him. "Only that they're bad people that steal women ... Mum thinks they took Lyssa. I don't know anything else about them ... except that they can make lightning and throw it at people." He gasped again, this time in horror. "That means the Giant can make lightning!"

"This is not good," Erin muttered.

The Red Lady held up her hand. "Tell me about this ... 'Giant.'"

Zane related the story to her, too busy editing out Dev and getting the rest of the details right to see that he now commanded her full attention. He went on to tell her about when Lyssa was taken and the lightning. "Until today, I didn't think that the Giant was connected at all," he concluded.

Titus said nothing while the Red Lady drifted over to one of the windows, letting the voile brush her cheek as she looked out into the courtyard. There was a slight tremor of her hand as she rested it on the windowsill.

"Is that where the dream ended?" she finally asked.

Titus nodded and then quietly added, "Yes."

The sounds of the people outside training and working crept into the room to mingle with the heavy silence within. Zane worried that he'd said too much, that the Giant was planning to steal his mother next, and that now Erin wasn't safe either. After a long pause, the Red Lady turned and looked at Titus.

"I'll help you to get your sister back," she stated simply. All three children responded with a wide-eyed silence. "I'll see to it that my people keep their eyes open when hunting. Any information you receive, pass onto me and when we have a location, my best Hunters will help you retrieve her." There was no coy smile, no teasing glance, only determination.

Titus finally managed to find his tongue. "Thank you."

She nodded. "You may leave now, but Erin, I want you to stay behind a moment."

Zane considered whether to risk a kiss, but somehow the atmosphere seemed too serious to try it. "See you soon," he said hopefully, earning only a brief smile and nod from the Red Lady. He suppressed a sigh and followed Titus from the room.

No opportunity for the three to talk in private presented itself for the rest of the day, and so that night, Zane and Erin were pulled into the dream room. At first there was an awkward silence until Erin stuffed her hands in her pockets and leant against the windowsill, stating, "Well, something weird is going on. With the Red Lady I mean." That piqued Zane's interest in particular. Erin continued, "The Red Lady never, ever offers to do anything for someone outside of the gang unless it's a deal."

Titus raised an eyebrow. "Really?"

Erin nodded. "She didn't make you promise anything in return for helping you find Lyssa, did she?" When he shook his head, she spread her hands. "There you go then. Weird."

Zane frowned. "Not weird, *kind*."

This time Erin's eyebrows were raised. "The Red Lady, kind? Hah!"

"Why not?" Zane retorted, angered by Erin's sarcastic tone. "Maybe she just wants to help."

Erin chose not to reply, simply rolling her eyes. Zane looked to Titus for support but the boy merely shrugged his shoulders.

"I don't know, or care, what her motivation is. I just want to get Lyssa back. And Zane, next time, try to be more careful about what you say ... telling her about what happened to Lyssa meant you had to talk about Jay ... I don't think Jay would like that."

Zane stuffed his hands in his pockets, hunched his shoulders, and began to gently kick at one of the legs of the captain's chair in frustration. "I thought it was important that she knew what happened. If people were more open, things would be much easier."

"Told your mum about the Giant yet then?" Erin asked, making Zane blush and scowl. "Thought so," she muttered.

The three fell back into silence, Zane hating the tension between them. He understood that Titus was tense about Lyssa, but he couldn't understand why Erin was so negative until he recalled a question he'd been wanting to ask her all day.

"Why did the Red Lady want to see you alone? Is that why you're grumpy?"

"I'm not grumpy!" Erin snapped, but when she saw Zane's concern, she deflated and perched on the edge of the captain's chair with a long sigh. "Sorry Zane. I shouldn't give you a hard time because you're soft." Zane didn't know whether to be insulted or accept the apology, so he just let it go. She continued, "I'm not sure if I'm allowed to talk about what the Red Lady said."

Titus frowned. "Why?"

Erin shifted nervously. "Because neither of you is in her gang."

"Neither are you," Zane pointed out and she nodded.

"True ... but she wants me to be ... and soon."

The boys looked at each other. Zane couldn't quite understand why, but the idea of that made him uncomfortable and Titus seemed to feel the same way.

"I'm not sure though," she continued. "I really like it there, and she's really tough and I like that. And Father thinks that I should be in it–there's no doubt for him that I should–but ..."

Her voice trailed off and Titus picked up the thread. "But it might make it harder for us?"

She looked up at him standing by the window and nodded. "Yeah ... I mean, it's already hard living near the Bloomsbury Boys, cos when you go over there they won't let me go in with you because of who my father is. And he keeps telling me they're horrible, but I can't see why if they're your friends, Zane. I can't see you getting on with horrible people. You're too nice."

Zane smiled half-heartedly, his eyes still sad.

"And if I join the Red Lady's gang," she continued, "then it might make it even harder for me to spend time with you, especially when your training is over. And that might be soon cos Dad's desperate to move back to her place. Then I might not see you much at all."

They all thought about this. "I like seeing you every day," Zane said quietly. "It feels right for us to be close together. Even when things are hard, like at the moment."

Both Titus and Erin agreed strongly. "And you're the first real friends I've ever had," Erin added sadly.

"I think gangs are stupid," Titus announced forcefully, making the other two look at him in surprise. "There must be another way for people to survive. Lyssa and I got by fine without any gangs for years. It's much better that way."

"But there were only two of you," Zane said. "And you didn't have a big garden to worry about protecting."

Titus sighed. "That's true, but I still don't like the idea of people feeling like they can't say things just because of what someone else might do about it." He looked at Erin. "You know that would get worse if you joined them?"

Erin didn't say anything, but she nodded after a few moments.

"Didn't you and Lyssa ever think about joining a gang?" Zane asked. "It must have been hard … it would've been safer to be in one."

Titus shook his head. "No, never. We stayed away from them. Lyssa said that it was better to be free and do what we wanted when we wanted." He looked pointedly at Erin. "If you joined, and the Red Lady didn't want you to see us anymore, you'd have to do what she said."

Erin turned away and Zane stepped forward. "We don't have to worry about that now," he said, desperate to alleviate the tension. "Do we? Or did the Red Lady say something about it happening soon?"

After a long pause, Erin spoke. "She asked if we were all getting along ok. I said we were, but I didn't say much more than that. You have to be careful around gang leaders." She looked pointedly at Zane. "She said that I'd settled in well and that Luthor said I'd be a good Hunter one day. She said that she was always looking for strong people to join her gang, but that I had to forget my life before. That I should only look to the future or something like that. I said I couldn't just forget my mum, but then she went all cold and said that of all people, she was the one I should try hardest to forget."

Zane gasped. "She said that? But no-one should ever be told to do that! Mums are the best things in the world!"

Titus turned and looked out at the strange oak tree. Erin sighed. "I asked her why, but she wouldn't answer. She said it wasn't my place to question her ... which is right I suppose. But I couldn't just let it go ... and I felt angry ... I said that my mum was in just as much trouble as Lyssa so why couldn't we help my mum too?"

Titus looked back at her. "That was brave."

Erin shrugged. "Stupid more like. I just lost my temper ... it wasn't fair. She was so nice to you about Lyssa – why be so mean about my mum?"

She fell quiet. Zane went over to her and very slowly reached out and touched her hand. She looked up at him and tried to manage a smile but it didn't quite work.

"How did it end?" Titus asked.

"She said that normally she'd have someone thrown out onto the street for answering back like I had, but that she'd give me another chance, seeing as I was new to it all and because of who my father is." She glanced at Zane. "She didn't say it very kindly either."

"I suppose she was angry too," he replied half-heartedly.

She looked down at the floor. "I asked Father about Mum."

Titus turned back to look at her. "I suspect that didn't go well."

Erin began to bite one of her fingernails. "He said I wasn't allowed to talk about her. That she was a terrible person, and that she deserved everything she got, and if I ever spoke about her again he'd be very angry. He said I was lucky that he was willing to give me a chance even though she's my mother."

Her lip trembled and she hurriedly started to chew on a second nail. Zane squeezed her other hand sympathetically and looked to Titus with concern.

"It sounds like he thinks she did something in the past," Titus commented.

"She couldn't have!" Erin exclaimed, suddenly angry. "Mum hardly says anything, she just sits there for hours or cries or stays in bed. How could she have done anything bad?"

"Maybe she wasn't always like that," Titus theorised, so caught up in the puzzle that he forgot her distress. "And she must have known Luthor before, to have made you with him. So where was she when she knew Luthor?"

Zane cleared his throat and frowned at Titus to make him aware of his insensitivity. Titus realised this quickly and fell silent.

"No-one deserves to be left with the Gardners," Zane said softly. "I wouldn't want my mum to ever be unhappy. I'm sorry it's all so horrible."

Erin shrugged. "It's better than it used to be." She looked over at Titus. "Sorry ... we should be talking about the Giant and your dream about Lyssa, not my stuff."

"I did want to talk about it a bit," Titus admitted. "I want us to go back to the hospital." Seeing Zane's dismay, he continued. "I have to find out more about the Giant and what he was doing there. I think it's ... interesting that he was in your dad's room."

Erin gasped. "Maybe the Giant is your dad, Zane!"

Zane shook his head. "No, my dad's dead."

"Is he?" Titus said pointedly and Zane began to pick at the thread on the hem of his trousers. "We talked about that. Miri's lying–I think he's still alive."

"I'm right, then!" Erin grinned but Zane shook his head again.

"No, it wasn't him. I'm sure of it. He would have tried to speak to me, surely. And anyway, I'd be taller if I was a Giant's son."

Erin shrugged. "Whatever. I still think I'm right."

"In the pictures he doesn't look tall enough to be a Giant, relative to the other people in them," Titus added and she sighed, nodding in capitulation. He frowned. "We need to go back to that room and see if we can find out more about him though. And the Giant … maybe we could find something that will give us a clue to find the Unders. First chance we get, we go, agreed?"

Erin nodded and then Zane did too, albeit reluctantly. "But in the morning," Zane added. "Can you meet me in the garden before we start training? There's something I want to do. It's important."

Chapter 20
AN OATH AND A LIE

The next day was the first that suggested the end of the summer. A cold wind blew grey clouds across the sky and prompted Miri to unpack jumpers and blankets from their summer storage.

Zane found it impossible to settle to anything, constantly looking to the corner of the square to see if Jay and Callum had arrived before the morning training was due to start. When he caught sight of them, he beckoned them towards the garden and hurried into the house.

"Mum," he called, "Can you come to the garden?"

She followed him outside. "What's wrong?"

"Nothing," he said, seeing Erin enter the garden with Titus and, to his surprise, Luthor.

Luthor picked up on this, Zane still unable to mask his feelings. "Erin said something important was going to happen, so I thought I should be here."

Erin gave Zane an apologetic look, but he smiled good-naturedly, doing his best to ignore the tension between Jay and Luthor who stood as far away from each other as they could in the small gathering.

Miri smiled at Callum and Jay, and then looked quizzically at her son.

"Thanks for coming, everyone," Zane began. "I wanted you all to be here because I'm going to do something that's very important to me. It's an idea I had a while ago, it just took some time to find out the things I need to know." He glanced around at the group. "A long time ago, there were people called doctors," he began, not noticing Miri tense up. "Titus read about them, and when he told me more about what they were like, I decided that I wanted to be one too."

Both Callum and Luthor raised their eyebrows in surprise; like Miri, they were old enough to remember the time before

It happened and were no doubt curious to see where this was going.

"Doctors were nice people who made people better, knew lots about bodies, and took a special oath."

He glanced at Titus who gently prompted him, "The Hippocratic oath."

"Yes, that's the one," Zane continued. "Me and Mum already try to make people better." He smiled at Miri, who looked back at him affectionately. "And Titus has found me some more books so I can learn what all the things in the body are called. So that just leaves the oath. Some bits of it didn't make much sense, so I wrote my own version that has the most important bits in it. I'd like to take it in front of you all, just like a proper oath, so you can all see how much this means to me."

Zane fished out a piece of paper from his pocket and read out loud, "I, Zane Taylor, do most solemnly swear to always do everything I possibly can to heal the sick, to treat the wounded, and to try to save the life of anyone who is injured or dying."

Both Luthor and Jay bristled at this, but Zane didn't notice.

"I swear," he continued, "that I will remember that sympathy and kindness are just as important as bandages and ointment, and that it is the whole person that should be thought of, not just where they are hurt. If a patient tells me something in confidence, then I will not tell others. If I have the chance to save someone's life, then I will with thanks, but if I must let them die to end their suffering, I promise that I will do this in a humble and considerate way, and that I will not try to be more important than I really am. May I always heal and find joy in that task."

He finished and looked around the small circle of people. Titus and Erin beamed at him, whilst Miri dabbed at her eyes with her handkerchief, smiling proudly. Callum nodded at him with respect and Jay winked at him. Luthor stepped towards him.

"If an oath is to be one that binds you, then you should mark it with blood," he stated, drawing his knife, which made Miri take in a sharp breath. Jay moved forward but Callum put a hand on his shoulder, holding him back calmly.

Zane swallowed hard and looked at the steel tip in front of his nose. Luthor was clearly waiting for him to do something, but he had no idea what. After a brief pause, Luthor took his hand and pricked the end of his finger swiftly before Zane could pull away. He waited until a large drop of blood swelled onto the tip before giving it one firm shake to make the drop fall onto the soil.

Satisfied, he let Zane's hand go, saying in a loud clear voice, "With his blood, let the oath be kept."

All three children shivered.

Zane sucked the tiny wound as Luthor looked at him with something like respect. "One step closer to being a man," he said, looking into his eyes before stepping back.

"Now you're a proper doctor," Titus said with satisfaction.

When the gathering drifted apart, Titus quietly followed Jay to the edge of the square and held a brief hushed conversation with him about the link between the Giant and the Unders that ended in Jay leaving with renewed purpose.

Now that Zane had taken his oath and his nerves were subsiding, he considered going to tell his mother about the Giant, but then Luthor returned with an armful of practice weapons and he was soon swept along into the morning training.

It wasn't until the end of the day that they were given some time to themselves and the three gathered at the far end of the square near the hospital.

"Mum's sorting out a sprained ankle, one of the Bloomsbury Boys," Zane reported quietly. "We should have about fifteen minutes at least."

"Dad was called back to the Red Lady," Erin added, "He'll be gone a while."

"Good," Titus nodded. "Let's go then whilst we have some light."

They hurried into the hospital lobby, furtively checking that they were unseen. Once again Erin was in the lead with a dagger drawn, Titus close behind her looking just as alert, and Zane following a few paces behind, his heart thrumming so hard that he could feel his pulse in his throat.

They stepped into the stairwell and since it was clear with no new footprints, they steadily climbed to the third floor as quietly as they could. Erin opened the door into the corridor after looking through the round window first. The dust lay still on the other side, save the small swirls stirred by the eddies of air from the door's movement.

"Looks clear," she whispered and Titus nodded confidently.

"We're the only ones here," he whispered back.

"Why are we whispering then?" Zane asked tremulously.

"Best to be on the safe side," Erin replied and stepped through into the corridor.

The three crept to the office door, seeing their old foot-prints and those of the Giant still crisp in the thick grey carpet of dust. They entered the office, Zane shutting the door care-fully behind them and staying very close to it.

Titus scanned the room. "I don't think he's been back since the last time we came here."

Zane went to the wall of photos and Titus looked at them briefly too before drifting off to look through the filing cabinets. Erin was twitchy; she went over the window again, rubbing her temples.

Zane frowned at the images of his father and his name-sake. His father looked nice enough, happy and friendly, so why had his mother lied? Had he turned into someone horrible? Then another idea struck him and he regretted this one even more.

"Maybe he joined the Gardners," he said quietly. "Maybe that's why Mum lied."

"No silly," Erin said softly. "I would've seen him, and I didn't."

Zane gave a huge sigh of relief. "Oh yeah, I forgot about that."

Erin gripped the edge of one of the desks, shaking. "Um, are you going to be long, Titus?"

He gave a noncommittal grunt, concentrating hard on a file he'd found. Zane went over to Erin. "What's wrong?"

"Got a bit of a headache. Something about this place ... had one the last time we came. I don't like it here much you know."

Zane nodded. "I don't either. Maybe it's the old air making your head hurt."

She shrugged. "It's not a big deal."

They both watched Titus rifling through the papers in the cabinet for a few moments before returning to the wall of photos, drawn to the glimpses of life before It happened.

"The women looked weird back then," Erin mumbled. "Their lips are all different colours. Look at this one." She pointed to a photo of Zane's smartly dressed father with his arm around a woman in an evening gown. "Her lips are really bright pink."

Zane peered at it. "That doesn't look ... natural," he agreed. "Maybe she was ill. But her cheeks are really rosy ... I don't understand."

"Her eyelids are a funny colour too," Erin added, fascinated by the puzzle. "Maybe some women used to be funny colours."

Zane shrugged, captivated by the images of his father and his best friend. He tried to imagine a world filled with women who wore sparkling dresses and who seemed only too happy to kiss and hold hands with men. A world that was clean and shiny, with bright colours and strangely lit rooms. He wondered what the dirty water that they were drinking in many of the pictures tasted like and whether it made them sick. He knew his mother would never let him drink anything that was that colour. But more than anything, he wondered what it was like to be his dad's best friend, to be in those places with him laughing and talking and putting arms around women with him. He felt a heavy ache fill his chest.

"I wish I knew him," he whispered, too quietly for the others to hear.

"You nearly done, Titus?" Erin asked impatiently.

"Just one more minute," he said, giving up on the filing cabinet and starting to rifle through the drawers of the desk.

She returned to scanning the pictures with Zane. "There aren't any of the Giant in these pictures," she commented.

"That's a good thing, right?" Zane asked and she shrugged.

"Guess so."

Titus slipped a piece of glossy paper into his pocket surreptitiously as Zane and Erin focused on the wall. He sighed with frustration. "I can't find anything about the Unders or Giants anywhere here."

"We should go," Erin said and Titus nodded grimly.

He turned to leave, but as he did so a book mostly buried under the scattered papers on the floor around the filing cabinet caught his eye. He pulled out a leather-bound diary and flicked through the pages, filled with meticulous notes on the weather, compared planting techniques, and relative yields. He was about to dismiss it as nothing more than a scientist's experimentation with gardening when he noticed how the entries stopped abruptly halfway through the book. "Zane," he said after reading the last lines. "Look at this."

Zane went over to see the page that Titus held open to him. He scanned a few lines about planting carrots in an old bath to avoid pests, but then the notes broke off and a thick line carved the page in two, as if scored in by a knife. Scrawled in the same handwriting, yet with less care, was the only personal note in the book:

Miri's pregnant. Shit shit shit. Should've been more careful. What the hell do I do now?

Zane stared at it, Titus reading his face as easily as he had read the page. Zane then noticed the date at the top of the page: 21st March, 2017.

"But ..." was all Zane managed to say as Titus nodded.

"I was right," he said softly. "That date is five years after It happened. He didn't die then."

Erin's eyes widened. "So your mum was lying! Whoa, I never thought Miri would be like that." Zane shot her an angry glare and she patted the air with her hands. "Sorry, Zane, that came out wrong."

"You *must* talk to her," Titus urged. "You have to tell her about the Giant and find out why she lied."

"But it'll upset her!"

"But it might help us to find Lyssa!" Titus blurted out. "The Giant came to this room, *only* this room on this whole floor—there has to be a reason why! Maybe he knows your dad. Maybe Miri knows where he is and then we could find the Giant and then we could find Lyssa!"

Zane bit his lip, struck by the open desperation on his friend's normally composed face. "Okay," he sighed, "I'll talk to her ... I'll go and ask her now."

Chapter 21

UNCOMFORTABLE TRUTHS

Zane closed the front door quietly and went into the kitchen, finding his mother tending to the houseplants on the windowsill.

"Are you hungry?" she asked, not yet turning to face him. "I thought I'd teach you how to make that mash you like."

He didn't reply, unable to find the right words to start off the conversation he'd delayed so long. The long pause made her stop and look over to him.

"Zane," she said softly after a few moments, and he broke out of his thoughts. "Why don't you tell me about it?"

Zane looked down at the rug, his stomach twisted into one large knot. "Because I'm worried you'll get all upset," he replied quietly.

She frowned. "Well, you have to tell me now, otherwise I'll just worry."

He sighed and went into the living room, Miri following straight away. He flopped down onto the sofa so heavily that she went to sit next to him and gathered him into her arms. She eased his head onto her shoulder and stroked his long hair, just like when he was small and had fallen over.

He pulled away so he could see her face. "Mum," he began tentatively. "I didn't tell you everything about when I went to the hospital where I got Dad's picture from." It was clearly the last thing she expected him to say. "There was someone in there ... a Giant."

Miri blinked. "What? Start at the beginning."

Zane told her about the first encounter, taking care not

to mention Dev. He knew if he mentioned Dev, his mum would blame him for tempting him into the hospital. Whilst it was true, he didn't want his friend to get into trouble for it. Dev's life was hard enough. Instead, he glossed over his involvement and went on to tell her about Titus' dream about Lyssa and their realisation that the Giant must come from the Unders. By the time he'd finished, Miri's cheeks had drained to an awful grey green and his stomach twisted when he realised that it wasn't all he had to tell her.

She swallowed again. "We need to tell Jay ... and Luthor ... if the Unders are sending people here they need to know."

He couldn't bring himself to tell her that Jay had known for some time, and that the Red Lady had also found out about this before her. "Er, Titus is taking care of all that at the moment Mum ... there's more that I need to talk to you about." He took a deep breath. "I need to know about Dad."

He saw her look away, watched her eyes become distant for a moment, and then when she looked back at him it was as if she was somehow closed off from him. "I don't think it's very worthwhile to think too much about the past," she said quietly and began to get up to go and busy herself.

Zane caught hold of her hand to stop her. "Mum, please. I need to know because the Giant was in his office."

She sat back down but her eyes wouldn't meet his.

Zane sighed and decided that he had to pursue this or she would never tell him. "I know he didn't die when It happened."

Her eyes flicked to him, infused with guilt. She swallowed again but didn't say anything.

He shifted around so that he was facing her properly. "Why did you lie?"

Her hands began to shake and she looked up at the ceiling, swallowing again as if something had caught in her throat. "I just thought it was the best thing to do. I didn't want you to think about it all."

"Well, I am thinking about it, a lot!" Zane exclaimed. "He's my dad, and ..." He took a deep breath. "I want to know what happened to him."

He watched the muscle in her jaw work as she struggled to deal with the conversation. "I'm just not sure if it's something that –"

"Mum," he said, cutting her off, and she blinked at him in surprise. "Tell me. Please."

She looked back at the rug, but he knew she didn't really see it. She seemed to be looking at another time. "I met your father when I came here a couple of years after ... after It happened." She paused, trying to hold back her emotions that threatened to drown out her words. "Mum and Dad, your grand-parents, used to work at the homeopathic hospital across the square and we used to have picnics in the garden here when I visited. But when I came back of course it was very different. I was very scared and alone and I didn't really know what I was doing here. You see, I'd had this silly dream that they were still alive and it was so vivid that I walked here, just in case it was true. There wasn't any other way to find out."

"You mean, you didn't always live here?" Zane asked incredulously, finding it very hard to imagine a time when the square was different.

She shook her head. "I moved away from London when I was eighteen, and when It happened I stayed in the country as it was safer where I was. It was such a long way away it took me months to walk back. And I had to be careful and avoid the other people here—most of them were very dangerous." She paused, clearly recalling something unpleasant.

Zane reached across and took her hand.

"My parents were dead, of course, and I found myself here with nowhere to go, no plan or anything. I was beginning to regret it, but then I met James." She smiled a little. "We nearly scared each other to death."

Zane mirrored the smile and leant forward.

"I liked him straight away. He was so handsome, and he had a slight Irish accent which I just loved. It was really ..." Remembering who she was talking to, she paused and cleared her throat. "Really nice. We were just so pleased to find someone else who was still normal and not in a gang. He was camped out in this house, he let me stay, and I never left."

"Did you love him?" Zane asked quietly.

Miri got up and lifted the kettle of water up to hook it over the fire. She nodded, keeping her back to Zane for a moment. "Yes," she whispered. "Very much."

She took a moment to compose herself and went back to sit on the sofa. "I cleared out the garden–it was horribly overgrown–and began to sort it out, to make a life for us. We were happy for a while. We made sure we kept out of everyone's way. No-one else knew we were here for a long while."

She smiled to herself.

"What was he like?"

"He used to make me laugh. He was very kind and clever too." Miri reached across and tucked a few strands of Zane's hair behind his ear. "You look a lot like him. You've got my eyes, but the rest of you is definitely James."

Zane studied her face, saw the sadness. He felt relieved to hear so many good things about his father, but he found it difficult to see her so upset. He knew she was trying hard not to show it, but it was impossible.

"He told funny stories," she continued. "Lots about him and his best friend and what they used to get up to."

"The one I'm named after?"

She nodded. "They were like brothers. He used to go into the office they shared at the hospital every day. He said he still felt close to him there. Sometimes he would get upset, be in a bad mood for a couple of days, but mostly he'd be fine."

She trailed off and Zane saw her try to stop the tears from forming. He took hold of her hand again, beginning to feel tearful himself, but tried to keep them at bay like Erin or Titus would if they were in his shoes.

"Did … did the Gardners kill him?" he asked in a whisper.

She shook her head and the tears spilt down her cheeks. "No, no, Zane. Nothing like that." She fished her handkerchief from a pocket in her long skirt and wiped her cheeks. "I can remember that day perfectly. It was in the spring. I'd been feeling a bit strange for a while and that was the day I realised why. I was pregnant, with you."

Zane held her hand tight, trying to imagine her before he was born.

"I was shocked, but pleased," she continued. "I liked the idea of us having a little baby to look after. I thought it would make him happy. I came into the house and he was sitting in that chair." She nodded over towards the armchair nearest the fire. "He looked at me, and I'll never forget it. He said 'You know, if I had a son, I'd call him Zane. I think he would've liked that.' I was pleased, and I told him that maybe he'd have the chance. He didn't quite get it, and I went over and kissed him and …"

She started to cry. Zane wrapped his arms around her, feeling guilty that he'd made her talk about it. She managed to regain control and pulled back to continue.

"I kissed him and told him that I was pregnant. I thought he'd be pleased, but he just stared at me, and he went so white. He said he had to get some air and walked out."

Zane thought of the diary entry and frowned to himself. Those words hadn't been written by a man that wanted to have a son.

"I thought he'd just had a shock, and that he'd come back and we'd talk about it. We'd find a way to get through and it would all be fine." The tears ran freely down her cheeks as she stared at the rug, looking at that time again. "I waited for him the rest of the day and when he didn't come in for supper, I was a bit concerned. But I just thought that he needed some space to think about it. I went to bed, and when he didn't come back by the next morning I really started to get worried."

Zane remained silent, getting up to lift the kettle off the fire as the steam began to plume out of the spout. He returned to the sofa and took her hand again.

"I looked for him everywhere I'd ever been with him. I even went into the hospitals." She shivered. "But I couldn't find him anywhere."

"Did the Bloomsbury Boys help you to look?" Zane asked, imagining her worry at that time.

She shook her head. "No, Zane, there were no Bloomsbury Boys back then."

"You were all by yourself?" Zane gasped. "What about the Red Lady?"

"I didn't know anyone else at all," Miri replied quietly.

Zane was horrified. He tried to imagine what that would have been like, and even though he could only guess, he knew it would have been frightening. He couldn't bear the thought of her being so alone.

"He never came back," Miri said flatly. "Every day I thought he'd come through that door, but he never did."

Zane was aghast. "Never?" He watched her shake her head as she dried her eyes. "But why?"

She shrugged. "I don't know. I suppose he couldn't cope with being a father. I wondered if he'd died. But I thought I'd know if that had happened, that I would feel it somehow. I know it's silly, but I don't think he died. I think he just ran away."

Zane thought of those words in the diary again. A new emotion began to bubble up in his stomach when he thought of his father. Contempt. "He just left you alone, when you were going to have a baby?" he asked, unable to conceive of how his father could do that.

She nodded. "It was very hard, especially late on in the pregnancy. And the labour ... that was hard too."

Zane saw his mother differently all of a sudden. He'd never thought of her as brave before. He'd only seen obvious acts of bravery, like the Boys facing off against men twice their size, but hadn't appreciated how she had been courageous too, in her own quiet way.

"You were all by yourself when I was born?"

"Yes. I bit down on a stick so I wouldn't scream ... I was scared that the Gardners would hear me, or the Sweepers- they were quite close at the time."

"Who?"

Zane watched his mother wrestle with her first instinct to brush the question aside, not wanting to fill his head with the terrible things outside of the garden. But with relief, he could see that recent weeks were forcing her to realise that she simply couldn't do that anymore. "The Sweepers are one of the most dangerous gangs I know about. They haven't been in London for years, but if you ever hear people singing loud songs about God or a holy fight, run away as fast as you can and hide." She smiled sadly at Zane's diligent nod. "Never mind about them." Miri patted his hand. "What's important is that you were a strong, beautiful baby." She drew him close and they held each other tight for a few moments. "And you were a happy baby," she said, kissing him on the forehead. "I was very lucky. You didn't cry very much at all."

Zane had read about birth in the medical encyclopaedia that his mother kept. He imagined her having to cope with it all alone. The tears welled up in his eyes and she embraced him again.

"I'm sorry, Mum," he croaked. "I'm sorry Dad was so rubbish. I'll never mention him again."

She nodded and wiped her eyes. She noticed that he'd lifted off the kettle. "I'll make us some tea," she said and went to get the mugs.

He saw Titus walk past the window but he didn't knock on the door. Zane briefly wondered where he was going but then Miri came back in with the teapot and mugs. After she'd poured the water into the pot to let it brew, he went over and hugged her tight.

"I love you, Mum," he said into her hair. "I'll never leave you."

Chapter 22

TITUS MAKES A CONNECTION

Whilst Zane consoled his mother, Titus walked purposefully towards Jay's square, the overheard conversation fuelling his determination. It didn't even occur to him that listening at the open window had been a breach of privacy. After learning that about him, he knew that Zane would never allow anyone to speak to the Bloomsbury Boys about his father, not only because of not wanting to upset them, but now also because he was ashamed of him. Zane wouldn't want anyone to know that his father could be involved, so Titus knew that if he wanted answers about how he was connected to the Giant, he'd have to find them out himself.

For Titus, there was no moral quandary; it was simply a matter of getting answers without Zane finding out. Then his friend wouldn't get upset, and he would be one step closer to finding Lyssa. Quite frankly, ending her suffering was much more important than whether his friend was upset or not. As he marched, he considered a flickering feeling of guilt at the back of his heart, realising that no-one other than his sister had made him feel this way before. But then he dismissed it as an irrelevance. How could he let his sister stay in that place he saw in the dream a minute longer than necessary? Her dying alone, in pain, was a far worse outcome than Zane being merely upset.

He was challenged at the entrance to the square by Smudge who grudgingly agreed to ask Jay if Titus could speak with him. As he was admitted, Jay strode over from the steps of the Russell Hotel.

Titus didn't smile in greeting as Zane would have done, and Jay was too busy swaggering to worry about such things, so only a curt nod was exchanged when they met.

"Titus." He looked down the street. "You by yourself?"

Titus nodded. "I wanted to ask you something."

Jay appraised the serious young man in front of him. "Alright, go on."

"I want to talk to the new Boy-Squeak."

Jay raised an eyebrow. "What about?"

Titus paused, not wanting to disclose this, but realising that Jay wouldn't let him without knowing why. "I wanted to see if I could help him. I think I might be able to."

Jay frowned deeply, searching Titus' eyes. "Why'd ya wanna do that?"

Titus maintained eye contact, unperturbed by Jay's scrutiny. "Two reasons. The first is because it isn't very nice when you're having problems. The second is because it upsets Zane when he sees how scared Squeak is of him."

Jay considered this carefully. "Alright, but I stay with you the whole time."

Titus nodded after a beat. "Agreed."

Jay started to walk off, but Titus stopped him. "Jay, Zane isn't to know about this, at all. I don't want him to feel embarrassed."

Jay paused and then nodded in agreement. Satisfied, Titus followed the young leader across the square. Squeak soon came into sight, huddled in the doorway of one of the large Georgian houses that lined the square.

Jay halted Titus and went to speak quietly to the Boy, who eyed Titus with open suspicion. The child gave a reluctant nod and Jay beckoned Titus over, standing back to allow him to sit opposite the small Boy.

"Hello, I'm Titus. I just want to ask you a few questions." The Boy looked at Jay and then nodded, chewing the sleeve of his jumper.

"Good," Titus said softly as he reached into his pocket. He pulled out something that he'd taken from the desk in the hospital office, a photo of Zane's father. He steeled himself as he held it ready in his hand. This was going to be difficult.

"Do you remember where you were before you came here?"

Squeak shook his head rapidly. Titus frowned.

"Are you sure?"

The Boy nodded and glanced nervously at Jay.

"I've asked him all this before," Jay sighed. "He don't remember anything."

"He's lying," Titus said back to him unemotionally.

Jay's eyebrows shot up. "You callin' one of my Boys a liar?" he said, taking a step forward.

Titus nodded. "Yes, because he is." He ignored Jay's threatening stance and turned back to Squeak, too set on his goal to be distracted by petty posturing. "There's no need to lie, no-one will send you back there. Is that what you're afraid of?"

The Boy chewed furiously on his sleeve, making squelching sounds as he looked from Titus to Jay and back again. He finally nodded slowly.

Jay knelt next to Titus. "I told ya, you're one of us now, you don't have to go anywhere else, and no-one's gonna get ya."

Squeak looked down at his tattered trainers that were far too big for him. Jay sighed and looked at Titus, who was silent, considering his next question.

He could see how intimidated the Boy was and how their proximity to him was making him nervous. He tried to think of a way to broach the subject of Zane's father without being too obvious for fear of the Boy clamming up even more.

"Do you remember anyone else being where you were before?" he finally settled on and the Boy shook his head.

Titus' keen mind latched onto the way the Boy's eyes looked away briefly as he nodded, the way his shoulders tensed just a little more. He was certain he was lying again.

He turned to Jay. "His lying is not making this any easier."

Now intrigued by the questioning, Jay looked at Squeak sternly. "If he tells me you're lyin' once more, I'll be pissed off. Have the others told you what happens when I'm pissed off?" Squeak nodded nervously. "Well then, stop messin' us about and tell the truth."

Squeak pulled the sleeve from his mouth and swallowed hard. "Sorry," he whispered.

Titus smiled, but it was only to make the Boy feel more at ease. He read the Boy's reactions carefully, noted how that smile didn't seem to help much. If anything, it seemed to make him more nervous. He let it fade from his face. "What do you remember?"

"Grey walls," the Boy whispered after a few moments.

Titus nodded in an effort to encourage him. "Good, that's a start, carry on."

The Boy pointed up at the sky. "No blue, only grey, low down."

"We don't think he was ever outside," Jay added in a whisper. "He gets a bit freaked out about the weather and he don't like being in the middle of the square. Come to think of it, quite a few of the Boys are like that when they first arrive."

Titus nodded, pushing back memories of the dream he'd had of Lyssa in an attempt to stay focused. He looked back at Squeak. "What else?" The Boy fidgeted nervously. "Were there any other people there?"

The Boy stared off into space briefly and then nodded. Titus noted how he'd started to shake.

"Bad people," the Boy spoke in barely a whisper. "But sometimes Eve." The deep lines of worry that were nestled between his eyebrows lifted when he spoke her name.

"Who's Eve?" Titus asked, intrigued.

"Like me, in the bad place. Eve opens the doors, even after the bad people lock them." He pressed a dirty forefinger to his lips. "But it's a secret." He took a deep breath and made a show of swallowing deliberately, then pointed at his stomach. "Keep it down, keep it quiet."

Titus frowned as he considered the Boy's behaviour. He suspected that the Boy's words and actions were a pattern ... a habit, similar to the way that he checked all of his pockets before he left the house to make sure he had the most important things, just like Lyssa had taught him. Then there was a flash of intense emotion as the longing to be with his sister surfaced briefly before he put it aside to concentrate on the task in hand.

"Never heard that name before," Jay commented.

Squeak shook his head. "No, cos Eve's a girl. Only boys here," he said forlornly. "I miss Eve."

"How did she open doors?" Titus asked. "Did she have a key?"

Squeak shook his head. "No, she didn't need one." He looked up at Titus. "She was special." He looked concerned all of a sudden. "But you mustn't tell anyone! It's secret—keep it down and quiet, in your belly."

He swallowed hard again, waiting for Titus to do the same, which he did to allay the Boy's fears and encourage him to speak more. Titus consciously filed the information about Eve away; it interested him greatly, but he didn't want to focus on that. "Did you see another girl there? A bit taller than me, with eyes like mine?" The Boy shook his head and the brief hope that Titus had harboured faded quickly. "What else do you remember?" The Boy went back to chewing his sleeve. "What about the bad people—what were they like?"

Squeak looked fearful again at the mere thought of them. Titus saw this but still wanted to pursue it, his goal taking precedence over the child's emotions.

"They kept the doors locked," he whispered. "Kept me in the room. Did bad things." The shaking started again, this time more intense.

Titus didn't let that change his line of enquiry. "What things?"

The Boy chewed fiercely on his sleeve, staring into space just past Titus' shoulder. He decided to change his tack.

"What did they look like?"

The Boy's face scrunched up. "Don't want to talk about them."

"But it's important," Titus pursued.

"Sayin' stuff about them won't bring them 'ere," Jay said reassuringly. "I got my blades, see? If they even come close I'll kill 'em before they even see you." He patted the hilts of his knives and Squeak looked at them. "If you tell us what they look like, I'll know who to kill, won't I?"

"But most of them are very big," he whispered. "Much bigger than you."

This piqued Titus' interest. "Do they have square heads?"

The Boy nodded, huddling back further into the corner of the doorway, glancing around the square as if they might arrive at any moment.

Titus began to get excited. "Have you shown him the picture of the Giant?" he whispered to Jay.

Jay shook his head. "He gets freaked out about stuff too easily," he whispered back.

Titus turned back to Squeak. "The people with square heads, did they breathe strangely, like this?" He tried to sound like he was wheezing, thinking hard about Zane's description of the Giant and what he saw in the dream.

Squeak nodded more quickly, eyes wide. "You know them!"

Titus shook his head. "No, but my friend has seen one."

"All of them were like that apart from one." The Boy shuddered. "He was the worst."

Titus held out the photo of Zane's father that he'd held hidden in his palm up until this point. "Did he look like this?"

Squeak looked down at the photo and drew in a sharp breath that lodged in his chest. An expression of absolute terror leeched away the little colour in his cheeks and he froze in a paroxysm of fear. He couldn't tear his eyes from it, and Titus felt a brief triumphant thrill at the fact that his private theory had been proven. But then something very strange happened that took him by complete surprise.

One moment he was watching the Boy's reaction; the next it was as if he were in a small grey room with featureless walls and a solid metal door that was set flush into the one opposite where he was. It was exactly the same as the one in which he'd seen Lyssa imprisoned in the dream, but this time it was like he was lying where Lyssa had been. The door was closing, and he realised that someone had just entered. He was lying on some kind of bed, and when he tried to move, he realised he was strapped down. He couldn't think; his mind was flooded with the purest feeling of terror as he heard footsteps approaching him.

The man was dressed in a white coat. His hair was dark with a peppering of grey, his small beard neatly clipped. He looked just like he had in the photos, only paler and older. If it hadn't been for his blue eyes, he could have been an older version of Zane.

He held something in his hand, something narrow and sharp, filled with clear liquid. He pushed the air out of it with the plunger and Titus felt himself begin to struggle frantically, hearing a boy's high pitched voice begging the man to stop, and realising with confusion that it was coming from his lips.

"Shhh," Dr Shannon said gently. "Just a little scratch, it won't hurt a bit." He smiled, which sent Titus spiralling into an abyss of fear, somehow knowing what was going to happen next.

There was a pinch on the back of his hand, and a horrible feeling of cold fluid racing into his veins. No matter how hard he struggled, he couldn't stop the feeling of numbness beginning to spread as his cries died in his throat.

"There there," Shannon was saying softly, smiling all the while. "See, soon you'll be asleep."

But he wasn't, and he knew he wouldn't be. He felt his eyes become glassy, unable to move them away from the doctor's smile. His body was utterly limp, no matter how much he willed it to try to break free. He could feel the straps holding him down, the pressure of the bed against his body. All physical sensations were still present, but he was simply unable to move. Then a hand reached over, shutting his eyelids, and there was the sound of the door opening, a harsh mechanical wheeze, and loud metallic footsteps entering the room.

"He's ready," Shannon said.

There was the sound of something being opened and the scrape of metal against metal as some kind of instrument was pulled out of something. Then the awful sensation of something beginning to slice into his arm.

Titus screamed and found himself stumbling backwards, arms flailing, heart pounding painfully in his chest.

Jay grabbed his arms and held him up as he almost fell. "Titus!" he yelled. "Titus! What the hell happened?"

Titus looked around, utterly confused and bewildered to find himself in Jay's square, and not in the grey room. He struggled to regain his composure but let Jay hold his shoulders, as his legs were like water beneath him.

"Are you alright?" Jay said, trying to make eye contact with him.

Titus looked past him at Squeak who was staring into space, eyes wide, distant and terrified. Titus knew where the Boy's mind was trapped, realised what had just happened. He'd shared his memory; somehow it had penetrated his mind and he had experienced it with the same intensity. And now the Boy was replaying that memory over and over again, unable to break out of it.

"Say something!" Jay urged and shook his shoulders a little.

"I'm ok, I'm ok," Titus said, trying hard to break away from remnants of the flashback. He forced some distance between himself and the emotions that still echoed inside him. He reminded himself that it didn't happen to him, that it had been a memory, someone else's memory, nothing more.

"I gotta get Squeak inside," Jay said, looking round the square. "I don't want the others seeing him like this. He'll be like it for a while, it's 'appened before. I'll talk to you later."

He gently let Titus go, who staggered a little and then braced his hands on his knees, lowering his head to get some more blood into it.

Jay picked Squeak up gently and carried him away, cradling him tenderly as the Boy shook violently.

Titus noticed the photo lying on the ground nearby where he must have dropped it. He picked it up, stuffing it quickly into his back pocket, checking that neither Jay nor any of the other Boys saw what he was doing. He paused to take a few more deep breaths before making his way home on shaking legs that hardly felt like his own.

Chapter 23
OF UNKNOWN ORIGIN

All that evening, Titus sat alone in his house, not rising from the sofa to light candles when the darkness closed in around him. When Zane called round he ignored the knocks on the door, staring up at the ceiling that had disappeared into shadow. He remained almost motionless until sleep drew its veil over him.

Zane also lay awake for some time after going to bed, his mind just as active as his friend's and thinking about the same person. He wasn't surprised when he was pulled into the dream room to find Titus waiting for him.

"I called round but you weren't there," Zane said, relieved to see him. When Titus didn't respond immediately, he frowned. "Is Erin coming too?"

Titus shook his head. "I don't think she's asleep."

"She's at the Red Lady's," Zane replied. "Maybe something's going on there."

Titus leant against the edge of the table, trying his best not to reveal how uncomfortable he felt, but Zane was too sensitive.

"I spoke to Mum," he began, thinking that Titus was reluctant to ask him. "Dad left when he found out she was pregnant. He never came back. She doesn't know where he is."

"I do," Titus said quietly, flatly.

Zane blinked. "What?"

Titus forced himself to look at Zane. "I didn't know whether to tell you or not. But it seems wrong not to, now that we're here. Do you want to know?" After a brief pause Zane nodded. "He's in the Unders."

Zane opened his mouth to speak but no words emerged. Finally he managed to force the question out: "How do you know?"

"Squeak, the Boy who's scared of you, told me," Titus replied coolly, not betraying a hint of there being any more to it. "He's scared of you because you look like your dad."

"But ... but why be scared of him?" Zane whispered hesitantly, not even sure he wanted to know the answer.

"Because he hurt him. He frightened him. He's helping the Giant. Your Dad is helping the ones who have Lyssa ... the ones who are hurting her."

Zane shut his eyes, his hands moving to clutch his stomach as it twisted into a spasm of nervous pain. "Oh ... oh ..." he mumbled as he tumbled from the dream and woke curled into a tight ball in his bed.

He sat up and lit the candle at his bedside, the flame growing tall and bright in the still air, outlining in amber the tears rolling down his cheeks. He got out of bed, slipped his dressing gown and slippers on as the tears fell with fat splats onto the rug. Taking hold of the candle holder carefully, he padded out of his room and crossed the living room towards his mother's door. But as he was about to knock on it softly, he was interrupted by a loud pounding on the front door behind him.

"Miri! Miri!" Jay yelled through the wood and Zane heard the creaking of his mother's bed as she rose quickly.

Frantically wiping the moisture from his face, he went to the door and opened it as his mother emerged in her thick woollen nightgown. Jay rushed in, battering the flame of Zane's candle with the sudden movement of air, a small figure in his arms who was dressed in the same pale blue pyjamas as Zane had seen the other new Boy wearing the day he was found. Zane shuddered violently and took a step back. Something about the Boy frightened him, something unseen, subtle, inexplicable.

Jay laid the boy on the sofa as Miri hurriedly lit candles and lanterns around the room. Zane steadied himself as his vision began to shift in a way that was now becoming familiar. The boy's blue aura was very pale and it was clear that he was having trouble breathing. There were other areas, one on his left arm that was hanging down limply over the edge of the sofa, where the aura was practically gone. There was a sense of something odd, something chilling about this boy, just like the other.

"We just found him," Jay panted, holding his side in discomfort as Miri knelt by the sofa and began to check the child for injuries.

The boy was as pale as the first snowdrop in spring and his hair was so short that it was little more than a dark fuzz over his head. He was thin, with gaunt cheeks and dark circles around his closed eyes. He was older than the other new boy, appearing to be around nine years old. His breathing was laboured, with a disturbing rattling sound that emanated from his chest with each exhalation. There was a large bruise fading on his left upper arm.

Zane began to approach but then stopped and just stared, shaking slightly. Behind him, Titus appeared at the front door, wanting to see what the noise was about. He entered silently, unnoticed by those already in the room as he closed the door quietly behind him.

Miri took the boy's pulse and watched his breathing. "Jay, build up the fire. I need some boiling water. Zane, get me the large glass bowl from the kitchen and a tea towel."

Zane didn't move, and just as Miri was about to repeat her order more loudly Titus said, "I'll get it!" making her jump as he hurried through the room into the kitchen.

Titus reappeared at the doorway, bowl in hand, and watched Zane moving over to the sofa fearfully, lips pale, eyes wide and fixed on the child.

"There's something inside him," Zane muttered, coming to kneel next to his mother.

"What?" she asked, now checking that the boy's mouth was empty and lifting the pyjama top up to the boy's chin so that she could listen to his chest more closely.

"Something ... in his chest, his lungs ... something bad and wrong," Zane said, his voice trembling.

He could see the boy's veins, his heart beating rapidly. But it was the substance, black and unnatural, spreading out like thick spider legs from a lump at the bottom of his lungs, that was clearly impeding his breathing. That dark substance was terrifying–not simply the fact that it shouldn't be there, but somehow the very essence of it.

"What do you mean, Zane?" Miri asked, disturbed by her son's behaviour.

Zane didn't reply, but slowly reached out to lay his hands on the boy's chest. When he made contact, a ripple of coldness travelled up Zane's arms, making him take in a sharp breath as if he had plunged his hands into icy water.

Zane knew that he had to get the substance out of him; every instinct he had was telling him that it was killing the boy. Trusting those same instincts, he moved his hands down and pressed his fingers firmly on the boy's abdomen, just below his diaphragm and the point where the black substance seemed to radiate from.

Zane began to shake as Jay and Miri watched in tense silence. A droplet of sweat ran down his temple as he began to push his fingers upwards towards the boy's chin, staring at the substance that no-one else could see and willing it to be pushed up too. When his fingers came level with the lump, the cold spread up his hands again, but this time he was ready for it and focused on pushing it away from himself. All the while, the boy was struggling to breathe, his lips starting to take on a blue tinge.

The black lump started to move, as if repelled by Zane's fingertips, edging away from them like a fearful creature. The dark threads that were spread out through the spongy tissue shrank inwards, retreating to the originating mass. Slowly and steadily, Zane pushed it towards the top of the lungs until it formed a large glob at the bottom of the boy's windpipe. When it was all in one place, he swiftly pulled at the boy's shoulders until he was sitting up and darted around Miri to get behind the child. He wrapped his arms around him, made a fist under his ribcage, and pulled hard with a quick upwards thrust.

The black substance shot out of the boy's mouth in one fat globule, splatting onto the floor at Titus' feet. The child drew in a huge breath and gasped, coughing and spluttering as the air flooded back into his lungs.

No-one spoke, staring first at Zane and the boy, then turning to look at the black matter on the floor. Zane leant heavily against the arm of the sofa, trembling. Jay went to examine what had been expelled whilst Miri absent-mindedly rubbed the new boy's back as she stared at Zane, slack-jawed. The boy struggled to breathe normally, looking uneasily at the blob on the floorboard.

It resembled a lump of crude oil, thick and shiny, unlike anything they had seen before.

"What the hell is that?" Jay asked, but no-one had an answer. Zane peered over at it, keeping half an eye on the boy and his recovery.

"Don't touch it," Zane said. "Whatever it is, it's something nasty." He realised now that the chill the boy had caused before had been because of this, not the child himself.

"Ugh!" Jay yelled and jumped back as he saw the lump stretch a little and then contract, moving an inch or so like a fat caterpillar. Miri gasped and scrambled to her feet as Titus stared at it in disbelief, frozen to the spot.

It slid again, moving towards the corner of the sofa. Jay

grabbed the thick glass bowl from Titus' hand and slammed it down over it.

"Get it out of my house!" Miri shrieked and Jay frantically looked for something to slide under as the globule continued to inch slowly across the space under the glass. Titus ran into the kitchen and re-emerged with a thin chopping board that Jay took and swiftly slid under the bowl, trapping the black matter securely. He gingerly lifted it up and took it outside as Titus went and collected a lidded saucepan from the kitchen and followed him out.

Miri watched from the door as Titus held the saucepan open and Jay carefully slid the strange black matter into the pot. Titus banged the lid down and put it on the floor, holding the lid on tight as Jay found a large stone and put it on the top, both of them shuddering in disgust.

"That'll do for now," Jay said and they both hurried back into the house. "It's not going anywhere, Miri. I'll get rid of it. Don't worry."

She nodded, and looked at Zane who was slumped against the sofa, exhausted.

"I dunno what you did, Zane," Jay said. "But it was cool."

Zane just nodded, his eyes heavy with fatigue. The boy on the sofa was breathing more normally and looking around the room in confusion, his pyjama top still gathered under his armpits.

Miri, seeing how disoriented he was, smiled at him and said, "You'll be alright now. We'll look after you." She pulled his top back down again but stopped when she noticed something. She beckoned Jay over. "What's that?"

Jay peered down and frowned at a mark just visible near the base of the boy's spine. "Lean forward a second," he said to the boy, who did as he was asked without complaint.

A small dark rectangle, looking something like a tattoo was inked on to the boy's back. A series of numbers, small and difficult to read, ran along the bottom of it, with different width stripes running along above them.

"My God, it's a barcode," Miri gasped.

"A what?" Jay asked but she didn't reply. "Where'd you get this?" he asked the boy with concern.

"Get what?" he replied, drowsy and disoriented.

"Let him rest, we'll talk to him later," Miri said quietly, picking him up and carrying him to her bedroom, the child falling asleep in her arms as she spoke. By the time she came back into the living room, her son was fast asleep too. "Perhaps you should come back later, Jay," she suggested. "Just don't tell anyone what you saw, please."

He nodded. "I'll get rid of that stuff," he said and left the house. Titus lurked in the corner of the room, observing everything silently. Miri looked at him.

"It's alright, Titus. It's over now," she said reassuringly, draping her shawl over Zane.

"I won't tell anyone either," he promised, watching her shaking hands ease a cushion under Zane's head.

She nodded, looking down on her son's sleeping face. "I'm not even sure what I saw," she mumbled to herself as Titus slipped out of the house.

He drifted outside and watched Jay carrying the saucepan away at arm's length in the first light of the dawn. He listened to the birdsong, watched the grey palette of the garden beginning to take on the first hints of colour in the strengthening light. He glanced back towards where Miri watched over Zane, sighed, and then walked back to his house, alone.

That evening Jay returned to Miri's house with a troubled frown. He was welcomed into the living room and offered a bowl of stew that he accepted gratefully. Zane was now awake but still looking somewhat drained, and the new boy was sound asleep in Miri's room.

Jay perched on the edge of the sofa and wolfed the stew down, not saying a word until the bowl had been scraped and then licked clean. He put the bowl down and ran a hand through his hair.

"Sommat weird is goin' on," he said after a few moments. "The stuff that came out of the new boy had to be burnt for a couple of hours before it was gone. 'Ent never seen nothin' like it before." He fidgeted. "It tried to get out of the pan when it was getting hot ... almost like it was an animal. 'Ent natural." He shuddered.

"At least it's gone now." Miri tried to sound as comforting as she could.

"That's not all," Jay sighed. "I got all the lads together and checked them for that mark. Ten of 'em have got it. That's most of my Boys!"

Zane frowned. "Does the new Boy who's scared of me have one?"

Jay nodded. "Look ... I didn't want to ask them ... could you check me?"

Miri nodded and he stood, allowing her to check his back. "Nothing," she said in relief and he let out a long breath.

"Good. That freaks me out, my Boys being marked. I dunno what gang done it, but they don't remember anythin' about it, not even how they got 'ere."

"I should check them," Zane said quietly. "Make sure that they don't have that stuff in them." He thought for a moment, remembering that shiver that went through him when he first met the other Boy and then said, "I think the other new Boy might."

Jay nodded. "He's damaged, that one. Been through sommat really bad. He'll be alright one day, but it's hard work.

You know, I've always wondered where they all came from, but I never *worried* about it. If one turns up and he 'ent in another gang, we take 'em in and that's that. Now I'm startin' to wonder about it. Maybe they were in a gang before comin' to our patch."

"Do they always turn up in those funny clothes?" Zane asked.

Jay shook his head. "I think a couple might've done, ages ago, but they turn up in all kinds of things." He jabbed a thumb towards Miri's room. "This one alright to stay 'ere a night? Just so I know he'll be alright? I'll make it up t'ya."

Miri smiled reassuringly. "Of course."

"Tomorrow I'll come over and check the ones with the mark on them," Zane offered.

"Ta," Jay said and went to the door as Zane followed to wave him off. When Jay had left, Zane took a moment to look across to Erin and Luthor's house, but saw that it was still dark. Something about their being gone for over a day made him nervous, made him mindful of other people's lives being shaped in ways beyond his knowledge. Oh but how little he was aware of then! How little did he appreciate how the delicate thread of his life was already being woven tightly in the affairs of others.

Chapter 24
BIGGER THAN GANGS

Later the next day, Jay shut the door to the hotel room and went over to Titus and Zane, who were standing by the window looking out onto Russell Square.

"So ... whaddya find?" he asked, trying to seem nonchalant in an effort to hide his concern. It wasn't working. Zane noticed how tired he was and suspected that he'd hardly slept since his conversation with them about the markings the night before.

"Squeak has some of that black stuff in him," Zane began, his voice quiet and tired. "Only a tiny bit and he won't let me near him enough to get it out. I think some of the others used to ... not any more though."

Jay peered at him. "How'd ya know that?"

Titus stepped forward. "Jay, we have an idea about where they came from before they arrived here, where that mark on their backs comes from."

His diversionary tactic worked. Jay scratched his head. "Go on."

"The Unders," Titus stated calmly, making no attempt to soften what he was saying. "Squeak was definitely there and he has the mark."

"I dunno much about them," Jay admitted. "Why are the marks there? What are they for?"

Titus spread his hands and shrugged. "I don't know. When the Boys with the marks were asked about ... certain things, most of the others had similar memories about being locked in rooms and the corridor that Squeak told me about."

"All of them knew someone there called Eve," Zane added.

"And this Eve mentioned Lyssa to the newest Boy," Titus continued, keeping his face and voice as neutral and calm as he could, whilst tightly gripping the windowsill that he leant against. "Which confirms that she's down there now."

Jay leant against the wall, rubbing his face as if trying to wipe away something clinging to it. He dropped his hands to his sides. "I really don't know anything about this Unders gang—don't know their sign, their territory, nothin'."

"No-one knows much," Titus replied. "We know that the Giant comes from there, that they can make lightning, that they take people –"

"Women," Zane interjected, "Mum said they take women and they never come back."

Titus looked down at the floor briefly. "That too."

"How'd you know the Giant came from there?" Jay ran a hand through his hair, clearly agitated.

"The marked boys recognised the picture that Dev found," Zane replied, handing it back to Jay. Zane then looked to Titus, but he didn't add anything about his dream.

"Hell," Jay muttered. Then he frowned. "Hang on. If they were with the Unders, and locked in rooms like you say, how'd they end up out 'ere with us?"

Both Titus and Zane shrugged. "None of them can remember," Titus said. "They only remember waking up outside and you finding them."

"I don't like this," Jay muttered. "I gotta think this over."

Zane nodded sympathetically. "You know where to find us."

He and Titus reached the door and as Zane was opening it, Jay moved towards them with a jolt, as if he hadn't noticed they were leaving. "Er, look … thanks for this, for helpin' me out an' all. I won't forget it." Zane smiled and Titus gave a small nod.

"And Titus." Jay held him back with a brief touch on his arm that made Titus tense immediately. "I'll help you get Lyssa back. It 'ent right, what 'appened ..."

Titus examined the earnest expression on his face. He wanted to shout, "It's your fault this happened at all!" but he held it in. He forced that blame and suppressed rage into a tight ball that burned in his chest whilst he acknowledged Jay's offer with a curt nod. He left the room quickly, with Zane following silently.

"I wonder if Erin and Luthor will be back tomorrow," Zane mused out loud once they had left Jay's territory. "They've never been away for more than a day before ... do you think something is going on?"

There was a brief pause before Titus answered, his mind on other things. "Probably," he replied.

"Can we try to speak to her again tonight? She has to sleep sometime." Titus nodded. Zane looked at him. "It's good that Jay offered to help ... don't you think?"

Titus didn't respond. Zane sighed and left his friend to his thoughts. They parted with quiet goodbyes and went to their respective homes, Zane being greeted by his mother with an embrace and questions about the Bloomsbury Boys, Titus by silence and candles waiting to be lit.

"I wish Erin was here!" Titus said loudly, and Zane silently wished the same just as strongly.

And sure enough, Erin appeared at the centre of the dream room, looking asleep in the first moment, but then opening her eyes to look around herself in surprise.

"Oh!" she gasped, realising where she was.

"We've tried to get you here three times!" Zane said, smiling affectionately at her. "And last night too, are you –"

His voice trailed off when he noticed what she was wearing. Titus stared at her open-mouthed and she looked down at herself. She was dressed in red leather trousers and a linen shirt, the uniform of the Red Lady's Hunters. Even in the dream, her weapons were present, the bow and quiver strapped to her back, knives at her belt.

"What have you done?!" Titus exclaimed, immediately putting her on the defensive.

"What does it look like!" she retorted loudly, her fists balling.

Zane moved between them, holding his hands up. "Wait, wait." He looked at Titus who backed off. "Erin," he said softly, turning to face her. "We're just surprised, that's all." Her focus slowly shifted to Zane. "I've been worried, you've been gone for ages, and when Titus couldn't bring you here last night ..."

Just as she began to relax, Titus jumped back in. "Did they make you? Did she force you to join?"

Zane sighed in frustration as Erin pushed past him to face Titus. "Do you think I'm weak or something? That I would do something I didn't want to?"

"You *wanted* to join them?" Titus asked incredulously.

"So what if I did?" she shouted back.

"Stop it!" Zane yelled, putting himself between them again. "Don't be like this!" he exclaimed. "Don't fight. Please. Can't we ... can't we just talk about this?"

Zane was upset, not only because of the tension. More than that, it was seeing Titus be anything but calm. He hadn't realised how much he'd become accustomed to his friend's usual coolness until now, when it had gone.

Titus and Erin glowered at each other, but that gradually faded when both of them noticed the desperation on Zane's face.

"Please," Zane continued. "So much is going on. Stuff has happened whilst you were away, Erin, and we need to talk about it."

"But everything we talk about will go straight to the Red Lady now!" Titus moaned, gesturing towards Erin.

"Not if it's secret!" she replied, appearing to be hurt by the assumption.

"Really?" Titus raised an eyebrow. "Would you really lie to her about talking to us?"

The muscles in Erin's jaw tensed as she considered his words. She looked from Titus to Zane then back again, standing straighter and holding her chin up stubbornly. "Yes," she stated firmly. "Yes, I would, if I needed to."

Titus was surprised into silence.

Erin let out a long sigh. "You're my friends and that means a lot to me. I've never had this before," she said quietly. "It doesn't feel right to lose what we've found. I don't want to stop being close to you both, not like this."

Zane was heartened by her words. "I don't want that either. Surely you don't, Titus?"

Titus was contemplating his shoes. He shrugged. "No," he finally replied. "I just don't see how you can be loyal to us and to her at the same time."

Erin looked away, jaw set.

Zane chewed his lip, trying to see a way forward. "Anyway," he began, "most of the things we have to talk about are things the Red Lady will have to know ... if she is going to help us to find Lyssa like she said."

Titus nodded slowly. "I suppose."

"And even though it might be harder for us three to talk in the really real world, we still have this room here, don't we?" Zane continued.

Both Titus and Erin nodded and Zane sighed with relief, going over to flop into the captain's chair. Erin went over to the window and leant on the sill. Titus watched her carefully, sensing that she was holding something back.

"What is it, Erin?" he asked quietly.

Erin turned and stared out of the window into the void. He could see her trying so hard to keep it all in, gripping the sill tightly.

"I'm sorry I was angry. I promise we won't think you're a bad person, or strange either," Titus prodded gently. "You can tell us."

Erin lowered her head. "I've had a really bad couple of days. You were right Titus–they did make me join them. Sort of. They all got together in a big room and waited for me, and then she offered me a place in her gang when they were all watching."

"So you felt you couldn't say no," Zane said sadly.

Erin nodded. "I wasn't sure I wanted to join ... I sort of did, but I was worried about us three. But then I looked at my father and ..." Her voice trailed off.

Zane got up and went to her, taking her hand gently and squeezing it. "I think I would have joined too, if I'd been you." He let her hand go, wanting to embrace her, but sensitive to her dislike of it. "But it's not all bad," he said, trying to sound cheery. "The Hunters will teach you lots of things, and you'll always be safe, and you'll see the Red Lady lots too."

Erin looked into his eyes and nodded uncertainly. She forced a smile. "So what's been going on whilst I was away? I promise I won't tell anyone about it unless you want me to."

Between them, Titus and Zane told her about the events regarding the Bloomsbury Boys, the black substance, and the markings on their backs, all the while stressing that the Red Lady was not to know about them. They told her what they had pieced together about the Unders and Zane even told her that his father was involved somehow. She listened carefully, saying nothing until they'd finished.

"What do we do now?" she asked.

"We wait until we have a sighting of the Giant again," Titus replied. "Jay has people out looking for him. When we have that, we may be able to follow him back to the Unders' territory."

Erin nodded. "That's when you'll have to tell Dad if you want the Red Lady's help."

Titus agreed, albeit reluctantly. "As soon as we have a chance of finding Lyssa, we'll need everyone we can get to help us." He was distracted briefly and then looked back to Erin and Zane. "I think someone's knocking on my door. I have to wake up," he said. "We'll talk more later."

Lunchtime the next day, Titus waited at a corner of Miri's square, deep in thought. Zane was drifting over towards him, munching a raw carrot, as Jay approached from his square too. Titus looked in the direction of the Red Lady's territory and took a deep breath to steel himself as he saw Erin, Luthor, and David striding towards him. Titus had deliberately positioned himself there; it wasn't possible for Jay to see the Hunters on their way.

Zane and Jay arrived first, Zane radiating curiosity and Jay doing all he could to look tough and in control.

"Watchya." He nodded to both of the boys.

"Thanks for coming," Titus said, taking care not to glance towards where the Hunters would soon come into view.

"S'alright," Jay said, leaning against the low wall next to Titus. "I told you everythin' the Runner said this mornin' though."

It was then that Luthor rounded the corner, David and Erin behind him. Titus was surprised to see David with them; of all the Hunters to send, why would the Red Lady pick the one with whom Luthor had the greatest rivalry?

"What the hell is this?!" Jay exclaimed, moving away from the wall, hands flying to his knives.

Luthor stayed icy. "Calm down, boy, and run home. We are here to speak with Titus, not you."

Before Jay could respond Titus stepped forward. "Actually, I invited all of you here to speak together."

David made a loud false cough and stood next to Luthor, looking amused more than anything else. Erin was obviously uncomfortable, electing to stand to the left of her father so she could be next to Zane.

Jay turned on Titus, furious. "You never said any of that bitch's mooks would be here!"

Luthor moved towards Jay, hand on the hilt of his sword. "Call her that again, and I will kill you," he growled.

"Oh yeah?" Jay spat back, drawing the knives, prompting Luthor to reveal half of the blade of his sword before Zane jumped in.

"Hey!" he yelled. "This is my mum's square! No fighting here!"

That made them pause, but it didn't stop them staring at each other balefully. Titus took the opportunity to speak.

"I want to talk to you about saving my sister. This has nothing to do with gangs. You've both said you'll help and that's why I asked you to come. We've found out where the Giant tends to move and we need to plan what to do next."

"The Red Lady said nothing about involving ... them," Luthor muttered.

"This 'ent none of her business," Jay sneered. "We don't need any of you 'ere, we can 'andle this ourselves."

"I don't think we can," Titus said loudly.

This angered Jay further, but he wouldn't take his eyes off Luthor, who chuckled menacingly.

"Titus is smart," Luthor said, smirking at Jay. "How could runts with toy daggers help here? Go home and play, and leave this to people who know what they are doing."

Jay pulled himself up but still fell short of Luthor's height. "I respect Miri's territory," he hissed through gritted teeth. "Unlike you, so I won't gut ya here and now."

David laughed. "You couldn't gut a dead fish."

Titus ran his hands through his hair, increasingly frustrated by the acrimonious distraction from his agenda. "Look, *both* of you are needed because of where the Giant was sighted," he said rapidly, before any more insults could be exchanged.

"No," Jay replied, "Me and my Boys are needed cos the Giant walks the edge of my patch–don't mean *they* need to be 'ere."

Titus struggled to keep his temper in check. "Jay, they have bows. They can kill at a distance so we wouldn't have to go near–can't you see that?!"

"I 'ent doing anythin' with these pieces of filth," Jay growled. "I 'ent takin' on a Giant with people just as ready to put an arrow in my back. That b–" He smirked. "Cow marked one of mine," Jay continued as Luthor drew his sword. He began to back away, lowering his blades but not his guard. "Miri don't want any blood spilt 'ere, remember? So I'm goin'. When you've got rid of them, come talk to me, Titus–else forget it."

"This is bigger than gangs!" Titus blurted, incensed by their blinkered vision. "Can't you see that?"

Jay merely shook his head in disagreement until a safe distance from Luthor and then strode off back to his square.

Luthor watched Jay leave, marking his movements like an eagle watching a mouse. Some moments after he'd gone out of sight, he dropped his sword into its sheath and looked at Titus. "I do not appreciate being tricked," he said quietly. "If it were up to me, this would end here and now."

"It isn't up to you," Titus replied coolly, not at all intimidated by the huge man. "The Red Lady said she'd help, so you'd make her a liar if you don't."

Luthor stiffened. Erin put a hand on her father's arm. "Titus wouldn't have asked Jay unless he had to," she said.

"We can't do anything about Lyssa unless we have access to Jay's territory," Titus explained. "Otherwise we'd have to risk going into Gardner territory or through the no man's land in the north and that's too dangerous. We have to work together."

"If the Red Lady wants it to happen, I will work with the runt," Luthor capitulated.

Titus nodded, considering this carefully. "I'll take it to her then."

Chapter 25
LOYALTIES TESTED

Late that evening, the three children were huddled conspira-torially behind the statue of the old Queen at the northern end of the garden. Erin was constantly alert for any sound of her father. "I don't have long," she said.

Titus nodded. "She took some persuading, but the Red Lady said to me that if we need to work with the Bloomsbury Boys, she'll allow it, and they won't be harmed."

"Jay won't budge," Zane said, giving Titus an apologetic look. "I tried every argument I could think of, and all the ones you told me too, Titus. He just doesn't trust the Red Lady."

Erin frowned. "That's stupid. If she says she won't hurt someone, she means it—she can't break her word. If a gang leader did that, no-one would ever respect them." She scratched her head, adjusting the braid at the nape of her neck and rubbing the skin there as if it were irritated. "She must really want to help you. I asked the other Hunters if they'd ever worked with another gang, and they haven't. Not even David can remember that, and he's been there for years and years."

"Why did the Red Lady send David with you today?" Zane asked.

Erin shrugged. "She told him to come with us when she knew it was a meeting about finding Lyssa. I suppose he's one of the best archers we have. Only Dad is better than him."

"But Luthor doesn't like him, does he?" Titus asked.

Erin shook her head. "They hate each other."

Titus scowled. "We don't need any more problems."

"Don't worry about them," she replied. "They can still work together. They go on the big hunts and help each other when they have to. It's only the first hunt of the season that really sets them off."

"We have to find a way to convince Jay to work with them," Titus said. "Every day that this stupid gang rubbish goes on is another day that Lyssa is trapped."

Erin didn't seem to like that, but before she could reply they all heard Luthor calling her name from the other side of the square. "I have to go," she whispered. "I'll see you tomorrow."

The next morning, the children were skinning rabbits that had been snared during the night as Luthor supervised and Miri worked in the garden nearby. Erin finished the task first and laughed at Zane's ineptitude, but it didn't dent the grin on his face.

"It's only a rabbit, Zane," Erin poked him in the ribs. "You look like you caught your first deer."

"I can't wait to take my first quarter of a catch to the Red Lady," he chirped.

"A quarter of that tiny thing?" Luthor bellowed with laughter. "They would shoot you at the gates before letting you take that scrap to the Red Lady."

Zane's shoulders sagged as he looked at the rabbit, noticing how thin it was for the first time. His despondency only made Luthor laugh more.

Miri appeared at Zane's shoulder, peered over to look at the haul. "Rabbit stew tonight, Zane," she said cheerily, kissing him on the cheek. "Well done."

Zane recovered some of his dignity and returned to the task, speculating about the stew, when a loud clanging noise interrupted him.

It was the Boys' alarm, the loudest and most urgent kind, indicating a Gardner attack. Just like every other time, Miri scooped her tools into her skirt and began to hurry towards the house, only pausing to grab Zane's wet hand as she passed.

Zane allowed himself to be pulled along until they reached the front door, then he stopped. Miri looked at him with confusion when he wouldn't let her pull him into the house.

"Zane! Quickly, come on!" she said urgently, dropping the tools onto the floor and beckoning to Titus and Erin to follow her inside.

Zane shook his head as the alarm grew louder and more insistent. "No, Mum ... it's not right, I made an oath."

White-lipped, she pulled him again with her shaking hand. "Come inside now, Zane, it's not safe."

He shook his head more firmly and broke away from her. "I'm sorry, Mum, I need to be there ... I may be able to save some of the Boys and I might get there too late if I hide now."

"No, Zane, don't!" she cried desperately as he ran off, clutching at her stomach as if it were being torn from her.

Titus watched him go. He thought a moment, looked at Miri, then back at Zane again. "Wait, I'll come with you!" he called and sprinted after him.

Miri began to cry with worry as Luthor walked away to his house on the opposite side of the square, not even taking a moment to reassure the distraught woman.

"Erin, come on," he shouted, turning when he realised that she hadn't followed him. Erin stood her ground, the rhythmic clamour of the alarm growing all the more urgent. Luthor jabbed a finger down at the path by his side. "Come. Here. Now." His voice was quiet and controlled, his eyes glinting like polished blades.

Erin looked at him, then up the road, catching a last glimpse of Titus and Zane as they left the square.

"It is not your fight, Erin," he growled. "You're wearing the Red—you must not interfere. You have no choice."

Her jaw tightened. "Yes I do," she said through gritted teeth and turned to sprint after her friends, drawing the dagger from her hip as she did so.

Erin soon caught up with Titus and Zane, and they entered Jay's square without interference; no Boy was stationed on that edge of the territory. They stopped as they looked down at the barricade across Montague Street, all three momentarily paralysed by the sight of the vicious fighting between the Boys and the Gardners.

Erin recovered her wits the fastest, her keen eyes scanning the men clambering over the top of the barricade as missiles of glass, bricks, and chunks of scrap metal rained down on them from Boys stationed in the upper storeys of the buildings on either side.

Zane's attention was purely focused on the injured, both Bloomsbury Boy and Gardner. His gaze briefly fixed on Len, who had been cut deeply across the chest by the swing of a Gardner's knife. Then it flicked to the attacker in the instant after he'd been hit on the head by a brick. His vision sharpened to focus in on the splitting skin and the hot blood rushing out from the wound as the man tumbled backwards, dropping the knife coated in Len's blood. In the next moment, he saw Dev cry out as he was knocked off by his opponent, a huge Gardner who had managed to get to the top of the pile of junk. Zane watched his friend land heavily and knew immediately that his head had struck the ground hard enough to knock him out, but not kill him.

Three Gardners were still on their feet and two dead bodies were slumped over the top of the barricade, but Zane had a feeling that more were dying slowly and painfully on the other side. Five Boys lay dead but he couldn't see who they were.

A cluster of the older Boys were at the foot of the blockade, desperately hurling missiles at the large man climbing over the top. It was the one who had struck Dev, now clambering down towards them.

Jay was fighting the other two men on the barricade alone, both blades out and holding his own impressively. He fought like one who had been born to do so, moving fluidly and gracefully, each parry quickly converted into a vicious attack. He yelled and swore at his opponents as he battled them, cursing their names, their leader, their mother, a torrent of abuse that was as fast as his knives.

One of the Gardners lost his footing, less sure on his feet than Jay, who rapidly exploited it to plunge a knife deep in the man's chest. As he cried out, a cheer erupted from the younger Boys higher up at the sides, and their efforts increased with renewed enthusiasm.

Zane rushed forward towards Len, who had fallen and was trying desperately to crawl away, one hand clasped over his chest, blood seeping between his fingers.

Erin hurried after Zane protectively while Titus hung back. Len had managed to put a few metres between himself and the worst of the fighting but then collapsed as Zane dropped to his knees next to him, rolling the Boy onto his back and tearing the Boy's shirt open to expose the wound. Erin planted herself between the rest of the fighting and Zane as he placed both hands either side of the deep gash and stared at it, willing it to close.

Jay was the only one left on the barricade that could fight up close, Mark and Grame long gone. Getting tired, Jay was finding it difficult to despatch his opponent and was helpless as the third Gardner, the one who'd hit Dev, managed to jump down into the square, firmly in Jay's territory.

The man, dressed smartly in his incongruous black suit, gave a yell of triumph. The Boys nearby backed away, frightened by his bulk. Smudge threw a brick that hit the man's chest but it only seemed to inflame him more. He grabbed the nearest Boy and lifted him into the air by his neck. As the Boy squealed in terror, kicking his thin legs desperately, the Gardner smashed him into the wall, and after an awful crack, the child's head lolled to the side, bloodied and lifeless.

The remaining Boys scattered and the Gardner sneered at their fear, searching for his next victim only to look straight into Erin's eyes. There was a flash of recognition.

"Erin!" he yelled over the din, looking down at the girl who held her knife tightly in front of her. "I thought I could smell girl." The foul man licked his lips, narrowing his dark, bulbous eyes that bulged over heavy bags beneath them.

"Stay away from me, Doug!" she yelled back.

He drew his knife, grinning at her. "Girly wants to play hard to catch," he leered. "I want some of what Harry had. It'll make Jonathan jealous!"

Erin readied herself. She leapt back when he swung the knife towards her, but she knew that he was toying with her, as she'd seen him fight before. Two more Gardners risked a look over the top of the barricade, having heard Doug shout her name, but were repelled by the Boys stationed at the windows on either side of the barricade, determined not to let another Gardner into the square.

Doug lunged for her again, and she darted to the side, trying to catch his arm with her knife as she did so but failing. He laughed and then saw Zane a few paces away, kneeling over the bleeding Boy.

Erin followed his eyes and hurried to put herself back between her friend and the attacker.

Doug drew his lips back, revealing his yellow teeth in the closest approximation to a smile that he could manage. "Does Girly have a friend?" he taunted, moving round and forcing her to move too in an effort to keep Zane behind her. "Would Girly cry if he died first?"

Erin's hand twitched as she struggled not to be baited by him. Helpless to act, Titus could only watch, silently willing her to be strong.

Doug was about to move towards Zane when he stopped and scratched the top of his head in irritation. He stepped closer to Erin and Zane, adjusting his grip on the knife in such a way that suggested he was no longer playing.

In the background, there was another cheer from the Boys as Jay's opponent fell. Doug lunged at Erin, who curved her body to the side, but not far enough. The blade sliced into her shirt and then a red stain began to spread through the linen. She drew in a sharp breath but stayed on guard, helped by the adrenaline surging through her. Zane seemed oblivious to the threat, entirely focused on saving the Boy in his care.

Doug chuckled and then licked her blood from the blade with his long, fat tongue, staring at her as he did so. He was about to lunge again when he scratched his head once more, this time to such an extent that Erin seized the opportunity to make a swipe at him that cut a button off his jacket cuff and nicked his hand.

"Bad girl!" he yelled and tried hard to concentrate more on her, but was still clearly distracted.

Neither of them had noticed Titus moving around the Gardner in a wide arc to position himself behind him. He was staring at Doug's head whilst wriggling his right index finger in front of him as if he were tickling a kitten. Every time he did it, Doug scratched at his head, becoming more furious at the itch.

"With the Red Bitch now?" he jeered. "How'd you make them take you in?"

"Shut up, Doug," Erin spat hatefully.

"Forget about your mother did they? Do your new friends know about her? She loves it with us now you're gone, she loves it."

Tears welled in Erin's eyes as she struggled to contain her rage. "Shut up!" she yelled, only encouraging him now he could see where the raw nerve was.

"Harry says she's lots of fun to spend time with," he jeered. "He likes it when they're quiet."

An animalistic roar leapt from Erin's throat and she dived for the Gardner. It would have been suicide, but at that moment Doug's attention snapped to his left even though nothing was there. Titus stood a few metres behind him, all of his attention focused on the man's head, making a flicking motion with his fingers as beads of sweat crept down his forehead.

Erin's blade plunged into Doug's lower chest and he bellowed, swiping her away from him as if she were made of rags. She landed several feet away with a loud thud and skidded back into a lamppost, the linen of her shirt being torn by the asphalt raking against her. But she was still so enraged that she barely noticed, her eyes rapidly fixing back on the Gardner as she scrabbled to her feet and lurched back towards him, her knife and hand glazed with his blood.

Doug had sagged onto his knees, an awful ashen pallor stealing the colour from his face. He spluttered and specks of blood appeared on his lips.

Erin was oblivious to the attention this was now being given by the rest of the Bloomsbury Boys, all other opponents having been repelled or despatched by Jay. He now stood halfway down the barricade, watching the scene unfold with disbelief, as did Zane, who had healed Len as best he could.

"Bitch," Doug gasped, readying himself for Erin's next assault as she sprinted towards him, screaming, now totally out of control.

"I'll kill you!" she screeched, "All of you!"

Seeing the wild hatred in her eyes prompted Doug to try to get to his feet, but he couldn't muster the strength as his injury stole breath from him. Instead, he raised his knife to aim at her as she hurtled thoughtlessly towards him, her own dagger held high.

Titus gasped, his face contorting with an incredible amount of effort as he made a motion akin to moving something aside in front of him. Doug's knife hand moved correspondingly, as if he were adjusting his aim at the last moment before release.

The blade flipped over and over in the air, slamming into Erin's shoulder, wide of her heart. Titus crumpled to the floor, his legs buckling beneath him, looking utterly exhausted.

Erin cried out, her steps slowed to a stop as her own knife clattered to the floor. But she was so driven by her fury that she didn't collapse—she simply swayed slightly on her feet, the hilt of Doug's blade held sickeningly still in her flesh.

Doug's eyes widened as she held his gaze, other Boys now moving closer but keeping a distance between themselves and the Gardner.

"Kill him!" Jay yelled from the barricade, thrilled by what he saw, and in moments all of the other Boys joined him with their steady chant. "Kill him, kill him!"

"NO!" Zane yelled, clambering to his feet. He could see the Gardner's punctured lung, how it was collapsing. "Erin! Stop, he can't hurt you now, look, he can't hurt you! Don't do this!"

Erin seemed oblivious to the chanting, the pleading, to the pain from her wounds. She simply stared at Doug, jaw clenched tight as she took one step, then another, then another, slowly moving towards the stricken man.

"Erin!" Zane yelled again, watching with horror as her shaking hand reached up and pulled Doug's knife from her own shoulder. "Don't! Don't!"

Doug spluttered again, falling forward onto one hand, large drops of blood oozing down from his mouth onto the pavement. He shook violently as Erin approached him with his own knife held in front of her, his head dropped as he lost even the strength to hold it up.

"Die," she muttered grimly and plunged the knife into his back as she herself struggled to stay upright. Doug collapsed at her feet and all around her the Boys went wild, cheering and whooping with delight, Jay leaping down over the lower bits of wreckage, waving his knives above his head triumphantly.

Zane turned away in disgust as the Boys closed in around Erin to pat her on the back and congratulate her. Titus looked on, unnoticed, captivated by the steady creep of the Gardner's blood seeping into a nearby drain.

Chapter 26
CONSEQUENCES

Early the next day, Titus sat silently in his living room, waiting for Erin to wake up. He replayed the fight in his mind, over and over, dissecting it carefully. He, like Erin, had been driven by instinct. He had distracted Doug, affected his aim at a distance, without even pausing to wonder how. It had just happened intuitively. He was certain no-one else could do that, otherwise they would talk about it and he'd have seen evidence of it. In all the books he had read, no-one had mentioned this ability. The same for Zane; Titus was convinced that his friend's healing skills were unprecedented. What was it about Zane and him that made them different, able to do these strange things?

He watched Erin stirring in her sleep. She was involved in this too; he was able to bring her into the dream room and no-one else. Not that he had tried with many other people, but the connection between the three of them was undeniable. He recalled the welt the three of them had the day they met her. He and Zane had dreamt her experience of training with Luthor, shared the same injury. Did this mean that Erin could do extraordinary things too?

She woke and was immediately alert, briefly confused before she recognised where she was.

"How are you feeling?" he asked.

"Just tired," she said, pulling herself up to sit upright and look down at her shoulder. She still wore the slashed and bloody linen shirt. "Zane's been here?"

Titus nodded. "He said you'd be tired from the blood loss. He healed the wounds but it made him pass out. He's sleeping it off now. There are Boys at Miri's house so I brought you here."

Erin sighed. "I can't believe I'm getting used to him being able to fix people like that. How is he? He … saw what I did, didn't he?"

"Yes. He didn't say anything."

She frowned at him. "You look tired."

Titus rubbed his eyes and nodded. "I'm okay. You know you slept through? It all happened yesterday."

Erin quickly moved to get up but Titus stopped her. "Your father isn't in the square."

Erin bit her lip, sinking back down into the sofa. "Does he know what happened?"

Titus shrugged. "I didn't tell him … I doubt anyone else would have. I know he's angry though."

She sighed, resigned. "Yeah, well, I knew he would be."

Titus leant forward. "Jay's agreed to help us."

Erin's eyebrows shot up.

"Because of what you did," Titus continued. "He said that if you were prepared to do that for him, he was prepared to work with the Hunters."

"But I didn't do it for him."

"He doesn't know that." Titus smirked. "He doesn't know you used to live with the Gardners. He was still fighting when Doug mentioned your mother."

Erin scowled. "I don't want him to think that I did it for him."

"It doesn't matter what he thinks," Titus replied matter-of-factly. "What matters is that he'll help us to get Lyssa."

Erin picked at the dried blood on her shirt, brooding. Titus watched her silently. "I just wanted to make sure you and Zane were okay," she finally said. "I didn't know that Doug was there or that I'd … end up doing that." She looked up at him, studied his face for a moment. "What do you think about what I did?"

"About you killing the Gardner?" He watched her nod, his face remaining unemotional. "You hated him. He was trying to kill you. It was self-defence." He was lying. He knew that Doug had been incapacitated and that she could have left him. "That's all any of the Red Lady's gang needs to know," he added. "You defended yourself."

She nodded slowly, taking in the veiled advice. "You don't think I'm a bad person?" she asked in a small voice. "I saw the way Zane looked at me. He thinks I am."

Titus gave this some thought and then shook his head. "I don't think you are. If Doug had been from the Unders and was talking like that about Lyssa, I would've done the same. Don't worry about Zane. He doesn't know what it's like to have bad things happen to anyone he loves ... he's never felt what we have."

She reached across and took his hand, unable to look into his eyes as she squeezed it tight briefly and then let it go.

"Besides," Titus added, "Lyssa told me once that there's no such thing as good people or bad people, only people trying to survive."

By the next day, Titus had arranged another attempt in the corner of Miri's square to have the two gangs and his friends discuss what to do about the Giant. Erin was nervous, not having had a chance to speak to Luthor beforehand, but Titus stayed close to her as he and David approached.

Luthor barely acknowledged her as they arrived, yet David gave her a nod and a warm smile that seemed to reassure her.

Jay soon arrived, walking as tall as he could and making a special effort to look straight into Luthor's eyes as he did so. The Hunter stared back until Jay gave a nod to David and a wink to Erin, which did not please her father at all. From the way he reacted, Titus suspected that he didn't know just how involved Erin had been in the fight.

Luckily, that was the moment that Zane arrived with Callum beside him. It surprised Titus to see the man, but it didn't upset him. With his detailed knowledge of the area, Callum was a good person to have on board.

Erin smiled at Zane uneasily, searching his face for a hint of forgiveness. Zane smiled back, but without his usual ease.

"Thanks for coming, everyone," Titus began, before any animosity between Jay and the Hunters had a chance to be expressed. "I need to tell you all what we've discovered about the Unders, and then I want to make a plan to rescue my sister from them. Jay, do you have the picture?"

Jay nodded, fished the newspaper scrap from his jacket pocket, and handed it over.

"This was found a while ago by one of the Bloomsbury Boys who first saw the Giant with Zane," Titus said as he carefully unfolded the yellowed paper. "He was seen in the hospital. We know that he comes from the Unders."

He held it out into the centre of the circle, allowing the adults to peer over at it.

"That's not a Giant!" Callum commented, sounding slightly amused. "That's just a person in a HAZMAT suit."

Jay and the three children gawped at Callum.

"You know the Giant?!" Zane asked incredulously.

"You don't understand," David spoke up. "This Giant of yours could be anyone. They look like that because they're wearing special clothes that are designed to protect them from the environment, from the air. What's the date on the page?"

Luthor peered at the corner. "About twenty years ago."

All three men said in unison, "When It happened." They nodded to each other.

"When what *exactly* happened?" Erin asked, confused. "No-one ever says what 'It' is."

"That's because we don't know," Callum explained gently.

"Lots of people died, all at the same time, but not everyone. Some people just seemed to be alright ... some people, like the person in this picture, had ways to protect themselves and survived that way."

David scratched his ear. "What I don't understand," he began, "is how someone could still be using one of those suits this long after. I mean, how are they replenishing the oxygen in the tank?"

"They must have electricity," Luthor muttered. He looked at Titus. "The Red Lady told me that when your sister was taken by the Unders, there was lightning used as a weapon."

Titus and Jay nodded. "But it weren't like normal lightning," Jay added. "It was blue, and it didn't come from the sky, but from people I couldn't see very well."

"This picture is in black and white, but I know that HAZMAT suits were yellow. If they'd been wearing a bright yellow suit that night Lyssa was taken, you'd surely have been able to see them," Callum said and Jay nodded.

"I reckon. But they weren't wearing yellow. I think they must've been wearing black, or just hidin' really well."

Luthor's brow folded above his eyes. "Then there may be others involved, either helping the HAZMAT wearer or being exploited by them. You're sure this person is in the Unders," he pointed at the picture whilst looking at Titus, "and that your sister is there?"

"Positive," Titus replied firmly.

"This Giant of yours won't be any problem," David stated confidently. "All we have to do is pierce the suit they're wearing and they'll either run away or die pretty quick, assuming that they can't survive out here without it. We won't even have to get close." He patted his bow.

"But what about if they have lightning?" Jay raised, "Or if they have friends that do?"

"And if we just kill them, we won't be able to find Lyssa," Titus added, eliciting a number of murmurs of agreement from the assembled.

"We need more information," Luthor replied. "What do you know about their movements?"

This time Titus searched a pocket and pulled out another piece of paper. "From what Jay has found out, I've marked on this map where the Giant has been seen several times over the last few weeks."

He gave the newspaper scrap back to Jay and held the map out in the centre of the group instead. It was from an old A to Z of the Bloomsbury area, with several crosses pencilled onto it, clustered around the far side of Jay's territory with a couple on the route to the hospital in Miri's square.

"I got Boys posted to look out for him, now we know where he goes," Jay said. "An' I been told that he only walks about at night, dunno why though."

Luthor peered at Jay. "Any idea why someone from the Unders likes to be so close to your territory?"

Jay frowned, leaning in towards Luthor. "You'd better not be thinkin' that we got somethin' goin' on with them," he said, his voice lowering. "Else I might take real offence at that."

"What matters here," Titus said quickly, hoping to deflect the flare up, "is that we can better predict where the Giant will be."

Callum rubbed at his chin thoughtfully. "Let's say that we watch and we see where this person walks. What do we do then?"

"We could follow them to where Lyssa is," Zane suggested.

Callum shook his head. "There's a reason for my friends calling them the Unders, it seems. From what Jay and Titus have told me, Lyssa is being kept underground. It wouldn't be like sneaking into a normal building. And even if we found her, we'd have to get her, and us, out again." He shook his head. "Not easy."

"Who are these friends of yours?" Luthor asked suspiciously.

Callum met his gaze. "Very private people," he replied. "And not in a position to help with this."

"Callum's right," Titus said quietly. "We need to get Lyssa to us, rather than going to where she is."

"That's easy," David said casually. "Capture your Giant, and exchange him for Lyssa. We just have to work out the details."

Zane frowned and exchanged a concerned look with Callum, but both remained silent.

Titus nodded slowly as he considered the idea. "Yes ... that could work," he muttered to himself.

"So I guess we just wait until the Giant decides to go out walkin' again," Jay said. "When he's sighted, I'll get one of my Boys over 'ere straight away."

Luthor turned to David. "Stay here in the square with us until we have a sighting, then we can go and watch what this person does."

Zane's back straightened. "You should ask my mum first," he said firmly, making Callum smile. "It's only polite."

Luthor agreed after the briefest pause and strode off towards Miri's house, gesturing to David to go with him.

"I guess that's that then," Jay muttered. He looked at Erin. "Er, can I speak with you for a minute?"

Surprised, she agreed and moved a few paces away from the others, Jay doing the same to give them some privacy.

He reached into his pocket. "I 'ad to fight the Boys off. They all wanted this, but I thought it should be yours. You earnt it." He pulled out a black tie. "Was off that biggun you killed for us." Erin stared at it, crumpled in his outstretched hand. "Take it then, it's yours an' all. 'Ent that many of us that get to say that." He patted his belt, made of several black ties plaited together and smiled wickedly at her.

She couldn't help but smile back, such was the glint in his eye. She took the strip of fabric and held it tight. "Thanks, Jay," she said quietly. "Just don't tell my father."

Jay smirked. "No problem, wouldn't wanna say more than I need to him anyway. Laters."

She watched him swagger off back to his territory and looked down at the tie briefly before stuffing it deep into a pocket and wiping her hands on her trousers.

That evening, Titus and Callum were seated in Miri's front room, enjoying bowls of fresh rabbit stew along with her and Zane. All were quiet, each contained within their own private contemplation of their discussion that afternoon about the loose plan regarding Lyssa. When the loud knock on the door broke the near silence, Miri jumped and went to answer it.

"Miri, is Titus with you?" It was Jay, panting and holding his side where the old burn was.

Titus was there in moments. "Is it the Giant?"

Jay nodded. "Tell them 'unters. I'll meet ya at the edge of my patch this side."

Titus bolted out of the room after grabbing a rucksack he'd brought with him, Zane running out behind him as Jay took off.

"Zane!" Miri called. "Come back inside!"

Callum put a hand on her shoulder. "I'll make sure they're alright," he said quietly and calmly.

"Don't let him go with them!" she begged as he moved past her into the doorway.

He simply smiled sadly and kissed her on the cheek. "I'll keep him safe, whatever he chooses to do. Lock the door."

Zane and Titus first went to Luthor's house. Within moments of the news he, David, and Erin were strapping on an extra layer of armour, plated with dull metal scales that lay flat and flexible over the leather. The three of them spilled out of the house, grabbing their weapons and quivers as they left. Titus and Zane fell into step beside them.

"What are you doing?" Luthor asked, not letting the distraction slow him down.

"Coming with you!" Titus replied as if it were a ridiculous question.

"No," Luthor said firmly. "You and Zane go home, leave this to us. It may be dangerous."

Titus ignored him and Zane stayed by his side as they all ran. But when the Bloomsbury Boys' territory came into view with Jay pacing at its edge, Luthor stopped and pulled Titus back.

"Go home," he insisted, his voice growing louder. "Both of you. I don't want to have to think about you and him when there are others to watch."

"But you might need me," Zane said and David laughed.

"He's right!" Erin yelled, making both Luthor and David look at her in surprise.

Titus fought to keep the flash of fear her words caused hidden from his face. His thoughts rapidly played through an imagined conversation where Erin would reveal that Zane could heal, how that information could reach the Red Lady if Luthor believed his daughter. Then a variety of imagined scenarios played out, ranging from Zane being taken into the Red Lady's gang through to the Gardners targeting him for death or forced service. All this happened in but moments, forcing him to re-evaluate his position. Before Erin could take a breath to explain herself, Titus had already run through several possibilities before settling on the only one that could achieve all of his goals.

"No, Luthor's right," he said quickly, eliciting incredulous looks from Zane and Erin. "You're all much better trained – we'll wait here."

"Good," Luthor muttered and then took off again towards Jay, glancing back to make sure that Erin was following him and David.

"I'll ... I'll tell you everything I see," Erin called as she left them, sprinting to catch up with her father.

Zane rounded on Titus. "Why did you say that!" he exclaimed. "I need to go with them – someone might get hurt!"

"Shush," Titus whispered, pulling him into the shadows at the edge of the street as he watched the Hunters reach Jay and exchange a few words. "We are going ... they just don't need to know that. Come on, we can't lose sight of them."

He pulled Zane down a street that connected to one parallel to the street that Jay was beginning to lead the others down.

Callum followed silently, keeping in the shadows. He was horrified by Titus' actions, certain that his desperation to find Lyssa was clouding his normally logical mind. "Stupid boys," he muttered beneath his breath.

A half moon high in the sky gave just enough light to avoid obstacles, but not to see much detail very far ahead, Zane's teeth chattering all the while despite the relative warmth of the late summer night.

"Titus," he whispered. "Has Erin talked to you about the Gardner she killed?"

"Not now, Zane," Titus whispered back, concentrating on tracking the Hunters and Jay. He needed to focus; the sense of others nearby was easy to lose. Ever since the day the Gardner came to Miri's square he'd been practising how to do this, but it was much harder when those he tried to follow weren't a threat.

When he concentrated, he had a sense of their movement, just as one might have an awareness of another person in the same room, only this was over a street away. Also present was the sense of Zane next to him, and Callum close behind them, but he was paying much more attention to tracking the others. As they weaved through the streets, he realised that his feel for Zane and Erin was much stronger, to the extent that occasionally he would have an intuitive grasp of her emotional state as it fluctuated between excitement, fear, and also pride. He had to force himself not to be distracted by that, or by the palpable fear that radiated from Zane.

At the end of that street Titus stopped and pressed himself flat against the wall of the high building that they had reached, pulling Zane to do the same beside him.

"We're close now," he whispered to Zane, who nodded back, taking a deep breath to try to control his nerves. "I think the others are climbing up higher," Titus continued, Zane too nervous to question how his friend might know that.

A minute passed, Zane shaking and Titus tense and alert, straining with all of his senses to determine what was happening. They both jumped when a soft metal clang ricocheted down the street that ran perpendicular to their position.

"It's the Giant," he whispered to Zane after a moment's concentration, "and they're coming towards us down the road around this corner."

"I hope the others can see him," Zane whispered back.

"They can–they're up high," Titus replied, tuning into Erin's anticipation.

They remained silent for few moments, listening to the muffled sounds of the Giant's metal shoes in the dust that occasionally made contact with something firmer. The footsteps grew steadily louder.

"What are we going to do?" Zane whispered urgently,

fighting the urge to run home immediately.

"Wait until they get a bit closer, then ..." Titus reached into his rucksack and pulled out a pocket knife, holding it up to Zane.

Zane frantically shook his head. "No!" he hissed. "We can't get close to them!"

"They won't be expecting it," Titus whispered back. "And they'll be too scared to risk me puncturing their clothes. No-one else is with them. It'll be fine."

"Let Luthor or Jay do it," Zane pleaded, "This is stupid."

Titus ignored him, flicking out the blade from his knife and readying himself as they could both hear the movement getting closer and now the mechanical wheeze of his breath.

Zane saw the knife and panicked, convinced that Titus hadn't thought this through at all, he was so set on getting Lyssa back. He didn't know whether to try to drag Titus away or just run or even alert the Giant so that Titus wouldn't have the opportunity to endanger them. But he was so paralysed by indecision that before he could decide, the Giant rounded the corner.

Chapter 27
HARD BARGAINING

"Stop!" Titus yelled, stepping in front of the huge figure as he jabbed the knife out in front of him, having it stop only inches away from the yellow outer shell of the suit.

The Giant stopped so suddenly that he nearly fell forward, and both boys heard a loud gasp from behind the smooth dark faceplate.

"Don't move or do anything unless I tell you, or I'll pierce your suit," Titus said loudly, keeping his voice steady despite his fear.

The Giant remained still, the only change being that the wheezing breaths increased in speed. Zane was relieved that he didn't seem to have any kind of weapon; he was only holding a small plastic case that looked large enough to carry some papers, or something else flat, but nothing more. He heard Jay swear from somewhere high above them and looked up to see his and David's faces peering over the top lip of the building that he and Titus were standing against.

Zane swallowed hard and looked to Titus for his next move, when the darkness was torn apart by an arc of blue lightning. It slammed into the wall of a building that was only metres from where he stood.

Zane yelled out in terror and Titus started, completely caught by surprise. He'd been so confident that no-one else had been with the Giant, but now he realised that he had been too focused on that one individual to the exclusion of anyone else. He looked in the direction of the lightning source but saw no-one, too shaken to be able to get a sense of where they might be by other means.

He clamped down on the fear broiling inside him, pushed it away from his thoughts. With his free hand, he pulled Zane close to him and took a step closer to the Giant. "They won't risk shooting him," Titus yelled at Zane. "Calm down!"

Zane trembled and looked wide-eyed all around him, not having the same ability to cut off his emotions as Titus did.

There was movement on the roof above them and the sound of arrows being loosed. "There!" Luthor shouted and then another volley. Their arrows slammed into a figure only made visible by the violent movement as the bolts hit. The person was dressed completely in black, impossible to see until the red-flighted arrows stuck out of him as he crumpled to the ground.

"Guardian down, Guardian down!" the Giant shouted, voice high with panic. "Hex? Hex! Guardian down!"

Titus frowned at the Giant, but then Callum was beside them, pulling Zane's arm towards a doorway in the building.

"In here, now!" he said, "I think more are on the way."

Titus allowed himself to be steered into the corridor of the abandoned office building once he had gone behind the Giant and ordered him to walk ahead, reminding him of the knife he held to his back.

"Zane, there are candles in my pack," he said once they were off the street.

Zane rummaged blindly, retrieved one, and followed Titus' direction to the matches held in his shirt pocket. The candle was quickly lit, revealing a dingy corridor with several doorways leading off it. Callum had gone ahead and appeared at the one to the first room on the right.

"In here," he said, beckoning to them all. "There's no window."

Zane hurried towards Callum, Titus urging the hostage on ahead to follow him.

"Oh God, oh God." The Giant wheezed rapidly as he entered the room after Zane, closely followed by Titus. His heavy steps were hesitant as they took in the surroundings, the suit he wore so cumbersome that he had to twist the whole of his upper body simply to be able to look from side to side. The candlelight didn't penetrate the shadows at the edges of the room, but there was enough light to reveal a desk and chair and a dusty floor covered with yellowed pieces of paper. The smooth glass of the faceplate reflected back the candlelight, making it impossible for any of them to make out any features.

"Sit in that chair," Titus ordered, but the Giant didn't move.

"I can't," he replied, the voice tremulous and higher in pitch than Zane had expected. "There might be splinters."

Zane gave his candle to Callum, took another from Titus' pack, lit it, and mustered all the courage he could to approach the massive man. He held it up to the smooth front plate of the helmet and peered at the face shielded within.

"You're a woman!" he exclaimed.

Large dark brown eyes, wide with fear, blinked at the flame and the boy. "Please, keep that candle away from me."

Zane drew back, still surprised to find that it wasn't someone as big as Luthor housed within the suit. Instead, the woman's pale face suggested a slender build beneath the layers. It was mostly the helmet that added to her height, that and the thick metal soled shoes that left the familiar footprints in the dust of the room.

In the moment he looked at her face, Zane immediately felt guilty. She was clearly terrified; her breathing was rapid and left a little patch of condensation on the glass between her and the world. He couldn't help but imagine how it would feel to be her, and he tried his best to smile reassuringly.

"We don't want to hurt you," he said gently and then Titus stepped in front of him, taking the candle from his hand to hold it up to her face again.

"But we will if you don't help us," Titus said in a flat voice that was somehow more frightening than one modulated by anger.

"I don't have much air. It was only going to be a short trip," the woman replied shakily.

"Don't waste it then," Titus replied unsympathetically. "Where's Lyssa?"

The skin above the bridge of her nose wrinkled as she frowned. "Lyssa? Who's that?"

"The one you took from Jay's territory!"

Zane watched a droplet of sweat run down between that furrow on her face. "I don't know anyone called Lyssa. I don't know where that territory is. Please, just let me go back–they'll be sending Guardians out right now. There's no need for there to be any more bloodshed."

Titus didn't flinch. "One month, three weeks and four days ago, some of your gang took my ... took a young woman and killed some of the Boys in Jay's gang. We want her back. If you don't give her back, we'll keep you here until your air runs out."

Zane fidgeted, not wanting it to come to that at all.

"Please, you have to understand that I don't have clear-ance to do what you're asking."

Titus frowned. "Who were you talking to outside?"

"She probably has a radio link back to her people," Callum said quietly.

"What does that mean?"

"It means they can hear what she says and they'll be able to talk back to her."

Titus scowled at her. "Is that true?"

She looked at the knife point and nodded slightly. She looked away briefly, clearly thinking as fast as possible. "Look, if you want this Lyssa, you'll have to let me go back to get her for you."

Titus took a step forward, looking like a small child next to the suited woman. His voice, however, was far from childlike; it was cold and measured. "Don't try to trick me or I will puncture your suit and watch you die."

"Titus!" Zane exclaimed, appalled at his friend's words.

Titus turned, fixing Zane with such a fearsome glare that he was silenced. He then looked back at the woman. "Speak to your gang. Tell them what we want—tell them if she's released, you'll be returned unhurt. She's called Lyssa, she's got violet eyes and brown hair and is a head taller than me. If you say anything else, you won't leave this room." He watched her glance down nervously at something strapped to her wrist. "You'd better hurry," he added, noting the dial and the one hand on it moving towards an amber segment.

She cleared her throat and said in a louder voice, "Hex? This is Radley. Do you copy, over?"

Then there was a pause, her eyes flicking up at the ceiling as she seemed to hear a response that was inaudible to anyone but her.

"No, the situation has worsened and … and they're making a demand in return for my release." She proceeded to give the details as Titus had said and then listened intently. Zane noted how much she was sweating, how her eyes darted from a spot on the ceiling to the knife held in Titus' hand. Then she looked at him. "They're … checking on her status. It may be a few minutes."

Titus simply stared back at her. "I'm not the one who has to worry about the time," he replied coldly, and then went to lean against the wall.

Zane swallowed hard, his stomach twisting with tension. "Um … is your name Radley, then?" He asked in as friendly a voice as he could muster, making the question seem ridiculous in such a situation.

The woman blinked at him and then swallowed. "Yes ...
Dr Radley."

"Doctor!" Zane exclaimed. "You heal people too?"

"Zane." Titus' voice was lowered to a warning tone. "Don't
talk to her."

Zane threw an annoyed glance at his friend and then
looked back at Radley.

"I ... I'm a doctor of microbiology," she replied nervously,
blinking away a droplet of sweat that had slid into the corner
of her eye. She then frowned at Zane. "You look familiar," she
mumbled and Zane was filled by a heady mixture of excitement
and dread.

"Zane!" Titus said his name so forcefully that he moved
away from Radley, shaken by her comment.

Titus moved swiftly to take his place in front of her
helmet. "Why did you take her? What have you done to her?"

Radley spread her hands, looking desperately confused.
"I don't know who or what you're talking about," she said shakily.
"Please believe me."

Titus stared at her, taking in the minutiae of her face.
With frustration he realised that she was actually telling the
truth.

"I don't know much about what happens in the other
spokes," she continued. "That's the – "

She cut off and looked up as she attended to something
else. Then her eyes shut and she let out a long sigh of relief.
"They have someone that fits that description, and they're
willing to make an exchange," she paused and then a frown
started to form. "I copy, Hex, stand by."

"What is it?" Titus demanded, his tension leaking into his
voice.

"They say that she'll die if she's brought up now," she
replied hesitantly. "They didn't say why."

234

Titus lowered his head, frowning. Could it be true? Lyssa had looked ill in the dream, but not so ill that moving her would kill her. But then, maybe she was worse now, and what did he know about that kind of thing anyway? He considered the Giant, considered Hex. They had stolen Lyssa, presumably because they wanted her for some reason. If they wanted her then, they probably wanted to keep her now and would lie to do so. Then he remembered Zane. Hex didn't know what he could do, so even if it was true, and Lyssa was that ill, Zane would be able to help her.

"I don't believe them," he said steadily. "They just don't want to let her go. Tell them you're running out of time."

As Radley responded Callum went to the doorway and looked out into the corridor. "I think the others are looking for us," he said to Zane. "Wait here." He hurried out of the room and within moments returned with Jay and Erin.

"What the hell is going on!" Jay yelled.

"They're bringing Lyssa for the exchange," Titus replied.

"She'll be at the end of the street outside in eight minutes," Radley said in a tremulous voice.

"There are other ones, wearing black, that have the lightning," Erin reported rapidly. "We've killed three, and we think there are more coming but they're hard to see."

Titus flicked his eyes back to Radley after taking this in. "Tell them that we can kill these 'Guardians' and we'll kill you if they send any more."

Radley obeyed as Jay nodded respectfully at Titus.

"Erin, Jay, can you keep an eye on her?" Titus asked. When they nodded, Jay drew one of his knives while Titus beckoned to Callum and Zane to step outside the room with him.

"You're playing a dangerous game, Titus," Callum said softly but Titus didn't respond.

"Will they really bring Lyssa?" Zane asked, the fear evident on his pale face.

Titus looked at him, sharing his concern. "We have to hope so. But I don't think they'll want us to get away. I think we need to have Radley in view, with one of the Hunters aimed at her so that if the Unders, or Hex-or whatever they're called-know that if they try anything, we can take her down."

Zane grimaced. "I don't like this," he muttered.

Titus ignored that. "I think we should tell them to leave Lyssa where Radley is, then we collect her and go."

Callum rubbed his chin. "I think we should exchange them near this building, seeing as we're committed to this now. I know this block-there are routes between the offices that I've made that they won't know about." Titus nodded and Callum continued. "I'll wait nearby to collect Lyssa. I don't think you or Zane should be too close, and I think Jay should be with you." When Titus looked as if he were about to object, Callum held up a hand to stop him. "No arguments, Titus. I know the fastest ways to get out of the area without going into the street any more than necessary. I'll get her into Jay's territory and you can meet me there."

Titus frowned as he considered Callum's words. "I could send Erin back up to Luthor and David to let them know the plan. They'll be able to defend you against those Guardians from up there, won't they?" At Callum's nod Titus added, "I need to stay long enough to make sure it's Lyssa, then I'll go with Zane."

Callum exhaled with relief. "Good. I won't leave her behind, Titus, don't worry."

Titus read Callum's face and was satisfied. "I'll go and tell Erin and Jay the plan, then I'll give Radley instructions."

As he went back into the room, Zane leant towards Callum and whispered, "I'm so glad you're here."

Minutes later, Titus stood with Radley and Callum outside of the building they had hidden within, with Zane and Jay waiting further down the street. Occasionally he could hear the creaks of bows being readied on the roof above Callum but no arrows were loosed. There was a brittle tension in the air, the only other noise being the mechanical wheeze and click of Radley's oxygen supply. The hand on the dial worn on her wrist was now reaching the end of the amber segment and he could see from her face how terrified she was.

Titus strained his eyes looking into the darkness in the direction Radley said they would approach from. When two figures came into view, one being half carried, half dragged by the other, he took a step forward.

"It's Lyssa!" he said to Callum after only a moment.

Callum nodded and watched their approach.

Lyssa looked barely conscious. The figure supporting her seemed to be male and one of the Guardians, judging by his black clothing that did indeed camouflage him almost perfectly in the darkness. He too appeared to be wearing some kind of helmet, but much less cumbersome than Radley's.

"Go now," Callum whispered to Titus.

Titus reluctantly backed off before forcing himself to turn away from his sister and run down the road to Zane and Jay. As soon as he reached them, the three of them increased their pace, Jay leading them back to safer territory.

When they reached the first crossroads, Titus paused to look behind him, noting that Radley was walking away from Callum who was now holding Lyssa and moving slowly backwards towards the door of the building. Just as Titus was about to continue, there was a yell from up on the roof, and then a volley of arrows loosed in the direction of the Guardian whom Titus could no longer see.

The night was illuminated by three arcs of lightning ripping through the air towards the roof. Titus cried out in despair as chaos erupted, blinking rapidly to try to see past the glowing afterimages left by the lightning. Jay grabbed his collar and yanked Titus round the corner, pulling him along roughly.

"C'mon, c'mon!" he was yelling, Zane sprinting alongside him.

At first Titus was dragged, but then he regained his senses and ran too, the three of them hurtling through alleyways and shadowy side streets lit by sporadic blue flashes in the distance.

Sometimes they heard shouting but it quickly faded, the loudest noise becoming that of their panting breaths. Soon they were back at Jay's territory, a line of Boys armed with makeshift weapons and knives waiting for them. When Jay was sighted a loud cheer went up and they closed around their returned hero.

"Stay smart-sharp, lads," Jay panted, bracing his hands on his knees to try to catch his breath. "May be more from the Unders comin' our way. And watch out for Callum. He'll be carrying someone–make sure he gets here safe."

The Boys dispersed to pre-arranged positions along the edge of the territory. Jay turned to Zane, who was shaking violently, and clapped him on the back. "Safe now, Zane, s'alright now."

Zane only nodded, also panting hard, and then noticed Titus' face, wracked with worry as he stared out in the direction they'd just run from, desperate for any sign of Callum. Zane went over and put a hand on his shoulder.

"Callum will bring her, Titus, he will," he said softly but Titus didn't answer.

When they had caught their breath, Jay insisted that they moved away from the border, but Titus would only move to the end of the street they were on, eyes still scanning the darkness.

Like a distant storm, the sky was lit intermittently by flashes of bright blue, but gradually it became less frequent and didn't seem to move much closer to where they waited.

The minutes ticked by and Titus started to pace. Zane sat on the edge of the kerb whilst Jay stayed nearby to direct wayward Boys to places where they could form a more useful defence. But none of the Guardians were sighted, and Jay began to relax.

"I reckon they've given up," he said and Zane nodded.

A familiar figure emerged from the end of a row of houses across the street and Titus ran over calling "Lyssa!" to the person cradled in Callum's arms.

Lyssa appeared to have the fragility of china, her face gaunt and white, her body painfully thin, making her skull seem larger, especially with her hair now cut very short. She was unconscious, and it was hard to make out her shallow breaths through the pale blue pyjamas that she wore. Titus took in her image wide-eyed. Even though he'd seen her in the dream, it hadn't fully prepared him for how she looked now.

"Let's get her into the warm," Callum said softly and Titus merely nodded.

Lyssa was soon laid on Miri's sofa with the fire built up and candles lit around the room. Jay hovered near the door, dividing his attention between looking out onto the garden cautiously and seeing how Lyssa fared.

Miri was boiling water for tea, leaving Zane to inspect the patient whilst Titus held his sister's hand as if it were a delicate piece of fine crystal. Callum watched from the corner near the window, also keeping an eye outside.

"Is any of that stuff in her?" Titus asked nervously.

Zane nodded, staring intently at Lyssa's left arm. "Not much, though. And it's in her arm, not her lungs."

Titus swallowed hard. "Is she going to die?"

The timorous quality of his friend's normally calm voice made Zane look at him and smile. "No, Titus, but she needs lots of looking after. She's not very well."

Titus allowed himself to relax just a fraction, watching as Zane moved the sleeve up Lyssa's arm, revealing a cluster of pinpricks and bruising at the inside of her elbow. He quickly lowered the sleeve again.

"There's Erin!" Jay cried and opened the front door as Erin stumbled in, immediately followed by Luthor, who had barely broken into a sweat.

"We did it!" she cried, seeing Titus holding Lyssa's hand. She punched the air triumphantly. "Yes! Oh Titus, you should've seen us. They sent loads more of those people, and there was lightning all over the place, and I got one of them right in the face, didn't I, Dad?"

Luthor nodded, patting her shoulder. "You did well," he said and she looked as if she might burst.

It was only then that Erin detected the sombre atmosphere in the room. "Will she be alright?" she asked quietly, trying to contain her exuberance.

Zane nodded. "Yes," he replied, but didn't elaborate.

When he looked back at Lyssa, his strange perception revealed the extent of her trauma. All over her body, patches of the blue aura around her were barely visible; there was extensive scarring over parts of her abdomen and evidence of healing after surgery of some kind. Zane didn't dare lift the fabric to see with his normal sight, as he didn't want Titus to see it. But of most concern to Zane were the black veins running through her arm. They seemed dormant, less aggressive than those that had been in the new boy's lungs, but it still disturbed him.

Zane resolved to deal with this when people had calmed down and when Titus finally went to sleep, whenever that would be, not wanting to upset him anymore.

"I will patrol the square, at least until dawn," Luthor said to Erin. "Stay here, in case the worst happens."

"Could they have followed you back?" Miri asked.

"Unlikely, but possible," he replied. "Best to be cautious. Erin, keep an eye out at the window. When David is rested he'll relieve you."

Erin went straight to the window and positioned herself to watch through the gap between the curtain and the wall as Luthor left the house.

"I'd better get back to the Boys," Jay told them and slipped out quietly as Miri brewed tea, filling the room with its reassuring aroma. She handed steaming mugs to Callum and Erin, placed one next to Titus who still hadn't looked away from his sister, and then put one into her son's hands. After draping a blanket around Titus' shoulders she went into the kitchen, Callum following her out of the room silently.

The three friends were left in the room with Lyssa, but no-one spoke. Erin didn't let her attention drop from the window and Titus studied Lyssa's features for any sign of consciousness. Zane sat in the armchair, watching Titus' vigil. He wondered how Dr Radley was, whether she had recovered from her ordeal. Guilt twisted his stomach when he thought about how terrified she'd been. As he regarded Titus now, he tried to decide whether his actions had been right or wrong. At the time, he'd been horrified at how he spoke to Radley, how brutal his threats were. But it had worked: Lyssa was with them now, he couldn't deny that. Did that make it alright?

Erin shifted position and sighed quietly, stealing Zane's attention away from Titus. He still hadn't quite come to terms with what Erin had done to that Gardner. It felt like it happened months before, but it had only been a couple of days. Luthor didn't seem to know about Doug's death, nor Erin's role in it. Zane wondered how he would react if he knew his daughter had killed a Gardner. He'd probably be pleased, he realised. Jay and the Boys were pleased and Titus didn't seem bothered by it at all, so why did it upset him so? He thought about the moment when she killed him and shuddered.

Callum's voice was so deep that its resonance carried sound without words through the kitchen door. He wondered what he was saying to his mother, reminding him of what Doug had said to Erin that made her lose control. If someone was hurting his mum, would he kill, even though he'd sworn always to save lives?

Chapter 28
DEATH OF A HERO

Several hours later, long after Callum had left and Miri had fallen asleep in front of the fire, Lyssa woke with a start.

"Lyssa, I'm here, you're safe," Titus said rapidly, stirring Zane from his dozing. Even though his muscles ached and various parts of his body had gone numb, Titus hadn't moved from her side.

Lyssa blinked at her brother with the same violet eyes as his. They looked large in their sunken hollows, her cheeks drawn and as bleached as her lips. After a brief hint of relief, her expression contorted with pain and she clutched her left arm.

"Titus," she croaked with a thin voice. "How ...? Where ...? Oh God, my arm hurts so much."

She drew it into her body, curling around the limb and losing herself in obvious agony as Zane hurried over, staring at the arm, the same one in which he'd seen the black matter. At the sound of his movement, Lyssa's eyes opened again and she stared at Zane with open suspicion.

"I'm Zane," he said gently, "Titus is my friend. I know why your arm is hurting, so will you let me help you?"

She shook her head, shrinking away from him. "No, no, stay back," she gasped and looked at Titus with terrified eyes. "He's in with them, Titus! He looks like one of them ... keep him away!"

Titus shook his head and put his hands on her shoulders. "He isn't the one that hurt you," he began. After a pause, he glanced at Miri and then turned back to Lyssa. "I'll explain some other time. For now, just trust me. Zane can help–he's my friend."

Lyssa searched Titus' face with desperation. It was clear that what he'd said hadn't convinced her, but the pain was such that she relented and nodded to Zane.

Titus moved aside for his friend to take his place. Carefully, and with movements that were deliberately slow, Zane placed his hands on Lyssa's arm and stared at it, *into* it.

"Mum, can you get me a pot with a lid and give it to Titus? Lyssa, you need to keep still and maybe shut your eyes."

Lyssa watched Miri return with a small lidded saucepan and hand it to Titus, who removed the lid. Zane coaxed Lyssa into extending her left arm towards him with a gentle pull. "I'm watching you," she said, her jaw tight. "Titus, don't let him stick any needles in me."

"Shhh," Titus whispered and moved the pot underneath Lyssa's elbow at Zane's mumbled instruction.

Within moments, the pinpricks in the inside of Lyssa's elbow began to bulge slightly, eliciting a horrified gasp from both Miri and Lyssa.

"What's happening!" Lyssa shrieked and tried to pull back, but Zane's grip was firm and his concentration intense.

"He's getting some bad stuff out of you," Titus replied, "Let him do it."

Lyssa stopped struggling and watched aghast, as thick black liquid oozed from the holes in her skin, each black thread joining with the others to form creeping rivulets that slithered down her arm towards the pan held underneath. The substance poured like treacle into the pot as Zane trembled with effort.

It didn't take long before the last of it was out and Titus slammed the lid onto the pot at Zane's nod. Miri, having seen the substance before, had found some thick twine and tied the lid onto the pot tightly as Zane slumped against the sofa.

Lyssa was staring at him as she experimentally moved her arm. "It feels better," she said quietly and Zane smiled sleepily.

When Miri had finished, Titus put the pot on the floor in front of him and rested a knee on top as he knelt forward to embrace his sister. They held each other tightly, silently, long enough for Miri to build up the fire and put a kettle of water on the trivet to boil.

Titus finally pulled away and kissed Lyssa on the cheek. "I'll take this outside, then we need to talk," he said. "Don't worry, you'll be safe here." He pointed at Miri. "This is Miri. She's Zane's mum and she'll take care of you." He then pointed at Erin. "That's Erin by the window – she helped you escape. Zane did too."

Erin nodded briefly, keen to stay focused on her task. Despite Miri's warm smile, Lyssa's suspicion was still apparent. Titus picked up the pan and hurried out of the house.

Miri was pouring tea when he returned, Lyssa now sitting up and wrapped in a blanket, watching her every movement. Zane hadn't moved but he was still awake. Titus returned to his sister's side and she scooped his hand into her own.

"This is Miri's house," Titus told her. Lyssa nodded, staring at the steaming mug that Miri had placed into her free hand. Titus smiled. "That's tea. It's nice – you should try it."

Lyssa blinked at him, dazed, and then out of nowhere, the shakes began. Titus took the mug away and then wrapped his arms around her as she shivered uncontrollably. Less than a minute later, she pulled away from him, wiping at her eyes with trembling hands as she apologised.

"It's okay," Zane said softly. "Something horrible happened to you. It's probably shock."

Lyssa shook her head. "It isn't that," she said, her voice wavering. She looked at Titus. "It's the others, the ones that are still there … I can't stop thinking about them, about Eve and …" She covered her face with her hands and shook violently as Titus looked on helplessly. He wasn't used to this; after everything that had happened that night, this was the most

245

frightening: his sister so weak and vulnerable. He breathed in and out, moving his emotions to one side as he focused on her and her needs. Keeping that worry inside wasn't going to help.

"Tell us about them," he said. "Tell us what happened to you. We ... I need to know." He watched Lyssa look at the others in the room uncomfortably and so he added, "They looked after me ... and they helped get you back, so they should know too."

Lyssa dropped her hands into her lap. "I don't know where to start. How long have I been gone?"

"Nearly two months," Titus replied and Lyssa's mouth fell open. Titus quickly realised something was wrong. "You didn't know it was that long?"

She shook her head. "No. I thought ... a couple of weeks, maybe. I don't remember ... maybe it was because I was asleep a lot."

Zane couldn't help but look at her stomach, remembering the scarring, but he said nothing.

Lyssa's eyes glazed over as she stared at the floor ahead of her. "Tell us about Eve," Titus prompted, putting the warm cup back into her hands.

"Eve ... Eve was wonderful. She visited me in the room they kept me in. She could unlock the door. I don't know how— she didn't know either." Titus noted how just mentioning Eve's name seemed to calm her.

Erin turned her attention back into the room at hearing this. "You were kept locked in a room?" she asked and Lyssa nodded. "If this Eve could unlock the door, why didn't you escape?"

"I was too sick a lot of the time," Lyssa replied.

"Was she sick?" Erin asked.

"Sometimes," Lyssa replied. "Not as much as me."

"So why didn't she escape?" Titus asked.

Lyssa smiled to herself. "I told her to lots of times. I begged her to. But she wouldn't leave us all behind. She told me that there were lots of children there, all prisoners like me."

"That's terrible!" Miri cried. "Why on earth would anyone do that?"

"Eve said that we were being experimented on. She'd heard some of the ones in the yellow suits talking about trials on the 'Compound' but we couldn't figure out what that meant. Oh, and she told me they talked about It too. They said everyone died because of something in the air, some kind of disease, and some people were immune or something. And the thing that killed everyone was still in the air, and that's why they have to wear those funny suits when they go outside and when they came to see us." Her voice trailed off and she started shivering again.

Titus barely seemed to take this in. "If she knew all that and could go in and out of locked doors, she must have been in the Unders' gang."

"Unders?" Lyssa shook her head. "I don't know who they are but she wasn't in any gang. She hated them and was just as scared of them as I was."

"The Unders is the name of the gang that took you," Zane explained.

"They might be called Hex," Titus added.

Lyssa shuddered. "Yes, Hex, that's the name of the place, I think, or maybe the people that run it. I heard it a lot when ... when they came."

"Who?" Titus asked, but he knew as soon as Lyssa's eyes flicked to Zane.

"The ones in the suits and ... the one that looks like him." She pointed at Zane.

Miri, who had been sitting on the arm of Erin's chair, stood up. "What?"

Seeing Zane's panic, Titus hurriedly said, "Tell us about the ones in the suits," in a futile attempt to deflect Miri's attention, but it was too late.

Lyssa looked at Zane, then at Miri and back at her son again. "Oh hell …" she muttered. "He's your father, isn't he?"

"James is alive?!" Miri shrieked. "In the Unders?"

Zane pulled himself to his feet and went to his mother's side. She clutched his arm. "Do you still have that photo?" she asked him urgently.

Zane sighed and pulled the photo of his father from his pocket. Miri plucked it from his hand and showed it to Lyssa, who only had to glance, nod, and then look away to tell Miri what she wanted to know.

Miri turned to Zane, her eyes glistening with unshed tears. "He's alive!" she exclaimed in a shaky voice. "He didn't leave me, they took him … he's a prisoner there too. That's why he didn't come back–do you see, Zane?" She began to almost laugh as she pulled Zane into a tight embrace. Over her shoulder, Zane looked at Titus with haunted eyes.

"No, he's not a prisoner," Lyssa said and Titus watched Zane's eyes squeeze shut as Miri froze. "He's one of them, he was the worst of them … he hurt me. He was the one that stuck the needles in me." Miri released Zane and turned to face Lyssa as she continued. "He didn't wear the same weird clothes and masks as the others did. He pretended to be nice, pretended that he would make me feel better. He said he'd take the pain away, but he always made it worse … he was the one who –" Titus cut her off with a pointed look as Lyssa's hand moved to the place on her stomach where the scarring was.

The photograph fell from Miri's hand and fluttered to the floor as an awful silence descended on the room. A shaft of light fell across her face and she looked to the glass panes in the front door that it had come from. "I don't want to hear any more," she said in barely more than a whisper. "The sun's coming up. I'll be in the garden."

They all watched her leave and shut the door behind her. Zane looked at the picture of his father lying on the rug but didn't move to retrieve it. "I didn't want her to know," he said quietly.

"You knew all along?" Lyssa shot at him. "I knew it! I knew you were in with them somehow!"

"No!" Titus shouted and Lyssa stared at him in surprise. "We suspected that he was doing bad stuff in the Unders– that's all, Lyssa. Zane is *not* like his father."

"Zane would never hurt anyone," Erin added.

Lyssa sighed and leant back. "I'm so tired. And this is all so strange. Titus, you know we never used to be friends with anyone from the gangs. I don't understand."

Titus sighed. "I live next door now. Let me take you home and you can get some sleep, then I'll tell you all about what's happened since we last saw each other."

She nodded wearily and let him help her to stand. Zane opened the door for them and watched them leave.

Erin watched them pass the window, then turned to Zane. "Why didn't you tell me about your dad being in the Unders?" she asked quietly.

Zane sighed heavily. "I think I was hoping that Titus was wrong. No chance of that now."

Erin looked as if she were about to reply when she saw something outside that distracted her.

"Father wants me to go home," she said. "David's coming out into the square, so you'll be safe. I'll see you later."

She left the door open behind her and Zane stood alone, staring at the photograph still lying where it had fallen. The breeze from the doorway teased at his hair; the sounds of bird-song drifted in with it but didn't make him smile.

He didn't even notice Titus at the doorway until he spoke. "You know what we have to do, don't you?"

Zane's eyes didn't leave the picture. "Huh?"

"You know we have to go after the Unders, stop what they're doing."

Zane nodded. "We have to get the other children out."

Titus stepped into the room. "Once Lyssa is well again, I'm going after them. Will you help me?"

Perhaps it was the conviction in his voice that pulled Zane's attention from the photo at last. "Yes," he replied, looking up at his friend. "I will."

Titus nodded with satisfaction. "Good."

Titus left and Zane remained motionless, staring at the image of his father and his friend, grinning out at him from a time he didn't understand. His fears now confirmed, he was assailed by a cacophony of emotions: shame, disappointment, disgust. But pervading it all was a crushing sadness. Silently, after one last look, he threw the photograph into the fire and watched the hungry flames consume his father's smile.

Outside, Titus watched Erin join her father on the steps of the house across the square. He didn't go home; instead, he went to a secluded corner of the garden where he took a penknife from his pocket and flicked out a stubby blade. He recalled the day that Zane swore to be a doctor, and Luthor's words. If what the Hunter said was true, this needed to be marked with blood. He pressed his palm onto the tip of the blade until a drop of blood slid down the metal and splashed onto the soil below. "I, Titus, *swear* that I will destroy the Unders. With this blood, let the oath be kept." Only when the blood had seeped into the ground did he wipe the blade clean and return it to his pocket as a cold blast of wind bowed the trees around him.

Chapter 29
EVE

Later that day, Lyssa woke with a start, eyes wide and alert, the tendons in her neck straining as she tried to get up before she had even registered her surroundings. She flopped back into the sofa cushions when she saw Titus and the room around her. As unfamiliar as it was, it was a world away from her previous prison and enough to take away that instinct to run.

Wordlessly, Titus held a glass of water to her lips and she drank long and deep.

"You're in my new house," Titus said, pre-empting the question. "Remember? It's in a place called Queen Square in Miri's territory."

Lyssa frowned and then made an attempt to get up that her weakened body simply couldn't realise. "Miri?" she croaked. "That woman with long hair?" Titus nodded and Lyssa frowned. "Why are you staying in her territory? What's the price you're paying?"

"No, you don't understand –"

"There's always a price," she interjected hoarsely. "Didn't I teach you anything?"

Titus scowled at the implication that he'd been lax. "She's different. A lot's happened."

"Evidently," she said wryly, looking at her emaciated arms. She sank back, accepting her inability to stand for the moment. "I think you'd better fill me in."

Titus paused. "Long or short version?"

"Short, I'm so tired. And hungry." Titus gave her an apple from a fruit bowl newly stocked from Miri's garden. Her eyes widened. "Wow, how many of these have you found?"

Titus smiled. "There are ten apple trees outside, and plums, pears, strawberries, raspberries, and *grapes*, Lyssa, actual, *real grapes* like in the pictures!"

She listened, enraptured as she sank her teeth into the apple's juicy flesh. He watched her bliss with open joy and then remembered what she'd asked.

"Do you remember us going down the road past Euston station that night?" She shook her head. "Oh."

"I remember us finding a house with a cellar and there being lots of good stuff hidden in it," she ventured between bites.

He frowned. "That was a few days before you ..." His voice trailed off as he realised just how much she had forgotten. "You don't remember Jay?"

"Who's Jay?"

Titus sighed heavily, remembering that night all too well. He tried to decide how much to tell her and decided to stick to fact rather than speculation. "He's the leader of the gang whose territory we went into by mistake. When he was –"

"Was there a storm?" Lyssa interrupted, her brow creasing as she struggled to recall that night.

"There was lightning, but no storm. It was made by guns. Do you remember that?"

Her chewing paused and she stared into the space above his left shoulder for a few moments. "No," she finally said. "Not really. I would remember that. How can lightning be made by guns?"

"You wanted the short version," Titus reminded her and she nodded, returning to her apple. He shrugged. "Ok then. You were taken by some people from a gang called the Unders. They have guns that fire lightning but they can't breathe the air, so they walk around in strange suits and look like Giants." Now set on his task, he continued regardless as his sister struggled to take in what he was saying. "I don't know what they did to you, but I think it was bad. And I don't think they fed you properly. You were gone for seven weeks and four days, but then we caught one of their gang and made them swap her for you."

Unchewed apple sat in Lyssa's mouth for a few moments. Finally she swallowed, quickly regaining her composure. "And what happened to you when I was away?"

"Miri and her son Zane looked after me when I was hurt. There's a big garden outside that they look after. They live in the house next door to this one, the one you woke up in when we brought you back. This one was empty so I –"

"You look ok now. Why did you stay? Did they help you to find me? Is that why?"

"They helped me a lot," Titus began but then was cut off by his sister again.

"What did you give them in return?"

Titus pressed his lips together, managing his irritation, and then said, "Nothing. They don't want anything from me."

"So they haven't told you yet." She frowned at him with obvious disapproval. "You didn't make a clear deal with them? I can't believe you were so –"

"No," Titus said firmly. "It isn't like that. They're nice people and Zane is my friend. And that girl, the one called Erin, she lives here with her father, though they're in another gang ... it's complicated. But the most important thing is that she's my friend too."

Lyssa looked at him as if he had said that in her absence he'd decided to hop everywhere backwards. "People are only friends when it suits them."

"They're different."

She peered into his eyes, searching, perhaps for the brother she remembered. "Just give me a few days to get strong, then we'll get moving again. It isn't right, any of this. I can't believe that you've been fooled so quickly."

Titus almost revealed the pulse of fury that flashed through him but managed to rein it in. "You don't know everything that's been going on … you wanted the short version."

Lyssa let her head flop back onto the cushion as she swallowed the last of the apple, stalk and all. "It'll have to wait. I just need to have a rest, just for a few …" And then she was asleep.

That night, the children met in the dream. Zane was pulled in first, then Erin. Each one of them had a good look around the room, as if to check that everything was in place and as it was before all of the drama of Lyssa's rescue. The shelves were still filled with the strange collection of objects, the captain's desk and chair were still there, and the window still looked out onto the tree hanging in the void, roots and all.

"How's Lyssa?" Zane asked Titus, watching his friend wander over to sit in the captain's chair.

Titus frowned. "She's … tired," was all he said.

"Has she said anything else about the Unders?" Erin asked, taking up her favourite spot by the window.

Titus shook his head. "She's been asleep most of the time. But Miri said she would be, so I'm not too worried."

Zane sat cross-legged on the floor and began to worry the hem of his trousers. "I think it will take her a while to get over what happened … it sounded horrible. Mum's still really upset about what Lyssa said about my dad. I heard her crying tonight after she went to bed. I'm not sure what to do about it."

Erin shrugged. "You can't stop her being upset."

Titus nodded. "I suppose you just have to be calm and patient," he offered. "You suspected this a long time before she did. It must have been a shock for her."

Zane nodded. "So what do we do now?"

"We find a way to destroy them," Titus stated firmly.

Zane frowned. "They're really strong, and they have guns that make lightning. And anyway, I thought you didn't like all that gang stuff."

"This isn't 'gang stuff'!" Titus was appalled. "We have to stop what they're doing to those children down there that Lyssa told us about. You've seen the boys when they arrive at Jay's patch. Surely you want all that to stop?"

"Of course I do!" Zane exclaimed. "But you said 'destroy' and that sounds a bit ... well ..."

"Violent?" Erin offered.

"Dangerous," Zane finished.

"Necessary," Titus returned. "It's necessary. If they're bad enough to do things like that to children, and Lyssa, then they don't deserve anything else."

"If my father's bad enough, you mean," Zane muttered and the trio fell into silence.

"We have to find out more about them," Erin ventured. "If you're going to hunt something, you learn about it first. That's what my father's taught me. You learn about how it thinks, how it moves, and what makes it attack or run."

Titus nodded. "Erin's right—we do need to learn more. I'll see what Lyssa says when she's better. But the one who I'd really like to speak to is Eve. The boys who get away talk about her and Lyssa told us about her too."

"Yeah," Erin agreed, staring out at the oak tree. "I'd like to know how she went in and out of locked rooms so easily. Maybe she was one of Them."

Titus shook his head. "No, she wasn't from the Unders, I'm sure of it."

"She was very brave by the sound of it," Zane said, not looking up from his trouser hem. "I'd really like to meet her too."

"If only we could talk to her here," Titus muttered, resting his head in his hands. "Then we could find out all we needed to know."

He looked up as someone touched him lightly on the shoulder and then cried out in surprise, jumping up so fast that the chair tipped over behind him.

A slip of a girl with strawberry blonde hair and deathly pale skin leapt away from him and silently cowered in the corner as Zane scrabbled to his feet and Erin sprang into a fighter's stance, hand on the hilt of her dagger. The three children stared at the strange girl dressed in familiar blue pyjamas.

"Eve?" Titus ventured and the girl simply nodded, with eyes just as large and surprised as his.

"Is this Uppabov?" the girl finally said, in barely more than a whisper.

The three children stared at her, until Titus finally regained some composure and said, "Where?"

"Uppabov," the girl replied, voice no louder.

Titus shook his head. "No. This is a dream. My dream. We brought you here."

The girl continued to look thoroughly confused. Zane blinked away the last of his surprise and gave her a warm smile. "I'm Zane," he began. "Hello."

"Hello," she replied and reciprocated with a nervous twitch at the corners of her mouth that didn't really make it to a smile.

"This is Titus." Zane waved a hand in his friend's direction. Titus didn't smile but continued to stare at the girl intensely. "And that's Erin," Zane added, pointing at her. Erin gave her a curt nod, similar to the way Jay greeted people when he wanted to seem impressive.

"Hello," said the girl. "I'm Eve."

"We've heard about you!" Zane said cheerily.

"More than that," Titus added. "We wished for you. We wanted to speak to you ... and you came." His voice trailed off as his mind began to work over the mystery.

Eve peered back at him. "You did? Why?"

"Because you know my sister," Titus replied, smiling at her for the first time. "And the boys who were in the Unders— they all talk about you."

Eve clapped her hands in delight. "The boys who went to Uppabov?!" she gasped. "You know them?!"

All three of them nodded and couldn't help but smile as she jumped up and down on the spot.

"They live near us," Zane said. "They're in a gang called the Bloomsbury Boys, but we know they came from the Unders, and that's why we wanted to talk to you."

Eve frowned. "What's the Unders? What's a gang?"

"The Unders are the people who keep you where you are," Titus began. "The ones who stole my sister, Lyssa—remember her?"

Eve nodded. "She's gone ... don't know where though."

"She's with us now," Titus began, but when Eve looked excitedly around the room as if expecting to find Lyssa, he added, "At my house, in the garden—not here literally."

"House?" Eve frowned. "Gar-den? I don't know what these words mean."

Titus sighed and exchanged a look with Zane. "What's important," Zane said, "is that Lyssa is safe with us and isn't being hurt anymore."

Eve nodded at that. "Yes. This is important—I'm glad. She's nice. Oh!" She pointed at Titus. "You're the one she kept asking about! I understand what a brother is now! It's a you!"

Titus smiled, charmed by her clumsy language. "We need to know why the Unders are keeping people prisoner," he pressed.

"Why?" Eve tipped her head to the side and regarded Titus with interest.

"Because we want to understand and learn how to stop them," he replied evenly, as if talking to someone much younger than she looked.

"Stop them hurting us?" Eve watched the trio nod. "Good, they hurt us a lot, it's horrible. But they say that it's necessary. I don't like *necessary*, it hurts."

Zane looked pointedly at Titus and then asked, "Do you know what the 'Compound' is? Lyssa said something about it."

Eve wrinkled her nose. "It's horrible stuff that they put in people to try to stop the air in Uppabov from killing them. They put it in some of the children, but it makes them sick. Sometimes it kills them, and then Hex stops doing things that hurt for a while whilst they talk about it lots. Then when they stop talking lots, it's always bad–then they come and do the really bad tests, where they take bits out of us and put bits in, and there are lots of needles and it all hurts really bad."

The trio listened with varying expressions of horror. Zane was the very embodiment of sympathetic distress, whilst Titus, at the other end of the scale, simply pressed his lips tight together as he took it in.

"They did this to Lyssa," he muttered, not at anyone in particular, but Eve nodded all the same.

"It's always worse for girls that they find in the Uppabov, cos girls are special cos of something they carry inside that's important to Hex."

"Zane?" Erin stepped away from the window. "Do you know why that would be?"

Zane shrugged. "Not sure. But I don't like the sound of it at all."

"It's to do with something inside that stops the stuff in the air from killing people, I think," Eve continued. "People in Uppabov have clever bodies. They don't get hurt, but people in Hex do, and if they go outside without these big yellow pyjamas and special hats on, the air gets inside them and they die.

"I saw one of them die once. He fell over and smashed the glass over his face, and so some of the air got in. He was screaming, and this weird kind of gurgle sound was coming out of his throat. And then there was blood coming out of his eyes and his nose and his mouth. And he coughed and it all went everywhere."

Encouraged by her enraptured audience, she continued, her voice still scarcely louder than a whisper. "Then he died, and then Hex sent lots of people in suits to the tunnel and they scrubbed everything lots and lots and lots with stuff that smelt horrible. And no-one from Hex went down there for a long time. They were scared to go down *that* tunnel."

"You saw this?" Titus questioned. "You were there?"

"Yes," Eve replied. "I was hiding, I saw all of it."

"And you breathed the same air?"

She nodded. "Yes, it doesn't kill me, or any of the children they hurt. We've got something called 'Immunity' and it means we could go to Uppabov and not die. But they won't let us go to Uppabov. Cos they want to test the 'Compound' and find a way to go to Uppabov without dying, see?"

Erin's eyes narrowed slightly. "But you can unlock the doors, can't you? So why don't you just escape?"

"I can't leave my friends!" she exclaimed, appalled. "I'm the only one who makes them feel better. I couldn't live in Uppabov when I knew they were in Hex and being hurt with no-one to talk to and keep secrets with. That would be horrible."

Erin seemed satisfied with the answer and her suspicion melted away to a look of respect. "Even though they hurt you too?"

Eve nodded and looked down at her toes, just visible past the hem of the pyjama bottoms.

"That's brave," Zane said quietly and smiled at her.

After a pause, Titus asked, "Do you know where Hex is?" At Eve's confused expression he re-framed the question. "Do you know anything about any places in Uppabov that are close to where you are?"

"Oh," Eve thought hard. "They talk about somewhere called Green Park sometimes. They talk about going up there,

259

so that must be a place in Uppabov."

Titus smiled broadly. "That's great, we have somewhere to start. We'll have to look on a map to see if the places we know they go to are near to this Green Park."

"How did I get into this room?" Eve asked, flicking a stray blonde hair from her eyes. "I went to sleep and then I was here. I don't understand."

"You're still asleep," Titus replied gently, patiently. "Your body is still where it was when you went to sleep, but your mind has come to talk to us."

Eve nodded, but not in a very convincing fashion. She began to take in the room properly. "It's very strange here ... I don't understand what all of those things are." She pointed at the shelves and the objects on them. "And why does the floor look so ... weird?"

Zane looked at the floor. "It's made of wood," he offered.

"Wood?" Eve crouched down and ran her finger along the grain. "There isn't anything like this in Hex. Is everywhere made of 'wood' in Uppabov?"

Titus smiled and shook his head. "No, there are lots of things made of lots of different materials. I'll show you, when we get you out."

Eve looked up at him and their eyes locked in a long gaze. She finally asked, "Are you going to get all of us out?"

"Yes, all of you," he replied. "All of the children. I promise."

Her head tipped to the side again as she seemed to study him. "Yes, I believe you." She stood and smiled. "I like you."

Titus blushed, relieved that she looked away to Zane and Erin. "I like you both too. I feel a bit funny, you're starting to feel ... far away."

Titus stood too. "You're about to wake up."

"Oh." Eve reached out to brush Titus' hand. "Can I come here again?"

All three nodded as Eve's form faded away.

"I like you too," Titus whispered, as the last remnants of her image disappeared.

"Can you hear something?" Erin asked and Zane strained to listen.

"It's the Bloomsbury Boys' alarm!" he exclaimed. "We need to wake up!"

Chapter 30
REDEMPTION

By the time the children had woken, thrown on shoes, and avoided various adults as they dashed out of their houses, the clanging alarm in Russell Square had stopped and a small crowd of Boys had collected at the edge of Herbrand Street. It was hard to see anything in the darkness; the moon was only half full and shadows clung to every building, every child, as they peered down the street, too afraid to go any farther.

"What happened?" Zane asked the nearest Boy as they ran up.

"Dev saw sommat on his watch, near where the Giants go," the boy replied excitedly.

"One of the Giants?" Titus demanded, standing on tiptoes to try to see past the throng of heads.

"Nah, some bloke I think. Not big enough for one of them Giants. Dev said 'e were carryin' sommat, then Jay went an' got a torch and now Jay's over there sortin' it out. Dev said this bloke were tryin' to leave sommat in our patch, but Dev yelled and he ran off before 'e could."

Whilst Zane and Titus quizzed the boy, Erin slipped away to climb up a rusting fire escape and look over the crowd. She saw an amber glow reflecting off the pale buildings at the end of the street. Jay came into view, his burning torch held high and in front of him with one hand, the other holding a knife firm. He swept the torch back and forth, peering in between rusting wrecks of cars and piles of wreckage left at the northern edge of their territory.

"Zane, Titus!" she hissed and beckoned them up to her. The rusting metal steps creaked in complaint as they climbed up to stand next to her and watch Jay's progress.

"Have you seen who it is?" Titus asked, following Jay's search just as keenly.

Erin shook her head. "By the way he's looking though, I think whoever it is has been trapped in that street."

"I'm going to look too," Titus said, "I don't want them to get away. They're probably from the Unders."

"It might be a Gardner," Zane cautioned, "You don't know who it is."

"Not likely to be a Gardner," Erin muttered back. "They never approach from the north. I think Titus is right."

"Come with me if you want," Titus said, as he began to climb back down the shaking steps. "But I'm not staying here and missing a chance to learn something about the Unders."

Erin nodded and leapt down to the ground from where she had been watching. Zane picked his way back down, fretting at the sound of the wall fastenings scraping against their loose housings. By the time he had reached her side, Erin had an arrow notched and Titus had joined her too.

The three children climbed through an overgrown garden to get past the dense cluster of Bloomsbury Boys and hurried down the street to Jay's position. Seeing them do this, a handful of the braver Boys broke off from the front of the crowd and began to follow them, eager to show Jay that they were unafraid.

When they reached the road that Jay was searching, Erin moved to the centre of the street, positioning her body at an angle ready to loose the arrow. "I won't let anyone or anything go past me," she stated.

Titus and Zane continued past her, but they had only moved a few metres into the road when Zane pointed to a pile of rubbish halfway down the street, close to where they could see Jay searching. "Someone's in pain behind there," Zane whispered. "I can feel it."

They watched Jay creep round the wreckage. There was the briefest pause and then he yelled, "What the hell are you doing?! Get away from 'im!"

"He's dying!" a man's voice retorted, but Jay leapt forward, pressing an attack. Both Titus and Zane arrived in time to see Jay slash at a man, forcing him back. He threw the torch down to draw his second blade, planting himself firmly between the intruder and the body of a child in familiar pale pyjamas.

The boy was shivering violently as ragged breaths rattled in his lungs. Zane rushed over to him, focused only on saving his life. He worked swiftly, knowing exactly how to draw the substance out of the boy's lungs.

Titus picked up the torch and held it towards the trespasser to try to identify him. Even though the man's face was barely visible by the flickering light, the resemblance was incredible.

"Zane! It's him!" Titus yelled as the man staggered away from Jay's blade.

"Stay back," Jay growled as Zane looked up and their eyes met for the briefest moment. When the man didn't withdraw farther, Jay gave a chilling cry and leapt at him, both blades flashing in the amber glow of the torch. Zane stared, struck dumb by the sight of his father desperately holding his arms in front of his head as he stumbled away down the street.

"I was trying to save him!" he cried out as Jay's knives slashed at his arms.

"Liar!" Jay shouted, "I saw you tryin' to kill him—your hands were round his neck!" He repositioned his blades in his palms as he stalked the man, slowly moving him further away from Zane and the new boy. "I'll kill you, Unders scum!"

"I'm not one of them!" he cried, now directing his desperate defence at Zane as well as his assailant. "I was saving the boy from them! You have to believe me!"

Zane stood, finding himself believing him, despite Jay's words, despite what Lyssa had said. He took a tentative step towards him. "Dad?"

"Jay!" Erin called out from the end of the street. "Get out of the way!"

Zane watched his father's face distort into an expression of abject horror. As Jay leapt to one side, Zane turned to see Erin taking aim at his father.

"No, Erin!" Zane screamed, the very moment that her fingertips loosed the arrow.

The arrow hit with a loud thunk and Shannon's legs buckled beneath him. He cried out before collapsing onto his back, the air knocked out of him.

Erin notched a second arrow as Zane hurled himself towards his prone father.

"Erin, wait!" Titus yelled, watching Zane fall to his knees, staring at the point where the arrow was embedded in his chest.

Erin came closer, not moving her aim an inch.

"Get out of the way, Zane," Jay growled. "He's the one that's been hurtin' my Boys, I know it."

"He was saving him!" Zane shrieked, glaring back at Jay with glistening eyes.

Titus nodded. "I believe him," he said, positioning himself between Zane and Jay. "Let us take care of this. The new boy needs you now." As Jay drew a breath to protest, Titus patted the air and said, "This isn't in your territory, Jay. It's no man's land here."

Erin drew up alongside the fallen doctor, aiming the arrow at his neck. "If they're wrong, Jay, I'll finish him."

Jay took the measure of her statement, and then a fearful whimper from the new boy snapped his attention away from the standoff. "Don't let 'im near my Boys," he hissed and then hurried over to scoop the frightened child up and take him to his square.

"Is he going to die?" Titus asked Zane in a hushed voice.

Zane was staring into his father's chest. "It's pierced his lung, but I think I can save him."

"Are you sure he was telling the truth?" Erin's bow creaked as she held the string taut.

"Yes!" Titus replied impatiently.

"But then why are they all so scared of him?" Erin pressed, not letting her aim slip.

Titus fell silent, recalling the memories he had seen in Squeak's mind. He shuddered. "I don't understand it yet ... but I know you shouldn't kill him."

Erin sighed and let the arrow slip down as she lowered the bow.

Shannon's face was pale in the moonlight, a sheen of sweat glistening in the silver light. Barely conscious, his breath was ragged, with an awful rasping sound. Zane placed his hands either side of the embedded arrow shaft and looked up at Erin. "When I say so, pull the arrow out as quick as you can."

Erin nodded and made herself ready. At Zane's "Now!" she pulled it out swiftly and Zane trembled with effort as he fought to close the wound. There was a brief spurt of blood as the barbed arrowhead was pulled free, but then no more. Within moments the tension in his father's body lessened and his breathing became stronger and steadier. The cuts on his arms began to close, the steady trickle of blood that ran from them also slowed to nothing.

Zane shook with exhaustion but smiled when his father's eyes opened and looked up into his. "Are you ok? You were –"

"Winded," Titus interrupted, giving Zane a pointed look.

The doctor only blinked for a few moments, then smiled weakly up at Zane. "Eve said she dreamt of a boy," he whispered, "A boy that looked like me with brown eyes."

Zane nodded. "That was me!"

"Miri's eyes," he whispered and the tears began to tumble from his own. Zane fell upon his father's chest and their arms locked around each other as both wept unashamedly.

Titus stood back, watching carefully as Erin took a pace back also, her nose wrinkling at the display of emotion.

"I thought such terrible things about you!" Zane cried. "But I was wrong, wasn't I? You saved that boy, didn't you?"

"Yes," his father whispered hoarsely. "I've been bringing them up here for years. Any time I could get one away."

Titus narrowed his eyes. "But you hurt them too."

The doctor released Zane from his embrace and sat up shakily. He looked down at his chest, confused, but then shook his head. "It's very complicated," he replied. "I don't have time to explain now. If I stay here any longer, Eve may get caught."

"You and Eve are working together?" Erin asked and he nodded.

"I couldn't do this without her." He clambered to his feet, Zane supporting him as he found his balance once more. Even though his wounds had been healed, it was clear he'd lost a lot of blood from the way he swayed when upright.

"Are you one of the Unders gang or not?" Erin demanded, her stance shifting as if readying herself to take aim once more. "You can't be both."

"I'm not one of them!" the doctor retorted. "I hate what they're doing!"

"Then why help them?" Erin threw back at him.

The doctor struggled to contain himself. "Because they force me to!" he spat. "If I don't do what they tell me to do, they will come up here and kill Miri and my son. Don't for a minute think that I have done any of these experiments willingly." The sudden rush of rage began to ebb as he swayed again. Zane quickly tucked himself under his father's arm and held him up. "I'm no monster," he whispered as he struggled to stay on his feet. "Please, son, don't think that I'm one of them."

"I don't," Zane replied and shot a warning look at his friends. "That's why you left Mum that day, isn't it?"

The man nodded, his head drooping. "They took me the day she told me she was pregnant."

There was an awkward silence as the three children took it all in. Zane didn't know whether to be overjoyed or upset.

"I have to get back to Eve," the doctor said. "But I'll come back, son."

Titus stepped forward. "You have to help us to stop them," he said, and the man nodded.

"I will, gladly," he replied. "I can't do it without help from people up here, but if you know people that are willing to take a risk …"

Titus nodded. "Yes, we do. Just tell us how to stop them."

"Two nights from now, I'll come back here at the same time," he replied, "And I'll tell you all you need to know."

"Everything will be okay now, Dad," Zane said hopefully. "I'll tell Mum and she'll be so glad and –"

"No," Shannon interrupted. "Don't tell her you saw me, not until this is all over."

"But she thinks that you're one of them!" Zane protested.

"Just wait until this is done," his father insisted. "If something happens to me, I don't want her to lose me twice." He placed a hand on Zane's shoulder and squeezed gently. "If I get the chance, I want her to hear the truth about me from my own lips. And if that's not meant to be … then you can speak for me." He glanced at Titus. "Gather all the help you can. You're going to need it."

Chapter 31
PLANS ARE MADE

By the time of the meeting, Titus was exhausted. Nothing about arranging it had been simple. Arguments about why they should meet, who would be there, where it should be held, constant bickering and posturing. Through this muddy frustration, his determination pierced like an arrow set on its target. He was so close, so close to understanding enough to destroy those who had hurt his sister. Those who had hurt him.

Zane had helped him as far as he could, but he'd been distracted by the anticipation of speaking to his father again and the sheer magnitude of the secret he was keeping from his mother. Several times, when he had heard her twisting and turning in bed, her mind too fraught with emotion to permit rest, he had almost gone to her. He wanted to reassure her, to let her know that the man she'd loved so much hadn't become the villain she thought him now.

It was dark when they assembled: the children, Luthor, and Jay. They met at the end of the street in which Shannon had been found, the end farthest from the heart of Jay's territory but still within sight of it.

Both Jay and Luthor arrived prepared for conflict, the Hunter in full armour. Erin was also armoured, on her father's insistence. They were very close to true no man's land, where no protection whatsoever existed against wild beasts and scavengers, some of the human variety.

They waited in an uncomfortable silence, the moon only partially full. It cast enough light in the breaks between clouds to outline in silver Jay's thumbs, hooked over the handles of his twin blades, and the tight grip of Luthor's fist around the riser of his longbow.

The creak of un-oiled hinges alerted them to the doctor's arrival. Before any misunderstandings could occur, Zane rushed to his father when he emerged from the shadows down the street. He was relieved to see how much better his father looked than the night they were last together. Their embrace was brief and tight as Shannon was clearly pressed for time once more.

"How long do you have?" Zane asked as he drew his father into the circle.

"A few minutes."

"Then tell us sommat first," Jay said in that voice, the one that always made Zane nervous. "Why should we trust you? What's in this for you?"

"I can't make you trust me," Shannon replied. "That's impossible in the time we have now. But I can tell you that I have everything to gain from the end of Hex. My freedom, my life, and the same for Miri and my son."

Luthor snorted. "You walked out just now freely enough."

"Not without huge risk," Shannon said patiently. "If they realise I'm gone, there will be repercussions."

"We don't have time to debate whether he's trustworthy or not," Titus spoke up. "*I* know he's sincere and that's enough for me."

"It may be enough for you," Luthor began but Erin touched his arm to interrupt him.

"Titus is good at this sort of thing," she said quietly.

Seeing Luthor's anger at Erin's intervention, Titus spoke quickly to divert his attention. "Where is Hex based and how do we get in?"

Shannon's eyebrows shot up. "You want to get *into* Hex?"

Jay, Luthor, and Titus nodded in synchrony. "It's the only way to be sure we got 'em," Jay explained. "Gotta get right in their patch and trash it. If we don't, they'll just keep doing what they're doin' to the other kids down there. How many other kids are there?"

"How many Guardians are there?" Luthor asked before Shannon could reply.

"Wait," he held up his hands. "Too many questions. Let's look at this in some kind of order."

Titus nodded at that. "Tell us where they are, that's a good place to start."

"Hex is contained in several old underground tunnels, predominantly the Piccadilly and Jubilee Lines," Shannon replied. "They're the deepest lines and the easiest to defend. The government was building underground bunkers extending from Westminster adjacent to the Jubilee Line for a long time before It happened."

"Them funny clothes they wear," Jay spoke up, "That's to stop 'em dyin', right?" Shannon nodded. "So do they wear 'em all the time?"

"No," Shannon replied. "All entrances to Hex are hermetically sealed, with rigorous decontamination procedures for any Guardians or scientists who come up to the surface."

"What does that mean?" Erin asked.

"That the doors are sealed so tight that air can't get through," Shannon explained. "When people come up here, they get washed lots so the bad stuff in the air doesn't stick to them."

"They do that to you?" Luthor asked but Shannon shook his head.

"No, I don't get to go into Hex proper. They keep me in the same spoke as the children. We all have an immunity to the virus, so they don't have to follow such strict measures for us, and that saves a lot of electricity, water, and chemicals."

"To keep the air clean, supply their suits with oxygen, those guns they use, that all takes electricity," Luthor commented.

"Where do they get it from?"

"Green Park," Shannon replied. "It's been cleared in the centre and is full of solar panels and wind turbines. All renewable sources, all out of sight from the streets around it. I know where the back-up generators are too."

All the assembled, save Luthor, and to a lesser extent Titus, looked somewhat blank at this discussion.

"The power from Green Park also runs Hex, I take it?" Luthor continued and Shannon nodded again.

"Air filtration, purification and recycling, waste disposal, door seals, everything," he elaborated. "It's an amazing system. Entirely self-sufficient and sealed from the outside world."

"The people in Hex," Titus was frowning, "They can't live up here because the virus would kill them ... and the electricity from Green Park stops the bad air getting in ... so it seems there's only one thing to do."

Luthor was nodding as he spoke, having come to the same conclusion. "Destroy the power supply so the door seals will fail and the rest takes care of itself."

Shannon nodded slowly. "Yes, I suppose you're right."

"Hang on, them Giants – I mean the Guardians – they'll still be able to breathe up 'ere," Jay interjected.

"We pick them off with arrows," Luthor replied. "The suits only need to be pierced once for them to die quickly."

"If you want to do this, tonight is perfect," Shannon advised. "Radley is collecting supplies and samples from St Mary's hospital and they've doubled the Guardians looking after her because of what happened with Lyssa."

"Excellent, then it should be tonight," Luthor said. "The Red Lady is keen for the Unders to be removed as a threat and has placed all of our Hunters under my command. I will post our best archers at various high points, and when the seals fail –"

"Wait!" Zane cried, and the group turned to him, noticing for the first time the look of total horror on his face. "If we break the door seals, won't everyone in Hex die?"

Titus blinked at him. "Yes. That's the point."

Zane's jaw was slack. "But … but that's terrible. How many people live there?"

When his son's eyes fell on him, Shannon's face showed the first signs of guilt. "About forty or so."

"Zane, they're monsters!" Erin exclaimed. "They took Lyssa, and they put horrible black stuff in children and cut them and –"

"Do all of the people in Hex do that?" Zane pressed his father, and watched him shake his head. "Then we can't do this. We can't kill them all. In fact, we shouldn't try to kill anyone – we should try to talk to them."

"Are you mad?" Jay snorted. "They don't talk, they shoot lightning! Remember?" He lifted his shirt to reveal the lurid scarring left by the burn on his torso. "They didn't talk when they did this. They just shot me, killed my Boys and nicked Titus' sister. You forgot all that?!"

"No, of course not," Zane sighed. "But can't we find a way to try to talk to them? Dr Radley – the one that Titus swapped for Lyssa – she didn't seem horrible or violent. How do we know that there aren't other nice people down there too?"

"We do not have time for this," Luthor growled. "It's irrelevant."

"It's not!" Zane retorted. "Titus, when we first met, you thought that me and Mum were bad people – you thought everyone was bad. But now you have us as friends, and you know people in gangs and that they aren't as bad as you thought either."

"So what?" Erin asked, before Titus could reply.

"So, it could be the same with the Unders!" Zane exclaimed.

Titus stared down at the ground, considering his argument. He was swayed by it for a few moments, but the doubts slowly crept back in.

"Zane, you cannot pick and choose who of them will live and who will die," Luthor stated. "This is a war."

"I see where you're coming from, son," Shannon said softly, "But if you want to stop what they are doing to the children, what they are forcing me to do, then you have to accept that others will die. To shut them down, we have to shut all of it down. All of it."

"But why do they do those things to the boys?" Zane asked, shaking with tension.

"Cos they're sick in the 'ead," Jay muttered.

"They're trying to find a cure," Shannon replied. "And they think that it's right to get that cure, no matter what the cost."

"But ... but what if we found that cure!" Zane exclaimed. "What if they didn't have to do that anymore? Then they could be our friends!"

"Shit, Zane, not everyone in the world can be your friend!" Jay yelled and the boy fell silent. "We gotta go in and take 'em down. Else we'll never be safe. Never. I gotta protect my Boys, and I gotta get the others that are down there out, and if some people die, well then fine. If they're the kind of people that let that kind of thing happen and don't say nuffin' against it, then they deserve it anyway."

"They've kept us apart all your life, Zane," Shannon urged. "They said they would kill you and Miri if I didn't do what I was told. These aren't the kind of people that care about making friends."

Zane turned to Titus, searching his friend's face for any signs of solidarity. Titus looked up from the ground, feeling that gaze, as a flash of Squeak's memories pulsed through him. In the next moment a flash of Lyssa's scarred body, the way she could barely walk, and the doubts were swept away like leaves by winter gales. His thumb traced the cut in his palm. He pressed it, feeling the sting.

"This is the only way," he stated coldly.

Crushed, Zane looked from Titus to his father and back again. "I can't do this," he said, eyes brimming with tears. "I swore an oath to save people, not kill them."

He spun on his heels and ran back towards Jay's territory, the group watching him go. Shannon took a step after him but Luthor grabbed his shoulder. "Let him run back to his mother," he said. "We need to plan and move tonight."

Titus watched Zane run around the corner. "I'm sorry, Zane," he whispered beneath his breath. "But I swore an oath too."

Chapter 32
THE EXPERIMENT

Three streets away, halfway between Jay's territory and the garden, Zane stopped and slumped against a wall, shaking.

"This is wrong, this is wrong," he muttered, covering his face with grimy hands and crying into them. He felt helpless and distraught; one moment he resolved to run to his mother and ask her for help, the next he almost went back to the others to try once more to persuade them to find another way.

Another way.

A thought struck him, one of those thoughts that is so big, so life-changing that even though it's terrifying it won't let go. It was so big that it filled him, making him drop his hands to his sides and his heart thud deep in him like a pestle against the mortar of his chest. He tried to forget it, but that was impossible. He tried to change it, to wriggle away from it, but he knew there was only one thing to do.

"I'll show the Unders there's another way," he whispered to the moon. "I'll show them why they don't need to hurt the children any more. Then no-one else will have to die."

Then he was running, his body moving faster than his fear could catch up. He knew where Radley was, he'd heard his father say it. If he could find her and show her that he could heal people, then maybe together they could find a cure to the disease. If they could find a cure, then the experiments would stop and the threat would be gone. His imagination laid tracks into the future that carried him towards a peace for everyone that would begin tonight: Radley would tell Hex to stop the experiments and release the children, and he would find the others and stop them before they got to Green Park. It would take time for Luthor to gather the Hunters and get them into position, plenty of time for him to convince Radley and stop all of this.

The hospital wasn't far out of Jay's territory, and he had seen it marked on the map that tracked all of the Giant sightings. Zane had never been out at night alone, yet his mind didn't have time to be frightened.

As he sprinted down shadow-filled alleyways, he remembered how frightened he'd been that night at the hospital with Dev. How he'd thought it was a terrible Giant with huge metal feet that would crush him. And all along it had been a woman in strange clothes, just as frightened as he had been.

The hospital came into sight and he slowed down, the fear now slamming into him from behind and making him shiver. He almost turned back, but then he thought of all of the people in the Unders dying and it kept him moving forward. He crouched down and kept in the shadows, watching for any signs of the scientist.

He saw a flash of light from a second floor window that was instantly recognisable: Radley's torch. From the way it moved, it looked like she was coming down a stairwell with long windows. He stopped and hunkered down, waiting for her to emerge, biting his teeth hard together to stop them chattering.

It seemed like an eternity until she came out, the familiar metal clang of her boots ricocheting off the nearby buildings. She had a case in her hand, like before, and he could hear the wheeze and click of the oxygen being drawn in.

She moved down the street, walking slowly and carefully around the rusting wrecks, taking care not to get snagged on anything. Zane stayed down as long as he could bear, listening carefully for Guardians, but none could be seen. He waited until she was a matter of metres away, took a deep breath, and stepped out into her path.

She yelped in surprise, dropping the case, and in moments black-clad figures materialised as if from the night air itself. They closed around Zane as he spread his hands in front of himself, trying to appear as non-threatening as he could.

"Dr Radley!" he said hurriedly, the fear making his voice crack. "I'm Zane. I want to talk. I won't hurt you."

He could hear the wheeze and click more rapidly now, her eyes wide as they peered through the glass visor at him.

"Down on the ground!" one of the Guardians yelled. "Down on the ground now!"

"Please, let me talk to you!" Zane begged, painfully aware of the guns being pointed at him.

Radley studied him for a moment and then said, "Hold on, hold on, don't shoot him. He's not here for a fight."

"Check the area, secure it," said the one who had yelled at Zane, and half of the Guardians broke away, fanning out with bright torches. Never taking his eyes off Zane, he said, "Keep your hands out in front of you, don't move."

"I'm by myself," Zane said in a quavering voice. "I wanted to speak to you."

"How did you know I was here?" she asked, beginning to look more intrigued than terrified.

"It doesn't matter," Zane answered, looking at the lightning guns trained on him. "What matters is that I think I can help you to find a cure to the disease that killed everyone."

Her surprise was evident, even though he couldn't see all of her face. "Well, I wasn't expecting that," she commented.

"I know about the experiments you do on the children, and I thought that if we found a cure, you wouldn't have to do that anymore, and then we could stop being afraid of each other."

There was an awkward pause. "Children?" Radley finally asked, and then smiled and said, "Oh! You mean the orphans! The carriers. You must mean the children who are carriers that they take care of in one of the spokes."

Zane swallowed, his tongue sticking to the roof of his mouth. "You don't know about what they do to them?"

Radley frowned. "You make it sound like they do something sinister there. I'm sure they don't." Zane didn't argue. "Did you say your name was Zane?"

Zane nodded.

"Look, Zane, I don't have a long time on my air left. Tell me something I can take back to Hex, something I can use to discuss this with them."

"We can take him with us," the Guardian said. "Secure him outside of the clean area, in the spoke with the carriers."

"No!" Zane and Radley said in unison.

"No," repeated Radley. "He came here to talk, he hasn't threatened me or any of you, so back off. He's just a boy for God's sake."

Zane chewed his lip, watching the exchange. He couldn't think of anything that he could tell her that she would believe, let alone anyone in Hex. Now he was here, talking to her, the idea he'd had before seemed significantly less plausible. But now he was committed.

She looked back at him. "Well? What can you tell me that Hex won't know about the virus already?"

"It isn't about the virus," Zane began, desperately trying to think of how to say what he needed to. "It's ... it's about me. I can heal people, I can make them better, and maybe, I could heal people with the virus."

She rolled her eyes. "Look, this isn't wrapping a doc leaf on a sting. What do you know about medicine?"

"Um, quite a bit actually," he replied in a small voice. "More than you might think. And I didn't mean that I do first aid. I mean that I heal people ... in a ..." Erin suddenly came to his mind and he said, "In a weird way."

She sighed and looked at the guardian. "Let's go."

"Wait!" Zane shouted. "I'll prove it! Shine the light onto my hand." When a torch was trained on his hand, he moved it slowly towards the nearest car. With a swift downwards thrust, he sliced his palm open on a jagged piece of metal, making Radley gasp. "I know this looks weird," Zane said, wincing, "But please, please let me show you why I'm doing this."

He held his bleeding hand in front of him, and in the yellow light of the torch they all watched as Zane dabbed away some of the blood with his sleeve to reveal the wound. More blood began to seep out, but then the gashed skin began to close and seal itself in an impossible way.

Zane held up his hand, palm towards Radley. "That's what I mean when I say I can heal people."

Radley frowned. "It's a trick."

Zane shook his head. "No. It's not. I can do it for other people too, if they're hurt. But I can't show you that."

"Look I have no idea why you're doing this but –"

"We're taking him in," the Guardian interrupted. "Hex wants him brought in now." At Radley's incredulous expression, he tapped a small device on the side of his helmet. "Live feed back to base. Hex saw it–they want him in now." He moved closer to Zane, finger curled around the trigger of his gun. "Hands on top of your head, no sudden movements. I'll tell you where to walk. You do anything else, I'll fry you."

A thousand times on that journey Zane regretted his decision and then immediately persuaded himself that he was still doing the right thing. He clung to that idea like a child to a rock, watching the tide rising around him. He tried hard to remember the route they were taking but lost concentration as he battled his fear. The streets, shadowed and silent, all began to look the same.

At one point he was told to shut his eyes and he heard a door opening. He was told to walk forward, still with eyes shut, which made the fear bubble over into terror. When he heard a scraping sound behind him and the sound of a lock, his breath caught in his throat, but then he was told he could open his eyes again and he found himself, and his escorts, at the top of a dingy, narrow spiral staircase, lit only by their torches. Radley went ahead, making slow progress with her large boots. Zane was grateful that the pace was slow as his knees were trembling and his legs barely felt like his own.

The staircase was steep, and it felt like they went a long way underground. At the bottom there was a wider space, but he could see very little of the walls, being forced to look only where they shone their torch light.

A series of heavy metal doors were each unlocked and locked behind them, and then one of the Guardians pressed the tip of the gun into his back and told him to shut his eyes again. He did so and heard a very curious sound unlike anything he had heard before, melodious somehow, like his mother's singing, but not sounding like a human voice at all. The sound of an electronic keypad made no sense to him; he didn't even have a name for it.

A hiss, then a loud thunk, and the barrel of the gun in the small of his back pushed him forward. He was told to wait as the hiss and the thunk sound happened again in reverse. He wondered if they had trapped a snake in a heavy door but thought it better not to ask.

This process happened once more and then he was told he could open his eyes again. He found himself, Dr Radley, and three Guardians in a corridor unlike any he had ever seen. The walls were grey and smooth, the ceiling and walls blending into one another in one graceful arched curve. Doors were spaced at regular intervals, and he could see at least ten off the tunnel that stretched ahead. Each had a number painted onto the wall above it, and to the right of every door was a metal board with a piece of paper clipped to it with the same name at the top: Eve, followed by a number. Beneath each of these was a pad with numbers on it set into the wall, the use of which was entirely beyond Zane. But it wasn't that which took his attention. It was the light.

It shone from strips set into the ceiling, glowing so brightly he couldn't look directly at them. They fascinated him and yet frightened him at the same time, alien and artificial to a boy who had never lived in a world with electricity.

A door opened at the far end with the same click and hiss, and then several suited figures stepped through into the corridor. Zane heard Radley make a noise, perhaps of surprise but it was hard to tell. One of the figures was dressed in a suit like hers, but with some kind of symbol on the upper right chest; the other figures looked like Guardians. He could tell the one with the symbol was a man as he was taller than Radley, and that perhaps his hair was grey, but not much more. From the way the Guardians fanned around him, he seemed to be in charge. Zane recognised that behaviour from the gangs up above.

Zane was pushed along the corridor to meet them half-way, Radley staying near him. As he passed the doors, he took the opportunity to glance at the clipboards. He managed to pick out what looked like a patient's name, a temperature chart, and a couple of notes, but the writing was too small to read quickly.

"Doctor Radley," the man said. "It seems you've had another eventful evening up above."

"Yes, sir," she replied, and Zane could hear the tension in her voice, even through the helmet. "But I'm not sure this is anything that requires your attention. I mean, I'm not sure I believed what I saw."

He raised a hand and she stopped talking. Zane shook, gripping the edges of his sleeves tight in his hands. This man acted like a gang leader. Maybe he was the leader of the Unders gang. Maybe he would say that Zane was in their territory and then …

"It's not for you to decide what I should see or not, Doctor," the man chided, breaking Zane out of his fearful thoughts.

"No, sir, sorry," Radley replied nervously. "Shall I go to Decontamination?"

"No no, stay here. I'm sure you're just as curious as I. Besides, you've never seen this spoke, have you?"

"No sir."

"Then I'm sure it will be an enlightening evening for you." He switched his attention to Zane, peering at him through the visor as one would peer into a shop window full of curiosities. Zane could see now that his hair definitely was grey, and that he was old, at least as old as Callum. "Come with me."

He went to the nearest door and as he tapped numbers on the keypad, Zane read the clipboard. At the top of the page, printed in letters made by a machine rather than a hand, was "Eve 17. 15 year old female. Batch-21-trial-3" and it was all he could do to stop himself from being sick.

A loud click sounded from the door frame and the door swung open. Inside was a featureless room, containing nothing more than a wheeled hospital bed, a set of metal drawers, and a chair. It was brightly lit and smelt strange to Zane, his sense of smell not accustomed to chemical cleaners.

The man entered while Zane and Radley were shepherded in by the Guardians, some of whom remained outside as the room wasn't big enough to contain all of them. Just as Zane had feared, the girl he had spoken to in the dream room lay in the bed, stirring in a deep sleep. He noted the drip in her arm, recognising it from the medical textbooks he had pored over for years, and the bruising on the inside of her elbows just like Lyssa had.

The noise of the heavy boots woke her, and Eve struggled into an upright position, her gaze immediately falling onto Zane.

Before there was even the chance that anyone could guess that they knew each other, the man flicked a hand towards her and told the Guardians, "Hold her down."

"What are you doing?" Zane shrieked as two of them pressed down on her shoulders and ankles.

"Performing an experiment," the man replied calmly as he opened the top drawer with a key and carefully removed a large handled scalpel, locking the drawers again afterwards. At the sight of it, Eve began to whimper and struggle as a sheen of cold sweat shone on her forehead.

Zane instinctively moved towards her, only to feel one of the guns in his back again. "Don't," was all the Guardian needed to say, and the threat of the lightning froze him in his shoes.

The man held the scalpel above her arm, poised to cut, and then scrutinised Zane. When he was sure that Zane was watching, he sliced into her arm and she screamed out as blood emerged and chased after the blade.

Tears sprang from Zane's eyes as he watched Eve writhe in pain. "Don't, don't hurt her!" he begged and the man removed the blade, the incision several inches long and bleeding profusely.

"This is sick," Radley gasped, putting an arm out to the wall to steady herself.

"This is science, Doctor Radley," he replied. "Now we'll see if he's telling the truth."

"I need to touch her," Zane wept and the man beckoned him over, stepping away from him as he approached but staying close enough to watch.

With his tears dripping onto her clammy skin, Zane touched her arm on either side of the wound and pressed it together, then focused in that unearthly way. In moments, the cut skin closed and knitted itself together again, leaving only the drying blood as any clue that the harm had been done.

Both Zane and Eve panted for breath. Eve caught hold

of his hand and they squeezed tight, their eyes meeting and exchanging the fear they both felt.

"Interesting," the man finally said, prodding at the place where the wound had been. He stared at Zane, examining him as one would a slide beneath a microscope. "You said up above that 'maybe' you could heal people with the virus."

Zane couldn't speak; his mind was reeling. It was only a movement from one of the Guardians towards him that shook him out of his paralysis. "I ... I don't know."

"Have you ever healed anything other than wounds?"

Zane blinked. "No ... no I haven't. People don't get sick very often."

The man nodded. "The ones up above have remarkable immune systems."

"Oh my God, oh my God," Radley muttered, over and over again, clearly in a state of shock at what she'd seen. "It wasn't a trick. Oh my God."

The slightest frown crossed the man's face as she drew his attention, then it was gone. "I think it's time for the next experiment," he said, moving over to her, but continuing to stare at Zane. "After all, it seems to me that there's only one way to see if you can cure the virus."

There was barely a movement. They all heard it before they saw what he'd done. The quiet hiss of escaping air as his scalpel pierced Radley's suit, and then the sound of her screaming.

Chapter 33

INHERITANCE

The Guardians pinning Eve to the trolley threw themselves against the wall, forgetting their duty in the process. The other Guardian, the one who had been cool all along, backed off a few steps to the opposite corner of the room, leaving Radley to stumble into the far corner, clawing at the walls like a wild animal trying to escape a new cage.

Eve curled into a ball on the bed, covering her ears and head as tight as she could. Even the gang leader stepped away, taking care to hold the scalpel as far from the flailing arms of Radley as he could.

Zane, aghast at what the man had done, watched dumb-struck for several heartbeats before his gift focused his attention onto something else. Even though he didn't want to see it, his vision began to penetrate through the suit into her body and then into her lungs. Now he could see why her chest heaved, why she seemed to be gasping for breath; tiny blood vessels were spontaneously bursting, releasing blood into the spaces where there should be air. The virus was making her drown in her own blood.

Then he was moving; without another thought he launched himself at her, planting his hands on her shoulders in an effort to hold her still and make that connection with her body. At the contact, her hands grasped his arms desperately and her eyes, bulging with panic, bored into him through the glass visor. It began to steam up, then a cough splattered drop-lets of blood onto the inside of the helmet and her legs buckled beneath her.

Zane fell to his knees, maintaining the contact by half holding her up. Everything else, everyone else in the room ceased to exist as all of his consciousness worked within her. As if he had a thousand deft fingertips moving at once, he mended every ruptured blood vessel he caught sight of as fast as he conceived of it, the healing being so miniscule. But as fast as he healed one, another burst as the virus continued to attack, and all the while her breathing became more and more laboured.

He paused only to force some of the fluid out of the lungs with a swift upward motion of his hand, blood erupting out of her with a violent choking cough. She breathed in again, momentarily relieved as he returned his attention to stopping the bleeding, the man watching intently all the while as he fingered the handle of the scalpel.

Zane's body shivered with the exertion as his mind ignored the demands placed upon it and pressed on, intent on saving her life. He alternated a few seconds of fighting the bleeding with an occasional evacuation of the fluid, giving her vital breaths. But soon, for every vessel he healed, two would burst until more blood seeped into the lungs than he could push out in time. Then his own body, unable to withstand the effort any longer, made his head spin and muscles turn to paper.

Radley's body fell away from him as his vision pulled out of her into the harshly lit room. He watched her eyes rolling backwards, barely visible behind the glass panel slick with blood. He was dimly aware of an awful gurgling cough and then nothing, as his own vision tunnelled to a grey speck and he collapsed next to the dead woman.

After the terrible noise of her death had passed, the room was quiet again, save for the respirators of the Guardians and their leader. Eve stayed tucked in a ball but moved enough to peer out from between her shaking knees.

"Is he dead too?" one of the Guardians asked.

The man bent slightly to hold the scalpel blade an inch from Zane's mouth. At the sight of the mist condensing onto it, he stood and said, "No, he's alive." He looked around the room at the men, still pressed against the walls. "Have the cleaners remove the body and sterilise the room. Move her." He pointed at Eve. "Down the corridor." He looked down at Zane as one of the Guardians began to whisper the orders into his mouthpiece. "Put him on a gurney and take him to a high security cell. Have blood and DNA samples taken. And be careful with him. I don't want him damaged."

"They'll definitely be dead?" Jay peered through the doorway. His burning torch lit the black stairway slanting deep into the ground.

"The main power supply was cut, and the fail-safes," Shannon replied. "The virus incapacitates in less than a minute, kills within three to four minutes, if that. The seals were breached," he checked his watch, "over an hour ago and there just aren't that many suits and oxygen supplies down there."

Erin still held an arrow notched as she stood behind the men and Titus as they peered into the entrance to the Unders. The wave of Guardians who had emerged when the power went down had been despatched quickly by the Red Lady's Hunters, but that didn't mean that one wasn't biding what little time he had left on his air supply in the hope of catching them unaware. She watched her father returning from his sweep of the street and noticed how he nodded slightly when he saw her still alert. The adrenaline still coursed through her and his approval only added to the buzz.

"So the ones who's got them Giant suits," Jay continued. "They'll be dead too by now?"

Shannon sighed. "Yes. There may be one or two with spare tanks, but I doubt they'll be quietly waiting to defend one entrance after all this time."

Jay hung back, wily after years of fighting the Gardners, and tossed the torch into the blackness ahead of him. An arc of lightning rippled up from below and he yelped in surprise, hurling himself further back.

Luthor ducked into a crouch and fired an arrow down the stairwell. There was a tell-tale hiss and a soft thud as the arrow hit its target and Luthor nodded to himself in satisfaction.

"You said they'd be dead!" Jay yelled, shoving at Shannon in anger.

Titus shut his eyes as Shannon defended himself against Jay's insults. Learning everything he had about the Unders, and seeing what they did to his sister, had built up a large tank of fury inside him. But all of the death and ripples of distress sensed on another level had worn him down, depleting that reserve until he was left numb.

"You ok?" Erin whispered in his ear, pulling him out of himself.

He nodded. Then shook his head. "Maybe Zane was right," he whispered back, instantly regretting it.

"Zane doesn't live in the real world," she replied softly. "He doesn't know what it's like outside of his mum's garden. The Unders are worse than the Gardners. The world's better off without them."

Titus nodded but said nothing, not trusting the sound of his own voice.

"Remember Eve," Erin added, and then noticed the others beginning to climb down the stairs. "We're saving her and the other children, and this is the only way."

It was enough to bring back his resolve. Besides, he reasoned as he crept into the darkness, it was too late now, and as Lyssa had taught him a long time ago, regret did nothing useful.

Jay retrieved his torch at the bottom of the steps, rejuvenating the guttering flame. He looked at the gun.

Shannon followed his eyes and shook his head. "It's run out of power," he said, pointing at a dull red light next to a charge symbol. Jay swore beneath his breath.

Titus was relieved to hear that; he didn't like the thought of Jay with one of those guns. He found a wind-up torch near the Guardian and switched it on. The five of them moved slowly into the tunnel, soon reaching stout metal doors that were slightly ajar.

"These would have been hermetically sealed," Shannon whispered.

Titus saw the arch of the ceiling, the smoothness of the walls and a snippet of the dream he'd had about Lyssa when she had been a prisoner down here returned to him. He took a deep breath, pushing the memory away to focus on the silent corridor and its looming shadows instead.

Zane woke as if leaping out of a fire, muscles straining and heart racing. He was sitting up before he registered where he was or what was happening.

By the time he had the wherewithal to look around the room, he realised that something had scraped his arm at the elbow and that a substance had been forced into his veins. He just knew it, just like he knew he was drawing breath.

He had to squint; a bright light was shining in his eyes, then it moved away. He realised that the room he was in was dark, but that one of the people from the Unders was in the room with him, holding a torch. He could hear them drawing on the oxygen tank. In. Out. In. Out. He couldn't understand how he could feel so alert and yet so exhausted all at once. His disorientation began to fade and he realised he was sitting on something soft, a bed like Eve's.

"I didn't want to wake you that way." He recognised the voice; it was the gang leader. "It was a necessity. You may feel rather strange, it was adrenaline and caffeine and a few other stimulants. I need you to be awake."

Zane blinked at the floating disc of torchlight, unable to see much of the man in the darkness. "Why? What's going on?"

"It's finished, you see. And I need to tell you what you are inheriting."

"What has finished? What does inheriting mean?"

A sigh and then the scrape of a chair. The torch was placed on the floor, illuminating more of the man as he perched on it whilst casting strange shadows onto the featureless walls.

"Hex is finished. The people up above have cut the power supply, undoubtedly with help from someone inside. The auxiliary power supply and back-up system have failed too."

"No!" Zane cried out and slammed his hands down on the bed. "No, no! I tried to stop it! I wanted to stop it!"

"Shhh," the man said softly. "There's been enough screaming and crying and begging and regrets. Let's be civilised at least for these last precious minutes." He waited until Zane sat back again. "Good. What's your name?"

The question seemed so normal and yet so unusual in the context that it took a moment for Zane to answer him.

"Unusual name," he commented. "My name is Lieutenant Colonel Roper. Or Doctor Roper, if that is easier, as that's also true."

Zane did nothing to disguise his repulsion. "You're a doctor? Haven't *any* of Hex's doctors taken the oath?"

Roper frowned briefly, then made the connection. "Oh, that oath. Yes," he chuckled bitterly. "All of us did, in our idealistic youth."

"Then how could you kill her?!" Zane yelled, his response exaggerated by the drugs coursing through him.

Another sigh. "Necessity. I had to know what you could do after seeing your remarkable feat with the cut. Killing one more makes so little difference."

"One more ... how many people have you killed?"

He looked up at Zane, his features shadowed by the angle of the torch, making his eyes look like empty sockets. "All of them. All of the people that died from the virus. I made it, you see. I made it, I released it, and I killed them all. After one has killed several billion people, one more is barely noticeable."

Zane felt sick. His body felt unreal, all of it felt unreal. He pushed himself down the gurney until his back hit the wall, as far away from Roper as he could put himself.

"Don't you want to know why?" Roper asked after letting Zane's silence hang. Zane didn't reply, couldn't reply; his mind couldn't find the words for him to articulate all of the things he felt at once, all of the questions bombarding him.

"Strange," Roper sighed, "I never thought I would tell anyone. I never felt the need, never saw the point really. But here I am, using the last of my air, confessing to a boy I don't even know."

"Don't you feel guilty?" Zane finally managed, his curiosity finally surfacing, like a Bloomsbury Boy compelled to poke at a dead rat.

"No," Roper said flatly. "No, I really don't feel an ounce of guilt. Nor regret." He paused, as if waiting to see if an emotion was going to bubble up within. "Perhaps a slight sense of disappointment," he finally concluded.

"But ... but why did you want to kill everyone?!" Zane asked, barely able to conceive of such an act.

"Oh, I didn't," Roper replied. "Only some. The blacks, the Arabs. Only them." His mouth twisted. "Foreign filth."

Zane struggled to comprehend what he meant. "Do you mean the people who had different coloured skin?"

"Yes," Roper said. "I created a very selective virus. Only meant to kill certain races. It was very elegant and worked beautifully for a few weeks. Excellent transmission rate, very swift."

Zane swallowed down the bile that had risen in his throat. "How can you talk like that?" he whispered. "Like you made something beautiful?"

"But I did," Roper replied quickly. "It was beautiful. A beautiful, elegant solution to all of our society's problems."

"How can killing people be beautiful?"

"You can't possibly understand," Roper muttered sadly. "You weren't alive then—you don't know what it was like, what they were doing to our country!" His hand balled into a fist and he leant forward, swept up in the first emotional reaction that Zane had seen. "Something had to be done! The government was pathetic, too obsessed with political correctness. Then the terrorism started, the wars ... but I knew what I had to do. I created Hex, started it off as a government project." He guffawed. "And they paid for it out of taxpayers' money without the faintest idea! They just trusted me, and they were so damn afraid they didn't stop to think what else Hex could be used for. A bunker to protect against terrorism one day, an island of civilisation the next. Hah!"

Zane pressed himself against the wall as Roper ranted, not fully understanding everything he said. He didn't know the meaning of words such as terrorism, government, or taxpayers.

The speech ended and Roper came back to himself, looked back at Zane. "You couldn't possibly understand." He sighed again. "It mutated. The virus. Began to kill other people, ones I didn't intend to remove. And do you know why?!" He stood, jabbed a finger towards Zane. "Because they had bred!" he shouted. "Because they had spawned half breeds and it ruined everything. The virus crossed over to the pure race because of them, damn them!"

Zane slid himself into the corner, the bed shaking beneath him. He said nothing, waiting for the outburst to pass, hoping desperately to get out of this room alive.

Roper calmed himself. "I'm sorry," he said finally, seating himself down once more. "I'm sorry. I didn't mean to shout."

An awkward moment passed, until he said: "That's your inheritance, young man." Seeing the boy's confusion, he continued. "What I leave behind to you. An imperfect world. I've spent all these years trying to find a cure to what my creation had become, but it seems that the savages on the surface finally won. At least they're white. Such a pity you didn't come to us sooner. I think you may have been the key to the cure. You almost saved her, almost."

Zane shook, with rage, with exhaustion, with fear. "You never should've done that! You're not a real doctor!"

"And what exactly is a *real* doctor?" Roper scoffed. "What do you know about doctors?!"

"I know about the Hippocratic oath!" Zane yelled back, jumping off the bed to stand in front of the man. "I know that doctors swear to do everything they can to keep people alive, not kill them!"

"Who told you that?" Roper smirked, amused at the young man's zeal. "One of the savages up there?"

"No!" Zane retorted. "I found out myself, and I took that oath, so I know what it means! You broke it, not just with Radley, but millions of times over! You're the worst, the most ... the most ..."

Roper stopped smirking, studied Zane's conviction, watched him struggle to express his hatred. "You really took that oath. You really believe in it, don't you?"

"Yes," Zane replied, holding his hands up to his temples to try to ease the pressure in his pounding head.

"You swore to always save a life?"

"Yes, always."

Roper smiled coldly. "Then if you value saving a person's life above all else, save mine."

Chapter 34
HIDDEN GUESTS

"Did you hear that?"

At Titus' whisper, the group stopped, immediately switching off the clockwork torches they had collected en route. All strained to listen above their own heartbeats, the pitch blackness of the tunnel seeming to close in around them.

"Don't 'ear nothin'," Jay finally said. "What did it sound like?"

"Someone crying," Titus whispered back.

All that could be heard was the slight creaking of Luthor and Erin's bows as they pulled them taut, ready to fire at the first sign of anyone approaching.

Titus drew in a deep breath, focused. He was certain there had been something. In his stillness he realised that it hadn't been a sound he'd detected, but that sense of Other, of a person nearby who hadn't needed to make a noise for him to sense them. Without hearing them, he knew they were crying. Without seeing them, he knew they were cowering in some kind of nook, with a weapon in their hand, waiting for them.

He switched on his torch and shone the white beam back up the tunnel to a spot where it had forked. "I heard it again," he lied. "Back that way."

"But the children are this way," Shannon urged. "There's nothing back there, no-one to find."

Titus shook his head. "I know it." He started to trudge back down the tunnel, Erin falling in alongside him with no hesitation.

Jay shrugged at Shannon and jerked a thumb in Titus' direction. "We'd better stick together," he muttered to the doctor.

"I don't know what's in that spoke," Shannon replied as the group fell in behind Titus and Erin. "They never let me in there."

"Shhh," Titus urged and they progressed in silence.

Only a couple of minutes past the fork, through several sets of unsealed doors, the tunnel changed from one with featureless walls into one with doorways set at regular intervals. No keypads or clipboards were fixed next to them, but name plates were set into them, made of smooth white plastic.

Catherine, Monica, Mary. Titus read the names written onto them as he passed, growing more uneasy with each step. He felt his chest tighten as the tension of the person he felt began to leech into him. Then he realised that it wasn't just one, but several different patterns of emotional registers that were pressing in on him. Even though they felt distinct from one another, all of those minds shared the same terrified mental state. Taking another long, deep breath, he consciously drew a mental curtain around himself, thinking hard about where he ended and they began.

He stopped outside of a door with a plaque that read "Day Room." He pointed at it. "There's someone in there," he whispered. "More than one I think."

Luthor pointed a position out to Erin using the notched arrow and she stepped into place. Jay readied himself as they did this, holding his hand above the door handle. When all were ready, he shoved the metal door wide open, dropping straight into a low crouch in case of any response from within.

Some kind of metal baton swung at the spot where his face had been moments before. Luthor gasped as he saw into the room first, raising the angle of his bow at the last moment to loose the arrow high into the air. He shot out an arm to knock Erin's aim high as several shrieks erupted from the room.

A woman staggered into the doorway, carried by the momentum of her swing. She was partially lit by a few torch beams coming from inside the room; for a few moments it was hard to make her out with so many beams of torchlight waving around, but Titus finally centred his beam on her as she blinked out at them.

The fact that she wasn't wearing an environmental suit struck them first, then the paleness of her skin. Her hair was lank, her eyes shadowed, and her stomach round and large despite her small frame.

Luthor said nothing for a moment, simply lowering his bow to lean it against the wall, clearly shaken by how close he'd been to shooting her. "We're not going to hurt you," he finally replied. "We're here to rescue you."

Taking this in, she dropped the metal bar with a clang and threw herself forward, wrapping her arms around him to sob into his chest. He gingerly put his arms around her as other women came into view, peering out at the strangers in the corridor, all of them in various stages of late pregnancy.

"My God," Shannon croaked. "Who on earth are you? Are you prisoners?"

They all shook their heads. "No," one replied.

"What happened?" another shrieked hysterically. "They didn't tell us anything. Who are ycu?"

A hurried exchange of information followed, whilst the children stared openly at their swollen bellies. "We listened at the door," the woman with the weapon told Luthor. "We heard all kinds of awful things, then nothing, for ages. We thought you were coming to kill us. We've heard about savages on the surface ..."

"We're not going to kill you." Jay smiled, recovering from the near overwhelming delight of seeing so many women in one place. "We live up above." He slipped an arm around one of the younger mothers who was shaking with nerves. "You can come up too, live with me and my Boys. We'll look after ya."

"That is absurd," Luthor scoffed. "They will come with me to the Red Lady."

"Who says?" Jay rounded on Luthor, straightening himself up.

"You cannot honestly believe that you are strong enough to protect these women," Luthor replied in a hushed growl.

"Don't give me that crap," Jay snarled. "Me and my Boys can take care of 'em fine."

"Don't we have some say in this?" a red-headed woman spoke up.

Luthor guffawed. "No," he replied, making Erin scowl at him. "You don't."

"But that's not right!" Titus exclaimed, and the argument quickly escalated.

"Look, this isn't the time for this!" Shannon announced loudly, cutting through the hissed words of people trying to argue passionately but fearful of being heard. "Worry about what happens on the surface later. We need to find the children and get out of this godforsaken place. We're wasting time."

"Children?" a woman said. "What children?"

Shannon frowned and shut his eyes, pieces of an ugly puzzle falling into place. "I can only assume," he replied with obvious reluctance, "that they're your children."

The women looked at each other. "But they died," the redhead said, in a faltering voice.

"All of them," another added. "They said they were stillborn."

"They said it was the virus, that it was because we're carriers," the redhead continued. "They said that was a side ... effect." Her voice trailed off as she saw Jay staring at the gap between her front teeth. He exchanged a look with Shannon as he realised the same truth.

"They lied, didn't they?" she cried. "Oh my God, they lied to us!"

"Where are they? Where are our children?" a chorus of despairing mothers clamoured to be heard over each other.

"Quiet!" Luthor tapped the floor with his bow and a hush descended. He gestured towards Shannon. "He knows where they are and you can come with us, but only if you stay back and stay quiet. We think all of the Guardians are dead, but one or two may have extra air supplies." He leaned closer to Jay. "We'll finish this later." With that he picked up his bow and set off down the tunnel. "Besides," he muttered grimly to himself, "I can't think with all these women caterwauling."

They formed a strange line of people as Shannon led them to the tunnel where the children were kept, Hunters in front, Titus and the women in the middle, Jay guarding the group from the back. They saw several bodies, many of whom looked like they'd suffocated in their suits, but no-one else left alive.

At the tunnel that Zane had been taken to, they found all of the doors open and not one child there. Shannon, fearing the worst, went from one to the next, checking it with a sweep of the torch, but Titus knew they had gone.

"No bodies," Shannon muttered. "That's something."

"Maybe they went to the surface," Erin whispered. "No reason to stay down here in the dark."

"Maybe," Titus replied and looked at Shannon. "I suppose Eve knew the way from helping you."

Shannon looked doubtful. "She was afraid of the surface – all of them were. Let's keep looking." He glanced back at the women, most of whom looked ragged with fear. "Why don't you take them up above?" He asked Jay.

"I 'ent leavin' 'im to find the kids," he jabbed a thumb at Luthor. "We stay together 'til we find 'em."

They trudged on, sweeping the rooms with their torches, the only noises being their footsteps echoing off the curved concrete. At the end of the corridor, Shannon suggested they try another spoke and all agreed.

"I was never allowed into this one," Shannon whispered to them as they reached one of the heavy doors that formed airlocks between the spokes. "It was high security. Never knew what they did here."

Luthor's frown was deepened by the shadow-laden light. "Then if there are any survivors, they are likely to be here, where there may be something to protect."

"I think he's right," Titus muttered.

"Hear sommat again?" Jay asked. He raised his eyebrows at Titus' nod. "You got good 'earin."

Luthor moved to the front, putting himself between the air lock and Shannon. "Stay back," he told the women. "Erin, up here with me."

Luthor swung the heavy door open as Erin trained her arrow on the opening. It was immediately apparent that there were no Guardians in the tunnel. Squeals erupted from a gaggle of children who fled down the tunnel away from Shannon's torch beam, but one remained, squinting at the bright beam of light.

"Eve!" Shannon and Titus yelled in unison and she ran to them as they stepped into the tunnel. She stopped a few feet away and grinned at Titus.

"I knew you would keep your promise," she whispered to him.

"Are you all alright?" Shannon asked and she nodded.

"Everyone's afraid. We didn't know what was happening."

"What are you doing here?" Shannon asked. "Are you lost?"

She shook her head. "No, we're looking for Zane."

"Zane!" Erin and Titus exclaimed and then shot a look at each other.

"Zane's down here," Eve replied, her voice just as quiet as it had been in the dream. "The Guardians and a doctor brought him. And they cut me to see if Zane could make it better, and he did. And there was a very scary man—even the Guardians were scared of him—and he killed the doctor to see if Zane could save her from the illness, but he couldn't, and she died and then Zane fell over and they carried him away. The scary man told them to take Zane to a high security cell, and I knew that was probably here, so we're here looking for him." Her audience was too shocked to say anything for a moment, and she misinterpreted the silence. "I didn't want him to be left behind," she added. "Everyone else is dead."

"Eve!" a boy hissed at her from the far end of the tunnel. "We found him! Come quick!"

In moments, the children burst through the door the boy stood in front of to find Zane slumped in a corner, so pale that his skin looked grey, a sheen of sweat glistening on his forehead. Lying in the middle of the room was Roper, exposed to the air and having suffered the same fate as Radley.

Zane was staring at him, the only colour on his face being flecks of the man's blood drying in the stale air. His stillness paused his friends and father in the doorway, as they struggled to take in what had happened.

"Zane?" Shannon asked after a beat, but his son didn't look up.

"Zane?" Erin repeated, pushing her way into the room as people crammed into the doorway to try to see what had happened.

"He's in shock," Shannon muttered and went to him. It was only when he touched Zane's shoulder that the boy seemed to notice anyone else. He looked at his father, blinked once, and then his eyes rolled back to stare at the body as he began to shake violently.

"He must have tried to save the man," Erin whispered to Titus, but he didn't respond, only watched as Shannon scooped Zane up and hurried out of the room.

"He gonna be alright?" Jay asked as they passed.

"He will be," Shannon reassured. "Let's just get out of this godforsaken place."

Chapter 35
REUNION

They emerged from the stairwell in the hour before dawn, the birds starting to stir and call to each other. Their songs sweetened the air, softened the edges of the horror they had all lived through that night. The grey-blue light sketched out the buildings, the drifts of dust, the rusting cars, all strange, terrifying things to the new children. They clustered tightly together, many of them trying to hold Eve's hands, or at least be close to her. The huddle of children quickly separated themselves from the others, regarding them suspiciously.

The women, some crying, some staring silently, also clustered together and watched the other adults with as much suspicion as the children. Titus, Erin, and Zane, still in his father's arms, found themselves between the two groups as Jay and Luthor joined them.

"S'alright." Jay smiled at the children and said, "You'll love it in my patch and your mates are there already."

He said it in such a relaxed way, with that smile and such self-confidence that some of them nodded. Eve, caught in the centre of the huddle, watched Titus as if hoping for clues, but when none were forthcoming, she looked around at the tall buildings and then up at the sky and began to cling to the boys in return.

"It's all so ... big," she whispered, and several of the children began to whimper in fear.

"Everyone's like this when they first come up," Jay reassured, his voice gentle. "But believe me, you get used to it dead quick. And it's great up 'ere. Honest-like."

As he was speaking to them, Luthor turned to the women. "You should all come with me, and consider yourselves under

303

the protection of the Red Lady."

"Hang on!" Jay rounded on him. "You 'ent got the right to go claiming' them when we're this close to my patch!"

"Nobody should be *claiming* anyone!" Titus interjected. "Where do you want to go?" he asked the women.

Nobody replied straight away, many of them were looking at the children, studying their features in the dawn's light. Two were whispering to each other excitedly and the taller of the two stepped forward and said, "I think you're my son!" to one of the boys clinging to Eve.

The word clearly meant nothing to any of the Unders children and the boy in question simply clung onto to Eve more tightly, staring at the woman in such a way that stole the excitement from her eyes.

"They don't know who we are," the red-headed woman muttered and in that moment, it was as if their collective maternal yearning shrank back, repelled by the sight of their own children fearing them as strangers.

"But we should stay with them," the tall woman said tearfully. "Else they'll never know who we are!"

"You're more than welcome!" Jay retorted, flashing a triumphant grin at Luthor. But when he glanced back at the children cowering away from the adults, it quickly faded.

"That is an absurd idea," Luthor said to the woman. "His gang has no means to protect you or provide for you." He pointed at her swollen belly. "You need protection. We will give it. There is no debate here."

Erin stepped forward, eager to soften her father's words. "You won't be prisoners!" she urged. "The Red Lady's gang is strong, and we grow food and hunt, and have clean water. There's a proper kitchen and rooms with beds that are clean. Won't that be better for you whilst you're ill?"

"We're not ill," the redhead retorted. "We're pregnant." When she saw no understanding in Erin's expression, she added, "We're going to have babies."

Erin's nose wrinkled. "Oh. Well ..." She glanced at Shannon, but saw that he was setting Zane down on a nearby doorstep. "I don't know much about that ..."

"You will be vulnerable." Luthor stated. "You will need protection for you and your children. Come with us."

Jay was about to wade in again when he saw Hunters emerging from the next street, returning from their part in the plan. His hands flicked out the bottom of his jacket to rest on the hilts of his knives as he glowered in their direction, but he said nothing. It was no coincidence that he was the only Bloomsbury Boy to see the early days of adulthood; he knew which fights were worth the risk, and which were not.

"Fine," he said. "Take 'em. My new Boys don't like 'em anyway. We're all better off without ya!" He turned on his heels, jerked a thumb towards his territory. "This way you lot, come and see my Boys."

"But what about Eve?" one of the boys wrapped around her left arm squawked. "She's a girl!"

Jay stopped and looked at her, frowning. "That's true ..." He watched the way the collective mass hung on his response, nodded to himself, and said, "Well, I'll let her join too, if you think she's that great. But that don't mean any other girls can. Only Eve."

At that, they swept off, Jay marching ahead of them like the Pied Piper. With a slightly dazed expression Eve glanced back at Titus, who called out, "I live very close to Jay's square! I'll find you soon!" and then looked rather surprised at himself for doing so.

Once Jay had left with the children, the rest had been simple. Shannon asked to go with the women, having discussed something with Zane who was slowly coming back to himself. Luthor agreed, knowing that a doctor would soon be indispensable.

Erin didn't join her father straight away as she helped Titus to take Zane home, one under each of his shoulders. It was the first time that the three of them had been alone since it had all started, and even though he was struggling to walk in his exhaustion and aftereffects of the injection, Zane held onto his friends as tightly as he could.

"How did you get down there?" Erin asked at the end of the street. "Did they catch you on the way home?"

He shook his head. "I went to speak to Radley. I was trying to stop you all."

Erin and Titus stopped, bringing Zane to a halt also.

"I'm sorry," Titus said quietly. "I'm sorry we didn't listen. I should have guessed what you were going to do, but I was so –"

"It doesn't matter," Zane mumbled. "It's too late now. It's all over." His voice was flat. Titus and Erin both frowned as they watched him, sagging between them. "I was stupid to think I could've done anything."

"You're saying that because you're so tired," Erin said quietly. "It must have been horrible."

They started to walk again, their footfalls echoing off the buildings around them. "Don't say anything to Mum, about Dad I mean," Zane said as they neared the square. "He wants to see her himself, once he knows the women will be ok, and once I'm feeling better."

"We won't say a word," Titus affirmed.

"Promise," Erin added. "It's your business."

None of them were surprised to be met at the edge of the square by a ragged Miri who had spent a sleepless night imagining the worst. Titus outlined only the briefest version of the events as Miri crushed Zane to her. Callum soon joined them, helping Miri put the exhausted boy to bed, giving her a steady shoulder to weep her relief into.

Erin left quickly to join her father and the escort of the women, leaving Titus outside of Zane's house as the sky blushed red and the clamour of the birdsong reached its crescendo.

Lyssa emerged from the house, still rather frail and thin in her mismatched clothes. She pulled the blanket from her shoulders and wrapped it around Titus, making him realise for the first time that he was tired, and cold, and just wanted to stop. They embraced.

"They're gone now," he whispered to her, squeezing her tight and feeling her ribs under his hands. "They'll never take you again."

A strange, choked noise erupted from her and she began to sob, not only for the first time since they had got her back, but the first time that Titus had ever known her to. It frightened him to feel her body shake as she wept uncontrollably. Lyssa, his rock, the one who had always protected him, was now leaning into him, clinging to him for support. He realised in that moment that at some point since they had first strayed into this part of London, he had grown taller than her. He parted slightly to look at her, look *down* into her eyes. "I think we should stay here. Until you're strong again at least."

She nodded, sniffing, reddening with embarrassment. She attacked the tears on her cheeks with her hands. "Sorry. I'm just tired." Titus smiled at the lie. "Where's Eve? Is she ok?"

"She's fine. She's with Jay and the Boys."

"I'm not sure she should be with that Jay," Lyssa muttered and Titus nodded in agreement.

"That's something for tomorrow," Titus replied. "Right now, let's just ... catch our breath." With that, he led her inside the house and shut the door.

Zane slept all of that day, through the night, and woke with the next dawn. After breakfast, Miri took him straight into the garden to work by her side in the hope that a normal day would be just the thing to restore his spirits. She had no idea what had placed that haunted look in his eyes, what had stolen the boyish look from his face. She had no idea that Zane would never be the same again.

"Mum," Zane said as they both plucked weeds from between the herbs. "Why haven't you asked me what happened in the Unders?"

Miri paused, then rocked back onto her heels. "I wanted to. But you haven't seemed ready to talk about it. And right now, you being ok is more important than me knowing."

Zane looked away, picked some of the leaves off a weed. Part of him wanted to tell her, but once he started, where would he stop? Would telling her that one man had killed all of the people she loved make her feel better?

"I'm not ready yet," he replied.

She nodded slowly. "Alright," she replied reluctantly, pushing away that maternal urge to find out everything and make it better.

"But I do want to talk about Dad," Zane continued, taking her by surprise. "Why haven't you asked about him?"

She sighed. "The same reason. And, if I'm honest, because I'm scared to know." She drew in a deep breath. "Is he still alive?"

Zane nodded. "Yes. And he isn't what you think ... or what I thought too. They made him do the experiments and said they'd kill us if he didn't."

Miri pulled off her gardening gloves, laid them carefully on the ground in front of her. She swallowed hard. "Where is he now?"

"There were lots of pregnant women, down there in the Unders, and Luthor took them to live with the Red Lady's gang.

Dad went with them to make sure they're ok."

Miri pinched the point where the bridge of her nose met her forehead and massaged the small muscles under the skin.

"He's going to come and see you," Zane continued. "He just wanted to give me a chance to talk to you when I woke up."

"Miri," Shannon's voice called to her from the gated entrance to the garden behind him. She turned so quickly that she almost fell into the herb bed.

Zane got up and ran to him. They embraced as Miri got to her feet and wiped her hands on the apron and pulled the scarf from her hair.

"I told her, Dad. I explained it to her. Now you can come and live with us!"

He pulled away to look at the two of them taking each other in. He couldn't understand why they weren't running into each other's arms, why they weren't holding each other tight and laughing with delight. He had played the moment through in his mind many times – why wasn't it becoming real?

"Mum?"

She approached slowly, looking at Shannon in such a way that Zane wondered if she disbelieved her own eyes. "Zane, go and put some water onto boil," she said with a cracking voice. "We need some tea."

He didn't know what drew him to the room in the hospital. Perhaps it was the desire to see his father happier, younger, in another life filled with colour and laughter and friendship. With the Unders emptied and the Giant's mystique destroyed, the place no longer held any fear for him. Not even the words of his mother frightened him now. Even now he could hear her saying, "Never go into the hospitals, Zane," but its power over him had been burnt away like mist on a summer morning.

As his eyes searched the photos, he thought about Roper and the monstrous thing he'd done. He remembered the coldness in his mother when his father returned; he thought about Erin plunging the knife into Doug's chest. He sank into the dusty office chair. How could he not have seen all these things so clearly before? How could he have thought that people were kind underneath it all?

Now he knew what lay underneath. Hatred. Fear. And the desire to survive. Nothing more.

He wept.

The hand on his shoulder made him leap up and cry out. Titus stepped back as Erin spread her hands in the universal gesture of harmlessness.

"It's only us!" she exclaimed. "It's ok."

"What are you doing here?" Zane asked, frantically wiping the tears away with his sleeve in Bloomsbury Boy fashion.

"Finding you," Titus replied. "We knew you were here."

"We thought you might be upset," Erin said softly. "We wanted to make sure you're ok."

Despite his best efforts with his sleeve, Zane's cheeks remained wet as new tears fell. For the first time he felt angry that he was still crying. His cheeks burned.

"How can I be ok?" he spat, shaking with heaving sobs. "He killed all of them! And Mum hates Dad! And I thought we'd all be together! But what does it matter anyway? All those people! All those people!"

Violent sobs stole the breath away from any words that might have emerged. Titus and Erin watched, speechless, as Zane dropped back into the chair and buried his face in his hands.

"Who killed all of them?" Erin asked after a few moments.

"The man, the man in the room," Zane garbled. "He made a disease that killed everyone. That's what It was, s ...

something that man made to kill the people he didn't like."

Only Zane's anguished sobs filled the air. Titus leant against the desk and Erin frowned intently at the top of Zane's head, both of them struggling to take it in.

"Only," Zane continued, "only it went wrong and started to kill everyone, and it killed millions of people." He pointed at the pictures. "All of my dad's friends, all of those people." He broke down again, unable to speak.

"That man, the one you were with when we found you?" Erin asked and watched Zane nod. "Zane ... did you –" She stopped when Titus put his hand on her arm and shook his head. Zane didn't seem to notice the unfinished question, and even though she was desperate to know if Zane had let the man die, she saw from Titus' expression that now wasn't the time to ask.

So they waited as Zane's grief and anger flowed out of him with the saltwater. Finally he looked up at them, his face blotched and pale. "Sorry."

"Your mum is talking with your dad," Erin said gently. "Maybe they just needed to ... I dunno, talk about it all."

"Perhaps Miri is finding it hard to come to terms with," Titus offered. "She's used to the idea of him being gone – perhaps it's too much of a shock for her to be happy straight away."

Zane shrugged. Erin crouched in front of him, putting her eyes level with his. "It'll be ok," she said but his eyebrow rose in disbelief. It threw her, to see anything but trust there. "Um ... but seriously, it will be. I know all that happened with the Unders, and that man, that all that was really bad, but you know, we have us. And we got Eve and the children out. And your dad."

Zane sighed and nodded. "I suppose so."

Erin's hand shot out to take Zane's and she squeezed it hard. "Don't be like this, Zane!" she blurted. "If you stop being ... if you're not ..." Her words faltered and Zane simply leant forward and embraced her.

"I'll be ok," he whispered, feeling like a liar. "You're right anyway. It is good that the others are out, and we do have each other." He squeezed her tight, not caring about how awkwardly she held onto him. He glanced up to see Titus watching and forced himself to smile at him, to reassure him that he was alright. "I can hardly remember what it was like before you two came, it feels so right for us to be together."

Erin nodded and gently pulled herself away. "We'd better go before we get too soft," she muttered and left the room quickly.

Zane stood, noticing the dark spatters of his tears drying in the dust. "What next?" he asked, and looked to his friend.

Titus smiled slightly. "We recover, we get Eve, then we have two things we need to do."

Zane frowned, noting the seriousness of Titus' manner. "What things?"

"We find out what happened to Erin's mum, and help her if we can," Titus stated. "If we can bring down the Unders, then we can definitely do that."

Zane drew in a deep breath and let it out again with a sigh. "It's only right, we can't leave her with the Gardners." Titus nodded. "What's the other thing?"

"We find out why we're different," Titus replied.

"You mean me making people better, and the dream room?"

Titus nodded again. "Then we might know why the Red Lady is so interested in us."

"It's not just because she likes us?" he asked, crestfallen, and Titus laughed affectionately at the glimpse of the old Zane.

"No, it's not," Titus replied with certainty, steering Zane out of the room to follow Erin out of the hospital. "But we'll talk about that another time."

EPILOGUE

So now you know how the Four were brought together, and that there are no such things as Giants. I think that's enough for now. We can't spend all of our time in the past. You need to keep this fire going and find something to eat. All I ask is that you don't consign this book to the flames to warm your hands. Instead, perhaps you could be kind enough to leave this where others may find it, so they may also read this tale.

And remember, all of these events happened in these dusty streets around you, in this dead city. I know because I was there, watching. But then why trust me? You don't even know who I am. Perhaps you're curious about that, though in the company of those such as the Four, it seems an indulgence to tell you about someone as insignificant as I.

Of course, the story of the Four is far from over. I haven't had the chance to tell you about how Erin discovered her own remarkable abilities, and how Eve's talent for opening locked doors in the Unders was only a tiny part of her potential. And it doesn't end there for Titus either, who, having found his sister at last, turned his intellect towards discovering what bound the Four together and why they were different. Let's not forget Zane, and how he learnt that sometimes his healing wasn't enough to save loved ones. They don't talk about these things in the stories you've heard, do they?

If you want to learn what really happened, Joshua's part in all this, and how a father's death led to the crowning of the King, then look around you for another book containing the same handwriting as this one. I haven't forgotten what I promised to tell you. Heavens! You didn't think you would find all that crammed into this one little book, did you?

ACKNOWLEDGEMENTS

This book never would have reached your hands if it hadn't been for Sally Bassington, an intensely talented librarian with effortless style and great taste in clothes. Sally was a colleague at the school I worked in whilst writing the first draft, and she read every chapter as I wrote it. Sally, thank you for being so gentle with a blocked creative stumbling back into the world of writing. Thank you for badgering me relentlessly until I agreed to try and get this published. You made this happen, and changed my life forever.

Thanks to Peter, Rick and Amanda, without whom Zane, Titus and Erin would never have existed. I hope you like where I have taken them.

Many thanks to the small army of friends and family who read through the early drafts and gave just the right mix of encouragement and constructive criticism to get the book this far. In particular, Dan, I still remember your advice on my writer tics; you made me a better writer. Conall, your encouragement meant the world to me.

All of you have enriched my life immeasurably, I am many times blessed. Much love to you all.